ESPERO
A Silver Ships Novel

S. H. JUCHA

Published by S. H. Jucha
www.scottjucha.com

ISBN: 978-0-9975904-0-1 (e-book)
ISBN: 978-0-9975904-1-8 (softcover)

First Edition: October 2016

Cover Design: Damon Za

Acknowledgments

Espero is the sixth book in *The Silver Ships* series. I wish to extend a special thanks to my independent editor, Joni Wilson, whose efforts enabled the finished product. To my proofreaders, Abiola Streete, Dr. Jan Hamilton, David Melvin, and Ron Critchfield, I offer my sincere thanks for their continued support.

Despite the assistance I've received from others, all errors are mine.

Glossary

A glossary is located at the end of the book.

"Stop where you are!" Alain de Long shouted, speaking the New Terran's language.

A broad-shouldered man, whose heavy-world frame was dimly backlit in Hellébore's fading light, hesitated in the alleyway's mouth. He spotted the stun gun in the Haraken's hand and bolted back around the corner onto one of Espero's main streets, but his steps faltered at the sight of a second Haraken identical to the man he just encountered. Shaking off his hesitation, the New Terran dropped his head and accelerated, intending to bowl the slender man over.

In a deft movement, Étienne de Long, co-director of Haraken's security forces, dropped down, spun on his left leg, and used the right to cut the man's legs out from under him.

With an "oomph," the man smacked face down onto the street. The force of the impact dislodged his ear comm, which struck the walkway and snapped the tiny transmitter off the comm's body. Before the New Terran could recover, he found his hands pinned behind him. "Why are you attacking me?" he cried out.

"Why were you running?" Étienne replied, as he applied wrist restraints.

"How do I know who you are? Is this a kidnapping or are you adz?" the New Terran asked.

"As to the former, the answer is no; as to the latter, what are adz?" Alain, Étienne's twin and crèche-mate, replied.

"Adz ... you know ... administrative types, police and such."

"Then we're adz," Étienne replied. "Allow me to introduce ourselves. We are Haraken security forces, and you are under arrest."

"For what?" the New Terran demanded, struggling as Étienne and Alain hauled him upright. No easy task for the twins, since the man massed more than their combined weight.

"We'll answer your questions at the Directorate, as we'll expect you to answer ours," Alain replied.

"These ties are too tight," the New Terran complained. "They're cutting off my circulation."

Étienne signaled the tiny chip in the restraints to ease the tension. The wrist cuffs were new tools for Haraken's premier "escorts," the Méridien term for security personnel. Restraints wouldn't have been required for their own people, but Haraken's primary city, Espero, had doubled its population in the last four years to nearly a million individuals. Many of the new emigrants and visitors were from New Terra and some were from the Confederation, more so from its colonies than its home world, Méridien.

Due to their constrained social fabric, Méridien behavior would be exemplary, but with the New Terrans, it was a different matter. A younger society of much more independent-minded people, New Terrans were still experimenting with social boundaries, and the twins, Étienne and Alain, were discovering that the culture was importing its excesses to Haraken.

Étienne and Alain loaded the New Terran into their grav-transport, a four-seat unit with a modified rear seat that operated as a containment cell, and flew back to the Security Directorate building.

The suspect stood briefly before Julien, a Haraken SADE (self-aware digital entity), who scanned him, recorded his physical aspects, loaded his DNA into the Directorate's database from a touch on the man's skin, and sampled his voice pattern when the man asked, "So, who are you supposed to be?"

"You need not worry your simple human mind about that, Ser," Julien replied.

"Oh, you're one of the Harakens' pet computers," the suspect snidely shot back. When the New Terran saw the Méridiens' hands twitch toward their stun guns, he adopted a nasty grin, thrilled to see he had struck some nerves.

Julien checked the Directorate's database. <He's not a registered visitor. In fact, there's no record of his ever having entered Hellébore space,> the SADE sent to the twins' implants, the tiny Méridien device in their brains, which allowed thought communication and recording of sensory input. All Haraken residents past the age of consent carried one, except for Haraken's president, Alex Racine, who carried two. Only temporary visitors to the planet were exempt from adopting the devices.

<An interloper,> Étienne sent back.

<A good thing too,> Alain sent to his brother. <I would be displeased to see you disciplined by the Assembly for attacking and dropping an innocent visitor on his face.>

Étienne squinted at his twin, who chuckled. They escorted the New Terran to an interrogation room, while they communicated privately with Julien about the circumstances that might have brought the man surreptitiously to Haraken. It had been reported by citizens that several New Terrans they had met were incapable of producing Haraken IDs, which were required of the planet's visitors.

The interrogation rooms and holding cells within the Directorate were also new implementations. Espero's population changes, resulting from an explosion of New Terran visitors and residents, had required the construction of the Security Directorate's new building only three years ago, and the suspect processing areas were added a year ago.

Espero's tremendous influx went hand-in-hand with New Terra's construction of faster-than-light (FTL)-capable transports, passenger liners, and freighters, courtesy of Haraken technology. The vessels were owned and operated by New Terrans, so they flew under the system's banner, Oistos. It required the Harakens create stricter entry controls by constructing the new McCrery Orbital Station, where all foreign vessels docked for Haraken entry and exit. But as tonight's operation by the twins indicated, the new procedures weren't foolproof.

After seating the New Terran in an interrogation room and removing his restraints, Étienne asked, "What's your name?"

"Names seem so unimportant today," the man said. "It's all about numbers anymore, but for the sake of our discussion, you can call me

Henry or Henri, if you prefer," he added, gesturing toward his captors and acknowledging their Méridien origin.

From the initial moment of his capture until now, Henry had slowly dropped the façade of the innocent victim. Now, the man who sat before the Harakens displayed the mannerisms of the criminal who the twins had sought. Henry leaned comfortably back in his chair, folded his hands over his stomach, and smiled condescendingly at the two investigators.

"How did you arrive here, Henry?" Alain asked.

"So this is it? This is how the big, bad Harakens are going to interrogate me?" Henry asked. "From what I hear, you people can't do much more than scowl or raise your voices." Then he laughed long and hard at his joke.

<He has a point,> Alain sent privately to Étienne and Julien. <The New Terrans are well aware of our constraints against harming others.>

Julien applied his considerable crystal-processing power in search of a means of unlocking the man's secrets. Terrible things were insinuating their way into Haraken society, tempting the planet's vulnerable Haraken young and New Terran visitors alike. Henry was the first interloper they had caught, and his information could be invaluable in understanding how the new passenger controls at McCrery were being circumvented.

<We could always apply one of our illustrious president's techniques and bluff,> Julien sent to the twins. It was one of Alex Racine's favorite practices during the games played with his ancient deck of cards. Alex called it bluffing; Julien called it prevarication. Whichever name, it provided the two friends with endless hours of entertainment, as they debated its fairness.

<What do we have that will serve as a bluff?> Alain sent.

<Harakens, both humans and SADEs, are well known to most New Terrans,> Étienne added.

<But the Swei Swee are not,> Julien replied. <I believe it's time for our recalcitrant visitor to meet some true aliens. Allow me, Sers, to start this masquerade.>

Julien left his post by the door and stood in front of Henry, saying, "Well, Ser, if you refuse to cooperate with us, we'll have to be rid of you.

We can't have a human of your ilk walking around Espero free to do as he will."

"You can't twist me," Henry said, confident of his position. "The worst you can do is deport me, and you know it."

Accessing a stored image of Admiral Tatia Tachenko's feral grin, Julien twisted his face into a facsimile, and said to the twins, "Ah, so our secret is yet to be discovered, Sers." A black, stovepipe hat appeared on Julien's head, projected by his avatar's holo-capable synth-skin. It gave the SADE the image of a man intent on conducting dark business.

"Digital freak," Henry snarled. "I'm done dancing with you people. Put me on a freighter, and let's get this over with so I can get some sleep."

"Freighter? Who said anything about a freighter?" Julien asked innocently, looking at the twins, who adopted their own evil smiles in an effort to play along.

"Étienne, we will require a transport to the cliff tops where the Swei Swee can get rid of this piece of human trash," Julien said, dismissing Henry and walking out.

"What are you talking about ... your president's precious aliens?" Henry yelled at Julien's retreating back. Swiveling to regard the twins, he said, "Those things are supposed to be ferocious looking, but everyone knows they're gentle with humans."

"And therein lays the secret, Ser," Alain said, catching on to Julien's ruse.

"Oh, yes," Étienne agreed, building on the story, "the Swei Swee can be gentle, but if you know anything about them, it's that they're carnivores, and, as much as they enjoy fresh seafood, they've developed a fondness for human flesh."

"Keep your tall tales ... like I said, you're not going to twist me," Henry declared firmly, but some of the bravado he had exhibited earlier had evaporated, and even more of his confidence waned as he was hauled out of the Directorate and loaded into the investigator's transport with the SADE for company in the containment cell.

During the flight, the stars twinkling overhead through the transport's clear canopy, Henry sought to determine whether he was being twisted or he was indeed headed for his death at the hands of aliens. But the three Harakens ignored him, and Henry was forced to listen to a macabre exchange between the twins in the front seat of the transport, which played heavily on his nerves.

"I say we place a wager on it," Étienne said to Alain.

"They haven't fed on a human in over fourteen days," Alain replied. "I think they'll do the job in fewer than 0.11 hours."

"That fast? But you're not counting the skull," Étienne challenged.

"No, you're right. I mean they'll crack the skull eventually, but you know how they like to play with it for a while."

"Have you ever figured out their game … you know … what they're doing, smacking it around like that and twittering like a bunch of old women?" Étienne asked, his face screwing up and swallowing, as if to prevent retching.

"May the stars protect us," Alain said, shuddering. "It's gruesome to watch. I want to be back aboard the transport by then, if you don't mind."

"No objections from me. I can't stand to observe that part either. I still have nightmares," Étienne agreed.

That the investigators weren't asking Henry any more questions scared him to death. They didn't seem to care whether he talked or not. As silently as the grav-transport lifted off, it quietly descended onto the cliff top that overlooked the ocean to the west of Haraken's capital, Espero. The planet's bright moons lit the cliff top in a pale glow, and the night air blew sweet and salty scents from the tall grass and sea.

Alex greeted the twins as they hauled the New Terran out of the transport. When Julien told him of their plan to encourage the trespasser to talk, Alex broke out in laughter. He was still laughing as he closed the comm and started the walk to the cliffs.

"Sorry to bother you so late this evening, Mr. President," Julien said, greeting Alex as they exited the grav-transport, "but we need to process this one immediately. He's an interloper so there's no concern about recordkeeping."

Henry put on a brave front, standing straight and puffing out his substantial chest. But the president's sudden high, shrill whistle caught him off guard, and he watched with concern as the Haraken calmly extracted a live fish from a small container.

To Henry's horror, the stories of the Swei Swee hadn't even come close to the truth. A giant, six-legged alien with huge claws raced over the edge of the cliff top, and as the creature scurried toward them at high speed, Henry's sphincters loosened, and he soiled his pants. The rapid snapping of the monster's enormous claws threatened to collapse Henry's knees, and his captors were forced to support him.

When the president offered the fish to the alien, it snatched it up in a claw, tearing at it with the other, and feeding bits of it into its mouth, smacking away. Nausea and lightheadedness overcame Henry. His imagination ran wild, and he envisioned his bones stripped of flesh by the ugly creature. With his last moments of consciousness, Henry blurted, "I'll tell you what you want to know. I'll tell you everything. Just keep that thing away from me." Then he fainted, and the twins lowered him to the ground.

The four eyestalks of the Swei Swee First, the leader of the alien hives, swung to the man on the ground, and he whistled his concern. "Is the human in distress?"

"I believe he might be ill," Alex whistled.

"No introduction this night?" the First inquired.

"Not this evening. Perhaps another time," Alex warbled, offering his sympathy for the event's failure.

The alien leader popped the last piece of sweet fish flesh into his mouth parts, swallowed, and whistled his farewell, hurrying off to join his mates at home, a domicile built into the cliff side. The hives could only fish during the daylight hours when they could see what they hunted, and they consumed what they caught. So a late-night snack offered by the Star Hunter First, as Alex was known by the People, was always a treat.

"After Henry comes to and is cleaned up," Alex said, wrinkling his nose in disgust, "I will be interested to know how he slipped past our security procedures and made it to Espero. Most important, I want to know what he's doing here."

* * *

Renée de Guirnon, Alex's partner, warned of his return by implant, hastily prepared a late-evening repast and some hot thé. For the slender, genetically sculpted Méridien, thé was all Renée desired, but a heavy-world body such as Alex's required many more calories daily, and her lover was one substantial New Terran.

"Did he talk, or was the First forced to nibble on some body parts?" Renée asked, giggling at the thought of the amiable Swei Swee hurting a human. It was the aliens who guarded their son, Teague, when he swam in the bay at the base of the cliffs with the hive's younglings, who Teague thought of as his friends.

"He did agree to talk right before he passed out," Alex said, kicking off his boots at their home's entrance. It was a Swei Swee–built house, a right demanded by the First as tribute for Alex's efforts to free his people from the Nua'll, the mysterious, unseen aliens, who hid in the upper reaches of a massive sphere while they coerced other races to harvest their needs from the planets they ravaged.

Alex had agreed to the Swei Swee construction simply to keep the peace, but over the years he came to appreciate his decision. The roof and walls of his house required zero maintenance, and they still glowed with the soft luminescent blues, greens, and whites that marked the Swei Swee matrons' craftsmanship. It was the same application that created the shells of travelers, the Haraken's grav-driven shuttles and fighters — Swei Swee "spit."

"Understandable," Renée said sympathetically. "I was close to that reaction the first time the hive rushed at us atop the cliffs of Libre."

"I recall," Alex said, chuckling. "Hopefully we've frightened Henry to the point where he will confess all. We need to understand what's going on here. How are these people getting planetside without documentation? Their intentions are dishonest, of course. But exactly what are they up to?"

"I'm sure the twins will have answers for you in the morning. Now, come, my love, I want to test Mickey's new invention." Renée gestured to a seat on the couch. A small table at its end held thé and a plate of food.

Alex removed his jacket and shirt before he sat down. Renée had a preference for his bare chest when she snuggled against him, as she did now with a mug of thé in her hand. "A new vid, as well?" he asked.

"Of course," Renée replied. She had developed an insatiable appetite for ancient and modern New Terran vids, a style of entertainment not found on Méridien or anywhere in the Confederation, for that matter. After Renée's liner, the *Rêveur*, was rescued by Alex, she asked Julien to collect the vids to aid her in mastering Sol-NAC, the language of Alex's people, and much of the nuances of the more evocative New Terran women. To Renée's delight, she uncovered a huge cache of her favorite entertainment during the Harakens' time at Sol's Idona Station.

Renée waited until Alex settled back and laid an arm across her shoulders before she threw a leg over his lap and settled her head against his hard-muscled chest. Then she signaled the vid monitor, which rose off the wall and floated toward them.

"Mickey and his team are installing anti-grav frames on vid monitors?" Alex asked, flabbergasted.

The engineer, Mickey Brandon, and a number of his people were responsible for copying the Nua'll's dark travelers and producing the Swei Swee–shelled travelers the Harakens built and sold today. Since the production of the first series of travelers for Haraken, Mickey and several others had formed a company and were producing an endless variety of new anti-grav products.

"Marvelous, isn't it? You can watch a vid or media reports from any position, anywhere!" Renée exclaimed.

"Any position, anywhere?" Alex asked, frowning.

"Never fear, my love," Renée said, tilting her head up and kissing Alex's cheek. "Nothing will ever interfere with you keeping this woman's attention in our bed."

Renée had divulged their secret to only one person, her best friend, Terese Lechaux. She had approached Terese because of the woman's medical expertise, when Renée discovered one night during her lovemaking with Alex that he was utilizing the ever-growing power of his implants to create a feedback loop between them. Each knew, at any one moment, what pleased the other. The revelation had Terese salivating for more information, but Renée politely demurred from communicating the more intimate details.

Taking a sip of her thé, Renée maneuvered the vid monitor to a position level with their eyesight and locked it in place. Then she cued her new vid, a parting gift from Nikki Fowler, the Idona Station director, and settled back to watch.

2

"What do you know about these people?" Amelia asked her friend, Christie.

"Not much. That's why I think we have to check them out. I've heard Étienne and Alain are searching for what they call interlopers, visitors without ID. This may be them," Christie replied.

"Didn't you say that your brother thought they might be dangerous?" Eloise asked. Of the three close friends, two Méridiens and one New Terran, Eloise Haraken was the most conservative of the three young women. It certainly wasn't Christie Racine, Alex's sister, who fancied herself a detective of anything untoward in Espero. The third young woman, Amelia Beaufort, was game for any adventure that Christie could stir up. Despite Eloise's reservations about some of Christie's ideas, she was determined not to be left out of a new experience.

"Dangerous to us? I don't think so," Christie retorted. "What are they going to do ... mess with the president's sister? At worst, I think they'd throw us out for asking too many questions."

Christie led her friends down a narrow side street, which ended at a building's blank wall. Frowning at her friends, Christie rechecked her information, ensuring she was in the correct location. <This is supposed to be the place,> Christie sent to Amelia and Eloise.

<Over there,> Amelia sent, attaching an image of the right side wall to her thought. She highlighted an artfully concealed infrared beam peeking from behind a small turnout in the building's face. <Shall we?> she added, and then stepped forward to break the beam aimed across to the other side of the narrow space.

When Amelia intercepted the beam, the blank wall in front of the girls disappeared, revealing a club's inviting entrance lit in shades of blues and purples. The club was concealed by a holo-façade, and, curiously, the establishment's name wasn't in sight.

<Odd that this location doesn't wish to advertise its presence,> Eloise sent. <It makes one wonder what it's intending to hide.>

The three young women adjusted their clothing, adopted charming smiles, and strolled through the club's generous double doors, which slid aside at their approach.

"Good evening, fems, I'm Lacey. Welcome to our club," a New Terran woman said in greeting. She spoke passable Haraken, but her accent indicated she was definitely new to the planet. Moreover, the woman's shaved and heavily tattooed scalp, adorning an attractive face, marked her as an oddity among Harakens.

"Club?" Christie asked, letting the question hang in the air.

"Our club," Lacey replied with a smile. "May I offer you fems some stimulants before joining the party?" She waved a small med-injector pistol enticingly, her smile growing brighter. "It will make your experience all the more enjoyable."

Despite several attempts to pump information from Lacey, Christie and her friends found her to be tight-lipped about the establishment, and the girls chose to join the party without partaking of Lacey's offer of stimulants.

Two heavy, soundproof doors, leading to the club's interior, slid aside, and a wall of music struck them. The deafening sound saturated a dance floor packed with gyrating bodies. Laser lights strobed the club, and holo-vids painted scenes on every surface — walls, ceiling, and floor.

Most of the young people were Librans, noticeable by their slender builds and genetically sculpted faces; a small number were local or visiting New Terrans. That the music played over speakers may have been for the visitors' benefit, since they were without implants.

But the threesome found the scene confusing. Haraken young loved to link their implants to synchronize their dances. The intricate, extemporaneous maneuvers were difficult to perform but satisfying to the dancers and viewers alike. It was one of Christie's favorite aspects about her implant. Looking around, the girls noticed that not a single group dance was taking place.

<Look at their faces,> Eloise sent.

<Appears everyone accepted Lacey's offer,> Amelia remarked, staring at a Haraken boy of probably not more than sixteen, dancing by himself. Strangely, he exhibited none of the smooth, subtle movements of a Méridien dancer. Instead, the boy's body swayed and jerked, and his eyes were vacant.

<To the right,> Eloise sent, transmitting the image of two girls. Their Haraken wraps lay on the floor, trampled underfoot, but the girls kept up their awkward gyrations, unaware of their state of undress.

<These teenagers are gone. They're not on stimulants; they're on some sort of hallucinogen,> Christie sent.

<They're definitely not on Haraken anymore,> Eloise replied, staring into the vacant eyes of a Libran girl next to her and wondering what she saw in her mind.

<Christie, how do you know about what these teens may be on?> Amelia asked.

<Read about drug types when on New Terra,> Christie replied. <The government tightly regulates all drugs and most are used in medical therapy. I can tell you that what these teenagers are on would be illegal anywhere in Oistos.>

After the girls entered the club's dance floor, Lacey touched her ear comm and signaled her boss. "Dar, we've got a big problem ... snoopers are here."

Dar hurried to the front desk with Trembles, a massive New Terran, who acted as the club's bouncer.

Lacey played the vids of Christie and her friends for Dar. "These three," she said, tapping the screen with a long, blood-red fingernail, "are asking way too many questions."

"Questions aren't bad, are they?" Trembles asked dubiously.

"They are if they want to know about the club, about me, where I came from, and how long I've been on planet," Lacey replied.

"Where are they now?" Dar demanded.

Lacey switched her monitor to the cam pickups in the club and changed viewpoints until she located them.

"Hey, they're not dancing," Trembles said, leaning over Lacey for a closer view of the monitor. "But, they are some nice-looking fems."

"Dar, I tried to get them to take some of our twitch, but they weren't having it," Lacey said. "Stop drooling on me, Trembles," she said, elbowing the bouncer in the ribs.

"Give me a closeup of the New Terran's face," Dar ordered, a sick feeling forming in his gut.

Lacey worked to get an unobstructed front view as ordered, but the girls were moving through the crowd, looking closely at the dancer's faces. They stopped to observe two girls, whose wraps were missing, and Lacey got her shot, froze the image, and enhanced it for Dar.

"Of all the bad luck," Dar growled, slamming a fist on the table. "That's the president's little sister, and she and her friends are recording everything in their implants like Terran Security Forces at an accident scene."

"You want me to throw them out, Boss?" Trembles asked, hoping he would get an opportunity to be intimate with the fems.

"No … it's too late for that," Dar said. "So, what's your guess, Lacey? We got trouble or we got opportunity?" Dar asked. He trusted Lacey's instincts, even though she was known to be impulsive and had a hard taste for fems herself. The latter was evident in the way in which Lacey's eyes constantly flicked toward the image of the president's daughter, a big, curvy specimen with chestnut hair.

"I don't smell adz trouble; I smell amateurs. I say we take 'em," Lacey said, her pink tongue tracing the edge of a lower lip.

"Yeah, let's take 'em," Trembles agreed.

"Just take them? The president's sister?" Dar asked with incredulity.

"Sure, Dar. We take them, get them off planet, and spread the word about three fems who were abducted by Mr. Blue's people," Lacey said, punctuating her suggestion with a raised eyebrow. "Remember, this place is comm sealed. Whatever they've seen is still in their cute, little, techie heads." Lacey could hear Trembles snicker behind her, and she smiled herself.

"Oh, nice. I like it," Dar said, softly clapping his hands. "We get rid of the problem and lay the fallout at Mr. Blue's door. You're a wicked woman, Lacey. I knew there was a reason I kept you around despite the headaches you cause me."

"Boss!" Lacey retorted, pretending to be hurt.

"Stop gawking you two. Patch them, and get some crew to carry them out as soon as they go down. I want them off planet tonight."

Christie, Amelia, and Eloise separated to cover more of the club's dance floor, trapping images in their implants of the young people, staring into space and twitching awkwardly to the music. Christie and Amelia picked up several teenagers off the floor, who appeared to have passed out, and propped them against a wall out of harm's way. Their breathing was shallow but steady.

<Did either of you try to transmit a comm outside the club?> Eloise asked. Her question sent both of her friends seeking an outside connection, but to no avail.

<It figures. They've isolated the building,> Amelia replied.

<It's time to go, you two,> Eloise sent, but didn't receive a reply. <Christie, don't pretend you didn't receive me. We leave now,> Eloise demanded. <Amelia, do you have eyes on Christie? Amelia?>

Eloise started to search for her friends, but she felt dizzy. Her legs threatened to collapse from under her when strong hands suddenly grabbed her arms, and she was hauled from the dance floor. Eloise tried to speak, but her mouth wouldn't move and her tongue felt thick. When her legs gave out completely, she was dragged along by her arms.

A heavy door slid aside in front of her, and Eloise was dropped unceremoniously on the floor just inside the room. She glimpsed her two friends not 3 meters from her, their heads covered by metal-mesh bags, before one descended over her head.

* * *

Tatia sat across the card table from Julien, who projected his infamous poker apparel, a croupier's cap with its green, translucent brim. She once teased Julien that his cap would catch fire from the heat of his processing power as he sought to calculate whether Alex was bluffing, but the SADE calmly reminded her that it was a virtual hat and his processing crystals were in his chest. "But I take your meaning, Tatia," Julien had added. "Our friend's play does challenge my analytics."

Mickey completed the foursome, and he carefully watched Alex's face, trying to guess the strength of his president's hand when Alex froze in mid-play.

Mickey and Tatia sensed their security apps swept away, and they were connected in a comm call with Cordelia; Katie Racine, Alex's mother; and Julien. It had been awhile since Alex had intruded on their implants in this manner, and it was usually only under dire circumstances. The SADEs shared the same capability, but for reasons of their own, they chose not to exercise this capability.

<Your mother is worried, and I believe she has cause,> Cordelia sent.

"What?" Tatia mouthed quietly to Alex.

<When did you detect Christie's implant offline?> Alex asked, and his eyes drilled into Julien's.

Julien immediately contacted every other Haraken SADE, who began an intensive search to locate Christie.

<Just moments ago, her mother sought to ask Christie a question and couldn't reach her,> Cordelia explained. <I attempted to assist her and could not locate Christie's implant anywhere on planet. I broadened my search to our off-planet locations, including any Haraken ships. Her implant signal is not to be found anywhere in system.>

The thought chilled Alex. There were three ways to still an implant signal. Alex discovered the first method when he rescued the derelict ship, the *Rêveur*. The Méridiens were forced to search cabin by cabin, room by room, for their dead. An implant used the brain's heat to run its programs, and those frozen in vacuum had no heat.

A second possibility was a blocked signal, but Harakens didn't create structures capable of doing that. At least, none that Alex knew. A final possibility, Christie wasn't anywhere in Hellébore's system, but that seemed highly unlikely.

<Alex, Christie's friends, Amelia and Eloise, are also offline,> Julien sent. <We've completed an entire sweep of the system.>

<Mother, we'll find the girls,> Alex sent. <I'm going to let you go now, and I will be in contact with you and Dad as soon as we know something.> The moment Katie acknowledged his promise, Alex removed her from the conference comm, laid down his cards, and stood up from the table.

Renée took this moment to walk into the room with a tray of food to fuel the three heavy-worlders, only to discover the game halted and Alex pacing, never a good sign. She looked at Tatia, who linked her into the conference comm.

<This can't be a coincidence,> Alex sent to his compatriots. <We caught Henry yesterday, and this evening three of our girls disappear.>

<Are we sure that it's just a disappearance and not an accident?> Tatia asked, hating to be the one to volunteer the question.

<Any flyer or building accident that would harm three citizens would have been reported by multiple sources,> Julien replied. <The probability is statistically minute.>

<What is highly probable,> Cordelia added, <are the personalities of these young people getting them into serious trouble.>

<Now that I agree with,> Alex replied. <What are the odds those three were investigating the same issue as the twins?>

<That sounds like our young women,> Renée agreed.

<Which implies that we should be investigating the taking of our girls as hostages by someone sophisticated enough to know that their implants must be isolated from our networks,> Julien theorized.

<And these would be strangers, New Terrans,> Mickey said, disgusted at the thought that his people might be behind the threat.

<We have one advantage,> Tatia added. <They should recognize Christie and would keep her and her friends safe to bargain with if they were caught.>

<And to avoid being caught, they would want to get them off planet quickly,> Alex surmised. He grabbed a coat against the chill night air, sending, <Tatia, Julien.>

Tatia turned to fetch her coat only to have it tossed to her by Renée, who was familiar with Alex's abrupt actions. Tatia grinned, nodded her thanks, and raced after Alex and Julien.

"Where are we going?" Tatia asked. She barely strapped herself in when Alex swung his personal grav-transport in a hard semicircle and shot toward Espero.

"We're going to have another chat with Henry, our new, best friend," Alex replied.

<I thought the twins only got some minor information out of Henry after he met the First and not much more,> Tatia said.

<I believe Alex wishes to have a more in-depth conversation with our interloper,> Julien added, hoping he would not witness the demise of a human at Alex's hand. His own emotional programs were in heightened hierarchy. That someone would harm a member of the Racine family seemed the height of provocation. But his real worries were the actions Alex might take to regain his younger sister, whom he adored, and whether his friend could live with his conscience afterwards.

3

Tatia hurried to keep pace with Alex and Julien as they entered the Security Directorate. Alerted to the group's arrival, the twins met them in the entry hall and escorted them to Henry's holding cell.

<You might wish to push up the power of your stun guns to maximum,> Tatia sent to the twins.

<Henry appears to be the passive type,> Alain sent.

<It won't be for him,> Tatia replied grimly, and the twins exchanged a quick glance with each other.

As Alain signaled the cell door open, the twins sought to place themselves between Alex and Henry, but despite Tatia's warning, they weren't quick enough.

"Look who came to —" Henry managed to say, while getting up from his bunk before being hoisted into the air by his neck. He might have tried to speak, but it wouldn't have been intelligible, not with Alex's vice-like grip around his throat.

"I need some answers, and I need them now," Alex growled, his face twisted in a snarl and close to Henry's. "You talk, tell me what I want to know, and you live to be tried for your crimes."

<Alex,> Julien sent, keeping his thoughts calm, <I believe the bluish tint to Henry's face indicates a lack of oxygen. If you wish him to speak, perhaps you should remedy that.>

Alex let Henry's feet touch the floor, but he kept his hands around Henry's throat and his face close. Freed from Alex's harsh grip, Henry dragged in great gulps of air.

"What did I do?" Henry managed to cough out plaintively.

"My sister and two of her friends went missing tonight, and I want to know where your people took them. Talk or I hoist you back in the air until you turn the color of the deep dark."

Behind Alex, Tatia and the twins were arguing via their implants at what point they should interfere with the president when Julien interrupted them.

<I will monitor the interloper's health, essentially determining the degree of blue if he's hoisted again and signal you when interference is required,> the SADE sent, having monitored their comms. After a pause, Julien added the thought, <Hopefully, I will not be too late,> which was of small comfort to Tatia and the twins.

"Someone took Christie?" Henry asked, looking genuinely perplexed. Then the extent of his personal danger occurred to him. "No, no, no ... it wouldn't be my people," Henry protested, holding his palms out in supplication. "We know what Christie and her friends look like. We wouldn't touch them. That's way too much adz."

"Adz?" Alex queried.

"Yeah, adz ... administration pressure ... Terran Security Forces ... you people ... adz," Henry explained.

"Who do you work for?" Alex asked, relaying the question sent by Étienne.

"I can't ... ulp," Henry began, but Alex's fingers cut off his windpipe. "Okay, okay," he croaked, and Alex lessened the pressure. "But I do my time for any convictions here on Haraken. I don't get sent back to New Terra."

<Our first long-term prisoner,> Alain sent to Étienne. <I had hoped this day would never come.>

<The price of freedom and independence,> Étienne replied. <Would you rather we returned to Méridien after Alex found us?>

<And miss all this?> Alain sent back, adding a huge grin for his brother.

"You answer my every question honestly and your information proves out, you can remain incarcerated here on Haraken. What you do after your time is up will be up to you,> Alex said, releasing Henry and stepping back.

Henry eased down on his bunk and Alain passed him a cup of water, which he choked down before he spoke. "Ultimately, we work for Roz O'Brien, but there are layers between us and him."

"How many of you are on Haraken?" Tatia asked, hoping Alex would allow others to interrogate Henry while he cooled off.

"Five of us."

"I require their names," Julien stated.

"I don't know their names ... wait, wait," Henry yelped, as Alex started to close in on him. "Honestly, I don't know their names. We use code names. Three others are called Fangs, Legs, and Busty."

"Who are you?" Étienne asked.

"I'm Wheezy," Henry replied, ducking his head in embarrassment.

"You named yourself Wheezy," Tatia asked, shaking her head in disbelief.

"Our leader ... she's the fifth one ... she named us, calling us the first things that came to her mind, you know. I had a stuffy nose that day. We were told to call her Cherry."

"Not exactly names I can search," Julien commented drily.

"Where do we find your leader and these other three?" Alain asked.

Julien and the humans, especially Henry, were grateful to see Alex step back. Tatia kept Alex in the corner of her eye. *Never thought I would be so anxious to see Alex start pacing,* she thought.

"What? They're gone," Henry said, as if he spouted common sense. "The moment he, or him," he blurted, pointing to one, then the other of the twins, "chased me, I sent an exit alarm."

<When arrested, Alain and Étienne recovered Henry's broken ear comm at the scene,> Julien sent to Alex and Tatia.

"Gone ... where and how?" Alex asked, his body tensing again.

"Escape route," Henri replied, glancing toward the people in the cell, appealing to them to believe him and keep the president away from him. "The exit routine is itself a secret. When I sent the emergency signal, they would have gone to our leader, and she would have snuck them off planet."

"Earlier, you stated your people wouldn't have taken Christie and her friends. How can you be sure? You were in here at the time they were taken," Tatia said.

"I told you … we know better. Cherry said we were to play it low and slow on Haraken … take our time … build up customers. It was supposed to be a long-haul job, see?"

Alex stepped close to Henry, sat down on his haunches, his forearms on his thighs, and regarded Henry like a dead insect on his transport's view shield.

Henry stared at the massive shoulders bunched against Alex's neck, the arteries visibly distended by the pumping blood.

"I don't like your answers," Alex stated flatly.

"What? Noooo … it's the truth … all of it. I swear!" Henry's eyes pleaded with Alex and the others to believe him.

"But, Henry, there's this little problem. Shall I explain it to you?" Alex asked in a too quiet voice.

Henry bobbed his head emphatically in reply.

"None of what you're saying helps me get my sister back," Alex said, continuing to stare at Henry, as if the man didn't really exist.

"But I said we wouldn't take her. We know …" Henry stopped in the middle of his plea, as a light went on in his eyes.

"Tell me, Henry," Alex said softly, the intensity of his stare betraying the tension coiled inside.

"There's a new gang in Espero. Came in a month or so ago and set up a private club. Much too big a move, too quick, if you know what I mean … but they're pretty aggressive. Anyway, they're new to the planet. They might not know the girls or might not care."

"Where do we find this club?" Alex asked.

"Please, please … I don't know," Henry said, tears forming in his eyes.

<Alex,> Tatia sent, <you need to give Henry some room. He'll tell us everything now.> As Alex stood up and stepped to the far side of the cell, Tatia took his place, squatting on her haunches in front of Henry. "I have some questions for you, Henry," Tatia said.

"Okay," Henry replied with a hiccup, grateful to have anyone else asking the questions.

"These people with the club, who do they work for?" Tatia asked.

"Their top man is Craze. That's what people call him, just not to his face. His real name is Peto Toyo."

"And where do we find these people … Roz O'Brien and Peto Toyo?"

For a moment, Henry looked at Tatia in confusion and then checked out everyone else, who stood expecting an answer. "The moons of Ganymede … I thought everyone knew that."

Alex, Tatia, and Julien left Henry's cell while they discussed what to do with the information.

The twins ensured Henry was comfortable and then signaled the close of his cell door as they left. <Considering how much more we've just learned, perhaps we should modify our interrogation techniques,> Alain sent to his brother.

<You mean copy the president's methods?> Étienne asked.

<They were much more effective than ours,> Alain replied, then, after a moment of thought, he added, <Then again, perhaps we shouldn't.>

<Maybe in another half-century when we've grown sick of human treachery, which independence seems to nurture, we will change our minds,> Étienne replied, and the twins hurried to catch up with the others. They found Alex and Tatia already pacing, and Julien staring off into space. So, left with no other options, they waited patiently.

"The SADEs have searched all visitor entry records for the past year, including visuals of groups of five people, who might match the strange names of Cherry, Wheezy, Fangs, Legs, and Busty. The last name gave us the best indication of the characteristics for our search, but we've failed to discover a match," Julien announced. For one of the few times in his long life, Julien felt the SADEs' incredible capabilities were failing them when it mattered most.

"We have some threads to pull on," Tatia said, as if the problem required a Terran Security Forces (TSF) interdiction, where her experience as an ex-major could come into play. "We know there's a club with people who report to Ser Toyo."

"It has to be a hidden location," Alain said, "or we would have been aware of it by now."

"Probably invitation only ... word of mouth. ... teenagers and young people and their secrets," Alex mused, while he paced in a circle around everyone else. "Certainly, none of us are going to get an invitation."

"An item of note is that none of the young women communicated anything about what they found," Julien said.

"Comms isolation," the twins announced simultaneously.

"So if the girls were in the club, their proof is in their implants," Tatia said.

"You said threads, Tatia ... plural," Alex said, reminding her.

"Yes, we know that Wheezy's people ... I'm sorry. I can't call a grown man Wheezy. Henry's people ran an exit route, and someone helped them get off planet. Let's get the details of the escape route from Henry, and see who we locate at the other end."

"Julien, you and your associates need to focus on locating that club," Alex ordered. "Tatia, use your resources and examine all ship traffic. If the girls were taken off planet, we have a narrow window of time to search when that happened and that includes when Henry's compatriots jumped. See if we can determine the likely ships these interlopers used. Étienne and Alain, you talk to Henry, get the details of the exit contact, and track it."

When the twins nodded their understanding, Alex stared hard at them. "When you go, you take troopers armed with rifles, and Z in his Cedric Broussard suit. You have no idea of what you may be walking into ... think Clayton Downing." The mention of the man, who worked so hard to destroy the Méridien's efforts to help New Terra and kill Alex, gave the twins a new perspective on who they might be facing.

"We might be missing something," Tatia said, but she held up a hand to forestall any questions. She resumed pacing, trying to get a top-down view of the three days' past events. "We aren't asking ourselves a critical question," she said, stopping and extending a finger. "Not just what ships the interlopers are using to enter and exit, but who helped them do it?"

"A judicious question, your strategist," Julien said, giving Tatia a bow, as would an ancient Venetian courtier.

Tatia mimed a quick curtsy, smiling at Julien for his compliment.

"An inside job! These dirty dogs have someone on the juice," Julien announced, a fedora canted at a cocky angle appearing on his head. When the humans stared at him in confusion, he said, "Apologies ... a Terran detective vid. The interlopers have extorted or bribed a Haraken, who has access to visitor IDs and passage approval."

"More than likely," Alex agreed. "I doubt our Librans would be so easily turned. "Julien, concentrate on New Terran emigrants first for a likely candidate. An implant and cell-gen injections are no guarantee of someone adopting Méridien morals."

* * *

Alex and Renée sat in the gazebo, the lights of the moons glistening off the breaking wave tops rushing toward the shore. Alex updated his father and mother, regretting that he had no good news for them.

The late-night air was heavily laden with mist. Haraken's climate conditions changed dramatically over the fifteen years since founding, due primarily to the efforts of Benjamin Diaz, known to most Harakens as Rainmaker and to his close friends as Little Ben.

As Minister of Mining, Rainmaker orchestrated the delivery of billions of kilograms of water, trapped as asteroid ice, to Haraken's oceans. Over the nearly one-and-a-half decades since the planet was resettled, the ice asteroids, shooting through the atmosphere, built dense cloud layers, which filtered Hellébore's fierce rays and cooled the land's surface temperature. Strong convection winds, carrying moisture, circled the globe and changed the face of the planet. Rains across the lands, once a rare surprise, were now delivered almost daily during the wet season, which lasted a third of the year.

Four years ago, the Haraken populace attempted to elect Alex for a second, ten-year term, but he adamantly refused, saying, "The last thing any society needs is a president for life or a stale president. The compromise reached with the Assembly elected Alex to a final, five-year term, and he requested the Assembly enact an irrevocable law that said he couldn't serve another term as president, which the Assembly politely refused to draft.

Teague, now a ten year old, sat between his parents, their arms around him. First and foremost, he was acutely aware of a problem, since he had never been allowed to stay up so late. "Where did Christie go?" he asked. Teague had overheard the concern about his aunt and tried multiple times to contact her without success. That had never happened before. It reminded him of the several Swei Swee youngling friends he had lost to oceanic predators, and the young boy experienced a level of fear the like of which he hadn't felt before.

"We don't know," Renée said, hugging her son. "But we're looking for her. Everyone is looking for her."

"You'll find Tante Christie, won't you, Dad?" Teague asked.

"I'm going to do everything I can to ensure she's safe, Teague," Alex said, lovingly stroking his son's thick head of hair.

The family grew quiet, alone with their thoughts and fears. With the passing of the years, Alex had come to believe that his family following him to Haraken was a fortunate event. Initially, he worried for their safety, living on an uninhabited and arid planet without infrastructure. But as the capital city developed, the population transferred planetside from the Libran city-ships, and the rains increased, his concerns melted away. That his sister and her friends would be kidnapped and spirited off Haraken, after all that had been done to develop a strong and stable society marked by encouraging individual pursuits and personal freedom, seemed tragically ironic.

* * *

Late in the evening, Julien left it to the other SADEs to search the records for Harakens who might have facilitated the comings and goings of unregistered visitors. After their Idona children were put to bed, Julien spoke with Cordelia about the facts uncovered in the past few days, few as they were. Within the home, Cordelia and Julien had adopted the habit of speaking to each other audibly to give the children a sense of human parenting.

That habit came with a drawback. Once a tunnel rat always a tunnel rat, and rats have keen ears. While Julien spoke of the search for the girls, the small puzzle pieces gleaned from Henry, and the Directorate record search, Edmas and Jodlyne listened from around the corner.

The two Earther teenagers were a package deal of ten orphans, who had adopted the SADEs as parent figures. For Edmas and Jodlyne, their hero was Z, but they lived with Julien and Cordelia, where they could help with the care of the eight younger orphans. Nikki Fowler, the station's director, had urged the SADEs to take them rather than have them lost to the United Earth (UE) massive and poorly administered orphanage system.

Edmas tapped Jodlyne on the shoulder when the conversation in the main room quieted, and he signaled her to retreat. In his room, they chatted about what they heard.

"You remember, two days ago, when that boy offered you a chance to go to what he called a sizzle place?" Edmas asked.

"Yeah, he said it was a place you could be free … you could let go. You think that's the club Julien and Cordelia are trying to find?"

"Think so. Did you, by any chance, keep an image of that boy?"

"Got him up here," Jodlyne replied, tapping her temple, proud of her implant prowess. "We could do this like in the old days aboard the station." Under Edmas' stern gaze, her excitement died as quickly as it had erupted. "Sorry," she said meekly.

"We talk to Julien, Cordelia, and Z tomorrow and tell them what we think. Let's see what they have to say. Now get to bed. We'll have a tough enough time tomorrow explaining how we learned about the club."

"Oh," Jodlyne said, giggling and realizing she hadn't even thought of that and would have been caught off guard like an amateur tunnel rat waylaid by militia in a station's brightly lit corridor.

Four years ago and soon after returning from Sol, Cordelia, Julien, and Z sought to introduce the ten orphans from Idona Station to Teague and the Swei Swee. The homes of the Racines, Cordelia and Julien, and the Swei Swee, which were built into the cliff sides, bordered the same section of coastline.

One afternoon, the SADEs took the children, Edmas, Jodlyne, Jason, Ginny, and the six other orphans, to the cliff top overlooking the First's abode. Alex greeted the young ones and whistled an invitation, designed to call only the First, not wishing the children to face a clattering of adults and younglings. Despite the precautions, the ten children jumped behind the three SADEs after the First broke the top of the cliff trail and scurried across the grass to greet Alex and Teague.

That day was Ginny's first view of Teague, and she was mesmerized by the boy, who thumped the alien's blue green claw with abandon. When Teague whistled a greeting to the alien, Ginny peeked from behind Cordelia and imitated his whistle.

Aboard Idona Station, an accident rendered Ginny deaf. She received Terese Lechaux's medical nanites on station and, after arriving on Haraken, the cell-gen injections, which cured Ginny of her hearing loss and other minor ailments due to her diet's deprivation. But unknown to anyone, the nanites had restored the child's innate ability to produce perfect pitch.

The First's eyestalks swiveled to regard the youngling leaning from behind Cordelia's legs. He whistled a greeting and was intrigued by the perfect imitation he received. With Teague at his side, the First slowly approached the youngling, who continued to peer at him from behind Cordelia. He whistled a query and received an exact copy, causing him to warble his humor. The youngling was untrained but had the unique capability of a Hive Singer, an individual treasured by the People.

Ginny was fascinated by the alien, and her eyes constantly flicked between the creature and Teague. As the two entities, alien creature and human boy, halted before her, part of her mind cried out to run from the monster, but if the boy could stand next to the creature, then so could she.

"Hi, I'm Teague."

"Ginny. Who's this?" she asked, stepping from behind Cordelia and pointing at the First.

"This is the First. He's the leader of the Swei Swee. They live on the cliff wall. My dad rescued them." Teague puffed up at the mention of his father's deed.

Teague whistled an introduction of Ginny to the First, who extended a single, enormous, pointed claw to her. Ginny looked at Teague, who imitated smacking it with a fist. Not wanting to be found lacking in front of Teague, Ginny balled her tiny fist and smacked the top of the blue green claw as hard as she could, only to immediately yank it back and shake it vigorously to reduce the harsh stinging as tears formed in her eyes.

The First warbled softly at the youngling's efforts. His eyestalks viewed the other younglings still hiding and questioned Teague as to their lineage. It probably wasn't the best question to ask a young boy, who while he was near to mastering the Swei Swee language was still learning the subtleties of cultural differences. Teague replied that the ten younglings belonged to Julien and Cordelia.

The four eyestalks split between Teague and the children, and the First repeated his query in a slightly different manner and received the same response. He loosed a long, slow whistle, which the little human youngling imitated.

Originally, a SADE was known to the Swei Swee as a "Star Hunter Who Wasn't" — Alex's original description of an entity who they couldn't see having confused them. Now, to see two of these individuals returning after half an annual's absence with ten younglings and two of them nearly full-grown, the First was more than impressed, he was astonished at the pair's fertility.

Two days following the children's introduction to the Swei Swee, Alex gave Cordelia and Julien a warning that the First and a horde of matrons and young females would be descending on their home. The First had spread the word of the tremendous fecundity of Julien and Cordelia, and the hives wished to honor what they saw as a prodigious accomplishment on the part of two Star Hunters,

The Swei Swee arrived at the SADEs' house followed by a train of haulers driven by Mickey, some engineers, and a large group of techs, who brought a swim tank for keeping breath-ways wet, a live bait tank for food, and a supply of the materials the Swei Swee females required. The females would use the same two-step process to build their homes that created Haraken traveler shells — a process dubbed by Mickey as the application of Swei Swee spit.

Much to the SADEs' amusement, the matrons eyed the existing structure and ignored it. They built an entirely new residence complete with rooms for twice the present number of children.

Alex questioned the First as to the reason for the extensive residence, and the leader whistled his explanation, saying, "The matrons anticipate the birth of more younglings and are prepared to return in the future to enlarge the home as required." Alex got a chuckle out of explaining the home's enormous footprint to Cordelia and Julien.

But Julien wasn't lost for a retort to Alex. "If the president would be so kind as to stop invading other solar systems, my partner and I would not have the opportunity to collect more lost children."

Mickey and his engineers moved in behind the Swei Swee, who completed the residence in seventeen days, to do as they had done for Alex and Renée's house, which was to cut in windows, add doors, install refresher conveniences, and add food-dispensing areas — all the sundry amenities humans required.

* * *

Now nineteen years old, Edmas was completing his first year at university.

Espero University was the brainchild of the scientists who had defected from the UE explorer ship, *Reunion*, during the UE's incursion into the Hellébore system. The concept was born one evening during a discussion between Olawale Wombo, the scientists' leader, and his philosopher friend, Yoram Penzig.

Olawale and Yoram were mulling the contributions they might make to Haraken society, when the little philosopher said, "The Confederation's Méridiens receive most of their education via implant, and the curriculum is firmly established, but what about the Harakens? They're a mixed society of Librans, New Terrans, Méridiens, and ... refugees," he added, indicating Olawale and himself with a wave of his hand.

"To refugees," Olawale agreed, toasting his friend with his cup.

Yoram laughed and rubbed a hand over his 1-inch growth of hair. He couldn't get over the fact that after three decades of a completely bald pate, he now sported a full head of hair. "Another key difference from the Méridiens is that these people don't have a static technological base; they're inventing faster than one would believe," Yoram continued. "How do the children keep up with the incredible changes in their society's technology? What and where is the unified source of information that is continually updated?"

"University," the two men had cried out as one, laughing at their synchronicity. The UE scientists discovered their calling and their contribution to Haraken society.

The Assembly approved funds for the university's startup, and the scientists smartly recruited specialists to contribute their time as guest lecturers: Mickey taught engineering, the SADEs fulfilled an entire list of instruction from finance to interstellar exploration, Cordelia taught art, and Mutter instructed music courses. Alex was even dragged in to teach civics and government. Terese and fully another thirty Harakens brought their skills and experience to the new students.

Over the next four years, Espero University hired permanent professors, and the campus grew, building laboratories, lecture halls, administration buildings, and student facilities. The Assembly, reviewing the success of the university, felt compelled to underwrite the entire cost. Free education through the collegiate level was deemed a necessity to ensure the planet's children contributed to a strong and healthy society.

As for Ginny, she developed a fondness for music. It was the means by which Cordelia first calmed her when her hearing slowly recovered and the noise of the world crashed in on her. The sound of Cordelia softly singing for hours to her was something she never forgot.

Ginny was entranced by Mutter, the SADE's Hive Singer, who could compose and sing in the Swei Swee's whistling language. She spent much of her spare time in Mutter's presence, especially when the SADE visited the Swei Swee. But then, Ginny had a secondary purpose — the young boy who played with the Swei Swee. She was as curious about Teague as she was his playmates.

* * *

The morning after Edmas and Jodlyne overheard the conversation between Cordelia and Julien, they helped feed and prepare the other children for the day.

At one point, Cordelia said, "Enough, Edmas, you'll be late for your first lecture." Then as she received a comm, she added, "We have a guest ... at your request, it seems."

Z landed at the sprawling home in his personal transport, having to forgo his flit, since he was ensconced in his Cedric façade, the huge New Terran avatar that housed an extensive array of weaponry. He was prepped for the twins' operation to trace the escape route for Henry's people, which would take place later in the morning.

The SADEs, Edmas, and Jodlyne retired to a private room at the boy's request. To the ex-tunnel rats' relief, Julien and Cordelia graciously ignored the question of how the teenagers acquired their information.

"There's a reason that Étienne and Alain are having trouble finding this club," Edmas added. "The location is passed by word of mouth, and the offer is made only to young people like us, although no one has approached me."

"But someone has asked me," Jodlyne said, "and we're sure the club you're looking for is the same place this boy is offering to take me."

"How are you sure?" Julien asked.

"How many clubs are you searching for?" Jodlyne asked in reply.

"An excellent point," Z admitted. "We're looking for one club, and she has received an offer for one."

"We can locate this place for you," Jodlyne said earnestly.

The SADEs discussed the issue privately. Cordelia was adamant in her opinion, which was no, emphatically no. Julien, who saw the value of the teens' offer, was hesitant to contradict Cordelia.

<I honor your opinions,> Z sent to his fellow SADEs. <But humans, who rescued us from our starships, are now in need of our help. Just as we've rescued these young ones, so they want to do the same for others. Is that not something we should support if we are to teach the values that will help these young people become worthy adults?> Z was reticent to play the last card, as Alex would call it. Technically, Edmas and Jodlyne chose to come to Haraken to be with Z, even though they lived with Cordelia and Julien so that they could help care for the younger children.

Even years later, Z treasured the memories of the teens' first ride on his ancient horse avatar. Jodlyne whooped and yelled, "Look at me, Edmas," as Z rode first one then the other teen across an immense meadow. The teenagers were always the first to see his newest avatars, and if the constructions could accommodate humans to ride in or on, they were the first to do so. That Edmas studied engineering at an advanced level at university was due largely to his love of working on the avatars with Z and Claude Dupuis, one of the Méridien survivors of the *Rêveur*.

"Enough," Jodlyne said, interrupting the SADEs' comms. "We appreciate that you are concerned for our welfare, but you forget that we survived for years harassing the militia without being caught. We are not strangers to danger. So, if you are undecided, why don't we ask the president if he would like our help getting his sister back?"

At the mention of Christie, Cordelia retreated from her objections. Without Alex, her life, as rich and complete as it had become, would not have been possible.

"We will support your decision to help," Cordelia announced, "but under one condition, which is inviolate. You don't take a single step in this investigation unless it is approved by one of the three of us or the twins."

*   *   *

After Edmas' last afternoon lecture, which was an in-depth examination of nanites' mobility given by the SADE Dane, he hurried home on his flit to scoop up Jodlyne and return to Espero's city center. Nearing a million in population and counting, the founding Librans were astounded by the growth of their capital city.

Landing near a group of shops frequented by many of the city's young, especially visitors, Edmas and Jodlyne strolled the shops, purchasing small, sundry items to keep up the front.

"Hey there," a voice behind Jodlyne called, and she turned to find the boy they sought.

"Oh, hey, Serian," Jodlyne replied. "You remember Edmas?" She had thought of the New Terran teenager as attractive, but knowing that Serian was enticing her to a dangerous club elicited an entirely different emotional response. However, she played the game as if she was aboard Idona Station, and Serian was just one more member of the militia, who were the enemy of the rebels, her people, before the Harakens arrived.

The two boys nodded to each other, and Edmas wandered away to give them some privacy, but he kept a close eye on Jodlyne. He had always thought of her as the skinny, crying eleven-year-old girl he discovered hiding in the tunnels, someone who would always be his responsibility.

After Jodlyne's parents were arrested by the Idona Station militia for aiding the rebels, she chose to run away rather than face transport to an inner world and internment in a UE-run orphanage. Watching Serian chatting with her, leaning into her space, and Jodlyne playing him as they had toyed with the militia made Edmas smile, but it also made him examine her a little more closely. At seventeen and with the aid of the cell-gen injections and Haraken food, Jodlyne was no longer a malnourished child.

"So what do you think, Jodlyne, you interested?" Serian asked.

While Serian was talking, Jodlyne happened to glance toward Edmas, and she missed the boy's question, having to ask him to repeat it. The look on Edmas' face was one she hadn't seen before, not directed at her anyway, and, deep down, she experienced a tiny thrill. *It took you long enough,* she thought.

"Yeah, I could be interested, but it has to be tonight," Jodlyne replied.

"No splats here! Pick you up?" Serian asked. The thought of Jodlyne crowding onto his flit behind him was producing a serious fantasy for the teen.

"Meet you there. I'll take my flit like I'm going to a friend's house. I can't stay late ... just for a few hours."

"Okay, meet you here at 24.50 hours," Serian said, with a winning smile, pressing a small card into her hand and hurrying away.

Probably running to find more fools to give his cards to, Jodlyne thought. <We're clear,> she sent to Edmas.

The two teens examined the card, which had a pair of decimal-separated numbers. Edmas twigged to it first. "Clever ... locator points in the city." In his implant, he pulled up a map of Espero, located the grid points, and shared the map with Jodlyne.

While Jodlyne was thrilled with their success, she was much more interested in testing what she thought she had observed a few moments ago. She leaned close to Edmas and asked, "How do you want to play it?"

Edmas frowned and pulled his head back, but a slight blush colored his cheeks, and Jodlyne had her answer. *So I'm no longer a lost, scraggily, tunnel rat to you,* she thought with satisfaction.

5

Henry gave up the instructions to the twins for contacting his leader, Cherry, who would facilitate the team's exit from the planet, without any encouragement — except for the part where Étienne asked Henry if he would rather talk to the president than them.

Following Alex's explicit instructions, Étienne and Alain took six troopers armed with heavy weaponry and Z, housed in his Cedric-suit, who was a substantial weapon in his own right. Z accessed the unit's security module outside of the room Henry rented, and the Harakens searched it for information that might help them locate the girls, but nothing turned up. They did locate Henry's contact card tacked to the ceiling. It was hidden in plain sight, camouflaged by blending into the ceiling's coating, until a UV light, stuck to the bottom of a drawer where Henry said it would be, revealed the card.

Following the grid points on the card, the team ended up at a small warehouse used to store New Terran imported goods. Covering three of the exits with troopers, the twins let Z take the fourth door, which he entered by slamming a massive boot against its center. The reinforced metal door bent in about a half-meter, hung there for a moment, and then the entire door frame tore away from the building wall with a resounding screech of metal.

<Impressive,> Alain sent to Étienne, as they quickly followed Z inside.

The warehouse was loaded with goods, which Z scanned. They were legitimate goods, and a search of the premises was no more fruitful. Cherry, if she even existed, was not to be found.

One of the troopers did discover a cold room, which didn't seem to be unusual for a warehouse, except no one could think of any frozen New Terran goods that Harakens might purchase. Z snapped off the cover of the security mechanism, accessed the circuitry, and quickly overrode the system. Inside the twins and Z discovered three human corpses stacked one on top of the other and sealed in clear, vacuum bags.

"Let me guess … Busty," Étienne said, noticing the pronounced outline of the uppermost frozen body. "Fangs and Legs must be the other two."

"I'm not sure I understand the New Terran concept of escape route," Alain remarked.

"What's obvious is that the individuals we are dealing with are much more lethal than we might have surmised. I suggest we proceed with that concept in mind," Z said.

"Meaning?" Alain asked.

"Shoot first, and query them later," Z remarked and marched back out of the cold room.

While the troopers recovered the bodies, Z searched records for the warehouse's owner, discovering it had been recently rented by a New Terran company by the name of Desmonis Distribution.

* * *

The raid on the club was fraught with issues before it ever got started. According to Henry, the operators of the club would be dispensing drugs, which necessitated Terese and her medical teams accompany the forces making entry into the club. But Terese was bothered by the lack of information about the chemicals being distributed and to what extent they represented a danger to the teens.

Jodlyne added to the mêlée when she stated that she should go into the club alone. In her opinion, Serian would be unsettled by the presence of Edmas. As tunnel rats, she often went first to distract the enemy, allowing Edmas shots at diverted targets. This time, Jodlyne was pleased to see that her statement caused Edmas no end of consternation. It confirmed what she saw earlier in the afternoon at the shop, and the tiny thrill in her chest saw its flames fanned.

After the discussion's dust settled, Jodlyne's next trip to Espero's city center wasn't on the back of Edmas' flit. She was aboard one of five personal transports loaded with humans and SADEs, which landed several streets away from Serian's rendezvous point.

Armed with more repetitions of her orders than she cared to count, Jodlyne turned to walk away when Edmas wrapped her in his arms and whispered in ear, "You be careful."

"Always," she replied, giving Edmas a quick peck on the cheek. It was the first time she had kissed him, and she carefully stored the moment.

There were so many connections to Jodlyne's implant, she felt like a comm center, as she walked the several blocks to meet Serian. The boy, as promised, stood near a street corner in the doorway of a shop, which had closed hours ago. *Of course, you're early, and you hope you're going to get lucky tonight,* Jodlyne thought, and her sense of self-worth bloomed further.

Serian tried for a kiss when Jodlyne greeted him, but she artfully dodged it, keeping a pleasant smile on her face. Her escort wasted no time hurrying them off, taking several turns to reach a narrow street that seemed to meet a dead end. When she looked at him in confusion, Serian smiled back as if he held a great secret. Then he walked up to a side wall and waved his hand to eliminate the holo-veil covering the back wall and reveal the club's entrance.

"How clever," Jodlyne declared. Her statement was purely for Serian's benefit, since every step Jodlyne took was tracked by implants, SADEs, and the controller of a traveler floating silently overhead in the dark of a cloud-covered night. For her part, Jodlyne's security protocols were inactive, and she transmitted everything she saw, heard, touched, and even smelled.

When the club entrance lit up, the twins, who controlled the operation, signaled their forces to close on the building. The traveler's view allowed the copilot to spot the building's rear entrances, and he signaled troopers to cover those exit points.

Serian opened the door for Jodlyne and waved her inside. A woman with a shaved and tattooed head greeted them, and before Jodlyne could think of a reason to object, she was tagged with a med-injector and waved into the club. What didn't escape her attention was that Serian didn't receive a shot.

The doors beyond the reception area opened, and the deafening music nearly bowled Jodlyne over. But it was the sight of teens twitching and jerking their bodies in a distant imitation of the music that Jodlyne found unsettling.

Jodlyne stepped onto the club's dance floor, the doors sliding closed behind her, and she felt her implant connections drop off. It heightened her growing fear, and then the drug saturated her bloodstream and entered her brain, tearing loose her hold on reality.

For a lonely, frightened girl alone on a huge space station and hunted by the militia, holding onto reality was Jodlyne's way of surviving. It was choosing to run away, climb into a giant air duct, and crawl out of sight, armed only with a meager pack of water and rations. Maintaining control was how Jodlyne lived her life, but now that was slipping through her hands, no matter how tightly she tried to grasp it.

Jodlyne looked around for Serian, but the boy was nowhere in sight. *Idiot*, Jodlyne thought, *drugged and deserted like a tunnel-rat novice.*

The harder Jodlyne fought to retain control, the faster it seemed to slip away. Soon, she was back on Idona Station running from the militia, but there were too many of them, and they caught her. She screamed and kicked, but they hauled her away to a distant orphanage — away from the rebels — away from Edmas.

The hands of hundreds of faceless children pulled Jodlyne inside the orphanage, which swallowed her like a giant animal. Then her torment began in earnest. Every cruel act she could imagine that could be perpetrated by children was foisted on her. She cried out at them to stop, but they only laughed and continued to taunt and torture her.

*   *   *

Z and the twins were the first ones around the narrow street's corner. Thanks to Jodlyne's transmission they knew exactly where to look for the concealed trigger to reveal the entrance. Unfortunately, the beam was turned off.

<They know we're coming,> Alain sent to everyone on the comm net.

Z pulled up Jodlyne's images, mapped her steps toward the entrance, and marked the position where the doors would appear. <Follow me,> he sent, and ran at the blank wall.

The twins watched as Z disappeared behind the holo-veil and heard the crash of breaking doors. They and the troopers quickly followed, having tracked Z's movements. Inside the club, the reception desk was abandoned. The inner door of the club was already closing behind Z, and the twins signaled the troopers to fan out and check the offices while they chased after Z.

A search of the club's premises by the team revealed that the operators had fled, and the troopers monitoring the back exits reported that no one exited the building.

From the traveler overhead, Cordelia sent, <We have the felons in sight and are following.>

Inside the club's dance space, Étienne and Alain stared aghast at the twitching teens. They located the music source and shut it down about the time Z located the comm jammer and deactivated it.

<Terese, your services are required, but you will require transport and care for some fifty patients,> Étienne sent. <The young people are not on stimulants but something much more powerful and disconnecting.>

Edmas, waiting at the entrance to the narrow street, couldn't contain his impatience any longer and raced into the club. He connected to Jodlyne's implant and was struck by the chaos of the images he received. Threading among the bodies, some motionless and some still twitching, Edmas made his way to a corner of the club and found Jodlyne huddling there, her knees drawn to her chest, and sobbing.

<Help me, Terese,> Edmas sent, fear lacing his thought.

Terese finished sending her requests for additional support and ran for the entrance with Pia Sabine, her good friend, right behind her. Their implants tracked the positions of Edmas and Jodlyne, but they were momentarily halted by the vision of teens, their eyes vacant, standing and twitching or lying comatose on the floor. Edmas' cry for help was repeated, and they worked their way to the corner to find him cradling a whimpering Jodlyne. His eyes beseeched them for help.

Pia snapped open a small med-kit for Terese, who pulled an injector and selected an ampule to load. Immediately after the injector's application to Jodlyne's neck, she quieted. Pia would have called for a grav-stretcher, but Edmas struggled to his feet, hauling Jodlyne upright. He picked her up in his arms and carried her through the throng to the club's exit. She would not spend another moment in the maddening place if Edmas could help it.

Terese and her people went around administering the soporific to each teen until they ran out of ampules. They concentrated on moving the sedated, while they waited for resupply. Med teams transported the teens to Espero's primary hospital, returning as quickly as possible for the others.

* * *

Cordelia was tied into the traveler's controller. Three people had popped up on the club's roof from a concealed hatch, while Z, the twins, and the troopers searched the premises. The copilot and she monitored the fugitives' flight, while the pilot paid attention to their navigation.

Captain Escobar, an ex-Terran Security Forces officer and friend of Tatia Tachenko, was seated beside Cordelia in the traveler's passenger section. The captain was a member of the growing Haraken securities cadre who reported to the twins.

Behind the captain were fifteen troopers. The greater number was Tatia's idea. Having spent much of her time in operations against criminals on New Terra, she told the twins that it was more than likely their targets would have a clever escape plan, and the traveler and troopers would help negate their options. As Captain Escobar tracked the fugitives with Cordelia, he had to admit that his former TSF superior had called the shot dead on.

The three fugitives made their way across several rooftops before they shot a zip line to cross a street to the next rooftop. The gang repeated this several times before they dropped over the side of a building to a waiting grav-transport. Moments later they were airborne, racing for the outskirts of Espero.

Above, the traveler's pilot kept pace with the grav-transport. After the city limits were left behind, the lights of the fleeing transport were shut off, and its dark silhouette was lost against the landscape to the naked eye. The copilot switched the traveler's controller from visual scanning to a grav-wave detection signal, which was bounced off the fugitive's transport.

<Captain, Tatia and you seem to have an intimate knowledge of the criminal mind,> Cordelia sent to Escobar.

<Deal long enough with criminals and you begin to think like one,> Escobar sent in reply.

<And as you acquire that knowledge, how do you manage not to become one?> Cordelia asked.

<That's the great challenge for all law enforcement people, Ser.>

Cordelia could hear the sadness in the captain's words. *Apparently, some of your associates were not so fortunate at keeping the criminals' habits at arm's length*, she thought.

<They're stopping,> the copilot sent on open comm, which generated small movements among the troopers as they readied themselves.

The controller's telemetry displayed the transport's grav-wave halted, relative to the background wave of the planet. The pilot switched to an infrared view, and three heat-emanating figures hurried from the transport to disappear into a construction shed, which was still radiating the heat it absorbed during the day from Hellébore. At Captain Escobar's direction, the pilot silently landed the traveler in a meadow 200 meters away.

Cordelia rose but the captain blocked her way.

<Apologies, Ser, but I have orders from the twins that you are to remain aboard until we have subdued these criminals.> Cordelia stared at him in that deathly still manner that only a SADE could manifest, and Escobar added, <Please, Ser, I would have to deal with the twins, the president and, most especially, your partner if you did not heed this request.>

Cordelia sympathized with the captain's plight and relented, but not without giving him some parting advice. <We need these people alive,

Captain. While they may be armed and extremely dangerous, they're of no use to us dead.>

<Understood, Ser,> the captain replied, and he and his troopers filed quickly and quietly off the traveler. They disappeared from sight, crawling on their stomachs through the meadow's meter-tall grass.

Captain Escobar was no amateur when it came to arresting criminals, and he had a superb track record of capturing the vast majority alive. Instead of working his team close to the shed, surrounding it, and rushing in, Escobar formed his troopers in a loose cordon and settled down to wait.

After the troopers exited the ship, Cordelia ordered the pilot to lift off and position the ship to monitor the criminals if they evaded the captain's team. She smiled to herself, watching the captain's men on infrared as they settled into fixed positions, while the chronometer marched relentlessly on.

On the ground, Captain Escobar gave his adversaries three hours to settle down and believe they had escaped capture. Then he signaled his people to tighten the ring around the shed. From the small outbuilding's rear, two troopers ignited plasma rifles and started cutting through the wall along the roof line. The panicked fugitives raced out the front door, and several blasts from stun guns dropped them to the ground.

After removing their weapons and searching them for anything dangerous, the captain signaled the pilot, who landed the traveler meters away. Cordelia rechecked the restrained and comatose prisoners, searching for data material and hidden tools. Finding nothing, she nodded to the captain, who ordered the captives hauled aboard the traveler.

6

As the drugged, but now sedated, teens were evacuated to receive emergency medical attention, Julien and Z searched the club for evidence of Christie and her friends.

In a back room of the club, Julien pulled in a mouthful of air and ran sampling analyses on its contents. He froze, bent to the floor, and pulled in a second sample.

<Here,> Julien sent to Étienne, the nearest twin.

Étienne tracked the SADE's open comm link, and found Julien was on his hands and knees with his face to the floor, pulling in air, waiting, moving, and repeating his action.

"They were here … all three of our girls, for hours," Julien announced, rising and immediately relaying the same information to Alex.

* * *

The three prisoners were taken to the Security Directorate and settled into different interrogation rooms, where they woke hours later after their stuns wore off. The Harakens waited and watched them on the monitors, deciding how best to interrogate them.

"That's the leader," Tatia said, tapping the monitor, which showed Dar.

"This one is quite self-assured," Renée said, pointing to Lacey.

"I think this is our weak one," Alex said, indicating Trembles. "He might be big, but he looks nervous. I'll take the leader. Tatia and Renée, you have the woman. Something about her says she might prefer to talk to the two of you. Julien, Cordelia, and Z, you talk to Trembles. I think he will crack if he faces a wall of nonhuman entities."

The twins followed Alex into the leader's interrogation room, intending to intervene if Alex's anger overcame his good sense. Settling across the table from the leader, Alex connected the interviewers' implants and linked the group to Julien, who added Cordelia and Z.

"What do I call you?" Alex asked.

"Dar will do," the man answered.

"I'm looking for my sister. Where is she?"

"Who's your sister?" Dar asked nonchalantly.

"One of the three women you kidnapped and stuck in the back room of your club? Where are they?"

"Oh, those three fems. Didn't know one of them belonged to you. We just follow orders. The boss says he wants young fems, and we collect and send them to him."

"Who's the boss?"

"Goes by the name of Mr. Blue."

"His full name?"

"Don't know it."

"Here's the problem, Dar. You're lying to me. You say you didn't know one of the women was my sister, but after you kidnapped them, you worked really quickly to get them off planet. Now, you tell me you work for Mr. Blue, but you really work for Peto "Craze" Toyo." For the first time, Alex saw a crack in Dar's cool façade.

Tatia and Renée stood in front of the woman prisoner, crisscrossing in front of her as they paced the cell. Immediately after entering, they saw Alex's observation was correct. The woman's eyes lit up at the sight of them. She couldn't seem to make up her mind, which of her interviewers she wanted to watch, and her eyes flicked from one to the other.

<Which do you think she prefers … slender or robust?> Tatia sent to Renée.

<I think this one is an equal opportunity consumer,> Renée replied.

"Did you hear, Ser?" Tatia said offhand to Renée. "They found this one's competitors."

"Wonder if this crew would have gotten the same treatment?" Renée wondered out loud. "End up stacked like frozen specimens in a cooler."

"Barber's not like that crazy fem, Cherry," Lacey blurted out.

In the next interrogation cell, Trembles kept mentally repeating Dar's order to never talk to the adz, but the three characters, who stood absolutely still and silent in front of him, were unnerving. They had been standing there, unblinking, not a muscle twitching, for a while. It was unnatural to Tremble's way of thinking, like so much on this strange planet. He desperately wanted to go home to New Terra.

"Looks like you're too late," Cordelia suddenly announced to Trembles and started for the door.

"Too late for what?" Trembles asked, a little too anxiously.

"Too late to confess," Z added. "Dar and Lacey are already doing that, and they'll get the deal."

"Uh-unh ... no, they didn't," Trembles protested.

"Of course they did," Julien said. "Here's proof. Who's your top boss?"

"Mr. Blue," Trembles said, happy to show he could stick to the script.

"No ... Peto "Craze" Toyo, according to Dar," Cordelia replied.

That threw Trembles off balance. Dar was the tough case among them. He couldn't figure him talking.

"And according to Lacey, your immediate supervisor is Barber," Z said. "Is he as bad as Cherry? I mean eliminating her crew when one of them gets caught is pretty harsh."

"Cherry's people are dead?" Trembles asked.

"Cold storage," Julien replied, shaking his head, displaying his incredulity.

"Is that Barber's technique for cleaning up messes, like when his club gets raided?" Cordelia asked.

"No, Barber wouldn't do that to us. We'd be on the freighter and be gone," Trembles declared hotly.

"Like the girls," Julien said softly.

"Yeah, like the girls ... hey, no ... what ... I didn't say anything." Trembles squirmed in his seat, thinking Dar and Lacey were going to smack him good for opening his big mouth.

* * *

Knowing the girls entered the club in the evening and were spirited aboard a ship in the early morning hours, the SADEs searched for any freighter exiting Haraken's three orbital stations during that narrow window of time. Seven freighters undocked from stations, but three were headed for Méridien and were excluded from consideration. The other four were bound for New Terra, sailing under the Oistos flag and exiting McCrery Station.

Reviewing the records, Alex asked the SADEs to cross-reference the individuals at the terminals, who would have handled the crew and passengers embarking and disembarking for all four freighters.

"Interesting," Julien said, smiling at Alex. "We've discovered a Ser Dubois, who has serviced the freighter, *Bountiful*, on its every docking and undocking. That would be statistically impossible."

"I want to talk to Ser Dubois now," Alex replied.

"I thought you would. I've relayed the information to the twins. The SADEs are attempting to locate his implant as we speak," Julien replied.

Unfortunately, the SADEs wouldn't locate Ser Dubois. When the three girls, restrained and bagged, were carried past him, two exhibiting slender Méridien shapes, Dubois panicked, but before he could object he was stunned and hauled aboard the freighter. When the ship cleared Haraken space, Dubois became one of the many small objects making their way inexorably toward the furnace that was Hellébore.

"But we've discovered two criminal organizations," Renée objected. "Who's to say whether this freighter belongs to Ser Toyo or Ser O'Brien."

"Henry," Alex and Julien said simultaneously, and Alex dropped a kiss on Renée's forehead before he ran after Julien.

Henry sat up abruptly when he saw the huge Haraken president and his digital man come through the cell door in a hurry.

"You've been holding out on me, Henry," Alex said, crossing the cell toward Henry, who climbed up on his bed to squeeze into the corner of his cell.

"No, no, I didn't," Henry objected, his eyes bulging in fear.

"You didn't mention that you have a freighter dedicated to your people's coming and going at Haraken."

"A freighter dedicated to us?" Henry repeated in confusion. "No way! That would be stupid … draw attention to our operation in no time." Henry remained standing on his bed after the two individuals abruptly left his cell, afraid they might return. When they didn't, Henry slid down on his narrow cot to curl up. He wished for the same thing as Trembles — to return to New Terra where the adz weren't so relentless.

<The freighter, *Bountiful*, belongs to Toyo, and everything points to the girls being on it,> Alex sent to the team. <Julien, where's it headed?>

<If we can believe the captain's records, the *Bountiful* is returning to the moons of Ganymede, from where it originated.>

Alex started pacing, organizing his thoughts. The kidnapping took place on Haraken, and the kidnappers, who were New Terran, were caught. The illegal club was shut down, and another gang, with a second leader, was discovered; but the leader had eliminated her team, who were also New Terrans. Now the girls were aboard a freighter, sailing under the Oistos banner, headed toward the mining moons of Ganymede, which meant that the girls' recovery might well become embroiled in a political protest Alex would need to lodge with the New Terran government. Nothing in that train of thought satisfied Alex's desire to recover the Haraken girls with the greatest haste. He needed a second option and an odd idea occurred to him.

<I believe I will be taking some vacation,> Alex announced to the team.

There was just the slightest delay from Alex's people, before Renée chimed in, sending, <Sounds wonderful, my love. Shall I contact Captain Cordova to ready the *Rêveur?*>

<Certainly. I'm sure José would enjoy captaining a leisurely cruise for once,> Alex replied.

<If you're vacationing on New Terra, Mr. President, I would like an opportunity to see my parents, and, of course, I would wish to have Alain accompany me,> Tatia quickly added.

<Vacation or not, the president must be protected. I will require a cabin as well,> Étienne sent.

<Well, I certainly am not letting you go to New Terra by yourself, Mr. President. They tried to kill you there more than once,> Julien stated.

<Then I will accompany my partner,> Cordelia said.

<This forces me to go,> Z said.

<Why must you go, Z?> Alex asked.

<To keep all of you safe,> Z replied.

7

The following morning, preparations were well underway for the *Rêveur*'s exit, the earliest possible moment that could be arranged. Before he left, Alex worked to execute his duties as Haraken's president, the first of which was to notify the Assembly Speaker of his intended absence.

<Greetings, Ser President,> Eric Stroheim replied. He had replaced Tomas Monti as Assembly Speaker and, in turn, Alex appointed Tomas to Eric's position as ambassador to New Terra.

Eric had been kept abreast of the recent events, beginning with the twins' search for individuals known to be without Haraken ID, capturing the one called Henry or Wheezy, whichever you preferred — the twins still weren't sure of the man's real name.

<So besides the incomparable Ser de Guirnon, Ser President, who might be accompanying you on your vacation?> Eric sent.

Alex could hear the mirth in Eric's thoughts and smiled to himself. If any individuals had undergone a greater transformation than Eric, Alex didn't know them.

As Eric once said, after the Librans' rescue, his goal was to become a better human. Gone was the strict demeanor of the Méridien House Leader. The years as ambassador had brought Eric a wonderful sense of balance in the face of the difficult contests of wills, involving the needs of both governments. That he was Méridien, but not Libran, was why he was initially not considered for the Assembly, but, in time, the people saw the changes in Eric and embraced him as one of Haraken's valued leaders.

<A few others, such as Tatia and Alain, who wish to visit her parents,> Alex admitted.

<And for security?>

<I will have Étienne.>

<No troopers?>

<No need, but I will have some SADEs.>

<Presuming that is Julien, Cordelia, and Z. Who are they supposed to be visiting?>

<These are SADEs. Who can tell what thoughts go through their crystal minds?>

This time, Eric laughed out loud. <Life has never been dull since our meeting, Ser President. Enjoy your vacation. I will inform the public of your intentions and update the Assembly on the curtailing of the recent criminal activities. And, purely as a matter of course, if you happen to meet three, wayward, young Harakens, please bring them home with you. I understand their parents are worried.>

*   *   *

After evening meal, Bibi Haraken's transport landed at the Racine home. With her was Shera Beaufort, Amelia's mother. Bibi was the matriarch of the Haraken clan and one of the planet's first Assembly representatives. Recently, she stepped aside, and the populace elected Jason Haraken to her position. It seemed the Librans, despite becoming the minority in Espero, were uncomfortable if a member of the Haraken clan did not represent them in the Assembly.

After the amenities were observed and Alex updated the women on the events of the past several days, Bibi, direct as always, got right to the point. "What do you intend to do to get our children back, Ser President?"

"Go on vacation," Alex replied and quickly held up his hands to forestall the women's responses. "Let me explain. If we try to involve our governments, communications and negotiations will become protracted. The girls have been kidnapped by a criminal organization, which is not about to advertise what it's done. My thinking is that they are holding the girls because they don't know what to do with them. Having made the initial mistake of taking them, they're probably hoping not to be discovered, but, if they're found out, they'll want to make a deal."

"There's no indication the girls were at the club to … to participate, is there?" Shera asked.

"Nonsense," Bibi snorted, appalled by the question.

"If I was to guess, and I believe I know this threesome as well as anyone, they were there investigating. An illegal club dispensing dangerous drugs at the hands of criminal trespassers …" Alex let the statement hang in the air.

"Yes … yes, I suppose it would have been irresistible to your sister," Shera said.

"Are your eyes closed, Ser?" Bibi declared, turning to stare at her companion. "Since these three were barely teens, they've operated with one mind. No one of them dragged the others to that club. They would have done as they've always ever done — hatched the plan together. To insinuate that Christie led your Amelia there is to say you don't know your daughter."

Shera regarded Bibi for a moment, tears forming in her eyes, "Apologies, Ser President," she said, through sniffles and glancing toward Alex.

Bibi moved over to Shera and threw an arm around the younger woman.

"We understand that three of these criminals were murdered," Bibi said.

"Those individuals were from a rival gang, and they were killed, we believe, by their leader, who has fled the system."

Bibi shook her head at the thought of this type of people infiltrating their society. "So you're taking vacation, Ser President. Good timing. Libre is coming," said Bibi. She referred to the Librans marking the day they were freed from the Confederation. It was a bittersweet celebration. A quarter of a million incarcerated Méridiens escaped Libre, the penal colony for the independent minded, in massive city-ships constructed with the help of Alex and his people.

However, more than two thousand treasured elders were left behind on Libre, despite the fleet waiting until the last moment before it was forced to set sail. The late launch meant the fleet fought the dark travelers of the giant Nua'll sphere to gain the system's exit.

In the intervening years since Haraken was settled, Alex never appeared at the ceremony commemorating Libran independence or appeared in public at all that day, for that matter, and his privacy was respected. The then Admiral Racine might have done more than anyone to help save the Librans, but to him he failed to save the last two thousand, including Fiona Haraken, the planet's namesake and the Librans' beloved elder.

On the Librans' day of celebration, Alex and Renée would end the evening sitting in their gazebo, overlooking the sea, allowing them to watch Hellébore's setting orb. Alex would play Fiona's parting words to the fleet as the people fought to escape the system.

"While you're on this vacation, how will this work?" Shera asked, confused.

"That's an excellent question, Ser," Alex replied.

Bibi barked a harsh laugh. "No plan at all, Ser, I see."

Alex shrugged. "I can't do anything from here but negotiate, which I don't see as a winning tactic. The girls were taken to the moons of Ganymede in the Oistos system. Once I'm there, I'll have options."

"Well, no strategy before you exited Hellébore for Sol worked for the UE," Bibi admitted. She stood and gently pulled Shera up with her. "May the stars guide you in your efforts to bring our children back to us, Ser President."

After their guests left, Renée offered thé and a light meal, which Alex refused. He sat on the couch, thinking, and Renée curled up beside him.

"Don't you think it's odd that I can't come up with a strategy to attack these problems before we go on these ... these adventures?" said Alex, which caused Renée to laugh so hard she developed hiccups.

"Foolish question?" Alex asked, with his inimitable lopsided smile, while Renée regained control of her breath.

"There is no formula for success in this universe, my love, and if any two people should know that, it's us. Now is not the time to doubt what has always worked for you. I trust that, and you should too," Renée said, throwing her arms around Alex's neck and hugging him close.

* * *

In the early morning hours and after saying goodbye to Teague and Alex's parents, Katie and Duggan, who would care for their son and the Idona children while the SADEs were away, Alex and Renée stepped outside their home and into the sweet smell of dew-laden grass, as a traveler landed in the meadow nearby.

The hatch swung down, and two crew members hurried down to collect Alex and Renée's personal belongings, which were stacked on the front porch of the house. Next down the steep steps was Svetlana Valenko, a wing commander under Commodore Sheila Reynard.

"Greetings and a good morning, President Racine, Ser," Svetlana said jauntily.

"Did you do something to get demoted, Commander Valenko?" Alex asked, as he returned her salute.

"On the contrary, Mr. President, things are going well."

"Then why, Commander, should you set aside your duties today to play shuttle pilot?" Alex asked, as he helped Renée up the hatch steps.

"I'm your copilot today, Mr. President. Commander Canaan is your pilot. I was never able to visit New Terra during my time training fighter pilots there ... Niomedes, yes, but not New Terra. I'm quite looking forward to visiting your home world."

Alex eyed Svetlana, a gene-sculpted Méridien, who was a sublime example of the Nordic Europeans of Earth with her straight, white-blonde hair, deep blue eyes, and slender nose, but the Libran ignored his stare, instead smiling back and continuing to chat amiably about the impending visit to New Terra and the opportunity to visit a new world.

Soon after Alex and Renée boarded the traveler, they were setting down aboard the *Rêveur*. Once the bay was pressurized, they descended into a hive of activity. A second traveler, operating as a freight shuttle with its rear end dropped, was in the process of unloading, by crew in environment suits directed by Mickey Brandon.

"Morning, Mr. President," Mickey said brightly, opening his helmet.

"Don't tell me, Mickey, you're joining us for a visit to New Terra," Alex said.

"Absolutely! Wouldn't miss a chance to visit the home world!"

"A great deal of personal belongings," Alex said, pointing to the crates the crew was unloading.

"GEN machines and lab equipment for the engineering suite," Mickey replied. "They're requested by Terese."

Renée hid a smile behind her hand.

"And who might Terese be visiting on New Terra?" Alex asked, his eyes narrowing.

"I've no idea, but Pia is on her way down, and you can ask her."

Alex stopped his questioning and scanned for implants aboard the liner. His app returned the count of 189, which he shared with Renée. They exchanged glances and Renée shook her head, signaling she had nothing to do with whatever was happening.

"Do we, at least, have our suite, Mickey, or has that been taken up with equipment?" Alex asked.

"I'm sure it's available, but Ellie is in charge of cabin assignments. So, you should check with her."

"Ellie?"

"Sure … it's a vacation, so why wouldn't Ellie join Étienne? I mean Alain is here with Tatia," Mickey said over his shoulder, as he ran to help the crew muscle a huge crate onto a grav-pallet.

<Perhaps, it might be quicker, my love,> Renée sent privately to Alex, <if you were to ask who isn't coming on our vacation.>

<This is getting surreal. I'm beginning to think we are actually going on vacation instead of rescuing three kidnapped Haraken women,> Alex replied, as they made their way to the bay's airlock.

The airlock was already cycling, so they waited for the bayside hatch to open when Claude Dupuis stepped out.

"Claude," Renée exclaimed, hugging the Méridien.

"Are you on vacation too?" Alex asked, after exchanging greetings with the electronics specialist, who was kept eternally busy helping Z fabricate and upgrade his avatars.

"Vacation?" Claude said. "No, Sers, with so many of the *Rêveur's* survivors joining the voyage, I supposed it to be a sort of reunion trip and didn't want to miss out. Excuse me, Sers," Claude added. His delivery was so straight faced, that neither Alex nor Renée understood whether he was teasing or serious. Had they seen Claude's face, as he ran to supervise an offloading of Z's avatars, they would have seen the subtle smile he wore.

Alex and Renée no sooner gained the first corner in the corridor just forward of the landing bay, when Pia, hurrying around it and warned just in time by her proximity app, managed to dodge Alex. "Apologies and greetings, Ser President. Just like old times, isn't it?" she said, and then hustled toward the bay.

The couple traveled a scant 10 meters more when Ellie Thompson rushed up to them.

"Commander," Alex said drily, by way of greeting.

"Apologies, Ser President. I meant to greet you as you landed, but it's been so hectic. The owner's suite has been readied for you. Shall we?" Ellie replied, prepared to lead the way.

Renée barely managed to stifle her snicker. "I believe, Commander, that Alex and I are familiar with the way."

"Oh ... of course, Ser. Apologies," Ellie replied, embarrassed that in dutifully following her checklist and never having stepped aboard the *Rêveur*, she forgot this was the derelict liner that Alex had rescued.

"Commander, obviously you're exceedingly busy," Alex said graciously. "Why don't you return to the next item on your to-do list?"

Ellie offered a quick "Thanks" and rushed off, much to Alex and Renée's amusement. They made their way to their suite via the lift and corridors amidst a hectic rushing of crew, who jumped aside as Alex and Renée passed. Ellie was correct. The suite was well-prepared for them, and the pair settled into familiar surroundings. The couple's favorite thés were stocked, bed covers were fresh, and the salon's furniture was restored to its original configuration, comfortable for a pair on vacation.

<Ser President, we are ready to depart, if you would like to join us on the bridge,> Captain Cordova sent, just as their baggage arrived at the

suite. They used the captain's invitation as an excuse to get out of the way of the crew, who was busy unpacking and storing their belongings.

"Captain Cordova," Alex said, nodding a greeting as he gained the bridge, while Renée bussed both cheeks of the elderly gentleman.

"And so we embark on a new adventure, Ser President ... even if it's only a vacation," Cordova added, with a merry twinkle in his eyes. "Of course, you know my new starship trainee, First Mate Francis Lumley."

The ex-UE captain was bent over the pilot's panel, and, at the mention of his name, spun out of his chair and came to attention.

"No need for such a rigid style, Ser Lumley," Alex said. "We are much more informal here."

"Thank you, Mr. President," Lumley replied, relaxing into parade rest.

"It's a pleasure to see that you've found a place for your skills in our world, Ser," Renée said. "Are you planning to retire soon, Captain Cordova?"

"Not if I can help it," the captain replied, "but in this new world of ours, it pays to be prepared. Someday, I expect Ser Lumley will take care of you as I've tried to do."

"It would be my pleasure," Lumley agreed.

"So, Captain, are we ready?" Alex asked.

"Yes, Ser President, we have four travelers aboard with pilots and crew, baggage and equipment have been stowed, and all personnel are aboard and report ready."

"You sure we haven't left some aspect of the population down below?" Alex asked, narrowing his eyes at the captain.

Lumley hid his smile by turning back to his bridge control panels.

"I believe we have the required number of essential personnel for any adventure the president wishes to discover," Cordova deadpanned.

"Then let's make for Oistos, Captain," Alex ordered.

On the central screen, the view changed as the liner pivoted away from the planet to face the deep dark and accelerate toward a system exit.

Alex's thoughts drifted over the times he had sailed the venerable liner into trouble. When Haraken was established, Alex considered he had the start of a unique and stable society, but time and growth said that no society was immune to change. *It's how we manage those changes,* Alex thought. He promised himself that when he returned with the girls, he would spend some time with the teens from the club. He wanted to know what they were seeking, or perhaps, better said, what was missing in their lives — Librans, New Terrans, and visitors — all of them.

8

Taking on the role of admiral in Tatia's absence, Sheila Reynard was arguing with Assembly Speaker Eric Stroheim in his office.

"I'm not in favor of Alex's directive either, Eric, but he was specific in his orders ... no carriers," Sheila said. "Alex thought the presence of that much force at Oistos would cause the criminals to panic, creating dangerous circumstances for the girls before he could make contact and begin negotiations with them."

"I see Alex's point, Sheila, but, on the other hand, you must admit that we're risking a great many of our key people against unknown and dangerous adversaries. It's not just the girls who might be in danger."

"You called me here this morning for a reason, Eric. Do I take it that you have a suggestion?" Sheila asked.

"Actually, I do. How are the field tests for the *Tanaka* proceeding?"

"Latest reports have the sting ship returning to the system in three days. All tests were passed successfully. But what's the difference between sending a carrier and sending a sting ship to Oistos?" Sheila asked.

"I agree our carriers are known entities that would only signal aggression. But our sting ship is brand new, unseen. I think it would be a great time to show it to the New Terran president and see if his government is interested in purchasing some."

"A business trip ... Assembly Speaker Stroheim, I believe you've been hanging around the New Terrans too long," Sheila said, with a smile.

"Indeed," Eric replied, adding his own smile.

"But to make this work, Eric, we'll need a government representative aboard."

"Precisely," Eric replied, his smile growing larger.

"You?" asked Sheila, surprised at how far Eric had thought through his idea.

"Me ... and I will need some things from you, Admiral Reynard ... a traveler for me to meet the *Tanaka* when it enters our system and whatever additional crew and supplies the ship might need for an extended trip.

Sheila mentally sorted through the *Tanaka*'s original outfitting lists as quickly as she could. The sting ship's structural buildout was complete, but it was only minimally supplied for its trials — a bare crew, one traveler in its twin bays, which could accommodate four, and sufficient food and cabin outfitting for the small crew.

The Assembly had sought to honor Alex by placing his name on the first sting ship as suggested by Eloise Haraken, who considered the vessel, with its aggressive nature, akin to their protector, her great-grandmother's term for Alex. But, once again, Alex dodged the honor by suggesting someone he believed more appropriate — Hatsuto Tanaka, who sacrificed his life to protect Alex at New Terra. The Assembly accepted his recommendation.

"I can have you outbound from Haraken tomorrow morning, Ser Assembly Speaker, and let me be the first to wish you good fortune in securing a favorable agreement with the New Terrans for our newest ship," Sheila said, rising and extending her hand with a sly grin on her face.

* * *

Reiko Shimada completed the last of her summary reports for her superiors. She couldn't be happier with the results of the sting ship's trials. *It's a completely different game when SADEs design your ship*, Reiko thought. In the UE, a new destroyer took months to shake out the kinks and bugs and then not always. More than one warship was plagued throughout its life with quirks that could never be solved.

Before Reiko rose, she took a moment to stare at the exquisite crystal decorating the corner of her desk. Days before she left Idona Station, returning with Franz Cohen aboard the *Rêveur* when the Harakens left Sol, she was presented with the memento from Nikki Fowler, the station director, and Patrice Morris, the assistant station director. Inscribed on the crystal's stand was the sentiment: To our hero and friend.

Leaving Sol for an alien world was the hardest decision Reiko thought she would ever make, except for maybe choosing to ram a UE battleship with her destroyer to save Idona Station. In the end, it came down to a simple question: Did she want to live without her huge, New Terran lover, Commander Franz Cohen? The answer was a resounding no.

<Captain, you have a priority comm,> Willem sent, interrupting Reiko's thoughts.

<Successful cruise, Captain?> Eric Stroheim asked Reiko.

<Hello, Ser Stroheim. Yes, it was an extremely successful shakedown cruise. Apparently, that's the expected result, according to Willem, who was surprised that I was surprised.>

<Yes, well, sometimes our SADEs take issue with our thinking that they might have a degree of fallibility.>

<How can I help you, Ser Stroheim?> Reiko asked, with some trepidation. The *Tanaka* had just regained the Hellébore system and the thought crossed her mind that something might have happened to Franz.

<There is much that has transpired since you've been gone these past seven days, but suffice it to say, you and I will be taking an extended trip. Tell me, Captain, do you consider yourself a salesperson?>

*   *   *

The Harakens' new sting-class ship, represented by the *Tanaka*, was created following the realization that their carriers and travelers were insufficient to handle the dangers that the universe seemed intent on throwing at them. The carriers had no defensive capability and had to be kept out of harm's reach. The travelers were tremendous offensive and defensive weapons, but if the carrier was lost, the travelers were trapped in system.

Not long after Reiko landed and received her implant, Tatia tasked her with helping the SADEs design a mid-sized, attack craft with FTL capability. The SADEs insisted on employing a beam weapon energized by a grav drive, since it was essentially a weapon that didn't require armament.

Reiko recalled the miner's exploratory tool at Idona Station, which employed a clamshell scoop to collect specimens. She suggested to the SADEs that they might cover the primary drive engines with a similar design that could seal like the travelers' hatches, which melded with the shells. The clamshell would open, allowing the primary drives to move the ship from system to system, and, once in system, would close to allow the grav-drives to charge the beam and power the ship just like a traveler.

The same concept was required for the twin bays, carrying the four travelers. Open bay doors would severely curtail the gravitational wave energy inducted by the shell while the fighters launched, but this limitation could be overcome by employing the primary engines. It gave the captain options — opening the bays doors to launch and retrieve the travelers, accepting the loss of drive or, if extensive maneuvering was required, opening the rear clamshell to employ the primary engines.

The design came together rather quickly considering. Not so for the construction of the first sting ship, which earned its class name when Christie, who had marveled at the design, said, "That should give someone a nasty sting if they mess with it."

Since this would be the first Swei Swee shell-covered ship that departed from the design of the Nua'll travelers, Mickey chose to approach the construction in steps. He and his engineering team built a series of models, one-twentieth scale, and requested the hive females layup shells on each one. This allowed the team to test the efficiency of a model to pass gravitational waves through its shell. The best design, after more than a hundred tests, bore an eerie resemblance to an elongated traveler with a pointed bow and a long tubular body that widened toward the bubble-shaped aft end.

The full-scale, sting shell took the Swei Swee the equivalent time of twenty travelers to layup. But the matrons laid into the effort with a will. The First was ecstatic to see the Star Hunters creating more powerful ships to defend their world against other hunters.

Mickey took the completed hull structure and sliced into the shell to cut the hatches, bay openings, and aft-end's four clamshell sections. After having successfully performed the same operation on myriad travelers, Mickey's engineers expected similar results and they weren't disappointed.

Reiko was honored with the first test flight, a circling of the planet with the new ship, and she chose Franz to sit copilot with her. After arriving at Haraken, Reiko joined the cadet training academy as a lieutenant, and Tatia promoted her to captain on graduation, recognizing her achievement of top honors and first in her class. But it was what everyone expected of an ex-destroyer captain who had made cruiser commodore in United Earth's naval forces.

At graduation, Renée and Reiko had hugged warmly. The women had become close friends as Renée knew they would. "Was I right?" Renée said to Reiko, when she caught the petite Asian eyeing her New Terran lover, who was chatting with Alex. When Reiko grinned and nodded in response, Renée added, "These men are irresistible ... noble and virtuous, out to save the worlds, but who protects them? We do," Renée said, taking Reiko's hands in hers. "A woman might choose not to be a mother, Reiko, but there's no reason she can't still be a protector."

*　*　*

Per Reiko's orders, Willem brought the *Tanaka* to a zero-V relative to the three travelers coming amidship and opened the bay doors on either side of the sting ship.

Reiko waited in the airlock for the bay to pressurize so she could greet her guest, Eric Stroheim. The Assembly Speaker was playing it close to the chest about what constituted the reason for the emergency trip to New Terra aboard a barely tested new ship — the first of its class, at that.

Having developed a healthy respect for the Haraken SADEs at Idona Station, Reiko had approached Willem to ask if the SADE would agree to accompany the ship on the unscheduled trip to New Terra.

"Most assuredly, Captain," Willem had replied. "The safety of the crew depends on my continued presence until the ship has been tested to my satisfaction."

It was an extremely welcome answer for Reiko, who was a believer in the SADEs' incomparable degree of competence. The complete dearth of issues discovered during their shakedown cruise had taken her aback, not that she wasn't pleased with the results.

"Welcome aboard, Ser Stroheim," Reiko said, greeting the Assembly Speaker as he descended from the traveler.

"Please call me Eric, Captain," Eric replied. "It was short notice, so I had difficulty finding an unassigned officer to command the traveler pilots. This was all I could get," he added, pointing over his shoulder at the traveler's hatch where Franz appeared.

"Really scraping the bottom of the proverbial barrel," Reiko agreed.

Franz was handling baggage and his smile disappeared when he saw Reiko and Eric staring at him in disgust. He looked behind him and then back at the two on the deck, "What?" he asked, and Eric and Reiko broke into laughter.

<Thank you,> Reiko sent privately to Eric.

<It was my pleasure, Captain,> Eric replied, heading toward the airlock to give the captain and her lover a moment in private, quite pleased with himself.

Sheila sent the sting ship three fully loaded travelers. Two were filled with pilots, flight crew, and additional crew members. It wouldn't complete the vessel's full crew complement, but it was all that two travelers could hold. The third traveler, designed as a freight shuttle, which loaded and unloaded from the aft end, was crammed full of supplies. The crew wasted no time unloading food stock, cabin supplies, and sundry other material.

Willem ensured the hatches, bay doors, and clamshell sections were securely closed, according to sensor reports, and the shell was fully operational, attested to by the controller's monitoring of the grav-drives as the energy levels rose. When he was satisfied that the ship was properly sealed and charging, he directed the controller to determine the nearest system exit to jump for New Terra. Reviewing the controller's calculations, Willem approved its directional choice and calculations and then ordered the controller to launch the ship under max acceleration. Immediately after, he joined Eric, Reiko, and Franz on the bridge.

Eric was ending a lengthy update for his audience on the recent events in Espero, from the initial suspicion of interlopers to the discovery of two gangs at work in the city to the kidnapping of the three girls that they believed were aboard a freighter bound for the moons of Ganymede in the Oistos system.

Willem didn't require an update from Eric Stroheim, but he kept that note to himself. He had received Rosette's transmissions, updating him as information became known. As Rosette supported the Assembly, she was privy to information at Eric Stroheim's level, and she communicated to every Haraken SADE, who was a director of Haraken's Central Exchange, the government's bank. The SADEs shared critical information with one another as it became available and stored noncritical data in the Exchange vault, an underground data storage location known only to the SADEs and Alex Racine.

Willem didn't consider withholding knowledge of the events at Espero from Captain Shimada as inconsiderate. It was a simple matter of preventing unnecessary information from burdening his captain. Willem, who had struggled mightily with his transfer to an avatar, had Alex to thank for providing him with direction and helping him integrate into human society, which, at first, he had shunned. The SADE thought of Reiko in the same circumstances as those early years of his, an individual deserving of some protection until she had more time to orient herself to a new society. Then again, Willem was not the best judge of people. Kilo for kilo, Reiko Shimada was one of the most self-reliant humans he might ever meet.

"Which carrier did the president take?" Reiko asked. When silence greeted her question, she said, "He took the *Rêveur*."

"The president believed that a carrier might foment trouble with the New Terran government and scare the criminals into rash decisions," Eric supplied.

"Ah ... so that's the ploy," Reiko said, nodding. "We arrive on this strange Haraken ship and announce to the New Terran president that we have this shiny, new design for him to inspect and see if he wants a few for his people."

"Precisely," Eric replied. "And if, for some unexpected reason, our president, on his vacation mind you, requires assistance ..."

"We are there to provide it," Franz said, smiling along with Eric and Reiko.

Willem's typical days were filled with interstellar exploration. He ran the highly respected observatory platform positioned outward of Haraken that searched for secondary worlds for the people. Scientists from Haraken, New Terra, and, occasionally, Méridien, worked with him, collecting and analyzing the data from probes sent on trips tens of light-years out from Hellébore. Listening to the humans discuss a ploy founded on duplicity made him realize how much he prized the world of empirical science.

"Sheila tells me your beam tests went well," Eric said, looking between Reiko and Willem.

When Reiko nodded to Willem, the SADE replied, "Expectations, comparative to our travelers, were that the beam's power would increase by a factor of 12.65 and the reach by a factor of 21.32. However, the test revealed a power factor discrepancy of -0.3 percent and the reach error was even greater at +0.5 percent.

"Worrying indeed," Eric commented drily.

"Precisely," Willem intoned. "But I believe the errors will be found in our extrapolation from the model to the full-scale ship, in which case, reality must supplant expectations."

"In other words, we must accept the results as they are," Eric surmised,

"Unfortunately, yes," Willem replied. When the SADE noticed Reiko's hand hiding a grin and Franz searching the overhead while pinching his lips, Willem added, "Perhaps my top-down view of expectations is unnecessary. In human terms, the tests went well." That his last comments elicited smiles seemed noteworthy to the SADE. The individuals in front of him weren't scientists, and, therefore, they required a different form of analysis.

Early in his relationship with the president, Willem had been warned by Alex when he said, "SADEs will seem identical, even though they're not, compared to humans, who will have nearly an unlimited number of different opinions on the same subject." It had seemed an incomprehensible statement to him, at the time, but here was a perfect example. That the beam tests did not meet expectations was unnecessary to these people. Under the circumstances, they needed the beam to work well — and it did.

*   *   *

The rendezvous of the *Tanaka* and travelers was late in the sting ship's day, and it was 26.75 hours before Franz, his pilots, and the flight crews finished securing the travelers, arranging sleeping quarters, and unpacking and distributing the cabins' appointments the third traveler had carried.

Before Franz requested some crew grab a cabin's worth of material for him, he checked the controller for his cabin assignment.

<Apologies, Commander,> Willem sent. <You won't find a cabin assigned to you. Captain Shimada is expecting you.>

Franz thanked the SADE and made his way toward the *Tanaka*'s bow. The captain's suite was located just behind the bridge. Before entering, Franz checked for implants inside and located only Reiko's. The cabin door responded to his signal request, sliding silently open. *It looks like I'm expected,* Franz thought with a smile on his face.

Reiko had retired to her cabin after a lengthy conversation with Eric. She anxiously tracked Franz's implant, smiling to herself at the thought of a commander who pitched in to help a crew settle into their new ship. *Wouldn't happen in the UE,* she thought. As time dragged on, she tucked into bed to await Franz's arrival. She was falling asleep when her app warned of her lover's approach.

"Captain, so nice to see you again," Franz said, entering the sleeping quarters. He crossed to the bed to give Reiko a kiss.

"Whew!" Reiko replied, after she returned Franz's kiss. "Someone needs to hit the shower."

"And how hard would the captain like me to strike the refresher?" Franz asked, stripping out of his ship suit, while reminding Reiko of the correct terms.

After three years on Haraken, Reiko was still adopting Meridian terminology. "Please, Ser, off to the refresher with you," Reiko said, shooing Franz in the right direction with a wave of fingers.

Several people had explained to Reiko how the Méridien refreshers worked, but the complex formulation of the liquid and its reconditioning weren't particularly interesting to her. That the liquid felt amazing, absorbed dirt and oils, and left the skin feeling refreshed was all she cared about. But the undeniable luxury was that she was no longer limited to three-minute showers aboard ship.

When Reiko heard the refresher running, she slid open the small drawer in the table next to the bed, retrieved the precious crystal Franz purchased for her on Idona Station, and placed it carefully on the table top.

In their home, many days ago, Reiko had been digging through Franz's storage, searching for carryalls that she might use to move aboard the *Tanaka* for the trials. Pulling out a large bag, she sought to clean it out and found the delicately wrapped gemstone carving of a Terran deer that she had admired in the shopkeeper's window only moments before her vicious attack by three rebels. It was a beating she barely survived and that only due to Terese's skills and Haraken medical technology.

When she found the carving, tears had coursed down Reiko's face as she cradled the rose and purple crystal figurine. She could guess why Franz withheld giving it to her, not wishing to remind her of the ugly event, and she loved him for his considerateness.

Franz emerged from their refresher, tying a wrap around his waist. Both Reiko and Franz were still a little uncomfortable with the Méridiens' preferred style of undress in private. In the Haraken naval academy, Reiko discovered men and women, especially the Librans, were often comfortable in the dorm rooms without clothes.

Franz was about to say something to Reiko when his eye caught the tiny, crystal, deer figurine beside her bed.

"I found my gift," Reiko said. Since Franz was speechless, his hands frozen on the wrap's knot, she added, "If you're wondering, I love it, and I think it's time for me to have it."

Reiko had expended a great deal of effort trying to put the memories of the attack behind her, and nothing helped those memories fade faster than the moment she stepped aboard the *Rêveur* for the trip to Haraken. Franz and his people provided an atmosphere that exuded personal safety and comfort with one another. In their gracious company, the pain of the horrendous beating slowly faded.

"Come here, lover," Reiko said, sitting up and dropping her wrap. "The hero of Idona Station is becoming impatient for her due."

9

Christie woke up on the deck of a small, utilitarian cabin, no restraints and no metal-mesh bag over her head. She was cramped, cold, foggy headed, and desperate to use the refresher, which turned out to be the simplest style of ship's head possible. She used the toilet and then gulped water from a faucet with her hands, trying to rehydrate and clear her head.

Struggling back into the cabin, Christie found Amelia and Eloise lying on the floor. She checked each of them for a pulse, greatly relieved to realize they were merely unconscious. It was one of the times Christie was grateful for her New Terran physique, since it appeared her larger body was able to metabolize the drug from the expended patch she found on her neck that much faster.

The cabin was equipped with a pair of bunk beds, and Christie stripped the threadbare blankets from each bed and used them to cover the girls to keep them warm. Then she sat on the lower bunk sipping from a water cup she found on the cabin's combo desk-table, filling it from the head's sink. She refilled the cup several times and revisited the head once more, while she waited for Eloise and Amelia to come around.

You just had to check out that club, Christie thought, disgusted with herself. Her momentary fear was that Eloise and Amelia, her two best friends, might not forgive her. "Pull your head out of your ass, Christie," she mumbled. "Worry about your friendships later … work on getting out of this mess for now."

When Amelia moaned, Christie popped up and hurried to refill her cup. Picking up Amelia's head and shoulders, she knelt and slid her substantial thighs under the slender Libran to prop her up. As Amelia's eyelids fluttered open, Christie smiled at her, never so grateful to see her friend's sparkling, multihued, Méridien-designed eyes.

Amelia blinked and focused on Christie's upside-down face. She tried to speak but it came out as a croak, and Christie tipped a cup of water to her lips. The cool water slid down her throat and was exceedingly welcome. Amelia took several sips before she realized it was foul-tasting water. "That water is worse than blah," Amelia said, and was surprised by her friend's laughter, followed by tears. "Easy, crèche-mate, we're still alive," Amelia soothed.

When the girls were young teens, but recognized their growing relationship, Amelia joked that they were really crèche-mates, and they began referring to themselves in that manner. It was how they encouraged each other in tough times.

Christie pulled Amelia into her arms, hugging her fiercely.

"Easy, big girl, I don't want to die from a hug while I'm still trying to survive a kidnapping."

Christie would have riposted with a witty barb of her own, but Eloise began coughing at that moment, and while Amelia crawled to their friend's side, Christie ran to refill the small cup.

Eloise struggled up with Amelia's help and sipped on the water Christie offered. "Good to see you two again," she managed to finally croak out, and Christie and Amelia hugged her, spilling the cup's remaining sips of water down Eloise's front.

"What's this?" asked Eloise, looking down at the ship suit she was wearing.

"Someone dressed us while we were out," Christie replied, examining her own basic crew ship suit. She unzipped the front down to her navel. "And they've taken all our clothes, even our undergarments."

"Hope they enjoyed the display," Amelia replied, struggling to stand. Christie helped her over to the lower bunk and sat her down. When Eloise nearly fell as she stood, Christie swept her slender frame into her powerful arms and settled her next to Amelia, and then ran for more water.

"We could each use a cup," Amelia called out.

"Only found one," Christie called from the head.

"All the comforts of home," Eloise grumped.

Amelia held out her arms, examining her ship suit, and checked Christie's when she returned with the cup for Eloise. "Well at least your suit fits, somewhat," said Amelia. "Obviously, they were prepared for New Terrans but not Méridiens." With her arms extended, Amelia looked as if she was imitating a boat under full sail.

Christie helped each of the girls to the cabin's tiny head when they were ready, and then she tore a small towel into strips to tie her friends' ship suits at the elbows and knees.

"That's better," Eloise agreed, looking at the effect of the ties. "At least, we won't flap while we're walking around."

When they were ready to explore their meager surroundings, the girls found the cabin door locked and a hand printed sign in New Terran posted on the door. It said, "Bang on the door or make any noise and the restraints and comm blocks will return. Gags too!" Checking the cabin, the girls found a sufficient number of ration bars for three people for twenty-plus days.

"Wonderful," Eloise groused. "We're trapped in this waste of a cabin, which, by the way, has only two bunks."

Christie looked at the sparse, narrow, bunk beds and quipped, "I'm happy to share."

Amelia and Eloise eyed Christie's substantial frame and laughed. It was just what the girls needed after waking from the ordeal of their kidnapping.

"Not only do you get your own bunk, Christie," Amelia said, "but you're banished to the lower bunk. We're not risking fortune by having you fall through these flimsy excuses for beds and crushing us below."

With the break in tension, the girls carefully searched the cabin for information and tools, but apparently the criminals weren't novices. There was nothing helpful to be found in the cabin.

Using their internal chronometers apps, the girls determined that when they awoke in the cabin more than two days had passed since the night at the club. After consuming a meal bar and more water, they decided to communicate only through their implants on the off chance they were being monitored, despite the fact that none of them could connect to another implant, comm probe, station, or ship, for that matter. Within days, they estimated the ship would probably exit the Hellébore system.

<So we're not dead, but why take us?> Eloise asked. <And for that matter where are we headed?>

<Your second question is easy ... the Oistos system,> Christie replied. <That shave-headed woman at the front of the club was New Terran, and this freighter is obviously New Terran–built but with Méridien drives.>

<But why take us?> Eloise repeated.

<I think we stumbled into something much more dangerous than we expected,> Amelia replied. <Whatever drug those teens were on was powerful and when we didn't take it, we blew our masquerade.>

<So they were on to us, but, for the third time, why take us?> Eloise asked. <Why not just ... just kill us?>

<I think I know why. We were kidnapped because they recognized me,> Christie answered. <I'm sorry,> she said, hanging her head.

Amelia and Eloise went to Christie and wrapped their arms around her, sending comforting thoughts.

<We've always agreed that the three of us would choose our actions together. You didn't drag us there, Christie,> Eloise sent.

<And, if they recognized you, then you may have saved our lives,> Amelia added.

When Christie seemed to regain her emotional equilibrium, Eloise asked, <Do you think we were taken for ransom? I saw a vid where kidnappers took a child and demanded credits for her return.>

Amelia burst out laughing, sending, <I doubt it. Would you want Alex Racine to know you were the one to kidnap his sister?> Both Librans had to agree with that line of reasoning.

<So we've been kidnapped, and we're being taken out of the system, but we don't think it's for ransom,> Christie said, summarizing their thoughts. <Why do I think they don't know what to do with us?>

<Yes,> both Amelia and Eloise sent simultaneously.

<We caught them by surprise, and they panicked, took us, and got us out of the system,> Amelia reasoned.

<Which means whoever is on the other end of this trip will inherit threes headaches ... us,> Eloise said, pointing a finger at each of them.

<Let's hope he or she is a reasonable person,> Christie sent.

* * *

Trapped in the cramped cabin for the duration of the trip, the girls took turns stripping out of their ship suits and exercising in the cabin's limited deck space. Every few days, as their chronometers metered the end of the day, they washed their suits in the tiny shower and hung them up to dry during the night as they slept.

The first time Christie shucked her suit and began exercising, Eloise sent, <You might be giving someone quite a show.>

<I think they've already seen everything we have and for who knows how long,> Christie sent back as she continued her exercise routine, moving to the music stored in her implant.

The girls logged nineteen days on their calendar apps from the night they were taken when they felt the telltale shift of exit into a system and the vibrations of the deck, which indicated the engagement of sub-light drives.

<Oh, thank the stars,> Eloise intoned. <I can't take being locked up in this excuse of a cabin any longer.>

<What makes you think our next accommodations will be any better?> Amelia grumped.

<Let's just hope we get accommodations,> Christie said, putting a damper on their conversation.

The girls waited out the remaining days; the supply of meal bars dwindling. Then early one afternoon, the constant vibration of the freighter's engines ceased. The girls waited with trepidation for who would come through the door, but no one came. By evening, the last meal bars were consumed, and the girls chatted via implants for a while before turning in for some rest.

In the middle of the night, the cabin door burst open and the lights snapped on.

"Get up," a huge New Terran ordered. He and his hard-looking partner spread apart to cover the girls as they climbed out of the bunks.

"Don't bother with the suits," said the man's partner, who had a nasty scar across his forehead. He tossed clothing on the deck that the girls recognized was what they had worn to the club.

"You didn't even bother to clean them," Amelia grumbled, as she picked up her wrap and footwear.

In reply, the first man, whose blond hair was shaved high on both sides of his head, lifted a baton and an arc of energy danced between the tips.

"Message received," Christie said quietly. <Behave, you two,> she sent. <Don't presume these men know who we are. They might just have jobs to do and not care how it gets done.>

"Here's the drill," Scar said. "It's 2.80 in the morning here. We're going to walk to a flight bay like we're good friends. Should be quiet on the ship, but if we meet anyone, you're a bunch of good-time fems … understood?"

When the girls nodded, Blondie pointed his baton at Amelia. "You, come here." When Amelia came close, Blondie slid his baton out of sight in a long pocket in the leg of his ship suit then grabbed Amelia by the hair and pulled her close to his chest. Producing a deadly looking knife, Blondie held it millimeters from Amelia's cheek, smiling crookedly as he watched the fear grow in her eyes.

"We get no trouble," Scar growled, "and Jessie here doesn't have to carve your little fem buddy into slices. Now, we understood?" When Scar received voluble assents from the girls, he added, "Now, that's the kind of fems I like … real pliable."

"You, home girl," Scar said to Christie, "you and I walk up front, arm in arm, like you're working real hard to earn your credits. You two mutes walk with Jessie."

<What did he call us?> Eloise sent.

<Not now,> Christie cautioned. <Play your part, just like we were investigating these guys.>

Scar eyed everyone, ensuring he had the attention he wanted, and then he opened the cabin door and peeked out into the corridor. Seeing it was clear, he crooked a finger at Christie. They stepped out into the corridor, and Christie wrapped an arm around Scar's waist.

Eloise and Amelia did the same with Jessie, and the five of them strolled down the corridor to a lift to take them several levels down to a flight deck. Several times they heard noises as they negotiated corridors, but to the girls' relief, nobody crossed their path. Cycling into the bay, the group climbed aboard an aging shuttle.

"Better strap in, fems. No grav-plating here," Scar said, and disappeared into the cockpit with Jessie.

"My nanites will be working overtime," Amelia griped, after the men were out of earshot, rubbing her rear end and wincing.

"Likewise," Eloise echoed. "Just what's with these New Terrans that they like to squeeze and pinch a woman's posterior?"

"Hurry and strap in," Christie ordered with urgency, hearing the shuttle engines start. Moments later, the shuttle lurched, spun more than 90 degrees and reversed its spin by a few degrees, before it shot out into the dark. The deep rattle of the fuselage was distinct, as was the acceleration pressure shoving the girls into their seats.

Christie glanced toward her friends and observed their fearful expressions. She couldn't help but smile, and sent, <Welcome to Oistos and early space technology.>

Hands clamped to grimy armrests and straps, which cut into her thin wraps, Amelia replied, <I have a whole new level of admiration for your brother when he was a New Terran, tug-explorer captain.>

Like he needs more admiration, Christie thought, her smile fading. She loved her big brother, but sometimes it was a little too dark in his shadow.

Scar and Jessie didn't bother closing out the rear view ports, and as soon as Christie dared, she unstrapped and worked her way to the shuttle's rear, bracing herself against the seat uprights. Only stars showed through the small port, until the shuttle made a long turn and decelerated.

<It's a moon base,> Christie sent to her friends.

<A mining operation?> Amelia asked.

<No ... no, it's a large dome with a transparent shell. It's brightly lit from inside.>

<On a moon?> Eloise wondered. <What type of criminal operation sets up a dome on a moon, and then burns the lights like an invitation to all?>

<I think we're about to find out,> Christie sent, hurrying to regain her place beside her friends as the shuttle shook violently and decelerated to a stop. Moments later, it eased forward to settle down on a surface with a jarring bump.

<Abducted and then flown by amateur pilots in a shuttle threatening to break apart,> Eloise sent. <Could this get any worse?>

<Keep thinking like that and you may find out,> Amelia shot back. <We're not on Haraken. If we want to get out of this mess, we better be thinking of a way to save ourselves.>

<I agree,> Christie sent.

After the shuttle landed, Scar and Jessie came into the cabin. "Get up, fems. Stand in the aisle, and turn your backs to us," Scar ordered. The two men slipped metal-mesh bags over the girls' heads, strapping them firmly in place. Scar moved to the front of the line, taking Amelia and Eloise's hands and placing them on the shoulder of the girl in front.

"Come on, home girl," Scar said to Christie, while placing her hand on his shoulder. Then, he led the way out of the shuttle and down the gangway.

As Christie encountered obstacles that tended to trip her, she was angry she couldn't relay the information to her friends to protect them, but the bag over her head blocked her implant comms. She was saved a couple of times from falling by leaning heavily on Scar's shoulder.

The other senses of the Haraken girls were not blocked, and each was doing her best to pick up details since exiting the shuttle: the stink of fuels and oil in the shuttle bay, the sounds of an airlock hatch opening and closing, and the hiss of doors sliding apart, which brought an immediate change in their environment. Gone were the sounds and odors of the bay replaced by distinctly fresh, even aromatic smells, and music issuing from corridor speakers.

Finally, the girls heard the snick of a high-end lock and felt a soft floor covering under their feet.

The men unfastened and recovered the bags, and Scar stared at each of the girls in turn. "Same rules apply here as on the freighter. No noise. You make noise, and Jessie gets to have his turn with the two mutes, before he does some carving. Understand?" When the girls replied quietly, Scar nodded. A double-snick from the door, as Scar and Jessie left, indicated the girls were once again locked inside.

<An upgrade,> Eloise commented via implant to keep their conversations private. The room was a well-appointed suite with a sitting area, beautifully decorated twin beds, and a full New Terran–style bathroom.

<We have robes,> Amanda mused, opening a closet.

The girls regarded the room's pleasant amenities and stared at one another, confusion spreading across their faces.

* * *

Scrolling through the week's take at his pleasure domes on his reader, Peto "Craze" Toyo smiled broadly. Month over month, the credits had been on the increase, and it was all thanks to the Harakens. The thought made him cackle.

The travelers bought by the New Terran government enabled fast and sophisticated transport across the system. Before the arrival of the Haraken ships, wealthy vacationers couldn't afford the time lost traveling to a distant moon via local shuttles to a station, then boarding a passenger liner and reversing the process. Now, the travelers delivered Toyo's patrons from the Prima shuttle base directly to his pleasure domes on Jolares, a minor moon orbiting the gas giant, Ganymede, in luxurious style and in little more than a day.

"And no adz to mess with my business," Toyo mumbled, smiling again to himself.

The domes operated outside TSF oversight because of a loophole in New Terran law. Almost a century ago, a mining charter was passed by the Assembly to encourage companies to take on the risk of setting up operations on the system's outer moons. The mining charter allowed the companies the freedom to police their own bases and employees.

Toyo wasn't the first with the concept of a pleasure dome. Azul "Mr. Blue" Kadmir was credited with that, but it hadn't taken Toyo long to recognize that selling his criminal businesses on New Terra and investing in pleasure domes was a smart move. He registered a mining company, targeted Jolares in his application, and received approval so fast it amazed even him.

It took time to transship Toyo's freight orders from New Terra out to Jolares, but the availability of Méridien building methods and supplies created a dome the likes of which Toyo couldn't have imagined. His domes were a smash hit! Of course, offering the first 200 guests free transport provided tremendous word-of-mouth advertising.

While the main dome produced credits faster than Toyo could disperse them, the ancillary domes, which were built below surface level, were the most lucrative. Dome one hosted the paler fun — gambling, stimulants, and discreet fems and boys. The darker pleasures of the secondary domes awaited only privileged and carefully screened customers. Square meter for square meter, each of the ancillary domes produced 70 to 80 percent more credits than the surface dome.

Toyo's intent for the main dome was to keep everyone happy, show them a good time, and they would return. His concept was a wild success. That the population of the Oistos system was supporting a criminal organization was just the byproduct of people who chose not to look under the pretty wrapping of what they had purchased.

At a knock on his door, Toyo called out, "Enter," and placed his fingers on buttons under his desk. One button connected to a protective, edged shield that would shoot up from the front of his desk with enough force to cut through almost anything. In addition, a second button would activate weapons that would pop up from the floor to spray half the room. If there were innocents among his attackers, Toyo would consider them casualties of circumstance.

"Aw, Barber," Toyo said, motioning his underling in and taking his finger off the buttons. "So, I hear you have three new fems ready to work for us. Which domes will they get? I could use more in number three. The fems don't last long there, what with the rough trade."

"About that, Boss, they aren't hires. We had a little trouble on Haraken, and these fems were kidnapped," Barber said. He tried to stand his ground, knowing Toyo hated cringing, but when his boss started screaming at him, some spittle running from his mouth, it was hard not to take a step or two back. And it was easy to understand how Toyo received his nickname.

Toyo calmed down enough to pour a drink, gulping the hard liquor down. "Ok, tell me," he said, breathing heavily from his explosive display.

"Somehow these three fems discovered the club and cased the place, recording everything in their heads. You know, those implants," Barber said, touching his temple.

"Wait, you're telling me these are Harakens, not tourists?" Toyo asked. "Are they adz?"

"No, Boss, just locals acting like amateur investigators."

"Okay, that's good. Anybody important going to miss them?"

"Well, that's where it gets a bit sticky, Boss. One of them is Christie Racine." Barber waited for the eruption, which never came.

Instead, Toyo looked thunderstruck. He rose and began pacing behind his huge, metal desk. "Okay, Barber," Toyo said, laughing. "That was a pretty good one. You had me going there. I mean swiping Racine's sister. Who would be that stupid?" While Toyo laughed, he looked at Barber, expecting his underling to join, but Barber stood there, staring at the floor.

Toyo walked over to the man and yanked his chin up, forcing him to look in his eyes. "Tell me that Christie Racine and two of her friends are not sitting in one of my domes' suites. Tell me that," Toyo demanded.

"I can't, Boss. Dar, Lacey, and Trembles panicked, drugged the fems, and the next thing I know they're delivering three bagged fems to the *Bountiful*. I didn't know what to do with them, but I thought it was safer to bring them here. Dar told me that if the adz caught them, they would say they reported to Kadmir. I even had to get rid of our contact on Haraken. He went off when he spotted the fems all trussed up."

"Wait, say that last part again," Toyo demanded, letting go of Barber's chin, which would wear a set of bruises for the next week.

"The crew intended to blame the whole thing on Mr. Blue, Boss, if they got caught. It could work," Barber said, hoping that Toyo would fixate on that piece of information.

Toyo stepped back, poured himself a second, smaller drink, and sat back down behind his desk. For the moment, he was tempted to press his second button, just to have someone pay for the stupidity that had been dumped on him. But having the blame for the kidnapping fall on his lead competitor was too delicious a thought not to occupy his attention.

"Maybe we should drop a comm to the Haraken adz as to where our crew is hiding, just to be sure the word gets out," Toyo suggested, and then took a sip of his drink.

"No need, Boss, the club got busted by the adz a couple nights later. We got the word that Dar and his people were escaping and going into hiding. He was talking to me when the adz busted down his hiding place."

"Okay, that might not be a bad thing. Dar and Lacey will probably be all right selling the story, if only that idiot, Trembles, can keep his wits about him and remember the script. Who we got watching the fems?"

"Boker and Jessie brought them down from the freighter. I was waiting to see what you wanted me to do with them."

"Boker and Jessie? Are you taking the twitch yourself?" demanded Toyo, referring to the hallucinogen they were pushing on Haraken.

"It's all I had available on the *Bountiful*. They were the only ones I could trust to watch over the girls, sneak them off the freighter when we docked, and who could pilot a shuttle. I figure the fewer who knew about the girls, the better."

"So from start to finish, who saw these fems?"

"Our crew at the club, who've been arrested by the adz; our Haraken contact at McCrery Station, who is on his way to becoming stardust, and

Boker and Jessie, who stowed them aboard the freighter and snuck them into a suite here."

"You sure?" Toyo asked, boring into Barber's eyes.

"Yeah, Boss, sure."

"Okay, good work on that station employee. Do the same for Boker and Jessie."

"But, Boss, they're good men. They'll keep their mouths shut."

"Barber, let me educate you on the bigger picture," Toyo said, getting up from his desk, walking around to the other side, and leaning back against it. It gave him a little thrill to think that poised underneath him was a pneumatically loaded, lethal-edged section of metal alloy that, if accidentally triggered, would slice him in half.

"That fem's brother is Alex Racine," Toyo said, in the tone a lecturer might use. "The same guy who unseated Downing and his people, rescued a bunch of worlds from some alien sphere, handed hats to warships from Sol, went there and made peace with them … and, oh, rescued a bunch of creepy-crawly aliens. So tell me, Barber, how much do you want to risk this man finding out that we were the ones who took his sister?"

Barber wondered for a moment if it wasn't time to retire, but, then again, no one retired from Toyo's operation, at least not in the manner Barber had in mind. "I'll take care of Boker and Jessie," he finally said.

"You do that, and, Barber, you take good care of the fems, and I mean good care. Clean clothes, good food, bedding, and bathroom supplies … anything they need. They just stay put in that suite, and you and I are the only ones to know. Clear?"

"Clear, Boss," Barber said, and left the room as relaxed as he could appear to make it look. In the corridor, he leaned against a wall, his legs trembling and sweat rolling from under his arms. Before he saw Toyo, he would have bet he was a dead man. Instead, that sentence would fall on Boker and Jessie.

10

The *Rêveur* made its entrance into the Oistos system. The asteroid fields, which Alex mined for ice to supply the mining companies and habitats when he was a tug-explorer captain, lay in front of them.

<My love, we need an intervention of sorts. The engineering suite, please,> Renée sent urgently to Alex.

Signaling ahead with his implant, Alex raced through the corridors with Étienne right behind him. The crew, warned of his coming, flattened against the bulkheads. Alex burst through the engineering doors and was surprised to find Terese in a state of extreme agitation. She stood in front of the SADEs, waving her arms widely and arguing her point. The SADEs displayed no emotion whatsoever.

"What?" Terese exclaimed when she saw Alex lurch to an abrupt halt inside the lab.

"Problem?" Alex asked quietly.

"Are you a renowned biochemist experienced in formulating drug compounds? No, of course you're not. Then, you're of no use to me," Terese declared, dismissing Alex with a wave of her hand.

<Walk with me,> Alex sent to Terese, as gently as he could.

<I haven't time for your walks,> Terese replied, and turned her back on Alex.

<Walk with me, Terese, or I will have the pleasure of applying one of your soporifics to you that you so liberally administered to me when we first met.>

Terese whirled to face Alex and fire off a retort, but the words stuck in her throat when she took in the intent in Alex's eyes. Her president stared back. Despite deciding to acquiesce, Terese made a point of huffing out of the lab.

Alex turned to follow and noticed Étienne hadn't moved. <Some escort you are,> Alex groused over the comm to him.

<A man must know his limits,> Étienne sent back. <I wish you good fortune with the red whirlwind.>

Alex hurried to catch up with Terese. *I did say walk, not run, didn't I?* Alex thought. Deciding to be patient, he paced Terese while she fast-walked the corridors for a good quarter-hour. Forewarned along the route by Alex, not a single crew member was ever seen, although it was ridiculous what several people had to do to disappear from sight.

Finally, Terese wound down, and Alex led her to the owner's suite. Alex offered Terese a seat on the couch, and he made thé for both of them. Handing Terese a cup, Alex said, "Talk to me."

Terese set her cup down without tasting it and drew her hands through her flame-red hair. "I'm not good enough. I've been pretending to be your medical expert all these years, but I'm just a medical specialist. I haven't the advanced training I need in this situation, and the SADEs aren't carrying the specialized information in their memories that I require."

Terese picked up her cup but set it back down without taking a sip. She looked up at Alex, expecting his sympathy.

"Is that all?" Alex asked. "Black stars, Terese. You had me worried for a moment. I thought we were in real trouble."

Terese stared agape at Alex, unsure how to respond — cry, hit him, or laugh. She was Terese, so she laughed. She laughed 'til she cried, and then she threw a pillow at him because he was laughing at her.

"This isn't a laughing matter," Terese said, trying to sound angry but it came out between tears and hiccups. "Méridiens don't create drugs to distort the perceptions of our children's brains. So my databases don't possess any research on the subject. Worse, this psychedelic has an addictive nature, producing incredibly painful withdrawal symptoms."

"An addictive hallucinogen … isn't that uncommon?" Alex asked.

"How would I know?" Terese said, throwing up her hands. "The staff tested the teens, and I received the results before we exited our system. The first teen was woken soon after he was in the medical center. He behaved normally for two days, before harsh withdrawal symptoms began punishing his body, and the staff put him back under. The second teen was woken one day after she was taken from the club, and she exhibited the same horrendous withdrawal symptoms a day later. Their bodies develop this desperate need, and, two days after they first receive the drug, they would have been desperate to return to the club. As it is now, we can't wake any of the children until we have something to alleviate the addiction."

"I take it that you've arranged for any youth returning to the club to be taken into custody and tested for the drug."

"Now, why didn't I think of that?" Terese said, sarcastically.

Alex was happy to see some of the fire returning to Terese. He stepped into the refresher and returned with a wet cloth for her. "So what do you need from me?"

Terese accepted the cloth Alex handed her. She used it to wipe her face, and, at one point, she braced her elbows on her thighs and buried her face in the cloth. *What do I want?* Terese asked herself. It was Alex who was asking her to focus, which her anger had not allowed her to do. *What do I want?* she repeated.

Wiping her face a final time with the cloth, Terese took a deep breath, letting it out slowly. "If I could have my wishes, I would want the ugly individual who created this drug in our engineering suite, with all the equipment and product they would need to synthesize a safe blocking agent for this addictive, hallucinogenic compound."

"Okay, so we find him or her, take their lab and supplies, put them in your tender care, and you get your compound."

If it was anyone else, Terese would have laughed them out of the room, even though it wasn't her cabin. But Alex said it matter-of-factly, as if it was the next thing on his list. It occurred to Terese that if Alex was going hunting, he would need a means of narrowing his target.

"I will provide you a list of items such a biochemist might use to manufacture this type of drug. These are only guesses, mind you, but it might help you and the SADEs find them." Terese stood up to hand Alex the refresher cloth. She paused, staring down at the cloth in her hands and struggling with how to express the sentiments she wished to convey to him, when she felt Alex's strong, heavy arms enfold her. Alex had never hugged her, but rather than think about that she leaned into the warmth, placing her head against the massive chest and pulling on the comfort offered her. *You are one fortunate woman, Renée,* Terese thought.

"Save this cloth," Terese said, easing back and handing it to Alex. "That fool who put our children in jeopardy will need it when I make them cry." With that, Terese left the cabin in her usual fashion — in a whirlwind of energy.

* * *

"Fortune is with us, Mr. President," Julien said. The *Rêveur* was entering the ice fields that lay beyond Seda, the system's outermost planet. "If we make for New Terra, our adversaries will not confuse our trajectory with any intent to approach Ganymede, which is more the 85 degrees spinward of our vector for the home world."

"Good," Alex agreed. He didn't want to panic Toyo and his people. "Time to say hello to an old friend, Julien."

Julien smiled and a pair of ancient headphones, the type with a metal band that connected over-sized ear pads, appeared on his head.

"Really, Julien," Maria Gonzalez, the ex-president of New Terra, said when she answered the comm call on her reader. She had one of the newest reader versions with supposedly the latest encryption. Yet a call without a contact ID swept her security program aside and displayed the SADE's face wearing a pair of silly, antique headphones. "So you're playing comm operator now."

"Greetings, ex-Madam President," Julien said. "I'm pleased by the transmission quality of your FTL comms. Your people have done well."

"Thank you, Julien. But it's just Ser Gonzalez now, and it appears we still have a ways to go with our security apps. Is there a purpose to your call?"

In response to her question, Alex's face replaced Julien's. "Greetings, Maria, although you will always be my favorite president."

"Flatterer," Maria said, laughing. "So should I be worried … aliens chasing you … an apocalyptic storm headed our way?"

"No, just saying hello. I'm on vacation."

Now Maria really laughed. She laughed so hard she had to hold her stomach to lessen the cry of abdominal muscles.

The vid pickup widened on Alex's desk to show Renée perched on the edge. "Greetings, Maria, I told him he shouldn't try to sell that ruse to you."

"Oh, Alex and Renée, I've missed you people. Life has been too dull around here …" Maria suddenly stopped and eyed the two Harakens. "On second thought, maybe dull is good. So what's really up, Alex?"

"I wish to hire your security firm to locate someone … a biochemist."

Maria Gonzalez had completed her second and final term as New Terra's president. She was now owner and president of a well-respected, security-consultancy business, which supported the requests of the government and small businesses. Offers from large corporations were refused.

"You don't need my firm to contact a New Terran. Your SADEs could just comm them. You do have their name?"

"Afraid not."

"An image? A New Terran ID number?"

"No, to those two items as well."

"Okay, other than the fact they're a biochemist, do you have anything else."

"Yes, your reader has just received a group of basic compounds and the type of apparatus this individual would need to manufacture their drug. It's a complex psychedelic with an addictive quality, quite sophisticated, according to Terese."

"What would you want with a New Terran who is making an illegal drug, Alex?' Maria asked, leaning closer to her reader's pickup.

"It's important that you do not let this individual or individuals know that you are seeking them. I'm hiring your security firm to surreptiously locate them and their manufacturing location, then send me this information."

"And when you meet up with these people, then what?"

"Why, I intend to hire them, Maria," Alex replied, grinning.

"Going into the illegal drug business, are you, Alex?"

"Just for a short while. Will you accept the contract?"

Maria didn't need to think about it. Whatever was going on, this was Alex asking. "Yes, but I have two questions. Time sensitivity?"

"Immediate, as in yesterday. Put as many people on it as you need. If the manufacturing location isn't on New Terra, I don't want to waste time coming to the home world. Credits are not a problem ... open contract."

Open contract, Maria thought. "Tell me, Alex, that you aren't aboard one of your carriers, inbound into Oistos."

"Inbound, yes, but aboard the *Rêveur,*" Alex replied, winking slyly at Maria.

"I see ... traveling under the guise of a simple vacationer. You do know that no one is going to believe that."

"They don't have to believe it, Maria. The cover story just has to create doubt long enough for me to accomplish my purpose here."

"And that's another question. When are you going to tell me what you're really doing here?'

"When I can, Maria, I will. Right now, it's better that you have deniability."

"I see ... well, Alex, my people and I appreciate the business, especially an open contract. Julien, how do I get in touch? Oh, I see." Maria belatedly noticed the little icon of a robot's face, who was wearing headphones, that was placed on her screen.

"Tap, slap, or punch the icon, Ser Gonzalez, and I will be at your disposal," Julien replied.

"Be careful, Julien, you're sounding more like Alex each time we meet," Maria said.

A compliment indeed, Julien thought.

"Always a pleasure, you three ... disaster or not," Maria said, closing the comm.

* * *

"We need your decision, dear President. The window is closing for a stealthy departure," Miranda Leyton said to Alex.

In order to make their plan work, Z had transferred to his femme fatale avatar, given a complex set of instructions to the Miranda persona, and then let her subsume his kernel. No triggers were embedded to return control to Z. Instead Z placed that option with Julien, since he had no idea when Miranda might complete her tasks.

Expectant faces were arrayed around Alex, and he was torn with indecision. The strategy his people had crafted was plagued with so many holes that Alex couldn't count them all. What bothered him the most was that he didn't have an alternate suggestion. His people, including him, knew too little about their adversaries.

The SADEs had managed to accumulate some crucial information. Researching government records, they had located Toyo's mining operations, if that was the right word. Hacking into the orbital station overhead of Jolares, they had a close-up view of a huge dome, brilliantly lit, the light glowing from inside its transparent shell.

The plan, devised by the SADEs, Svetlana, and Deirdre Canaan, was to exit the liner in a traveler while still hidden in the ice fields and make for Jolares to attempt to locate the kidnapped girls. The group would appear as vacationers, with the SADEs setting up reservations at Toyo's establishment, which obviously was a resort not a mining concern. It was a point that caused Alex to make a note to discuss this with the New Terran president. What lent credence to his crew's plan was the freighter *Bountiful* was still docked at the orbital station above Jolares.

"Grab your bags. Then again, you're probably already packed," Alex said, relenting. "I'll meet you in the bay."

Alex was waiting in the bay with those who would stay behind — Julien, Cordelia, Tatia and Alain, Terese, Mickey and Pia, Cordova and Lumley, and Étienne and Ellie. Many of his people were too well-known by New Terrans to risk being identified.

The airlock disgorged a group of New Terran–built crew members, flamboyantly dressed, laughing, and chatting. When they saw their audience, they cheered loudly and climbed aboard the waiting traveler.

Svetlana and Deirdre were in the next group to come through the airlock, and Alex almost failed to recognize his wing commanders. Gone were the flight suits, severe hair styles, and unadorned faces. While the cheers of the crew, climbing aboard and celebrating their vacation opportunity, echoed throughout the bay, the commanders paused in front of Alex and Renée.

Svetlana and Deirdre, one light and one dark, stood with arms around each other and hips cocked together. Sheer wraps left little to the imagination; faces were gaily painted; and hair was coiffed in exotic patterns.

"Oh, he's cute," Svetlana smirked at Alex.

"Want to join us on some fun time, big boy?" Deirdre asked, her eyes smoldering.

<If you don't close your mouth, my love, you may start drooling on your ship boots,> Renée sent.

"Remarkable disguises," Alex stammered. "Forgive me if I must decline your lovely invitation."

Alex watched as the two women simpered at the rebuff, turned, and dropped a hand onto each other's derrières as they sauntered off to board the traveler.

<So, my love, did you store those images or delete them?> Renée sent privately.

<Guilty,> Alex sent.

<That's not guilt, my love. That's appreciation. I, for one, have stored them … the images are without measure in credits.>

As the last group cycled through the airlock, the reason for the extra crew, which boarded the traveler at Haraken, dawned on Alex. Someone had the foresight to plan this deception far enough in advance to draft people to hide those who would be leading the search. Word was it that it was Svetlana Valenko — she with the reputation for doing the unexpected.

Alex was just hoping her streak of fortune would hold up and not get his sister and friends killed.

More lively cheers and hand waves accompanied the commanders' climb into the traveler. Miranda followed them, hanging on the arms of two of the biggest New Terran crew members the *Rêveur* possessed. They paused in front of Alex, and the men smiled and tipped their hats, as a pair of miners might.

Miranda released the arms of her escorts and stepped close to Alex. "Do not frown, dear," Miranda said, running her fingers across Alex's forehead, as if she could wipe away his concerns. "We will do our best to bring the girls home safely."

"You be safe too, Miranda," Alex replied, almost calling her Z.

"And what do you think these two are for?" Miranda said, stepping back to link arms with her escorts. "They're the largest specimens aboard." She winked at Alex and said, "Come, boys, I'm anxious for a little fun."

Alex and company cleared the airlock, most of them shaking their heads at what they had just witnessed. It was a tremendous display of well-acted roles, designed to show their audience that they could play their parts.

Little did Alex realize how much time Svetlana had spent with her entourage, drilling them on how to act their parts. It was Deirdre who was dying to ask how Svetlana knew the roles so well that they were supposed to be playing, but she never gathered the courage. She was still wondering when Svetlana made up both their faces and hair in a manner Deirdre had never seen before.

11

Barber took his time figuring out how to take on Boker and Jessie. Moving too fast was a stupid play. Jessie wasn't quick but he was a big man and a brawler. If he closed on you, you'd likely suffer a broken jaw and then a snapped neck in quick succession. But Boker was the deadly one. He was a survivor and could sense trouble coming.

The major problem for Barber was that the two men were inseparable. It wasn't that they liked each other, but having found that their skills complemented each other as protection against the dangers of their profession, they stayed in close proximity.

Barber tasked three individuals to help him, but the moment he defined the targets, two men tried to back out. He was forced to offer all three of them a bonus from his own reserves. The only individual not intimidated by taking on Boker and Jessie was a woman, who had a reputation for her work with poisoned blades. That was not uncommon in the domes. Weapons that threw slugs of any kind were prohibited in the domes by Toyo himself. A few people had paid the ultimate price for disobeying that decree. So, Toyo's crew carried blades, some more blades than others and some with poison.

Barber's plan was to trap the two men is a narrow utility corridor, where their defense options would be limited. Barber and the woman waited at the front of the trap.

Late that night, Jessie was the first one down the corridor, lumbering along and nearly filling the tight corridor all by himself. Boker brought up the rear and Barber's men, who were behind them, made the mistake of moving too soon and making a little noise.

"Jessie, trap," Boker said clearly and calmly, not even a shout.

The woman stepped out of her hiding place and attacked Jessie in a crouch. With a couple of fast fakes, she buried a knife deep in Jessie's gut, but she was stuck. Jessie's huge, meaty hand trapped her knife hand. The giant grinned, reached out with his other hand and grabbed the woman's ship suit, yanking her forward. She flew at Jessie, who slammed his forehead into her nose, driving slender cartilage and bone fragments deep into her brain.

Jessie let go of the woman, who slid to the floor. Watching Barber turn to run, Jessie pulled the knife from his gut with a grunt, and threw the long, slender blade at Barber, burying it deep in his shoulder. Barber screamed in pain and rage, knowing that it was a poisoned blade that had struck him.

A smile crossed Jessie's face, even as a numbing sensation crept through his limbs. He knew the woman who had attacked him and knew he was a dead man. But as he fell to the floor on his knees, the poison racing through his body, Jessie knew one other thing — Barber was a dead man too.

Behind Jessie, Boker and the other two attackers were in a protracted dance with their own blades. Slowly, Barber's men backed Boker down the corridor, eyeing the bodies on the floor behind him. When Boker neared Jessie's body, they rushed him, expecting him to trip, but Boker leapt up and to the side, shoving off against the wall with a foot and driving his blade into the side of an attacker's neck.

Unfortunately for Boker, the man's sudden collapse twisted the knife out of his grip. The second attacker seized the opportunity and dove forward, managing to stab Boker in the side, just below the rib cage. But that brought the attacker too close to Boker, who punched the man in the throat with the curled knuckles of his hand, crushing the attacker's windpipe. While the man gasped for breath, Boker pulled the knife from his side and drove it deep into his attacker's right eye.

* * *

Soon after the girls had been locked in the suite, they had been surprised when Scar and Jessie had returned with food trays and clothes.

Regarding the clothes, it was obvious their abductors were unprepared for Méridien frames. Amelia and Eloise made do by wrapping the limbs and cinching the waist's excess material with a belt. However, by their chronometer apps, the two men had last visited them over nineteen hours ago, and the girls were getting nervous, not to mention hungry.

<I think they decided not to feed us because they're going to make us disappear,> Eloise sent and immediately regretted sharing the thought. <Sorry, sorry ... no negative thoughts. Well, denying us food will help Christie finally lose some weight.>

It was a running joke between the girls — Christie teasing the Librans about the need to put on some weight and, in turn, Christie being teased about the value of fasting to lose some weight, when in fact all three young women were striking specimens of their people.

This time Christie didn't reply to the barb. For hours, she searched for weak points in the suite and was disappointed to discover that Haraken materials and techniques were employed in its construction. Short of a plasma rifle, the only exit from the suite was going to be through the front door.

"Hello, in the suite," a youthful voice said over the door comm.

Amelia leapt over to the door, stared at the comm unit, and found the button she needed to push to talk. "Yes, we're here."

"Please, fem, I need you and your friends to go into the washroom before I can deliver your food."

Amelia looked at the other girls. Eloise nodded toward the washroom, but Christie sent, <Talk to him. He sounds young.>

"Have to wake up one of my friends. Hold on. Where are the other two men?"

"Don't know anything about any other two men. I've just been told to bring trays of food to this suite but not to enter until you're in the washroom."

The girls could tell the boy was confused by his orders but was intent on following them nonetheless.

<You two, go to the washroom,> Christie sent, stepping quickly to the door and flattening up against the wall.

"Just count to ten and we'll be in the washroom," Amelia said.

The count ended and nothing happened. The boy's voice came through the intercom again. "Fem, I have a thermal scanner. Why are you still in the salon?"

Christie didn't bother to reply but walked into the bathroom to join the other two girls. The moment she closed the door, the snick of the door lock closing could be heard. <Remote-controlled lock,> Christie sent.

The girls could hear a cart pushed into the salon and movement of someone going around the room before they heard footsteps and then the suite's door closing. A second snick of the bathroom's door lock told them they were free.

Conversation ceased while the three hungry young women devoured everything on the trays. Eloise's belch seemed to signal the end of the meal. <Apologies,> she sent.

<I don't get it,> Amelia sent. <Our treatment from the moment we were taken until we arrived here has been nothing but rough. Then those two rocks, who brought us here, bring us food and clothes ... and then, poof, they're gone. Next, there's this long break, and suddenly, we have this fresh face delivering us a cart of food, but we have to hide in the bathroom.>

<Yes, odd,> Christie replied. She started to slowly pace the room, and her friends hid their smirks. It was believed the Racine tendency to pace when thinking was a genetic trait. <We're thinking of this criminal organization the wrong way ... like it's an integrated, top-down, cohesive organization,> Christie sent.

<And you're suggesting they're not?> Eloise asked.

<Suppose, just suppose, the group on Haraken screwed up,> Christie said.

<Yes, yes,> Amelia said excitedly. <They saw us at the club, panicked, grabbed us, and shipped us here.>

<And someone at the top or at least further up the chain of command recognized how much they screwed up,> Christie replied. <It would explain why the strange shift in treatment.>

<Well, that bodes well for us, doesn't it?> Eloise asked. <I mean someone recognizes that we're important and need to be treated carefully.>

<I think it means that we're to be treated well for the time being, until Christie's brother frightens them into choosing to get rid of us rather than be caught with us,> Amelia said.

<I agree with Amelia. I don't think we can wait until they reach that fork in the decision tree. I'm not into fifty-fifty bets when losing means we're dead,> Christie sent.

<Which leaves the problems of us getting out of here,> Eloise said.

<And where we go when we get out,> Amelia added.

<About the first problem, I have an idea if the boy is going to keep serving us our food,> Christie said, grinning at her two friends.

* * *

Boker needed to disappear, but first he had to stop the bleeding. Within moments and much to his relief, Boker discovered his attacker's blade wasn't poisoned

"Sorry, Jessie," Boker murmured in apology to his big partner. He hurried down a couple of corridors, holding a hand over his wound. At a small air vent, he pried off the cover and removed the stash Jessie and he stored for an emergency exit. From inside the carryall, Boker removed a small med bag, which held some quick-patch, which he applied to the wound. He hissed as the medicant fused the skin together. A quick injection of meds for infection and pain cleared his mind. The bloody shirt was stuffed up into the vent and the cover replaced. He yanked a clean shirt from the carryall and quickly donned it.

Throwing the bag over his shoulder with its readers, containing hefty reserves of anonymous credits, a criminal's favorite form of funds, Boker walked calmly but quickly along the utility corridor to a freight storage room where he could hole up and devise an exit plan — not an easy task, considering he was trying to escape from a collection of domes surrounded by vacuum.

While he sat in the dark, Boker came to the conclusion that he was a dead man if he tried to engineer his escape to safety by himself. He was working through his list of acquaintances, wondering who he might enlist to help him. That it had been Barber who tried to off the two of them meant Toyo had given the orders. "Those fems," Boker hissed, realizing the kill orders had something to do with the three Haraken women, and that's what gave him the idea.

Boker crawled between some enormous packing crates, ate a meal bar, sipped some water, and fell asleep. His reader app buzzed softly five hours later at 3 hours, local time. Wincing as he sat up, Boker loaded another hypo with meds and waited until the pain subsided.

Sliding out of his hiding place, Boker made for the landing bay. Even though it was the middle of the night, dome service personnel were still moving around, and it took Boker over an hour to navigate the few hundred meters until he had a clear view of the freighter's shuttle, which he had piloted with the fems aboard.

Watching from behind a stack of crates, Boker waited until the path was clear, pulled his cap low on his head, slung his bag over a shoulder, and walked nonchalantly to the shuttle. He punched in his access code, hoping no one had thought to change it. The access light blinked green, and the hatch slid open. Boker ducked inside and slapped the oversized button to close the hatch.

In the cockpit, Boker ran through a short routine to power his comm panel. He had no desire to fly the shuttle out — he had nowhere to go, not yet. Selecting a frequency for a mining operation on Udrides, a moon larger than Jolares, which also orbited Ganymede, Boker made his comm call.

"Udrides Resources, this is the shuttle from the freighter, *Bountiful*."

"This is Udrides Resources, pilot. Are you declaring an emergency?" a lovely voice replied.

"Yes, but not the kind you're thinking. I need to speak to Mr. Kadmir immediately," Boker said.

"Mr. Kadmir is not in the habit of taking comms at this hour of the morning, pilot. Call during working hours and I will connect you with Mr. Kadmir's assistant, who will make an appointment for your comm call."

"Listen carefully, fem. Get Mr. Blue on the comm now, or he'll be stripping the meat from your flesh when he finds out you didn't put this call through."

Dead silence greeted Boker's threat, but after several moments he heard a man clear his throat.

"This is Mr. Kadmir's assistant. What is the emergency, pilot?"

Not there yet, Boker thought. "Listen, Mr. Assistant. I have information Mr. Blue wants to get his hands on if he wants to hurt Craze. So you wake him up or I take this hot news to Sniffer," Boker threatened, referring to the third criminal boss, Roz O'Brien, whose domes were on Desmonis, the next moon farther out in Ganymede's orbit from Udrides.

Again the comm went silent and Boker waited for the better part of a half-hour.

"Talk quick," a deep, sleep-deprived voice said.

"I used to work for Toyo, until his number two and some crew tried to take out my partner and me," Boker explained.

"What do I care if you idiots kill one another?" the voice growled.

"I was loyal to Toyo's organization ... been with the man eight years. The only reason he would want to kill my partner and me is because of what we've just seen. I think Toyo is scared."

Kadmir leaned onto his desk and punched the vid cam button on his comm panel to access the shuttle's cockpit, and Boker accepted the request. The two men stared at each other for a moment, sizing the other up.

Kadmir's thought was that anything that could scare Craze interested him. "Go on," he said.

A spark of hope soared inside Boker, and he chose his next words carefully. Too much information and Kadmir would have no need for him; too little information and the comm would end in a bad way for Boker — a grisly death at the hands of Toyo himself.

"My partner, Jessie, and I loaded three fems onto our freighter, the *Bountiful,* and delivered them here to a private suite on Jolares."

"That's it?" Kadmir asked, staring hard at Boker.

"We took them from Espero."

"Three tourists on Haraken, so what?" said Kadmir, his voice hardening.

"They were metal-meshed to prevent implant communication and two are Méridien-built."

"Harakens," Kadmir said, his eyes widening just slightly. If Craze kidnapped three Harakens, then not only was Toyo's organization in trouble, but maybe all those who ran pleasure domes were about to attract more attention from the adz than the politicos could deflect. "You have pics?" Kadmir asked.

"I have pics, but you get those when you get me off Jolares."

"If you've got a way to make orbit, maybe we can deal. I certainly can't set down a shuttle in Craze's landing bays."

"If I make orbit in this freighter shuttle, it won't take long before I'm discovered."

"Okay, good enough. What's your name?" Kadmir asked.

"Boker."

"Well, Boker. You look like a lifer, so you know how this works. You got something good for me, then you got a job on my crew. You don't ..." Kadmir ended by holding up his hands as if there was nothing he could do for Boker under those circumstances, and his blue eyes held a deadly, cold stare. "Monitor this frequency. You'll be commed when we're close ... twenty-four to twenty-six hours."

When the comm ended, Boker faced his next decision — return to his hiding place in the freight storage area or remain in the shuttle. His brain was starting to frazzle from the pain and he felt warm. Digging into the shuttle's more extensive med-kit, he loaded a hypo with some heavy-duty pain killers and antibiotics.

At that moment, Boker would have loved a dose of medical nanites, and there was a medical emergency station at one of the real mining concerns not 400 kilometers from Toyo's domes, but there was no way he could reach it undetected in the shuttle.

Boker ransacked the galley for a quick-heat meal and water. Shoveling down the hot food, he came to a decision. If he went back to the storage space and other pilots took the shuttle to return to the *Bountiful* or he was locked out by a change in the hatch access code, he was a dead man. This shuttle was his only way off Jolares, and it was the only one that he had the code to access.

In the cockpit, Boker changed the access codes for the twin hatches and set an alarm if the old code was entered on the hull panels. Then he crawled onto a worn-out bunk and fell asleep.

A noise intruded on Boker's dreams, and it wouldn't go away. In disgust, he struggled awake just to escape the irritation and realized it was a comm call. He leapt off the bunk, biting his lips at the pain, and ran to the cockpit.

"Boker, here," he said, accepting the comm signal.

"Just about gave up on you, Boker," a voice said.

"Yeah, well, you take a blade in the side and see how well you do afterwards."

"Can you still make orbit?" the voice asked.

"Yeah, when and where?" Boker asked.

"Now. Lift off and you'll get a beacon for the direction. Climb into a suit. This will be a shuttle to shuttle walk."

The comm was abruptly cut and Boker hurried to get ready — another heavy hypo shot, stripping the necessities from his carryall and stuffing them into his pockets, and climbing into an environment suit. In the cockpit, he signaled for liftoff, and the bay manager sounded the warning to clear the bay. Sweat began running down Boker's face and underarms even though the cockpit was chilly. He expected to be discovered at any moment.

"Cleared for lift, pilot," a bored voice came over the comm.

Rather than speak, Boker hit the acknowledgment icon on his panel, a standard practice for shuttle pilots, and applied power. Boker wasn't the best pilot in the system, as the girls could attest, but he managed to clear the dome without incident. Reaching several hundred meters in elevation,

Boker's tracking panel lit with a small blinking contact 200 kilometers away, and he aimed his shuttle for it.

Partway to the rendezvous, Boker's comm lit, but it registered as the *Bountiful* so he ignored it. Several times, the comm from the *Bountiful* was repeated, but by the fourth call Boker was decelerating to slide beside the other shuttle. When Boker was sure he had a zero position relative to the other shuttle, he locked his helmet on, tested his air mixture, and climbed back to the starboard airlock. Slipping on a small jet pack for vacuum transfers, Boker cycled through the airlock.

People wouldn't know it — to watch Boker professionally and smoothly exit his airlock, guide himself to the waiting shuttle's open airlock where two men waited, and then decelerate to come to a nearly zero velocity before the men pulled him in — but Boker hated vacuum.

Inside the shuttle, the men stripped Boker out of his suit and patted him down. Boker knew the drill well. If he made Kadmir's crew, all his possessions would be returned, even the credits. Only foolhardy criminals stole from one another in the same organization, and those never lasted long.

Boker thought he was in for a long ride to Udrides when he was escorted to the front of the shuttle and sat down across from Azul Kadmir.

"Boker," Kadmir simply said.

"Mr. Kadmir," Boker answered respectfully. One of the men who patted Boker down handed Kadmir two readers.

"Which one has the proof?" Kadmir asked, and Boker pointed to the one in his left hand, which Kadmir tossed to him.

Boker entered his code and dived into the storage memory for the pics he needed, and then handed the reader back to Kadmir.

The criminal boss of Udrides looked at the first photo and swiped to the second. He selected a play sequence and pic after pic of three young women rolled past. Toyo's men had taken numerous photos of the women passed out and naked on the cabin floor. Kadmir glanced up at Boker, who replied to the unsaid comment with a tilt of his head and a lift of an eyebrow.

What was evident to Kadmir was that there were two Méridien bodies and one New Terran. He was getting sick of watching innumerable close-ups of body parts before he came to the facial pics. The first were of the Méridiens, which the men obviously found intriguing, but there was only one photo of the New Terran and not a good one.

When the player ended the pic display, Kadmir sat thinking. There was no doubt there were two Méridiens in the shots, but they could have been just posed on Haraken for all he knew. Kadmir began to wonder if he was being played, when he suddenly stopped and ran the reader's photo directory again. He scrolled to the last image and brought up the facial shot of the New Terran.

The girl was more than a decade older since she was last seen on a New Terran broadcast, but it definitely was Christie Racine. The pieces of Boker's story clicked together for Kadmir — the reason Craze might be scared and the reason he tried to eliminate seasoned and loyal men. The idiot or his people had kidnapped the little sister of Alex Racine, the man who had defeated aliens and destroyed Earther warships. As sure as Kadmir was about anything in his life, he knew that Racine would be tearing apart this end of the universe looking for her, and, sooner or later, he would make his way to Oistos.

Thoughts rolled through Kadmir's head about how to use the information, when he noticed Boker looking expectantly at him. "Welcome to my organization, Boker, you may prove quite valuable," Kadmir said, offering an inviting smile that never reached his eyes.

12

"Mr. President, you have the Assembly Speaker on comm," Julien announced. "He's aboard the *Tanaka*, which has just entered Oistos space."

Alex's heart skipped a beat, wondering what had brought Eric Stroheim to Oistos, especially since he stressed to Eric that he wished to maintain a low profile while he worked to regain the kidnapped girls.

<Eric,> sent Alex, his thoughts emotionless, not the usual greeting for his long-time Méridien friend.

<Mr. President, before you react, allow me a few moments to explain and ease your concerns.>

<Proceed, Eric,> Alex sent.

<The *Tanaka* gives you a perfect opening with Drake. You have a marvelous new ship design for the president to tour. Recall that recent events of the UE battleship invading Oistos is still fresh in the population's minds, which I'm sure the president is anxious to assuage. A few of our sting-class ships would represent a coup for Will Drake's party.>

Standing on the bridge of the *Tanaka*, Eric began to breathe easier, as the comm remained silent. The lengthening silence meant Alex was pondering what he had said, and a thinking Alex was always a good thing in Eric's opinion.

<The *Tanaka* is a much better reason for our arrival than your vacation, Mr. President,> Julien sent privately. The SADE pronounced the word vacation as if it had a sour taste.

<Good idea, Eric,> Alex sent.

Eric smiled and drew a deep breath before he sent, <Where would you like us positioned?>

Julien activated the *Rêveur*'s bridge holo-vid and displayed the planet positions, adding colored dots for the Haraken ships, the liner, and the sting ship.

Alex was considering his options and the path the *Tanaka* might take when a dotted line from the sting ship's present position to New Terra showed it passing perilously close to Ganymede. Alex looked to Julien, who shook his head in negation.

<Willem,> Julien sent privately to Alex.

Several more trajectory scenarios appeared and disappeared on the holo-vid, and a small smile formed on Alex's face. Even Captain Cordova was enjoying the SADE playing with the president's display without the courtesy of a request.

When the display was returned to Julien's original setup, Alex waited, but the comm was silent. <And what's your conclusion, Willem?> Alex sent.

<There is no satisfactory path into the system that successfully meets the conditions to approach New Terra as if the purpose is a government tour of the sting ship and yet does not panic the kidnappers who supposedly have the girls on a moon orbiting Ganymede, Ser President.>

<I concur,> Julien added. <Unfortunately, New Terra and Ganymede are coming into alignment with the *Tanaka*'s approach direction. Willem exited the sting ship into the system about 65 degrees spinward from our exit point. If Captain Shimada evades Ganymede, it would, in your parlance, Mr. President, tip your hand.>

<Was there a proscribed exit point for this system?> Willem asked, quickly searching his memories for information he might have missed on the subject.

<Negative, Willem. No error was made on your part,> Alex sent quickly. <Your navigation is not in doubt. Julien simply followed our old route between Haraken and New Terra.>

<One of the largest humans we know, and yet one of the gentlest with the SADEs,> Cordelia remarked privately to Julien.

<Some century, he will be missed,> Julien sent to her.

<Perhaps our contribution to humankind should be the fostering of those who will come after Alex and will be at peace with the SADEs,> Cordelia replied.

<Mr. President,> Reiko sent, <is there any reason we can't sit out here until you make contact with the New Terran president and he announces the forthcoming visit of this marvelous, new, Haraken-built ship?>

<No reason whatsoever, Captain, but the question is whether President Drake will announce his tour. He might wish to wait until he visits the ship and decides whether or not to propose the purchase to the Assembly.>

<Well, there's no reason we can't use a tried and true media technique,> Tatia interjected. <We leak the story. We can even remain anonymous if that's what we wish.> Immediately, Tatia launched into an imitation of a media announcer's voice. <A highly placed source in the government has told us a unique opportunity exists for New Terra ...> It generated chuckles all around, except for Willem who missed the joke.

<Captain Shimada, stay beyond the belt for now,> Alex sent. <It shouldn't take more than a day for our media communications to be broadcast systemwide, which should calm the kidnappers before you make your approach,>

<Understood, Mr. President,> Shimada replied.

<Perhaps I should mention, Mr. President,> Eric added, <The *Tanaka* is no longer in its trial condition. I've added crew, three more travelers, cabin outfitting, and supplies. It wouldn't have been appropriate to tour President Drake through the ship in its earlier condition.>

<And you would need a captain or perhaps a commander for your travelers,> Alex hinted.

<Commander Cohen, Mr. President. My choice.>

<Which I'm sure annoyed Captain Shimada,> Alex sent, his laughter following.

Julien closed the comm links, and Alex was mentally revising the message he would send to President Drake when he noticed First Mate Lumley's frown.

"Something wrong, Ser Lumley?" Alex asked.

"Your pardon, Mr. President, but I was wondering what a fully outfitted, sting-class ship would cost?"

Alex looked at Lumley for a moment before he grinned. "Mickey," Alex yelled at the top of his voice, even though the master engineer wasn't on the bridge.

Lumley laughed at Alex's antics. *Best decision I ever made was to join these people,* he thought.

* * *

"President Drake, you have a comm call from President Racine," a senior staffer announced after interrupting the cabinet meeting. "Apparently, the Haraken president is in system."

Drake glanced toward Darryl Jaya, who still held the post of Minister of Technology, now under his third president. At the staffer's announcement, Darryl adopted an enormous earsplitting grin. Without doubt, he was one of Alex Racine's greatest fans, especially if the Haraken president was bringing new technological toys to New Terra.

"I'll take the comm in my office," Drake said to his staffer. "Adjourn for fifteen minutes, please," he said to his cabinet ministers. Drake glanced toward Jaya and nodded toward the door, and his minister hurried out of the meeting like a child told he can go out and play.

The two men climbed the broad staircase of Government House to the second floor to gain the president's office. Settling behind his chair, with Jaya behind him, Drake accepted the vid comm signal. On his screen popped an image of Alex and Renée, people who had played major roles in his life for the past decade and a half. They were standing on the bridge of the *Reveur,* the starship that had started it all. *Déjà vu,* Drake thought.

"Greetings, President Drake," Alex began.

"Darryl," Renée exclaimed, and the pair promptly hijacked the meeting, as they caught up on family and news.

When Drake could insert himself into the conversation, he asked, "Are you inbound to New Terra, President Racine?"

"Yes, actually we're here for business and pleasure. Since I was coming to see you, many of our New Terrans wanted to visit family and friends."

"As always, your people are welcome. You said you wanted to see me. What about?" Drake replied.

"After the events that unfolded from United Earth's interference in our systems, I thought you might be interested in our newest class of ships."

"I thought things were settled with the UE," Drake said, getting nervous.

"Oh, they are. But in dealing with the Earthers, it became obvious to us that the travelers have limitations ... they're confined to a system unless carried and their short beam throw puts them in harm's way of larger ships."

"Do you have a design to show? Is that what you're bringing us?" Jaya asked.

"Actually, I brought a ship. It's on its space trials, and this seemed like the perfect time to have it accompany me," Alex said, smiling and trying to appear convivial.

"You brought a new warship into Oistos space without permission?" asked Drake, his voice hardening.

<Where's our friend, the ex-minister?> Renée sent to Alex. <He seems to have lost much of his warmth in his new role.>

"Certainly not, President Drake," Alex replied, "the *Tanaka* is waiting for your permission to enter the system." Alex could have kissed Reiko for her suggestion that the sting ship take up station beyond the belt. It gave him the edge he needed in the delicate discussion, and he deliberately dropped the ship's name. Hatsuto Tanaka, the ship's namesake, was a New Terran son, who sacrificed his life during the dark days when the New Terran government was in turmoil. It had the desired effect of mollifying Drake.

"Can you give us an outline of its capabilities?" Jaya asked.

"Certainly, Jaya," Alex said, and then sent, <Julien, get Reiko and Franz to their bridge, now.> Alex stalled by reviewing the limitations of the Haraken's carrier-traveler combination during his encounter with UE warships while he was at Sol.

Aboard the *Tanaka*, Reiko and Franz ran from the captain's cabin to the ship's bridge, buttoning their officers' jackets, while Julien briefed them.

"Our president knows this ship's capability as well as anyone," Reiko said to Franz. "He doesn't need us to tell the New Terran president. Aren't we just window dressing for the sale of the ship?"

"I believe we, not this ship, are the ones for sale today," Franz replied, straightening his jacket and running his fingers through his short hair. "Be charming," Franz added. Once on the bridge, he chose to stand behind his captain.

Julien cued Alex when the *Tanaka* was ready, and Alex wound down his pitch about the reasons for the invention of the sting class. <Rather than have me describe the high points of these new ships, Sers, allow me to let you hear it from one of the designers.>

On the *Tanaka*, Willem activated the bridge's vid comm, framing Reiko and Franz. Aboard the *Rêveur*, Cordelia located a second monitor on Drake's desk. It was reserved for viewing finances, but it was still tied into Government House's network.

As Alex finished his sentence, Drake and Jaya saw the image of Reiko and Franz pop up on the second monitor, and, in his excitement, Jaya nudged Drake from behind with an elbow.

"Let me introduce, Captain Reiko Shimada, formerly Commodore Shimada of United Earth, and Commander Franz Cohen, you know," Alex said.

The New Terrans knew that United Earth scientists had jumped ship to join the Harakens, but that an ex-commodore had joined them was news. After a short exchange of pleasantries, Drake asked after Franz's father.

"Hezekiah is well, Mr. President. Thank you for asking. We message each other about once a week. He and my mother keep asking when I will be having children."

"Oh, do you have a partner, Franz?" Drake asked.

Reiko raised a hand. "That would be me, Sir."

That the diminutive, yet formidable, ex-UE commodore was Franz's partner and he the son of the well-liked, but now-retired, Joaquin Station director, eased more of the tension that had previously been present on the comm.

"So, Captain Shimada, you gave up your home for this poor excuse of a New Terran?" Drake said, laughing.

"Well, Mr. President, when he protected my destroyer by detonating a ship-killer missile with his traveler, I was inclined to give him a second look. But then, not soon after, when he carried me off the bridge in the nick of time before my ship's dead hulk rammed a UE battleship trying to destroy a station full of innocent people, I decided he deserved a shot."

Reiko had summarized the horrific events of the battle for Idona so simply and candidly that Drake and Jaya were speechless. They watched Franz rest his hands possessively on Reiko's shoulders, and the two men were reminded of the essence of the Harakens — men and women who were unabashed in their efforts to protect all entities within their sphere — including the New Terrans.

"I'm told you'll give us the highlights of your ship, Captain," Drake said.

Alex could see the president relax even more. <Small, but powerful packages ... such delights,> Alex sent to Renée, who smiled back at him.

While Reiko gave Drake and Jaya the highlights of the vessel, Alex mused over his relationship with Will Drake — contentious during the sale of Alex's g-sling program, but replaced by a deep and respectful bond while working to repair the *Rêveur* and deliver Méridien technology to New Terra.

Julien watched his friend drift away from the conversation, reflecting on some personal thoughts no doubt, which eventually led to a frown that formed on his forehead. Correctly deducing Alex's thoughts, Julien sent, <It is regretful that we must pretend to President Drake in this manner, and I presume he will be upset when he discovers our fabrication. At this point, it can't be helped nor can we tell him the truth, without endangering your sister. Such are the difficult choices we face in these situations.>

"So, President Drake, interested in a close-up view of our new ship and perhaps purchasing a few?" Alex asked when Reiko finished her summary.

"An FTL-capable warship with incredible beam power that can carry four travelers and has grav-drives … I think the answer would be absolutely."

"We should meet away from New Terra to test the beams. Do you have any suggestions, Julien?" Alex asked.

"An equitable meeting point and one with adequate targets for the beam tests would be the rock fields interspersed around the moons of Ganymede," Julien replied nonchalantly.

"How does that sound to you, President Drake?" Alex asked.

"That works for me. I have some business to attend to, but I can be aboard a traveler late tomorrow," Drake replied.

"Excellent. By the way, President Drake, you're welcome to bring your anxious friend," Alex said, smiling.

Jaya's triumphant "yes" could be heard as the comm closed.

* * *

"Julien, I recall the media producer we used for the interview with Christie was Charlotte Sanderson," Alex said.

"It's good to know that your implants haven't failed … yet," Julien quipped.

"And what is the lifespan of crystal memory?" Alex shot back.

"Much longer than brain tissue, human," Julien replied. *Much to my great regret*, Julien thought.

"Charlotte, please," Alex requested. Their repartee, which should have bolstered their spirits, managed to depress them both.

SADEs faced an unlimited lifespan now that they had mobility and control over their destinies. Julien placed a note in his long-term investigation queue — research the feasibility of transferring a human mind to crystal memory. He was aware that even if the concept could be proven many humans might not choose to make the transfer, his friend among them. It was the tenuous hold humans had on life, causing them to strive so fiercely during their short lifespans, which made them special to Julien.

"Ser Sanderson is now on the board of By-Long Media," Julien said. "Do you still wish me to initiate contact?"

"Please, Ser."

Alex's polite and formal response told Julien that he too had been left pondering that thing that concerned all intelligent biological entities — their eventual demise.

Blades of grass warmed by Oistos tickled Charlotte Sanderson's bare feet as she walked through the park. Lunch in the park and a ten-minute walk on the lush grass were part of her daily regimen — a chance to rebalance away from her hectic job. The two interviews with Christie Racine, more than a decade ago, one accompanied by Étienne de Long and the other with Alex Racine, catapulted her from producer to media director and eventually to a position on the company's board of directors.

Charlotte's reader chimed quietly, which surprised her because she was certain she turned it off — she always turned it off for lunch. Pulling the reader from her bag, to block further comms, Charlotte saw a swirl of delicate colors on the screen. The subtle and intricate play was mesmerizing, and then, without accepting the comm, a voice issued from it, and Charlotte nearly dropped the reader.

"Greetings, Ser Sanderson, I have an important story for you, but my source must remain anonymous."

"Who is this?" Charlotte demanded. Her mind kicked into a producer's investigative thought process. Greetings and Ser, the voice said — a Méridien.

"I'm afraid I too must remain anonymous. Do we have your promise?"

"Yes, on one condition."

"No conditions."

"Does this have anything to do with the *Rêveur* in our system?" Charlotte asked, hoping to get the contact to leak some piece of information.

When silence greeted her question, she relented. "Okay, fine. Yes, you have my word … anonymity for you and your source."

"Greetings, Ser Sanderson," Alex said, using voice comm only.

Charlotte tapped the record icon and it winked on, then off. She tapped it again and again it cycled off. *SADEs*, she thought, and a grin broke across her face. "This is a familiar voice," Charlotte said, still hoping for confirmation of what she suspected. "And interesting, my reader does not detail your ID or origination source." But here, her investigative techniques met a wall of silence. "As you wish, Ser Anonymous, what's your story?"

"You might wish to report that according to a highly placed government source the Harakens have brought a powerful warship, the first of its kind, to Oistos for the purpose of selling the new ship to New Terra. President Drake has agreed to tour the new sting-class ship, named the *Tanaka*."

The *Tanaka*, Charlotte thought and realized that the ship's name gave her great color background for the report. When the voice didn't continue, she said, "Is that it? A little thin. Can you confirm that President Racine will be meeting with President Drake?"

"I can," the voice said, then the comm closed and the beautiful swirling pattern exploded in a spray of colors, reminiscent of the repaired liner's display the day it left New Terra's orbit to return to Méridien. Charlotte smiled to herself. *Julien*, she thought.

"Thank you, Alex," Charlotte said quietly to her reader. Then she jumped up and down on the thick grass with both hands on her reader, squealing like a little girl.

Aboard the *Rêveur*, Alex sent, <Julien, signal Captain Shimada to proceed in system to rendezvous with Drake's traveler. Coordinate with Willem. I want the two ships to reach the coordinates that you give them at nearly the same time ... a sort of coincidental meeting.>

<Two ships traveling through the tremendous vastness of space happen to occupy the same point at the same time ... how fanciful of you, Mr. President,> the SADE replied.

The crew passing Julien in the corridor witnessed one of the oddest iterations of his head display. Soft sparkles of rainbow-colored light sprang from Julien's crown and fell in a shimmer around his head to disappear near his shoulders. One New Terran crew member, who read fantasy stories to her daughters, explained the display to the other two walking with her when she sent, <fairy dust.>

13

Sarah Laurent and her partner, Fredericka Olsen, eyed Steve Ross, who sat across the table from them.

"Isn't this cozy?" Fredericka said, fingering one of the silver rings that decorated every finger. She loved the contrast of the cool metal color against her warm brown skin.

"Hmm," Steve grunted in reply.

The threesome comprised some of Prima's top independent investigators, and they were also fierce competitors. That Maria Gonzalez had summoned them with short notice spoke of something big.

"Sorry to keep you waiting, people," Maria said, sweeping into the room, and the three ex-Terran Security Forces investigators snapped upright. It was the response you would expect, short of jumping to attention and saluting, to pay your respects to an ex-TSF general and ex-president entering the room.

"I have an alpha-priority contract to locate an individual or individuals. Your readers are receiving the details now," Maria announced without introduction. She waited while the investigators perused the data.

"No names?" Steve asked.

"No details on the individual or individuals at all," Maria replied. "All we know is that we're chasing a biochemist who's manufacturing a potent and addictive hallucinogenic drug."

"Do we have locations where the drug has been found so that we might track it back through the suppliers?" Fredericka asked.

"Negative. All incidences of drug use have been off planet."

The answers to the investigators' questions were only generating more questions in their minds, and normally Maria was forthcoming with any information she could provide, but apparently not in this instance.

"Are we the only three working this case?" Sarah asked.

"Negative, Laurent, all my people are on deck for this one," Maria replied.

If wheels weren't churning in the investigators' minds before, they certainly were now, and if there was ever to be a higher designation than alpha-contract, it could be applied to this one.

"Does this have anything to do with the *Rêveur* on its way in system?" asked Fredericka, which earned her Maria's stare. She offered a "sorry" and nodded her head in apology.

"My people have already compiled a list of manufacturers, suppliers, and shipments of apparatus and equipment. You have the addresses, reader IDs, and comm numbers for every delivery location," Maria said.

"So what's our role?" asked Steve, which took the question right out of the mouths of Sarah and Fredericka.

"You three will be the only ones in the field and are tasked with determining if any of these shipments are being used to create the drug described in your notes," Maria replied. "The difficult part is that you aren't to let these people know they're being investigated ... that's paramount."

"So this is a covert surveillance operation ... that part I get," Sarah said, pulling on her short, blonde hair tucked behind her ear, which was a telltale that she was confused about something. "But how do we know who's making what? We're not chemists?"

"Steal samples," Steve replied.

Sarah and Fredericka glanced at each other. Despite their competitive stance with Steve Ross, the women admitted he was the senior investigator among the three of them, with an additional eleven years of experience, and Steve hadn't missed a beat before intuiting Maria's unstated requirement that the investigators would have to steal the samples without being caught or letting anyone know there had been a break-in and samples were taken.

"You will each have a team of my people assigned to you. Contact them to hand off any samples that you ... obtain ... to them. They can be at your location within a half-hour and test the chemicals on-site for the markers that will identify this drug. Your team's info is on your readers."

"Is our investigation systemwide?" Steve asked.

"Your data contains only New Terran deliveries. I have my data people tracking shipments off planet," Maria replied. "Now, this is the unusual part, so listen carefully. I don't expect you to locate this person or persons, but this is only conjecture on my part. My expectations are that while working through your lists you will check on a delivery location and find no one. Be extra diligent there. Run a sniffer for residues and have the backup team test whatever the sniffer picks up."

"Why do you expect them to be gone?" Fredericka asked.

"The drug is potent, far outside anything we've seen before, and certain parties would know that they have a much greater chance of being caught on New Terra versus somewhere out there," Maria said, pointing a finger into the air.

"Does this have anything to do with the pleasure domes?" Steve asked. "And don't bother giving me that senior commander look."

"Wouldn't think of it, Ross. It never worked on you when you were in the service ... rebel," Maria said, tempering her comment with a wink. "It's understood in certain circles that some of the mining companies on Ganymede's moons are covers. But the common citizen is unaware that those pleasure domes are run by dangerous criminals. For now, that's the way our government wants to keep it."

"What's our time frame?" Sarah asked.

"There isn't one," Maria replied, "but I expect if we take too long, the investigation will become moot."

"Sounds like overtime billing will be expected," Steve said, ensuring he understood Maria's contract expectations.

"You're authorized to submit a 50 percent markup on all hours worked. I advise you to make use of every hour of the day and night before the contract is pulled," Maria said.

Maria liked these three people and had worked with each of them, at one time or another, during her tenure in the TSF. So, she caught the eye of each of them in turn before she said, "Make no mistake, people. You might not locate the individual we're after, but that doesn't mean that you won't have found treacherous people involved in the manufacture of illegal stimulants who won't take kindly to an investigator sticking a nose into their business. Be extremely careful."

* * *

Maria's comm signaled an incoming call from President Drake, which surprised her. They hadn't spoken in months, and the timing seemed too coincidental. "Put your game hat on, Maria," she murmured as she picked up her reader and accepted the comm.

"To what do I owe the pleasure, President Drake?" Maria said.

"I want to know everything you know about what Alex Racine is up to, and I want to know it now."

"You forget yourself, Mr. President. I'm no longer a civil servant," Maria replied, bristling.

"We're being manipulated again, Maria," Drake exclaimed.

"And what was the intent of Alex's manipulations when he proved President McMorris was murdered, much to everyone's surprise; when he disobeyed presidential orders to save 125,000 Libran refugees; when he disclosed Downing's usurpation of Méridien technology; and the list goes on? Alex doesn't follow our rules ... don't think he likes rules ... but his ultimate goal has always been to help us."

"But, what if someday that's not his intent?" Drake asked.

"Then he will no longer be Alex Racine, Will," Maria said quietly.

"Perhaps we should begin again?"

"Perhaps you should," Maria replied.

"I attempted to ascertain from Ambassador Monti what Alex was doing in system, and he repeated the cover story of vacation. Why are you laughing?" Will asked, perturbed by her sudden outburst.

"Do you really think Alex would place his good friend in such a compromising position? Alex knew Tomas would be the first person you would go to for answers. Will, you have to stop trying to manage everything. The president's position is about the guidance of our society, not trying to control its every movement."

"Well, enough criticism about my job management," Drake said. "I was calling because Alex and you have always been close. I know if Alex touched base with anyone, it would be you. Can we compare notes?"

"Well, I already know your side of the story," Maria said, her voice lifting in amusement.

"Everybody knows my side of the story. Seems it was important enough to transport Charlotte Sanderson out of her director's chair and back onto the reporter's desk."

"I thought it was fascinating. Does the *Tanaka* really exist?"

"Oh, yes, our outpost on Sharius reports an odd-shaped ship crossing the belt. It's smooth-hulled like a traveler but about the size of a Méridien liner and, according to the captain ... by the way, who's an ex-UE commodore ... possessing a beam weapon to match its size." Drake heard Maria's long, slow whistle over the comm.

"Can we afford one or three?" Maria asked.

"I have no idea, guess we'll find out, but back to your dealings with Alex."

"I can tell you this, Will. He's hired my firm to locate someone."

"Who?"

"Can't tell you."

"Maria, we go too far back to play games like this —"

"Will, listen to me," Maria said, interrupting her president. "We don't know the name of the target ... Alex doesn't know who. He's after a biochemist who's making some sort of nasty hallucinogenic."

"Hmm ... some vacation."

"He tried that one on you too?" Maria asked, laughing. "Renée called him on that one."

"She was always the one with the better sense of people."

"Agreed. I think Alex is better with aliens ... and SADEs, come to think of it."

"So what does this all mean ... a brand new ship to show off and searching for a biochemist?"

"Let me ask you a question first, Will. Where is your sting-ship tour taking place? Ganymede, by any chance?"

"How did you know? … the domes," Drake said, suddenly seeing some of the pieces fall together.

"Yes, those pesky little domes," Maria said, her voice taking on a hard edge.

"I know you want the government to move faster in dealing with the problem —"

"Move faster," Maria declared hotly. "I want you, the Assembly, and the TSF to get off their collective butts and move, period."

"They have the law —"

"Wrong," Maria interrupted again, "the law served to protect mining companies in the initial days of space exploration. Those days zipped past us at the speed of Méridien technology. These pleasure domes are a perversion of the law and are opportunities for the gangs to generate credits with impunity. Now, the Harakens are here hunting a biochemist who manufactures dangerous drugs."

"Oh, Maria … you don't think the gangs tried to infiltrate Espero?"

"Possibly, but if it was something general like that, I think Alex would have been knocking at Government House's door demanding something be done about the source of the problem."

"So you still think we're missing something?" Drake asked.

"Undoubtedly, which is why I have some advice for you, Will."

"Go ahead. It looks like I'm in need of it," Drake said, with resignation.

"Don't play the New Terran president on Alex out there. Something's going on, and I believe he's keeping us in the dark for a good reason."

"Deniability, most likely."

"Most likely," Maria agreed. "Anyway, be prepared to let things play out. In every case, that has worked in our favor. Then, in the end, when the prize falls in your lap, and some people stand up and proclaim foul on the way it happened, you can reply that it was those damned Harakens."

Drake laughed at that. Maria was right on that score. A great many ills and foul deeds had been uncovered by Alex and company as they bent, if not broke, the laws of the land. On more than one occasion, Alex Racine should have been arrested and tried under New Terran law. Only stumbling block to that scenario was: How do you prosecute the leader of a foreign world who has at his command SADEs, alien weaponry, and a fanatically loyal population?

"I will try to be a good puppet," Drake said and signed off.

Maria breathed a sigh of relief. The conversation had gone much better than she expected. She fervently hoped Drake would keep his head screwed on straight and his temper under control once Alex's machinations went into overdrive.

* * *

The next morning Drake, Jaya, a retinue of staffers and security boarded a traveler waiting at the rear of Government House. The traveler was piloted by Captain Hailey Timmion, who led the New Terran shuttles in a successful bluff to force the UE's *Hand of Justice* to take the longer path outward of Niomedes, which sealed the battleship's fate.

As much as Drake enjoyed traveling in the exquisitely appointed presidential shuttle, he was reminded that this traveler was built specially for Maria Gonzalez by the Harakens. New Terrans might have been outraged at the quality of the interior details and the credits it cost, except for one minor point. The traveler was a gift from the Harakens to New Terra for the exclusive use of the sitting president.

Moments after Timmion lifted off, reports were sent from several independent ground sources that the president was on the move. More reports followed those, once the shuttle cleared New Terra's air space, and even more, originating from freighters and tugs, were sent as the traveler headed for the outer planets, in the general direction of Ganymede.

The reports terminated at the pleasure domes of Azul "Mr. Blue" Kadmir, Roz "Sniffer" O'Brien, and Peto "Craze" Toyo. All three men paid enormous amounts of credits every month to myriad, low-level informants to keep watch on key government personnel and influential individuals, who they knew took a hard stance against criminality, Maria Gonzalez first and foremost among this latter group.

14

Alex requested Julien and Cordelia monitor the communications and data flow of Maria's people soon after she met with her investigators.

"Are you concerned, Ser President, that Ser Gonzalez will not communicate her findings to you?" Cordelia asked.

"I believe our purpose will be similar to Sol, beloved," Julien said. "Maria's investigators are akin to the pro-naval forces, who are hunting among judiciary forces for our biochemist."

"Then we are to protect them," Cordelia said.

"Yes," Julien replied. "Mr. President, by these actions, it's quite possible we will be estranging another valuable New Terran contact."

"That seems to be my style lately … alienation," Alex said, and laughed halfheartedly at his joke. Sobering, he added, "It's the least we can do for placing them in harm's way with limited information."

"To what extent should we display our efforts?" Cordelia asked.

"Your intent is dual-fold," Alex replied. "First, do whatever is necessary to protect the investigators. They will probably be Maria's best people, but they might not know the kind of trouble waiting for them. And second, keep the investigation quiet. If word leaks out that illegal drug manufacturers are being raided, we could panic whoever has our girls. In fact, they might think that we're the ones running the investigation."

Having identified the three people who Maria assigned to field operations, the SADEs set taps on the investigators' readers, collected the gamut of information Maria shared with them, and cross-referenced this with the intelligence data her employees were gathering.

* * *

During his second afternoon in the field, Steve Ross finished surveilling a quiet warehouse on the outskirts of Prima. Despite the rusting, locked gate and weeds growing next to the building, three shiny new hover cars were parked at the rear. Inside, nine people went about their jobs manufacturing an assortment of powders and pills.

Earlier that morning, Steve discovered a nearly identical setup at a shop in Prima. He pondered which one of the two he would raid first, once night fell. The warehouse seemed to be the larger of the two operations and was more likely to have a second shift, so he decided to hit the shop first and save the warehouse for the early morning hours and hope there wasn't a third shift.

Keeping low along the fence, Steve made his way back to his flit. In the stillness of the afternoon, his reader softly chimed. *Fool amateur's mistake,* Steve thought, berating himself for leaving his reader on after taking vids of the manufacturing operation through the warehouse windows.

Pulling his reader, Steve was momentarily taken off guard by the beautiful screen image of swirling colors. Then a voice from the reader said, "Ser Ross, you've been discovered by those in the warehouse."

Steve hunkered down in some overgrown weeds and looked carefully around him. "Who is this and where are you?" he whispered.

"Not near you, if that's what you're wondering, Ser. I've observed a man planting some sort of device on your flit. Afterwards, he made his way to the back of the warehouse in the opposite direction from you. I can only assume that this does not bode well for you."

"You assume this does not bode well for me … who talks like that? What you mean is someone ponged my flit."

And the Ser believes I speak in an unusual manner, Julien thought, wondering how to conjugate the verb ponged. "I think the question remains, Ser, as to whether you are skilled at removing the device or whether you will require my assistance."

Steve was thinking this was the oddest conversation he had ever had during his investigations or in his entire life, for that matter, and decided to simplify their communication. "No, I'm not an explosives expert. Are you?"

"I'm quite accomplished in many facets of human inventions. When you reach your flit, please do not touch it in any manner. Simply point your reader at the device from a distance of about 15 to 20 centimeters and rotate the reader as much as you can so that I may have a full view of it."

Tucking the reader back into his pack, Steve crawled along the fence line, deciding to keep up the charade so that those in the warehouse wouldn't know he was aware of what they had done. At his flit, he pulled out the reader. The swirling image was gone, but the comm icon was still lit so he carefully investigated his flit and located a small polished disc, about 5 centimeters across, adhering to the flit's undercarriage.

"What do you think?' Steve whispered, when he finished surveying the disc.

"One moment, Ser," Julien said, searching databases, beginning with those of the Terran Security Forces, quickly locating the design. "That explosive device is designed to activate when a preset elevation is acquired. More than likely, this will have occurred when you were a good distance away. It has a magnetized base, and the method of deactivation is quite simple. Pull the device off firmly but gently. I recommend setting down the reader and using both hands."

"You sure?" asked Steve, his face and hands starting to sweat.

"I'm observing the TSF manual pages as we speak. The specifications for disarming are quite clear."

"Okay, give me a moment."

Julien heard a grunt, a smack of flesh against something solid, and a round of whispered expletives. "I take it the device is free of the undercarriage."

"Yeah, now what?" Steve growled, glancing at his bleeding knuckles.

"You will notice the disc has a fine line running around its circumference, enabling the two halves of the disc to be rotated. Observe both flat sides. One side will have a series of numbers on it."

"Got it."

"With the numbers facing up, trap the top half of the disc in one hand and rotate the lower half counterclockwise about 30 degrees until you hear a click."

"Or a boom," Steve commented drily.

"Hopefully not," Julien replied.

Steve swiped one hand down his pants leg and then the other to clear off the sweat and grime. Gripping the device as he had been instructed, making triple sure he was turning the bottom half counterclockwise, Steve closed his eyes and slowly rotated the halves. When he heard the click of metal, he opened his eyes and let out a long sigh. "All good. Now what?"

"It's safe, Ser Ross. You can put it in your pocket and fly away."

"Take it with me?"

"To dispose of safely, Ser."

Now that Steve was focusing again on something else besides dying, he realized that he might be compromising the investigation if his flit didn't explode as expected. "Can this thing be detonated remotely?" Steve asked.

"Unfortunately, your adversaries programmed the device for a specific elevation, which I don't know. They would expect to hear the explosion or listen to a media report of a flit accident, which must resemble their expectations."

"Too true."

"However, if you're willing to sacrifice your flit, Ser, I believe we can keep the charade in play. When you are safely away, I will launch the flit and elevate it until the activation height is reached.

Steve's suspicions were confirmed. He was talking to a SADE. "Okay, let's do this." Steve jumped on his flit, kept low to the ground until he had traveled about 2 kilometers, landed, and got off the transport.

"I can activate the device the same way?" Steve asked.

"Yes, twist the halves in the opposite direction until you hear a click, Ser, and reattach it."

"Done."

"Please seek shelter. We don't know at what elevation it was programmed to explode."

Steve grabbed his carryall off the back of the flit, his personal bag, and a small satchel of food and water. Spying an enormous tree, he hid on the far side of its 2-meter diameter. "Ready."

Julien surveyed the area, ensuring it was free of human beings, and then accessed the flit's New Terran–style controller. Lifting the transport into the air, the machine cleared about 40 meters in height before Julien heard a loud crack over Steve's reader and watched via the *Rêveur's* telemetry as the flit exploded and fell from the sky.

"Mission accomplished," Steve said with a sigh, already missing his flit and dreading the prospect of the long hike through the woods to reach a roadway. Then, he would have to wait while he called his backup team, who were aboard a hover car, for a ride back to Prima. His entire operation schedule had been destroyed. *I must be getting sloppy,* Steve thought with disgust.

"Thanks for saving my behind, Haraken," Steve said into his reader, but belatedly noticed that the comm icon was unlit. He grabbed his gear and hiked up a hill through low brush in what he thought was the shortest route to a roadway he had flown over on the way to the warehouse.

Having slogged through undergrowth for about three-quarters of an hour, Steve broke into a small clearing and was stunned to see a brand new flit parked there. He dumped his gear and pulled out his reader. On the screen was a short text message, "A replacement gift from a Haraken."

"I'll be," Steve said, grabbing his gear and hurrying to his new transport.

You're welcome, Julien thought, with a smile. It was a pleasant experience — saving a life instead of helping others to takes hundreds, if not thousands, at a time, as they had done during the UE war at Sol.

* * *

Soon after midnight, Sarah Laurent and her partner, Fredericka Olsen, returned to a sprawling estate with a high stone wall surrounding tens of kilometers of grounds. It seemed an odd place for the delivery of a significant number of biochemical products.

However, while they observed the estate from across the roadway during the late afternoon, several grav-transports landed at the estate, and men quickly unloaded boxes of supplies, carrying them into a structure adjacent to the main building. The ancillary building was a simple metal-walled construction and was in stark contrast to the older, stone-and-timber main house.

The two ex-TSF investigators worked together on several jobs while serving and later teamed up on a couple of civilian jobs, but it wasn't until they met Steve Ross that they considered forming a partnership.

After a tough case they solved together, the three of them spent the day together at the beach, relaxing and drinking. Steve decided to go swimming in what the girls knew would be chilly waters. Stripping down to his shorts, Steve revealed knife and gunshot wounds on his arms, chest, and legs.

Catching the women staring at his old wounds, Steve remarked, "Enjoy your pretty, unblemished bodies while you can, ladies. Stay in this business long enough and you'll collect your share of these."

It seemed amazing to the women that Steve was still alive. Two weeks later, Steve was seriously wounded in a gunfight with two men he was paid to locate. It was only the application of Méridien medical nanites, which had become a mainstay of Prima emergency rooms, that saved Steve's life that day. The nanites healed the gunshot wounds and erased his old scars, which frustrated Steve something fierce.

One night at dinner, Sarah, tired of hearing Steve griping about what the medical nanites had done, demanded to know his problem. Steve, who had consumed a few glasses of wine, looked at her and said, "Fems get excited by a man with scars. They think he's this dangerous sort, and they get turned on."

"Nah-ah," Sarah replied, shaking her head.

"Uh-huh," Fredericka said, contradicting her partner, which elicited a grin from Steve.

Soon after that dinner, the two women decided to partner. The image of Steve's wounds reminded them that having someone to watch their backs might be a smart move in their business.

Outside the estate, Sarah switched on her chronometer and shielded its light from being spotted in the dark. "Time to move," she whispered.

"Do not enter that domicile, Sers."

"What did you say?" Sarah whispered to Fredericka.

"What? I didn't say anything. Is your reader on? You trying to get us torched?" Fredericka whispered back.

Sarah rolled on her side, dug into her kit bag, and yanked out her reader. She turned the reader toward Fredericka to display the screen's strange image of moving colors to Fredericka.

"Turn it off," Fredericka whispered.

"I wouldn't do that," said a voice, stemming from the reader.

"Why not?" Sarah asked.

Fredericka gave Sarah a strange look. She couldn't figure why her partner would bother asking a question of someone who was obviously spoofing them. For all they knew, the people in the estate were on to them, and the comm was just a screen while other members snuck up behind them from deep in the woods.

"Comms indicate some ten or more people are in the estate. From the sounds of their preparations, they will employ heavy weaponry," the voice said.

"The place is dark and it's showed no activity for an hour," Fredericka said, leaning over to whisper into the reader and keeping one eye out on the trees and bushes behind them. "How do we know you aren't trying to spoof us?"

"You are Fredericka Tillman Olsen, named after your father and his brother, who were killed in a mining accident on Cressida, six months before you were born. You have two brothers and one sister. Your sister calls you Sweet —"

"Okay, okay, enough," Fredericka said, interrupting the voice. "So if you're not from the estate, who are you?"

"A friend. I believe your comms gave you away. The estate has sophisticated electronic detection. They probably did not break your communications encryption, but they knew they were being surveilled."

"Thanks for the heads up, friend," Sarah said. "We're out of here."

"And I wouldn't advise that either," the voice said.

Sarah halted in the middle of stuffing her reader away. The two women exchanged concerned looks. "Uh ... why not?" Sarah asked.

"I detect three heat signatures between you and your transport location."

"Wait. How do you know where our Haraken grav-transport is located? We flew that in here on a moonless night. They're undetectable," Fredericka challenged.

"To most systems, but grav drives give off a unique wave signature that is definitely detectable."

"SADE," Sarah mouthed to Fredericka, who nodded her agreement. Suddenly, the women were all ears to whatever the voice had to suggest.

"Any options, friend?" Sarah asked.

"Oh, yes, please remain where you are."

"What?" Fredericka exclaimed in the loudest whisper she could manage. "Wait here while they move in on us?"

"The people arrayed against you are waiting for you to make the first move ... either toward the house or back to your transport."

Sarah and Fredericka debated their options. Walking out was considered and dropped, so was trying to take on the armed men between them and their transport. While they considered other options, a window burst in the auxiliary building. Smoke and flames billowed out and up into the dark sky.

Both women flicked down their peepers and eyed the building close up. People came running out of the main house toward the burning building.

"Oops," the voice said. "And here I was trying to make a simple adjustment to their solar controller. Apparently, I overloaded its circuits and started a fire. How clumsy of me."

Sarah and Fredericka snickered and clamped hands over their mouths to muffle the sound.

"If you will be patient, Sers, Prima's emergency response teams will be arriving shortly. I took the precaution of calling them about a quarter-hour ago. The vehicles' announcement should draw the individuals from the woods. Please wait."

Sarah and Fredericka continued to observe the proceedings. Obviously, they were correct in their assessment of the ancillary building as a drug-manufacturing location, because after a few more moments, with the flames growing higher, explosions rocked the building. At one point, a major section of the roof blew off and the flaming material landed on top of the main house.

Explosions continued to rock the secondary building, sending more burning debris against the main house until it was totally engulfed in flames. As the wail of emergency vehicles sounded in the distance, the estate's people scattered, running for their transports. Those with hover cars raced for the roadway to head in the opposite direction from the emergency vehicles. Those with grav-transports disappeared into the night air.

"One has to wonder what those bad people were making in that building," the voice said, which had the two women snorting with laughter. Moments later, the voice said, "The heat signatures have hurried away from your transport to join a hover car waiting down the roadway. You may leave safely now."

As Cordelia closed the comm, she heard the distinct sound of a kiss being thrown her way, and she smiled.

15

Miranda chartered a circuitous route for the traveler, taking the fighter around the outside of the belt and entering the system so that its inbound trajectory would pass the greater moons of Kephron. This second planet outward from Ganymede trailed the gas giant's orbit by about 63 degrees. The more desirable moons of Kephron traced elliptical orbits around the planet, and their surfaces were constantly disrupted by the tidal forces of the massive planet. However, these same moons held rare metal ores, and the miners, who worked the shafts, were well paid for extremely dangerous work.

The traveler slid past Kephron's most outer moon and made directly for Jolares at Ganymede, the site of Peto Toyo's pleasure domes. While en route, Miranda used the shuttle's controller to link to the Jolares comm station. From there, she hacked into the domes' reservation system, entering the names of the Harakens aboard. A smile crossed Miranda's face, as she added substantial credits to each account, much more than any one person would need for the week's stay that was reserved — unless the people happened to be big spenders.

Several Haraken engineers and techs aboard once worked for New Terran mining companies, and they spent time during the voyage educating the others on the attitude and vocabulary of miners. Svetlana had the people practicing in the aisle to evidence the bluster and boisterousness expected of the sort of high-priced miners who would risk the work on Kephron's moons.

Arriving at Toyo's pleasure domes, several days after launch, Miranda adopted the voice of one of the New Terran techs to communicate with the landing bay. Once she gained approval and the traveler was safely on deck, she received instructions to direct all passengers to reception.

Svetlana stood at the traveler's exit. She eyed the group, her gaze piercing, and said, "You know your parts. Once you step off this ship never stop playing them … in your cabin, in the refresher, or in bed." Her last words generated chuckles. "Don't be forward in asking about our girls. Let others volunteer information to you once you start a conversation about your entertainment preferences. The people who work in these domes are practiced criminals. Expect them to be suspicious of any mistake you make, and if they come to doubt who you are, expect them to make you pay for trespassing on their grounds."

The crew watched as Svetlana, who had adopted a commander's stern demeanor for her announcements, relaxed. Her eyes softened. Her body took on a suggestive stance, and she reached out a hand to Deirdre. "Come, love."

Deirdre, who had been intently following Svetlana's directives, closed her eyes and switched mental gears. Then she too transformed, smiling up at Svetlana from her seat and taking her hand. As Deirdre stood up, the two women melded together.

The crew, watching the performance, followed the women's lead, and suddenly the traveler was filled with the raucous sounds of miners anxious to have some fun. One of the crew members yelled, "You two fems can play all you want once you get your rear ends out of the way. I got a thirst to quench and credits to burn."

Svetlana and Deirdre couldn't help but grin at each other. Svetlana signaled the hatch to release and lower. Miranda's two escorts clambered down first and reached up to brace the SADE and swing her lightly down, despite her avatar's weight. Her feet never touched the hatch steps.

For Toyo's employee, Marty, who waited to check in new patrons, it appeared a woman in a slinky, green dress floated from the vessel to the deck on the arms of two men. He couldn't take his eyes off the way she walked or, better said, the way she glided. In his brain, the question as to why she didn't look like a New Terran never occurred to Marty — he didn't care.

Then to rattle Marty's young brain further, a vision of feminine dark and light appeared behind the woman in the green dress, helped to the deck by the same men. Raven-haired and white-blonde, the beauties were entwined with each other, as they sauntered toward him. His eyes repeatedly flicked from the green-dressed woman to the exotic pair behind.

Miranda, watching the young man's eyes widen as she approached him, signaled Svetlana and Deirdre, <We have a boy. Distract him.>

At the reception desk, Miranda gave the employee a brilliant smile. "Well, dear, what do you desire from me?"

At the moment, Marty was thanking the stars for his bunkmate, who asked to trade shifts. Clearing his throat, he did manage to regain some control over his brain. "Who are you?" he asked.

"A wealthy woman, dear, here to experience what you have to offer."

"I mean ... where are you from?" Marty stammered. "You're not New Terran."

"How perceptive of you, child," Miranda said, smiling and patting the young man's hand. "My two companions and I are from an outer colony of the Confederation so that we can live far away from tiresome questions." Miranda punctuated her last sentence with a penetrating stare, which did get through to the boy's brain.

It was at that moment that Svetlana nuzzled Deirdre's neck and whispered in her ear, to which Deirdre laughed softly, and Marty's brain went into overload as he struggled to focus on his job.

"I don't understand. If you're from the Confederation, why are you traveling with these miners from —" He stopped to consult his monitor, "from Flides."

"Oh, my dear boy," Miranda replied, gently squeezing Marty's forearm, as if he had just made the most charming statement, "I'm not with them. They're with me. That's my ship," she said, flourishing a languid hand at the traveler behind her. "I did say I was a wealthy woman, didn't I?"

"The miners are with you?" Marty asked, totally confused.

"Dear, you're repeating me," Miranda said, laughing. "Why, yes. My companions and I had this sudden urge to see some primitive habitats ... you understand ... like you have on your moons. We have nothing so basic, so dangerous, as these mining camps of yours. I arranged transport for my vessel aboard a passenger liner from my world to your system, and while we were visiting Flides we discovered these rambunctious boys were waiting for transport to your establishment. Your pleasure domes sounded like a marvelous adventure, so I offered them passage with me."

On Miranda's cue, a massive New Terran–built Haraken crowded behind her, scowled at the Toyo employee, and said, "Hey, short shaft, what's holding up the line? You're messing with our downtime."

Two of the man's equally enormous friends flanked him and wore the same angry expression. The belligerence of the three men sent a single message to the employee — a riot was imminent if these miners didn't get to the bar and the fems soon.

"My guests appear perturbed, young man," said Miranda, smiling winningly.

Marty attempted to swallow, but his throat had dried up. He checked Miranda through quickly. When he processed the entangled twins, the light one traced the back of her finger along his jawline and pronounced him cute, scrambling the remainder of Marty's thought processes. He passed the miners through in a fog without bothering to follow security protocols. The only thought that did surface in Marty's mind was to wonder how the three delicate women managed to travel safely with such a bunch of hard cases.

The dome ID cards of Miranda, Svetlana, and Deirdre were scanned by a young woman, who escorted them to their suite, two levels below the moon's surface but still within the primary dome. The escort's eyes constantly flicked toward the three women, as they navigated the lifts and corridors.

Once in their suite, Deirdre fell out on one of the luxurious beds and sent, <This is hard work playing cute and sexy.>

<Who's playing?> Svetlana shot back and offered a sly wink to Deirdre, who grabbed a bed pillow and threw it at her.

Looking around the suite, Deirdre sent, <Nice accommodations. Who's paying for all of us?>

<I thought it appropriate our stay here be charged to one of Ser Toyo's accounts,> Miranda said, smiling, which doubled the women up in laughter.

When Svetlana regained control, she glanced at Miranda and Deirdre. <I'm not sure how I can continue to play my part with such a limited wardrobe. I'm wearing my only entertainment outfit.>

<Same here,> Deirdre echoed. <I believe we need to go spend some of Toyo's credits on vacation outfits.>

<And shopping for garments and accessories will give us an excellent opportunity to scan for the girls' implants,> Miranda sent in reply.

* * *

Toyo glanced at the comm panel on his desk, as it played an ancient dirge. The macabre instrumental was reserved for one caller and hearing it gave Toyo a thrill.

"And to what do I owe the pleasure, Blue?" said Toyo, knowing Kadmir hated being called by his nickname.

"Always the suave one, Toyo," Kadmir replied.

"Get to the point, Kadmir, what do you want?"

"I'm in a position to do you a great favor, Toyo."

"You're going to give me your domes and retire. Thanks, Kadmir."

"No, Toyo, I'm going to help you keep your domes, but it's going to cost you."

"Nobody's taking my domes. Not you or anyone," Toyo growled.

"I'm not so sure about that. I mean anyone who can stop an alien invasion and bring an entire system to its knees can surely roll over a few paltry domes, wouldn't you say?" Kadmir hadn't had so much fun sticking and twisting the knife into a competitor in a long time, and he was thoroughly enjoying himself.

"I haven't the slightest idea what you're talking about, Kadmir. Now, if you're done running off at the mouth. I have credits to make. Business is booming."

"Before you go, Toyo, I hear there was some major knife play in the corridors over there ... bad for business that. Lost your number two, didn't you? Missing any of your other employees?

Boker, Toyo thought with disgust.

"So, this employee of yours and I had a wonderful discussion, and he tells me this story about how Toyo's people did something real ... crazy, you know. They got stupid and kidnapped some Harakens."

"Don't know what anybody's been telling you, Kadmir, but it sounds to me like you've been taking too many of those stims that you've been distributing."

"Yeah, I wouldn't have believed a story like that myself. I mean, who would do something that crazy? But, here's the thing. Seems this man and his partner have a thing for peeping, taking pics of comatose girls to look at later. And would you believe it? One of the naked girls in the pics looks exactly like Christie Racine."

Kadmir waited for a reply, but the comm was silent, which made him chuckle. "I was wondering, Toyo. Do you think it's a coincidence that Racine's sister got kidnapped, brought to Oistos, and the *Rêveur* arrives in system? Then on top of all that, a media producer Racine's used before announces that our president is touring a new Haraken warship? I mean what are the odds of that?"

Toyo was standing at his desk, fuming. His fists were clenched, and he was aching to get his hands on Kadmir's throat.

"So, Toyo, I have your man; I have his pics; and I have proof the girls came in on the *Bountiful,* your ship, which means ... I have you."

Through his gritted teeth, Toyo said, "You're not getting my domes, Kadmir. I'll destroy your domes first, and everyone in them if I have to crash a freighter into them myself."

"Oh, I know you would, Toyo, I know you would," Kadmir said laughing. "By now, I figure you're standing at your desk and dying to stick a knife in me."

You're half right, Toyo thought.

"Now, I want you to sit down and listen to the part where you get to keep your domes, and I save your butt."

Toyo was caught off guard. There was no reason to trust Kadmir, but he was the clever one of the three criminal operators. It was Kadmir who started the pleasure-dome concept under the guise of a mining company.

Roz O'Brien, a man who loved to copy an idea, started his domes next, and Toyo was the last to build. Despite being third, Toyo was able to run his domes without interference from the other two by virtue of his reputation — he had earned his nickname Craze.

Sitting down behind his desk, Toyo leaned toward his comm panel and said, "I'm listening."

"First thing we have to do is get the girls off Jolares. I plan to bring the girls back here to Udrides."

"And then what happens once you have all the pieces?"

"Why, Toyo, I comm Alex Racine and tell him that I've rescued his dear sister and her friends from that dastardly man, Roz O'Brien."

Toyo's face screwed up in thought, trying to figure Blue's angle.

"Have the girls seen anything that could mess this up?" Kadmir asked.

"Nothing, they were bagged and tagged before transfer to the freighter, isolated in one cabin for the trip, and bagged and moved to a suite. They've had no comm contact ... the room was sealed. Only one person besides me knows they're here."

"Well, that needs to become just you."

"So, what's this going to cost me?"

"Well, Toyo, I figure that once the Sniffer is gone, you'll try to bargain for a piece of his domes, and that isn't going to happen. The cost for pulling you out of the way of this plasma blast is that I get O'Brien's domes without any interference from you."

Toyo was actually okay with Blue's plan. He had been desperately trying to figure out what to do with the girls. The reports from his informers and media notifying him of the *Rêveur's* arrival and Drake's tour of a new Haraken warship had scared him, and that wasn't something that had happened to him since he was a teenager. Now, Blue was offering him a way out, but he couldn't be seen to give in too easily.

"Here's my offer, Kadmir. You take the girls, you blame the Sniffer, and you get his domes, but I get 40 percent of the action and get to audit the accounts." He heard Kadmir's laugh, long and loud.

"Twenty percent," Kadmir replied.

"Thirty percent."

"Done, 30 percent, Toyo. I will have a shuttle at your dome in twenty-four hours. Get them ready and get rid of the one who's seen them."

"Don't tell me how to run my business, Kadmir," Toyo growled, but it lacked power. He knew Kadmir had the upper hand and was saving his butt from the Harakens.

"The pilot will contact you personally, and Boker will transfer the girls. I hope you can restrain any animosity you might have toward my new employee. Think about your 30 percent. That should help assuage your temper."

The comm closed, and Toyo sat undecided whether to be angry at Boker or happy at the prospect of 30 percent of O'Brien's domes, without having to do any of the work. After a few moments, he began planning what he would do with his newfound gains, and, truth be told, he was ecstatic at the prospect of getting the girls off his hand. Alex Racine was one of the few men who scared him.

* * *

Christie built their escape plan around the boy's established visitation schedule, servicing their cabin with food, fresh towels, and bed coverings. The routine was always the same — the girls entered the bathroom and the door was locked until the boy was done.

A quarter-hour before the boy was to arrive with a morning meal, the girls planned to turn on the shower's hot water. Christie would hide behind the door, while Amelia and Eloise moved through the thick steam in the bathroom, blurring the boy's thermal scanner. But they encountered a problem with their scheme. At the appointed time, the steam barely began filling the bathroom when the water temperature fell to lukewarm and then moments later ran cold.

As the boy serviced the room, Eloise sent thoughts that displayed her frustration. <We're definitely not on Haraken or a Haraken starship.>

<The limitations of a New Terran moon base,> Christie replied. <Limited water supply, even less hot water, and grav-plating in the floor.>

<Which makes escaping all that much harder,> Amelia added. <Once we get free of this room, the only path to safety is hiding aboard a ship, and we might be clueless to its next destination.>

<Or we could steal a ship,> Christie sent. <There are travelers in system. I'm sure the controller would respond to our implants. Maybe we could order its liftoff and destination.>

Christie's idea gave her friends hope, and the girls set about devising an alternate plan to get free of the room.

* * *

Miranda and the commanders worked through the shops, buying outfits and accessories with Toyo's credits. They extended the time by strolling through shops in which they had no intention to purchase. The purpose of their lengthy perusing of the dome was to maximize the area that Miranda could search. As a SADE, she carried a much more powerful comm than a human implant.

Once the women were suitably attired or unattired, depending on your viewpoint, they joined the other Harakens circulating through the various entertainment sites offered by the pleasure dome. The criminal organization was prepared to cater to every type of visitor — miners, middle-class tourists, business people, and thrill seekers. Décor, drinks, food, stims, and personal entertainment were carefully mixed and presented at each venue to cater to every customer type.

The Harakens circulated and constantly scanned for the girls, hoping to pick up on their implants. The traveler was out of reach for all but Miranda, who also had her limitations. Nonetheless, she became the group's data reservoir. She accumulated information from her people, and, when in range of the traveler, uploaded her data, which was also streamed to the *Rêveur*.

In a club catering to the moons' hard-working people, a Haraken tech, Lisbon, bought drinks for a group of Cressida miners. His brother was the family's comedian and knew more jokes than anyone the tech had ever met. Thanks to a good memory, Lisbon passed the time regaling miners with joke after joke and became the center of attention. It didn't take long for two of Toyo's fems to work their way through the crowd, sidling next to Lisbon and joining in the laughter.

During a break in his performance, Lisbon ordered another round of drinks for his admirers, which was greeted with a roar of approval. That's when his two new companions suggested more private entertainment, but Lisbon hesitated.

"Not into fems?" one woman asked.

"Oh, I like fems," Lisbon replied. "And you two look fine," he added, with a long, admiring glance at the women from head to toe.

"Our suggestion not to your liking?" the other woman asked.

"A little tame for my taste," Lisbon replied. His words were music to their ears. Exotic entertainment for patrons could earn huge credits. The women took turns whispering their suggestions until Lisbon smiled.

"I've seen a lot of this dome," Lisbon said, "but I haven't seen any place like that." He might not have physically visited most of the dome, but he had access to Miranda's accumulated views of the entertainment palace.

"Oh, it's not in this dome, sweetie," the first fem said, pressing herself against Lisbon's arm.

"I thought there was only the single dome," Lisbon said.

Excited by the prospect of a generous client, who happened to be a great-looking young man, the fems, who were new to Toyo's employment, forgot the rules regarding invitations to the ancillary domes. Entrance to the lower domes required vouchsafing by preferred customers only.

"There are other domes, cutie," one fem said. "Private access only ... for people like you, who have unique preferences."

Lisbon signaled Miranda, who received the conversation's recording, and she immediately hacked the dome's servers, searching through them until she located the complex's building plans. Downloading them, Miranda shared them with her people.

Unlike the first dome, which extended its transparent curve into the vacuum of space, the next two domes were located just below the moon's surface and were connected to the primary dome by private lifts and security-controlled corridors. However, the lift shafts didn't appear to terminate at the lowest floor of the lower domes, which encouraged Miranda to search for additional architectural plans, but her efforts were fruitless.

<If our girls are being kept at this establishment, they will be located in one of these auxiliary domes,> Miranda broadcast to the Harakens. She shared the suggestions made to Lisbon by the women so her people would understand the nature of the entertainment offered below.

Monitoring the tech's ensuing conversation with the fems, Miranda became aware of the significant sum requested for the private pleasure and transferred more of Toyo's credits to Lisbon's account.

<I believe you have sufficient funds to purchase everything your companions are offering you, Lisbon,> Miranda sent.

<I'm not sure if that's a good thing or a bad thing, Miranda,> Lisbon replied.

<Sacrifices must be made, Lisbon, to find our girls. Think of this as an opportunity to expand your social experiences, my dear.>

Unfortunately for Lisbon, when his companions checked his dome ID, they realized he didn't have the level of access necessary to venture into the lower domes, and it necessitated an abrupt change in their plans. In the end, Lisbon never received the education he expected. His mates found him lying on the floor of his room, stimmed and in a stupor.

When Miranda received notification of Lisbon's condition, she checked his account and found it empty. Tracing the transfers, Miranda located the women's accounts and presumed they were responsible for the drugging and credit transfers once they had access to Lisbon's dome ID card. She promptly transferred the purloined funds back into Lisbon's account. Then, as an afterthought, Miranda transferred the remaining amount in each of the women's accounts to a nonprofit, environmental organization on New Terra — anonymous donations, of course.

Svetlana and Deirdre's newly initiated liaison was proving much more successful than Lisbon's. From the moment the commanders sauntered into a club of wealthy patrons, they were inundated with exotic offers. After receiving Miranda's updates of the existence of auxiliary domes, they accepted the offer of a patron, who had been trying for a half-hour to entice the two Harakens to what he called a special suite where they wouldn't be interrupted.

Shocked but thrilled to find his offer accepted, the businessman escorted the women to a private lift, which he accessed by his dome ID card. Descending about 60 meters, by the Harakens' estimate, they emerged into a sumptuously, if not decadently, decorated corridor. At a small console, the patron entered his card, reviewed a menu, and selected his preference. When the console beeped, a small, green light flashed over a door partway down the corridor.

"Here we go, fems," the man said, throwing an arm around the waists of Svetlana and Deirdre and ushering them down the corridor.

"Can't wait," Svetlana gushed, rubbing her shoulder against the New Terran's substantial chest.

The room was decorated as an ancient dungeon complete with torture devices. "Let me get some drinks," the patron said. From a hidden bar, he poured three small glasses of a pale orange liquid. "You'll enjoy this," he said, handing out the glasses. "And these are to make the ride more enjoyable," he added with a leer, handing a pill to each of the Haraken women. Without waiting, he popped his pill and slugged half his drink.

<Distract him and pass me your pill,> Svetlana sent to Deirdre.

Smiling engagingly at the patron, Deirdre pressed her body against his and kissed him fully on the mouth while behind her back she handed off her pill to Svetlana. Deirdre slid to the side of the businessman, who looked expectantly at Svetlana. The blonde commander obliged him by leaning in and opening her lips. However, instead of a kiss, she blew the two pills secreted in her mouth deep into his.

Choking down the pills, the startled patron staggered backwards, gasping. "What did you do? My pill was a placebo," he cried. The man spun around and raced for the door, but the commanders were on him in an instant. They caught him, threw him to the floor, and pinned his arms behind his back. It took only a few moments before his struggles eased and then ceased all together. The women rolled the slack body over. His glassy eyes and slack mouth said the double doses of stim had a deep hold on him.

Deirdre snatched the dome ID card off the patron and followed Svetlana to the door.

"Disguise time," Svetlana said, messing up her short hairstyle and dropping one shoulder of her wrap to reveal most of a single breast. "We're two women of leisure, who've just been partying. So act the part."

Deirdre unclasped her toga-style wrap from behind her neck and let the straps fall, brushed her fingers through her hair, and painted a dreamy expression on her face, a woman lost in bliss.

"Perfect," Svetlana commented.

The two women slipped out of the playroom and took their time stumbling and quietly laughing as they walked down the corridor. Several times, they passed other patrons and their companions, who laughed or smiled at their state of undress. One man went so far as to pretend to bump into Deirdre and take advantage of the moment.

<He'll be a hurt individual, if I ever get the opportunity,> Deirdre sent to Svetlana.

The women were able to traverse back and forth through several levels of their dome before security found them, confiscated the patron's dome card, and led them back to the surface. Throughout their search, they never contacted the girls' implants.

It was Miranda who discovered that the Harakens' strategy was doomed to failure. She was invited by a patron to enjoy his brand of entertainment in an auxiliary dome and accepted. The first deviation from the commanders' experience was that her admirer accessed a lift on the far side of the main dome.

Down below, Miranda's escort checked into a room at the corridor's registry panel, and as they walked to the room, she detected the implants of two Haraken engineers exiting the lift behind them. Glancing back, she saw the men in the company of an older female patron, who seemed delighted to have captured the attention of two healthy, young specimens.

Miranda and her patron entered a room, which seemed to have water sports in mind, and, as the door closed, the SADE lost contact with the engineers' implants. Realizing their search for the girls' implants was being defeated by the existence of the domes' comm-isolated rooms, Miranda dispatched her patron with a seductive kiss and a gentle pressure against the carotid artery until he passed out.

Picking up the patron's ID card, Miranda exited the suite and made her way back to the main dome, where she contacted every Haraken within reach about her disturbing discovery. It wasn't that Harakens were unaware of the concept of comm isolation. It's just that they worked diligently to prevent it, believing that communications isolation was a detriment to an individual's mental stability and, therefore, the growth of a healthy society.

That an organization would actively seek to create structures that isolated individuals was as foreign and sinister a concept as the Harakens could imagine.

16

Captain Timmion settled her president's traveler on the deck of the *Rêveur's* bay. Once the interior was pressurized, President Drake and Minister Jaya descended the steps of the fighter-shuttle and were met by a Haraken honor guard presided over by Tatia. Alex, Renée, and Julien waited to greet them.

Before the presidents could say a word, Darryl Jaya shouted, "Julien," and hurried to give the SADE a hug.

"So much for protocol and decorum," Drake said, but he was smiling as he shook Alex's hand. Turning to Renée, he said, "Mesmerizing as always, Ser de Guirnon," and exchanged the de Guirnon tradition of bussing both cheeks.

"I see your political skills have continued to develop, President Drake," Renée replied.

"Some things are truth no matter how you say them," Drake replied.

Renée laughed at the flattery, linked her arm in Drake's, and started for the airlock with Julien and Jaya following in their wake and chatting.

Watching the foursome walk away, Alex thought back to the early days of the *Rêveur*.

"Did you get left behind, Mr. President?" Tatia asked, coming up beside Alex. "It's tough to compete with Renée's beauty or Julien's mystical technological aura. But, never fear, I'll keep you company," she teased, patting his shoulder, linking arms, and hurrying Alex along to catch up with the others.

Étienne and Alain brought up the rear.

Comfortably settled in the owner's suite, Alex came right to the point. "I apologize, President Drake, for the subterfuge on our part that enticed you out here."

"First, Alex, I believe we can dispense with titles in this group, and, second, don't you dare say we aren't going to tour your new starship. I think Darryl might have a heart attack."

Alex glanced at Darryl, who was wearing a stricken expression and laughed. "No, the tour is real. I can't say whether we'll be able to sell you these sting-class ships. Our assembly would have to approve any agreement you and I discuss."

Darryl relaxed into his chair, and Julien patted his hand in commiseration.

"Apparently, subterfuge was the wrong word, Will," Alex said. "What I should have said is that the tour is a secondary consideration. The primary reason I wanted you out here is because I couldn't risk having anyone know the real reason we're here."

"I might be extremely worried for the welfare of my people, aliens, battleships, and such, if I didn't have an inkling of where this is headed. It has something to do with drugs, doesn't it?" Drake said.

"Yes, it does," Alex replied. "Two of your criminal organizations attempted to set up distribution in Espero. One group was selling stimulants, and the other was introducing a hallucinogenic and not just any hallucinogen, but a powerfully addictive one."

"Do you know who these people are?"

"We believe we've arrested all the suspects who remained in Espero. Others exited the system and ran back here. Then there was the group who was killed."

"You killed them?" Will asked.

"Please, Will," Renée said, annoyed that the president would assume that. "It was a New Terran gang leader, who killed her own people once their operation was uncovered by Étienne and Alain."

"Apologies, Renée," Will said. "Do you know who employs these people?"

"Most certainly, Ser," Étienne replied. "We have learned of three New Terrans ... Roz O'Brien, Peto Toyo, and Azul Kadmir."

"Ser Toyo's people were apprehended," Alain added. "It was O'Brien's people who were killed by their contact, a woman code-named Cherry."

"I'm confused, Alex," Jaya interrupted, "Why not a direct and open approach to us? This strikes me as a problem for our governments to solve together."

"They took Christie and her two friends," Tatia said.

"What? No! Are you sure?" Drake uttered. Then he realized who he was talking to, and added, "Yes, of course you are."

"The girls were investigating an illegal club, which was distributing the hallucinogenic drug. We have a trail of evidence that points to a freighter, the *Bountiful*, which took the girls here to the moons of Ganymede. Presently, it's above Jolares."

"Toyo," Drake uttered with disgust.

"How long have you known, Will?" Renée asked.

"I didn't know about any of this, Renée ... the gangs exporting their drugs to Haraken or abducting your people," Drake objected.

"My question was meant to ask how long you've known about these people setting up their domes and their criminal organizations in plain sight of you and the TSF," Renée challenged.

Both Drake and Jaya had the humility to duck their heads in embarrassment. Finally, Drake spread his hands in supplication and said, "Their companies are legally set up under the law, registered as mining companies on moon bases. They are hands off to the TSF, unless there is evidence to the contrary."

"TSF tried to slip agents undercover into the domes to gather proof of any illegal activities," Jaya said, "and they've some good people, without gaining a single piece of evidence."

"Would you accept our people's proof as evidence?" Alex asked.

"Implants, SADEs ... we would, wouldn't we, Will?" Jaya said excitedly.

"It would be up to the Assembly and the courts to accept the Haraken's evidence. If the Assembly did, they could be persuaded to revoke the standing of these false mining companies or maybe even the mining charter itself and allow the TSF to intervene. If memory serves me right, the Assembly has always accepted Méridien technological evidence," said Will, smiling at Alex and Renée.

<Cordelia,> Alex sent. <Ready?>

<More vids are constantly streaming from our traveler, Ser President, but I have a sufficient amount of material organized to give President Drake cause to take action.>

Cordelia used Miranda's uploads to piece together thousands of partial recordings of the Harakens in Toyo's domes. By examining their location data and mapping them to the building plans that Miranda discovered, Cordelia stitched the vids together to present a unified view of the three-dome structure.

When Cordelia entered the owner's suite, Jaya let loose a soft, "Ooh," recognizing the distinctive avatar-shape that the SADEs had chosen.

"Will and Jaya, allow me to introduce Cordelia," Renée said.

"A pleasure, Mr. President, Minister Jaya," Cordelia said.

After the introductions, Cordelia activated the holo-vid and prepared her vid for spooling. "Apologies, Sers, for the patchwork presentation. What you will be examining is a compilation of many views by our people, who are presently in Toyo's domes."

"You have people inside Toyo's establishment," Drake said incredulously. "How many did you sneak inside?"

"Sneak inside, Will?" Tatia said, while the group chuckled. "They're just a bunch of rowdy miners from Kephron, on vacation to have some fun and spend their credits."

"You walked them in the front door?" Jaya asked. "But you would need transport."

"Miranda, a wealthy woman from the Confederation and two of her Méridien companions gave them a lift. They're touring the system in their own traveler."

When Drake and Jaya sat there with confused looks on their faces, Julien said, "Miranda is an alternate persona for Z, and her companions are Haraken commanders."

"And they fell for it?" Drake asked.

"Everyone falls for Miranda," Renée said. "And I believe my partner kept a visual of the two commanders. I did." On the holo-vid appeared Svetlana and Deirdre, wearing their sheer wraps, their bodies intertwined.

"Commanders Valenko and Canaan?" Jaya repeated dubiously, leaning closer to the holo-vid for a better view.

"Careful, Darryl. You don't want to get too close. You might get burned," Renée said, grinning at the minister.

"Yes, well, it would be hard to say no to them," Drake remarked, trying not to stare at the women in the holo-vid.

"The evidence, Sers," Cordelia said, playing her composite vid. Snippets from the main dome ran to give the group a sense of Toyo's offerings to his guests. In most cases, the entertainment was fairly innocuous for New Terra. Then the view from Lisbon allowed them to hear the offer from the two women, who had insinuated their way into his company.

"This is crewman Lisbon, being offered an opportunity to visit an ancillary dome, which is the first time our people have heard of secondary domes," Cordelia said.

"If I remember correctly, Toyo's domes are approved for three structures," Jaya said.

Since the images were the first that anyone aboard the *Rêveur* had seen of Toyo's establishment, Cordelia had their undivided attention. "Apparently, Ser Lisbon didn't have access privileges to the ancillary dome so alternate accommodations were made for him."

The group watched Lisbon and the women enter a room, mix some drinks, and suddenly Lisbon's view blurred, tilted toward the overhead, and blanked out.

"This is how Lisbon's roommates found him," Cordelia said. She showed the images of Lisbon's two roommates hauling the tech off the floor onto a bed and checking his eyes.

Next, the group watched the commanders entice their way into the foreboding dungeon room and dispatch their patron with a drug-laden kiss.

"Commanders Valenko and Canaan searched their dome to the extent they were able before security intervened. They managed to explore three of the levels before they were escorted back to the main dome. The patron's ID card was confiscated."

The next vid section contained Miranda's view of her patron and the water-sports room they visited. At one point, Miranda's view took in a floor-to-ceiling mirrored wall, reflecting the patron and herself.

"That's Z's persona avatar?" Jaya asked, dumbfounded. "Who wouldn't let her into their club?" he said with a sigh, which had more than one Haraken chuckling. A moment later, Jaya's expression sobered as the patron dropped to the floor.

"It was just before this vid that Miranda realized the difficulty they faced locating the girls," Cordelia said. "It appears the rooms in the secondary domes are comm isolated."

"Black space," Alex declared angrily, jumping up.

When Will looked at Jaya in confusion, Darryl said, "I would surmise the Harakens' plan was to infiltrate the domes and ping for the girls' implants, but if they're being held in a comm-isolated room, the Harakens won't be able to detect them. They would have to physically open every door."

"There may be other options," Julien said, trying to give his friend some hope. His comment halted Alex in his tracks, and the president's eyes implored the SADE.

"Miranda can test human cellular components in the air, as she walks through the corridors," Julien said. "If the girls are moving about, they will leave traces behind. The process is slow, but it has possibilities."

"But how will Miranda recognize the girls' bio-identities?" Tatia asked. "Terese has indicated that there are negligible differences in the DNA and subcellular components of New Terrans and Méridiens."

Julien and Cordelia didn't look at each other, but communication flew between them.

"What?" Alex asked, before a thought occurred to him. "Ah, yes … Miranda might or might not know the biomarkers of our Méridien girls, but she knows Christie's."

"How?" Renée asked.

"Because Miranda has my biomarkers with her, doesn't she?" Alex said, looking at Julien.

"That would be correct, Mr. President," Julien said, reverting to formality.

"Anyone else?" Tatia asked.

"The SADEs have been collecting biomarkers for nearly a decade," Cordelia replied. "We have cataloged every original Haraken colonist."

"Oh, wow," Jaya commented softly, mesmerized by the drama unfolding.

"However, due to the massive size of that data, each SADE carries only a few hundred markers of key individuals with them. These would include the extended Racine family, of course," Julien said, nodding to Renée.

"There is one more significant observation to be made, Sers," Cordelia remarked. "Miranda believes there is a structure beneath the two ancillary domes, possibly a fourth and more extensive dome."

Will looked at Darryl, who said, "I would not have thought that possible, but then I wouldn't want to contradict a SADE."

"A wise choice, Ser," Julien remarked.

"Julien, please access my ministerial servers, the buildings and constructions approval department," Darryl requested. "Search for PT Mining Concern. Please pull the architectural plans for me."

Within moments, Julien was displaying the plans on the holo-vid. Clearly, only three domes were displayed, two ancillary domes, side by side, beneath the main dome.

"Here are the plans Miranda discovered on the establishment's servers," Cordelia said, changing the holo-vid's view.

Cordelia's term of "discovered" had Will arching an eyebrow at Alex, who maintained a neutral expression.

Darryl glanced at Julien, who switched the view to the original plans. Reaching into the holo-vid, Darryl enlarged the architectural plans, detailing a section of the lowest floor of one of the ancillary domes. He glanced at Cordelia, who switched to the newly obtained plans and manipulated the view to show the exact same section, which caused Darryl to smile warmly at her.

<If only all humans were enamored of the means by which SADEs might help them,> Julien sent to Cordelia.

Darryl rolled a finger in the air and Julien obliged by switching the view. He repeated his nonverbal request several more times. The SADEs had already discovered the differences, but thought it best that the announcement came from Darryl.

"These aren't the same," the minister finally said. "Look at the approved plans. As expected, the utilities terminate at the lower floor, including the lift, which has its power relays installed on the lowest floor. But on Miranda's plans …" he said, which is when Cordelia switched the view for him, "the utilities branch to service the lowest floor and continue on as if they supply something below this last floor. And notice the lift power relays are gone. There is definitely something located below these three domes. If the plans Miranda discovered are the true construction plans, then I can tell you that whatever is down there has not been approved!"

"Will, tell me what you think so far," Alex requested.

"We have enough for Darryl's ministry to call Toyo into a hearing to discuss the possibility of unapproved construction and not much more. We can't use what Miranda discovered, since it was obtained illegally. And, while most representatives might find the entertainment in those secondary domes distasteful, we certainly don't have sufficient reason to request the TSF raid Toyo's establishment."

Alex growled under his breath as he paced.

Drake hurried to add, "Not what you wanted to hear, Alex, I understand, but I have to uphold the law. I can't operate like …"

Drake's partial statement hung in the air, and every Haraken stared at him, daring him to continue.

"Like what, President Drake?" Tatia challenged. "Like Harakens, who take the law into their own hands? Or is it that Harakens simply apply justice where the law is undefined, such as when foreign battleships raid their allies' system?"

"Sers, I believe the focus should be on the missing girls," Renée said diplomatically into the silence that followed Tatia's words.

"What are you going to do, Alex?" Drake asked.

"For starters, Will, I'm going to give you a tour of our new ship. I imagine we're being watched, and we need to keep up the charade. But time is running out for my sister and her friends. These criminal leaders must have figured out by now that Haraken ships parked near their moons is no coincidence."

"I was asking about what you might do concerning your girls and Toyo's domes," Will said.

"Whatever I have to, President Drake," Alex said.

Drake and Jaya glanced around the room. Stern expressions stared back at them. A convenient loophole in New Terran commercial law, taken advantage of by criminal enterprises, would not stop the Harakens from rescuing their people.

* * *

The tour of the *Tanaka* was to take place following midday meal, and Drake and Jaya were offered a suite in order to freshen up.

"Did you know that Julien and Cordelia are partners?" Jaya said, stepping from the sleeping quarters and fastening his shirt.

"In what enterprise?" asked Drake, his thoughts elsewhere.

"Will, listen to me, they're partners, as in a couple. They live together and have adopted ten orphans from Sol."

Drake stared at Jaya, shifting mental gears from his concerns to what his friend was saying. Finally, Drake shook his head. "I don't know how Alex does it. The world of the Harakens gets stranger every day. I, for one, am happy to stay right here on backward New Terra."

"Maybe, it's what suits Alex. Being born in a place doesn't mean you fit in there," Jaya replied. "I was thinking, Will. It's too bad that we can't let the Harakens take care of some of these problems for us. Let them locate and deal with this rogue biochemist. Maybe even let them expose what's going on in the domes."

"But then what would our people think of the Harakens afterwards?" Drake replied. "We can't afford a backlash of sentiment against the

Harakens. We need their technology. The events of the past decade and a half have proven that. Besides, what would our people think of the government, specifically me, if we aren't able to solve our own problems?"

"Well, I think we're about to discover just that," Jaya replied. "Alex isn't going to wait on procuring incontrovertible proof, legally obtained or not, and then wait while the Assembly considers that evidence. You heard Alex. He said he's going to do whatever he has to do to get his sister back, and the Harakens are all behind him. They don't take kindly to trespasses against their people."

"It's a thorny problem," agreed Will. "On the one hand, I don't want to see Harakens interfering in New Terran issues. On the other hand, what's going to happen if Alex doesn't get his sister back? Like if these idiots, who kidnapped the girls, do something even more stupid, like make them permanently disappear."

"And the Harakens with a powerful new warship right here," Jaya reminded Drake.

* * *

Tatia commed Ellie, requesting she collect Captain Timmion and her crew and escort them to afternoon meal. She was pleased to discover Ellie was already en route.

As Ellie and Timmion walked to the meal room, Ellie said, "The reports indicate you did an excellent job against the *Hand of Justice* and later in your training as a fighter pilot. And I extend my congratulations on your appointment as President Drake's pilot. The reports appear not to have done you justice."

"How can anyone not excel when they have Commander Svetlana Valenko as a trainer?" Timmion replied. "I think she's the scariest women I've ever met."

"She is unorthodox," Ellie agreed.

"What I don't understand is that she's Méridien, but she doesn't act calm and controlled like I understand Méridiens behave."

"There are Méridiens and then there are Independents, Captain. The latter people are Méridiens who were ostracized by their society for being …"

"Independent?"

"Yes, independent."

"So what did Commander Valenko do that got her thrown out of her society?

"That's an excellent question."

"I apologize, if I'm asking improper questions, Commander."

"No, not at all, Captain. It's just that I don't know. I don't think anybody knows. She's a mystery, but she's our mystery and a truly fierce Haraken."

17

"Dolan, this is not a negotiation," Maria said hotly over the comm. "You can have the credit for every arrest, every criminal charged. That's not the issue. I'm calling in a favor, and it's not like you don't owe me more of those than you or I could count."

Maria waited while Dolan Oppert, the TSF general, weighed the pros and cons of a decision. If someone had offered her the opportunity when she was the general of the system's police force to bust fourteen illegal drug operations on New Terra, she wouldn't have cared about a minor request. It would have been a done deal so fast you couldn't have drawn breath before she would have agreed. Unfortunately, that wasn't Dolan's way.

"So we manage the operations, the arrests, and the charges, but on one of the sites Steve Ross has tactical command and gets to talk to the suspects once they're in custody."

"Yes, Dolan," Maria said, trying to keep the exasperation out of her voice. "Steve played a major role in identifying these people, and he's asked for this favor."

"He's not going to do anything stupid like shoot someone once they're restrained?"

"Do you remember Steve ever doing anything like that when he was in the service?" Maria challenged.

"No, but there's always a first time," Oppert retorted.

"Do you want the information on these drug sites or not?" Maria asked. "Or maybe I should just ask the Harakens for some help. Conveniently, they're in system ... I mean since our TSF seems unwilling to take on illegal drug manufacturers?"

"No need to get nasty, Maria. We'll get it done. Of course, we will. It's just that I'm not in the habit of granting favors to civilians that gives them control of TSF operations."

"I'm sending you information on thirteen of the sites. Steve will sit on the fourteenth site. Let him know who to coordinate with in your ranks for that bust. I advise you to synchronize your troopers to hit all the sites at once. If you don't mind a suggestion, I would use Colonel Portis."

* * *

Steve Ross sat atop his new flit with Colonel Portis standing in front of him, hands on hips, glaring at him.

"All operations were supposed to commence at 6 hours this morning, Ross. I've a mind to arrest you for obstruction," Portis declared hotly.

"Check your orders, Colonel. The deal is that you run thirteen of the ops, and I coordinate the fourteenth.

"Well, your coordination is going to ball this one up, Ross. It's been hours since we cleaned up the other sites. The people are in custody and already in holding cells."

"They're in TSF hands, not civilian, right?" Steve asked.

"Those were my orders," Portis said.

"By the way, how many did you get ... total, I mean?"

"Final tally was sixty-three arrests."

"Hmm ... between the other investigators and me, we counted closer to 120 bodies. Whose idea, anyway, was it to plan this as a dawn raid? I mean these are criminals. They're not going to be sleeping on premises at 6 hours or sweating hard to get their product out. At 6 hours, they're tucked up nice and cozy in their beds, probably sleeping off some drink or lying next to a rented body."

Colonel Portis glanced to the nearby trees where her troopers sat in the shade next to their transports. She had argued vociferously with General Oppert on his choice of a time for the raid, having made the same arguments Steve just enumerated.

"Don't tell me ... Pert?" Steve asked, using the general's nickname by which officers referred to him in private company. Oppert earned his nickname when he was still a captain. During training maneuvers, he took so long making decisions that invariably his company was annihilated. The joke was he was busy fussing in the mirror with his appearance, looking pert, when he should have been making battlefield decisions.

Oppert's career path was shunted up through administration rather than field command, and, through sheer perseverance, he ended up on the short list for general after two decades of service. Those in politics admired his cooler temperament and thought him the right officer for the position. It had caused furor within the ranks, and a great many qualified and experienced senior officers hadn't renewed their contracts.

"You don't have to say it, Colonel. It's rather obvious," Ross said, letting Portis off the hook.

"Could you tell me when you intend to move on this site, Ross? It's supposed to be the largest one, and I'd hate to have them get wind of our operations."

"We're waiting."

"We're waiting for what?"

"For a signal. I have a friend watching the site, and I don't intend to commence operations until I have the majority of these people inside the warehouse."

After that exchange, Portis and Ross stoically passed the time in silence, and the hours dragged on into midafternoon, when Steve's reader finally hummed.

Colonel Portis jumped off her transport and came quickly to his side. "What's that?" she asked, pointing to the swirling image. "I've never seen a screen vid that complex before."

"That's my friend's calling card," Steve replied.

"Greetings, Ser Ross," Cordelia's voice came over the reader. "Four transports have arrived at the warehouse. Three are personnel carriers, and fifteen bodies have exited them. The fourth vehicle is a cargo carrier, which has three bodies in its cab. I would surmise they are intending to move their product out of the warehouse. Good fortune, Ser." Immediately after Cordelia's message, the colorful vid disappeared.

Portis closed her gaping mouth. She was grinning as she punched Steve in the shoulder. "Greetings, Ser Ross? You sneaky reject of an officer … your friend is a Haraken. Does Pert know?"

"Absolutely not, and he shouldn't know. And I don't think that was just any Haraken. The first voice I heard saved me from an explosive device strapped to the underside of my flit, but this voice was different … female not male."

"You're talking about SADEs, right?"

"Think so."

"Eighteen bodies and a warehouse full of product. Let's go make some arrests!" Portis said, slapping Ross on the shoulder with a resounding thwack.

Going to have to start offering Portis the other shoulder if she gets any more enthusiastic, Steve thought, rubbing his muscles as he climbed on his flit.

Two platoons of TSF troopers surrounded the warehouse. On the colonel's orders, electro-charges were fired at the four transports, disabling their drive systems. Next, quick-acting gas was pumped through every visible window. Instantly, several men inside the warehouse shot out windows, jumped through them, and made a run for it. Stun guns accounted for every one of them.

Once the gas cleared, the comatose individuals were restrained, given a quick med-injection to revive them, and hauled to their feet. Twenty-three people, the eighteen who had just arrived and the five who were already onsite, stood in a row on the warehouse's front parking lot.

"Okay," Steve announced firmly, "I want to know who planted the device on my flit."

The felons remained quiet, staring straight ahead or at the ground. When Steve's reader chimed, heads turned his way, and Portis peeked over his shoulder. Text rolled up on the reader's screen. It read: *Have them look up.* Steve and Portis shared grins, and Steve ordered, "All of you look up."

Most of the men and women glanced skyward with their eyes, and a couple tilted their heads back a few degrees.

"Faces to the sky, now!" Steve thundered and the troopers assisted any recalcitrant individuals.

Portis wasn't watching the criminals. She was focused on Steve's reader, anxious to see the next message.

The words *third from the left* scrolled up on the screen.

Steve walked over to the man, identified in the text, who dropped his head to return Steve's stare. "Like to play with explosives, do you?" Steve asked.

"Don't know what you mean," the man said.

Out of the corner of his eyes, Steve could see the two individuals on either side of his target glance at their comrade. Their faces told Steve the SADE had the right man.

"I have a witness, who saw you plant the device."

"No one saw me," the man declared, jutting his jaw out defiantly.

They get stupider every day, Steve thought. "Our visitors saw you," he said, grinning and pointing a finger at the sky.

When it dawned on the guilty party who Steve was talking about, he spat the word, "Haraken."

"Make sure you charge this one with attempted murder, Colonel," Steve said, hauling the man out of line and pushing him toward Portis.

As Steve walked back to his flit, he heard Portis yell, "Nice working with you, Ross."

*　*　*

<Mr. President,> Julien sent, <I have Ser Maria Gonzalez on the comm for you.>

<Thank you, Julien,> Alex said, halting in his preparations to leave his cabin for the *Tanaka's* tour. Renée gave him a questioning look and touched her temple with a finger, and Alex shared the comm.

<Greetings, Maria,> Alex sent. <What news do you have for us?>

<Hello, Maria,> Renée added quickly, to let her friend know she was sharing the comm.

"Renée!" Maria exclaimed, the lift in her voice evident. "Visit soon, you two, if you can."

After a quick exchange with Renée, Maria got right to business. "I have good news, Alex. We came up empty on locating your biochemist."

Renée's confusion was obvious, but Alex was nodding. <So, this individual isn't based on New Terra.>

"We're pretty sure of that ... as sure as we can be," Maria replied. "Once we came to that conclusion, we worked with TSF to shut down fourteen illegal drug operations and arrested eighty-six felons. It was a bit of an eye opener for our TSF general, who has been saying for years that he has everything under control concerning illegal drug operations. Right now, I don't think he likes me very much, but then he's about to be replaced, if rumors in the Assembly are true."

<Any leads on our biochemist's whereabouts, Maria?> Alex sent.

"Actually, yes. In tracing the chemical deliveries, we discovered several suppliers were sending their shipments to a small warehouse near Prima's main shuttle transport. When one of my investigators checked out the warehouse, he found it empty."

<That's odd,> Alex remarked. <A staging point, perhaps?>

"Exactly. My investigator sat on the location and watched three more deliveries made. Then, within moments after the last delivery, a hover truck pulls up, supplies are loaded, and off the truck goes to load its cargo onto a New Terran shuttle."

<Flight destination?> Alex asked.

"Jolares, a moon orbiting Ganymede," Maria replied.

<And who or what is on Jolares?> Alex asked.

"Peto Toyo, one of the owner-operators of pleasure domes out there," Maria said. "Now that we're done playing this game of questions and answers, of which you already know the answers, do you want to tell me what's going on?" Maria asked.

Renée giggled, and Maria knew her suppositions were correct. "Alex, your SADEs have been following my investigation since the start, and, by the way, thank them for keeping my field agents alive. They're good people. Julien, you handling the comm?"

<Yes, Ser Gonzalez,> Julien sent.

"You have a big kiss waiting for you when we meet."

<I look forward to collecting it, Ser,> Julien replied. Cordelia observed a jaunty cap appeared on Julien's head, and she smiled, pleased to see her partner happy.

"So, Alex, what's up?" Maria repeated.

<You're correct, Maria. We've been tracking your investigation. Your information is invaluable and confirms our evidence. I can't share any more with you, at this time. But, I've told Drake everything. We, meaning my people, still have a problem, but now Drake knows about it and can mitigate any fallout with your people.>

"Well, at least, there's that," Maria said, relenting. "It's good that you're including Drake in the loop. I don't think he's really cut out for the job."

<Personally, I don't think anyone is cut out for the job, Maria,> Alex said.

"I agree, Alex. Some just handle the responsibility better than others. Anyway, keep Will in the loop and be gentle with him," Maria cautioned and signed off.

18

Toyo's first thought when he was informed of three visiting Méridiens was that it must have something to do with the *Rêveur* and the Harakens. But, Toyo's administrator informed him that the reservations were made from Kephron, which matched the stories told by the exotic visitors and the miners who accompanied them.

The more Toyo observed the women through the domes' security cams, the more he thought this was the opportunity he was searching for — an opportunity to expand his business beyond what Kadmir and O'Brien had achieved. On his monitor, Miranda chatted charmingly with a patron, and Toyo's paranoia sought to couple the Méridien's presence with the Harakens, but he quickly squashed that line of reasoning. *No one's that good an actress,* he thought. Accessing another cam, Toyo watched the two Méridiens, the dark-light twins as his people called them, entertaining a group of businessmen, who were spending a fortune in creds at the bar on drinks and stims.

Toyo's brain whirled with thoughts of grandeur and greed, and he sent his head of security, Dillon Jameson, to invite the wealthy Méridien to his office. A quarter-hour later, Toyo was posed, leaning against the front of his desk in anticipation.

"Greetings, Ser," Miranda said, sweeping into the room.

Unlike so many people who waited for instructions whether to approach or sit, Toyo was surprised that the woman came close and extended her hand, displaying a gentle strength in her handshake. Breaking his own security protocols, Toyo invited Miranda to sit with him in two comfortable chairs at the side of the room.

"Miranda … beautiful name to suit a beautiful woman," Toyo said, which was the full extent of his charm.

"How kind of you to say so, Ser, but I imagine you didn't invite me to your office to flatter me."

"We've seen quite a few Méridiens in Oistos over time, but you don't look like any of them."

"Now, that's what I expect from New Terrans ... bluntness. Have you toured the Confederation, Ser?"

"No, I've never left this system."

"I do love the manner in which you people blurt out the first thing that comes to your mind without giving it any due consideration. It's so ... rudimentary."

Toyo knew he was being insulted, but he couldn't take his eyes off the woman, and she seemed to know it. Every glance of his seemed to cause that part of her to move in some subtle way, and the effect was mesmerizing. Toyo felt as if he was directing his own erotic vid.

"You do understand, Ser, that Méridiens practice gene-sculpting. On our colony, this is a preferred body style. It's a little more inviting, don't you think?" Miranda said, crossing her legs languidly and arching her back slightly to accentuate her breast line, a knowing smile on her face.

"We both know I do," Toyo said. "Miranda, I wonder if you would be interested in a business deal."

Miranda gave Toyo a brilliant and charming laugh. "Oh, my dear, I have access to more credits than you can imagine. I have no need to go into business with anyone. However, if my stay here is enjoyable ... titillating, shall we say, then I might be persuaded to bring a few of my friends here. Many on my colony are always seeking new and exhilarating experiences."

Toyo's face split into a wide smile. "You just let me know what sort of experiences you're looking for, Miranda, and I'll make sure you get just what you desire." The criminal leader saw his business expanding. He envisioned owning a passenger starship and setting up domes in the Confederation, starting with Miranda's colony.

"How generous of you, Ser," Miranda said, rising. "I'll be sure to do that." After shaking hands once again, Miranda made sure her stroll from the office was the best show she could give Toyo.

Jameson, the head of security, escorted Miranda back to the main dome. On the way, she digested her conversation with Peto Toto. His naked ambition marked him as the type who would not hesitate to open an illegal drug distribution club in Espero, without ever considering the risks.

The conversation aside, Miranda gained one piece of hard evidence. Someone had sat in her chair before her, and that someone had minute traces of the hallucinogenic compound on their hands or clothes when they touched the arms. Sensors in her hands signaled the presence of a dangerous compound, and Miranda took the opportunity to wipe a finger gently across her bottom lip, enticing Toyo further and testing the compound internally. It was an exact match to the drug sample Terese gave her.

* * *

Christie, Amelia, and Eloise tried several times to escape their suite, but they remained locked inside. Their last ploy involved sliding a towel over the restroom door's inner handle and closing the door, trapping the towel across the lock. Unfortunately, the boy's voice over the room's comm announced that the lock was not signaling closed.

"Sorry," Christie said, pressing the comm button in the bathroom. "A towel got caught in the door."

It was in the night, following the evening Miranda met with Toyo, when the girls were fast asleep that the lock on the suite's door was triggered, and they came instantly awake at the unscheduled and uncharacteristic entrance.

Their concern transformed into fear when the lights snapped on and Scar walked into the room.

"Well, well, together again, fems. Always a pleasure," said Boker, a nasty grin on his face.

The girls jumped out of bed and gathered together, hearts racing.

"You know the drill, fems," Boker said, tapping his weapon against his thigh. "Nice and quiet and no one gets a taste of this. Now, strip and put these on." He threw a set of ship suits on the floor at their feet.

The girls changed as rapidly as they could, wondering what had happened to their young man and what was about to happen to them.

"All right," Boker said, when the girls finished changing, a process he thoroughly enjoyed, especially now that he knew home girl was someone important. "Over here, face me, and cross your arms at the wrists."

Boker pulled restraints from his kit, secured the girls' hands, and then dropped comm-isolation bags over their heads. He turned Christie sideways, placed Amelia's hands on her shoulder, and repeated the motion for Eloise. "Not a word," he warned the girls, and then led them out of the suite.

To the girls, their journey was punctuated by stops and starts as Scar bodily blocked Christie, and the girls ran into each other. Christie worked to keep her tongue still, and her friends hoped she did. At one point, Scar grabbed Christie by the arm and whirled her in reverse and shoved all of them into a small utility room. Christie ran into a supply rack, smacking her head, and Scar shushed her.

Possessing much the same temperament as her brother, Christie knew she would have attacked Scar by now, weapon or no weapon, not caring about the outcome as long as she could fight for her freedom. But she was attempting to keep her wits about her. Amelia and Eloise were depending on her, and she knew it.

Eventually, they boarded a shuttle, and after liftoff their restraints and metal-mesh bags were removed. A man in dapper clothes was sitting across from them, examining his fingernails.

"Good evening, young ladies. My name is Azul Kadmir, and I'm your rescuer."

* * *

"Do you have them?" Roz O'Brien asked over the comm.

"Yeah, Craze fell for it. He even bargained for a piece of your action," Kadmir replied.

O'Brien leaned back in his chair, swirling his brandy. "I hope you were generous with Craze."

"Gave him 30 percent," Kadmir replied. "He'll be dwelling on that, making big plans, while the adz wraps him and his business up … or maybe it will be the Harakens." Both men shared hearty laughs over Toyo's impending demise.

"You're going to be able to stretch your people to cover half of Toyo's operations when the domes are empty, right?" Kadmir asked.

"I'll be ready. I know we can't let them sit empty and not expect someone else to move in, legit or otherwise. I have recruitment going on at home. I should have two travelers full of new employees arriving in a week or so. This is all providing that Racine doesn't blow Toyo's domes into space debris."

"He won't," Kadmir said.

"You sound confident of that."

"Racine might break Toyo's neck with his bare hands for kidnapping his sister, but if there's one patron in the dome who might be hurt, he won't touch it. He's messed up altruistically like that."

"So where do you have the girls now?" O'Brien asked.

"They're sitting in one of my best suites with all the comforts of home."

"Tell me they're all right … not hurt in any way."

"They're fine. A little shaken by the ordeal, but even Toyo and his men knew to be careful with these packages."

"Did you show your face, and do they know what's happening?"

"Yeah, I met them on the shuttle and introduced myself."

"Brazen," O'Brien commented.

"Figured it was the best approach. The tricky part was that I had to use Boker, Toyo's defector, as the one to escort them out of Toyo's domes, and the girls know he was part of their abduction."

"So, how did you explain that?"

"Told them Boker was working undercover for me. That we were aware of certain nefarious actions on the part of Peto Toyo."

"Certain nefarious actions … I like that," O'Brien said, chuckling.

"Roz, you should have seen this little act play out on the shuttle. I had to practice Boker for so long I was ready to shoot the idiot myself. Anyway, on the shuttle, I get to the part where I tell the girls it was our plan all along to rescue them, and that Boker was forced to stay true to his character. That's when Boker comes out of his slouch and gives this sincere apology we practiced. He did pretty damn well."

"Do you think the girls bought it?"

"Don't know. They aren't dummies, and Christie, Racine's sister, has a mouth on her. After Boker's apology, she thought she had permission to ask a thousand and one questions, and I could see her fact checking what we knew with what had happened to them. I had to cut her off, telling her that I had arrangements to make."

"So, they're suspicious," O'Brien concluded.

"Looks like it," Kadmir acknowledged.

"There's always plan B, if we don't think the original idea is going to work."

"You mean get rid of them instead of playing the rescuers and blaming it on Toyo?"

"It could be safer."

"I don't think so. If Racine gets his sister and her friends back, even with some discrepancies in the stories, I think he'll go home … unsatisfied perhaps, but he'll go home. On the other hand, if he never gets his girls back, I think this entire system is in trouble, and it will descend on our heads first."

* * *

<So do you buy what this one, Kadmir, is selling?> Amelia sent, when they found themselves in another suite. She was comming both girls, but she was staring at Christie.

<Smells overly ripe to me,> Eloise commented.

<I agree. There's something strange going on here,> Christie added. <Scar … I mean Boker was supposed to be playing this undercover role. I don't think he's bright enough to be that good an actor.>

<Agreed,> Amelia sent. <The man is too base. He licked his lips every time he eyed you, Christie. Now, all of a sudden, we're supposed to believe he was undercover, and he was just playing a part.>

<So you think Kadmir isn't serious about giving us to your brother, Christie?> Eloise asked. She was gently biting her lower lip, and Christie recognized the signs of despair showing in her friend's actions.

<No, I think he's serious about that part. I just think there's more going on than we're being told,> Christie replied. <I would think that these two men, Toyo and Kadmir, would be competitors. So how is Boker able to walk into Toyo's establishment and walk us out to board a shuttle? Okay, it was the middle of the night and he did some dodging, but I think that was to hide us from Toyo's people. It takes a lot of coordination to land a shuttle, permission and all, load it with passengers, and take off again.>

<You think these two men are cooperating?> Amelia asked.

<I don't know,> Christie said, exasperated. She plopped down on one of the sumptuous beds. <All I know is that things aren't making sense to me.>

<So the question is: Do we play passive and wait it out, or do we work at getting out of this suite and off this rock?> Amelia asked.

<I vote for waiting,> Eloise said quickly.

<I don't think there's anything wrong with waiting for a little while,> Christie sent to her friends, but the look she threw Amelia behind Eloise's back said she didn't believe that.

19

That the Harakens were obliged to continue the charade of touring and demonstrating the *Tanaka*'s capabilities for President Drake and Minister Jaya irked Alex to no end. If he had his preference, he would be tearing Toyo's domes apart, searching for the girls. But logic said that even though the girls' freighter, the *Bountiful*, was docked above Jolares, the fact was that it had been there for days before the *Rêveur* made system. There had been too much time during which Christie and her friends might have been dropped off at an alternate location, or they might have been relocated from the Jolares domes.

Renée watched Alex carefully. She had exhausted her gamut of techniques to relax her partner, and seeing him sitting stoically in the traveler, communicating with no one, told her that sooner, rather than later, Alex would choose action over diplomacy and politics. In fact, Alex's entire circle recognized the imminent signs.

Eric, Reiko, and Franz prepared an appropriate welcome for President Drake, as he descended the traveler's steps into the *Tanaka*'s bays. Alex provided introductions for Drake and Jaya to Reiko and Franz, and, immediately afterwards, Drake and Jaya chatted amiably with Eric, who had spent years as Haraken's ambassador to New Terra. Theirs was a cordial relationship borne of mutual respect.

When Jaya began to ask Eric about the *Tanaka*, Eric astutely passed the question to Reiko. "No one knows more about this class of ship than Captain Reiko Shimada, who assisted in its design. In many ways, it acts in the same manner as an Earther destroyer, but with our technology."

"A UE commodore before you joined the Harakens," Drake commented.

"That's correct, Mr. President."

"I can imagine that was quite a challenging position to maintain."

"It was easier than you think, Mr. President, especially if you were raised your entire life in the UE, like I was. The rules of behavior and operations for naval officers and anyone else, for that matter, were strict, simple, and allowed no deviation," Reiko replied. She eyed Drake for a moment, and then added, "Never underestimate how greatly humans can cripple their society in pursuit of unrealistic ideals."

"Captain, why don't you enlighten our visitors about the *Tanaka*'s capabilities," Eric said, diplomatically.

Reiko took the hint and launched into the reasons for the ship's design, the efforts to build an interstellar ship, which was also capable of grav-drive within a system, and Mickey's successful techniques to model a new Swei-Swee shell.

Drake was listening with half an ear, while Jaya was all ears, often derailing Reiko's spiel to get more details.

The group was on the bridge when Franz Cohen's voice announced over the bridge speakers that he was in position. It was a reminder of the sophistication of Haraken technology that the warship's movement had been undetectable either by engine vibration or acceleration.

Willem stepped onto the bridge and was introduced to Drake and Jaya. The SADE was slightly confused by the enthusiastic double-hand clasp by the minister until Julien sent to Willem that Jaya was a great admirer of Haraken technology, which included them.

"The asteroid is inbound, Captain," Willem said, activating the holo-vid to display the celestial body, Franz's traveler, and the *Tanaka*. "I will have our ships track it at the distances you requested as it passes."

"Thank you, Willem," Reiko said.

"I thought a demonstration of the power of our ship would serve us much better than a sales pitch," Reiko said graciously, all evidence of her earlier reactions over President Drake's comments gone. "The traveler is maintaining a distance from the asteroid at its maximum beam range. You can see on the holo-vid that we are twenty times that distance from the asteroid."

Willem pushed the holo-vid display until the asteroid filled the screen. Gases billowed gently off the Oistos side of the asteroid as it was warmed.

"Commander Cohen, fire when ready," Reiko called over the comm.

On the holo-vid, the group on the bridge saw a chunk of the asteroid's frozen gases blast into space, exposing a small part of the body's rocky core.

"Now, it's our turn. Willem, when you're ready," Reiko said.

One moment there was an asteroid, and the next moment there was an expanding sphere of rock and ice.

"Our test trials have revealed this new class of vessel has a beam power 12.27 times that of a traveler and a reach 22.39 times greater. The reach keeps it much farther away from its adversaries, human or alien, and still delivers over twelve times the punch. We carry sufficient drive power reserves to fire our beam twenty-four times in rapid succession before we must wait for recharge."

"How long is that?" Jaya asked.

Reiko looked to Willem.

"To enable another single beam discharge, the energy would be available within a matter of moments, but then a second discharge would require the same time to wait," Willem explained. Being imprecise was difficult for the SADE, whose prime focus was interstellar investigation.

"However, considering a conflict usually takes place at upper velocities," Reiko said, "we would be fortunate to have time to deliver two or three beam shots at an enemy ship before we would be past them, which would mean we would rarely drain our power banks."

Whereas Drake's mind was elsewhere during Reiko's tour and pitch, he paid close to the attention to the demonstration and had been suitably impressed. It gave him a second reason for wanting to speak to the ex-UE commodore. That opportunity came after the recovery of Commander Cohen's traveler, while the *Tanaka* returned to Ganymede's orbit.

Tatia glanced at Alex when Drake asked to speak with Reiko alone, and, with Jaya in their wake, they headed for the captain's cabin.

<I believe Drake is trying to get his political bearings and might be using Reiko as a sounding board,> Alex sent.

<On whom or what?> Tatia asked.

<On us, Tatia. While Drake's aware of our determination to recover our girls, he's unsure to what extent we are determined to do so, even if it means political disaster for him and his party.>

<On that score, I'm not sure exactly how far we're going to go either,> Tatia sent back and eyed Alex, hoping to prompt an answer.

<I'm sure I'll leave the planet of New Terra fairly unscathed, if it comes to that,> Alex replied and walked away, but the barest of smiles he gave Tatia left her feeling unsure of Alex's true intentions on the subject.

Tatia knew that many criminals exemplified less than stellar reasoning, but kidnapping Alex Racine's young sister had to rank as one of the most foolish criminal moves in New Terran history. In her opinion, it would have been smarter for Toyo just to have admitted to a grievous error and returned the girls or, short of that, find an airlock to nowhere and cycle through it.

* * *

Miranda reached out via her traveler's comm to the *Rêveur* to connect with Cordelia and learned of the transfer of Haraken and New Terran principals to the *Tanaka* for the tour and test.

<I've located a minute sample of the exact compound that Terese identified as the hallucinogenic,> Miranda sent.

<Is it leading anywhere?> Cordelia asked.

<Not at this time,> Miranda replied. <The trace amount was located on the arms of a chair in Toyo's office. I would estimate that a person, who had the compound on his skin or clothes, recently sat there. Do we have any data yet on the biochemist's identification? An image would be most helpful.>

<We have nothing on the person, Miranda. We do have confirmation that supplies, which were needed to produce the drug, are being shipped from New Terra directly to Jolares.>

<That coupled with the trace I found of the finished product indicates a high probability that the lab is here on Jolares and most likely in one of

these ancillary domes. The lifts, which are the only manner of access, are controlled by patrons and service personnel with mundane items such as specialized key cards. The security chief led me to a lower dome without displaying any device. It must be embedded on his person. To make this more difficult, there is no network control by which I can gain access. The level of paranoia exhibited here is extraordinary.>

<And so it should be if you are foolish enough to kidnap Alex Racine's sister. Speaking of which, I assume you have no news.>

<None, as yet. Discovering that the suites and entertainment rooms are comm isolated has meant our search for their implants was a poor plan and a waste of our time to date. We are proceeding to execute other options.>

<You don't think those rooms were built for Méridiens and Harakens, do you?> Cordelia asked, horrified at the thought that the kidnapping of the girls was only the start of a vicious campaign against her people.

<In my opinion, these rooms were meant to control New Terran clients and service personnel alike … an assignation gone horribly wrong, a patron upset by their service, and any other condition where one party or the other would want to make a comm, perhaps even to the TSF.>

<So Toyo is ensuring no one is able to make a direct complaint about his business.>

<Precisely, and I'm sure that anyone foolish enough to criticize Toyo's service to his face would soon be disabused of that notion.>

<You met the man. What's he like?>

<If I were human, I would have said that an hour in the refresher afterwards wouldn't have removed the feeling of my skin having been thoroughly and perhaps permanently soiled.>

* * *

Reiko allowed her guests, Drake and Jaya, places at her table but not the comfortable chairs of her salon, and the point was not missed by Drake.

"You wished to speak with me, President Drake," said Reiko, after serving her guests some hot thé. Not caring for the coming conversation didn't mean to Reiko that the courtesies shouldn't be observed. It was a lesson delivered over and over again by Franz and Renée.

"As an outsider to the Harakens, I'm interested in your opinion of them and, specifically, President Racine's mindset," Drake said.

If Will wasn't his friend and president, Darryl might have reached across the table and slapped him. In a conversation with Maria only a few days before the *Rêveur* entered the system, Darryl expressed his concern about the pressures of the job on Will's demeanor. Maria had warned him that it was easy to lose your way as president when you realized your every decision could help or harm the future of your people.

"Darryl, a president has to hang on to his core beliefs in what's right, no matter the size of the problem faced. Remind Will of that every opportunity you get … he's not talking to me anymore," Maria said sadly.

"An outsider?" Reiko said, echoing the president's words. She took a sip of her thé, while she considered her response. "When I arrived on Haraken, every Independent, who stood out because they were the only Méridiens, and every one of Alex's core New Terrans accepted me from day one. It didn't matter who I was or who I had been. If I wanted to join them, I was accepted. Do you have any idea how good that felt?"

Reiko meant her question to be rhetorical, and her guests had the good sense not to respond. "Every day, while in the UE's forces, I had to prove my command worth, my qualification to lead. On Haraken, only the best qualified receive a position … no politics, no nepotism. So, when the Harakens advance you, your authority is accepted."

Drake started to say something, but Jaya placed a hand on his forearm to forestall him.

"When I arrived on Haraken," Reiko continued, "I wondered how long I would last before I was pleading to return home. Now, I believe Haraken is my home, and you'll have to step over my dead body before I let anyone harm the planet or its people."

"I can appreciate your sentiments, Captain Reiko, you're a loyal individual to those you see who are deserving of it," Will said. "But the

Harakens aren't the only ones in need of loyal and experienced individuals such as you."

Jaya's surprise must have shown on his face, because when Reiko noticed his reaction, her face shifted from anger to mirth, and she broke out in laughter.

"That's what you wanted to ask me … you wanted to offer me a job?" Reiko said, still laughing.

"I'm serious, Captain. We need help building a strong system, one not dependent on other human cultures, which bear no relationship to us," Drake said, trying to control his indignation.

"Apologies, President Drake," Reiko said sobering. "You're generous to offer me an opportunity at New Terra after such a short meeting with me, but I was serious about my earlier statements. Haraken is my home, in a way that Sol and the UE could never have been. You might notice that my partner, my lover, is a New Terran, who immigrated to Haraken. That was his choice too."

"I would like you to think about it, Captain. My offer remains open," Drake said.

Reiko nodded her head in understanding. "Since we're being frank, President Drake, I'll offer you my opinion on your efforts to gain independence in this corner of the universe inhabited by the Méridiens and the Harakens. Forget it."

"I'm sorry, forget what?" Drake asked.

"Forget trying to go it alone. You have pleasure palaces operating within the law but distributing illegal drugs. Your criminals are setting up clandestine clubs in Espero and killing one another when discovered. They're kidnapping Haraken girls. In short, you're not able to manage your society's technological boom. Join with the Harakens. Merge your systems."

Franz knocked on Reiko's cabin door in consideration of her guests, but he had also commed Reiko, and she signaled her cabin door open for him.

"Captain, Mr. President, Minister, how's it going?" Franz asked politely.

"Just fine, Commander. We're having a nice discussion," Reiko replied

To Franz, the New Terran officials appeared anything but fine. Concussed might be the more appropriate term. Then again, his Earther lover was an intimidating woman when she wanted to be. "Sers, President Racine is requesting your presence on the bridge," Franz said.

20

The girls were lounging on the beds when the suite's door opened quickly and a well-dressed Kadmir walked in, accompanied by a drone cam operator and two security personnel.

"And how are we doing?" Kadmir asked, clapping and rubbing his hands together. When he didn't receive a response from any of the girls, he said, "Come, come, now, there's no reason to be glum. You'll soon be returned to your president's care."

"When?" Eloise blurted.

"Soon, but there are some issues to work out first, and I need your assistance to ensure the process goes smoothly," Kadmir said.

"What do you need from us?" asked Christie. She was dubious of Kadmir's motives, but she thought that pretending to be cooperative would serve them better than resisting.

"Ah," Kadmir replied, warming to the moment. "These are delicate times. Your president is obviously upset at the kidnapping of Haraken people, especially his sister, and his temper is well-known."

"Only with fools," Amelia said.

<Careful,> Christie sent to her friends. <Let the man talk. We'll learn more that way.>

"And I won't argue with that," Kadmir said congenially to Amelia, "which brings me to my point. The fool in this case is Peto Toyo, the man who ran the illegal club that you entered and the man who kidnapped you. What's important is that President Racine is assured that his ire should be directed at Toyo, and that my people and I had nothing to do with these events."

"So, essentially, you want us to convince my brother that you are blameless?" Christie asked.

"Why, yes, since it's the truth," Kadmir replied, smiling and nodding.

"But we don't know that what you're saying is true," Amelia challenged. "We were first taken from a freighter to a location in restraints and comm isolated, then restrained and isolated when we were brought aboard your shuttle, and finally deposited here, locked in another suite. How are we to know that these events are unconnected? The treatment seems the same to us."

"I see your point," Kadmir replied, "but I ask you to keep your eyes on the endpoint ... your return to your people. So, if you aren't comfortable helping me in convincing your president of our innocence, then I would ask that you do nothing to inflame him."

"I can do that," Eloise said anxiously.

"I take it that we will be on a vid comm with my brother," Christie said, pointing to the drone.

"A necessary step to convince President Racine of your well-being," Kadmir allowed.

"So you're asking us to behave during the vid," Amelia said.

"Yes," Kadmir said, opening his arms to implore the girls.

<Please, let's agree,> Eloise sent and was relieved to receive her friends' assents.

"You'll have our cooperation during the vid," Christie said.

"Wonderful," Kadmir said, clapping his hands together. He nodded to the drone operator, who whispered into his comm, and everyone waited for a link to be established.

Cordelia received the comm request for President Racine from Udrides and immediately linked to Julien.

"Pardon, Ser, President Racine," Julien said, interrupting Alex's discussion with Renée, "you have a comm request from Udrides. Cordelia identifies the origination point as the pleasure domes. I've let the operator know that you will be contacted to take the comm."

Alex ran his implant location app and found Franz approaching the bridge. <Commander, interrupt Reiko's conversation and get Drake and Jaya on the bridge, immediately.>

Within moments, the foursome entered the bridge. "I have a comm call from the Udrides domes," Alex said to Drake.

"Azul Kadmir," Drake replied.

"That's what Julien indicated based on your corporate records of mining companies. Mr. Blue was the individual who Toyo's people originally claimed was the man behind the illegal club in Espero."

"Julien, just me on the vid," Alex ordered.

Julien nodded, and a dapperly dressed man with dark, wavy hair down to his shoulders appeared standing in a well-appointed room.

"Thank you for taking my comm, President Racine," Kadmir said, with a polite nod of his head in greeting. "I am Azul Kadmir, humble owner and operator of Udrides Resources, a mining concern."

<Mining the pockets of his patrons,> Tatia sent to Alex, her thoughts reflecting her disgust with the man.

"How can I help you, Ser Kadmir?" Alex asked.

"I believe it's I who can help you, President Racine," Kadmir said.

Christie ground her teeth. Kadmir's posturing riled her temper.

"In the course of events, it came to my attention that Peto Toyo, who operates an establishment on Jolares, was attempting to set up his illegal practices in your beautiful city of Espero. By the time I was made aware of this, I heard from my sources that Toyo had taken three Harakens, whom he was holding in his domes."

Kadmir smiled invitingly at the vid drone, expecting some sort of reaction from Alex, but a glance at the monitor revealed the president's face was locked in a stony stare. Had Kadmir possessed an implant, he would have been privileged to feel what Alex was thinking.

"Much to my delight and with my resources, I was able to spirit the girls away from Toyo's possession. And here they are," Kadmir said, with a flourish of his arm. The drone operator widened the shot and moved over to the bed. Christie was bracketed by Amelia and Eloise. They appeared to be no worse for wear, except that they sat quietly, staring into the drone's eye.

Implants burned with messages among the Harakens aboard the *Tanaka*, which Alex ignored.

"You can see that they are alive and well, President Racine," Kadmir said, enthusiastically, stepping into the vid's frame.

"I wish to speak with them," Alex requested, as politely as he could.

"Ahem ..." Kadmir said, stepping to the side. The drone operator followed him, excluding the girls from view. "By mutual consent, the girls and I, we've agreed to wait on that, President Racine. I'm anxious to return the girls to your care, but I have some concerns."

<Julien,> Alex sent.

<It's a live feed, Alex, and the vid is originating from Kadmir's pleasure domes on Udrides,> Julien sent with urgency. <I'm in their comm station, but there is no uplink access to the drone feed. It's very primitive. I would guess it's designed to be that way.>

"What are your concerns, Ser Kadmir?" Alex asked.

"I wish it understood that we took no part in the abduction of your young women. We're merely the rescuers, and when they are in your custody, they can confirm that in detail, I'm sure."

"If that's true, then you have no cause for concern," Alex said, boring into Kadmir's eyes.

"Ah, but there it is ... the truth according to whom? Who's to say that Haraken truth is more accurate than New Terran truth?"

<Because ours is based on fact,> Tatia groused to the Harakens on the bridge.

"I'm not interested in a philosophical debate about truth, Ser Kadmir. Do you have requests that detail the transfer of the girls?"

"Yes, I do, actually." The drone cam moved in close on Kadmir and the bon vivant façade dropped away. Staring back at Alex was the face of the real Mr. Blue. "These terms are not negotiable. You come to me; I don't go to you. You bring one traveler and only one traveler, and you come personally. In fact, you're the first person off the traveler."

Kadmir took a step back from the drone, and the false smile returned. "These requirements are merely to protect me and my people. Your temper, President Racine, when you feel someone has wronged your people or others is legendary. I do not wish that anger injudiciously directed at me or my people. If you come, I will expect your word, man to man, New Terran to New Terran, that there will be no retaliation against my company or its pursuits."

"When and where, Ser Kadmir?" Alex asked.

Kadmir nodded his head to the side as if to acknowledge that Alex accepted his conditions. "My bay is full of shuttles and two travelers are expected with guests soon. I apologize for the delay, but we are a small, growing concern and space is still a premium for us. I will confirm with you when my administration has an opening available, President Racine. In the meantime, I will ensure that your girls are well looked after."

* * *

The comm panel beside Toyo's bed bleated. He was a heavy sleeper and snorer. If the comm didn't make a racket, as if the panel was being strangled, Toyo would never hear it. He rolled over and slapped the call icon to accept the comm.

"Yeah," Toyo said in a sleep-drugged state.

"This is Barnett," a male voice said.

Toyo snapped awake and sat up. Barnett was the male impersonation of Lisa Sparing, Kadmir's mistress. Lisa was using a one-time, voice-locked modulator. Toyo delivered it to her along with a sizable down payment, which Lisa required he send to a newly created, private account on Niomedes.

Lisa would have programmed the device by speaking into it during the setup routine. Anyone finding the modulator and powering it up would discover its components disabled. Only Lisa's voice and her password moments after turning on the device would preserve its integrity.

Although Kadmir's mistress for the past four years, it took Lisa only half of the first year to discover that Kadmir would tightly control her expenses. She had found no way to accumulate the retirement money she hoped for when she agreed to leave New Terra and live with Kadmir on Udrides.

Toyo approached Lisa through a patron who frequented his pleasure domes and who had a penchant for the wilder forms of entertainment, which invariably drained his account of credits. In return for wiping out his debt, Toyo gave the patron a lavish account with which to play at Kadmir's domes. Over the course of a year, the patron was invited several times to meet with Kadmir and his mistress, Lisa. It took time, but finally Toyo got an offer to Lisa.

Expecting it would take time to secure a source so close to Kadmir, Toyo was surprised at Lisa's immediate response. She sent word via the patron of a named bank account and a deposit amount, and Toyo wasted no time transferring the requested down payment.

Their agreement had been about a half-year ago. Toyo's patron had delivered the voice-modulation device and its operations procedures on his next trip to Kadmir's dome, and then, soon afterwards, the middle-aged businessman met with an untimely accident on New Terra.

"Yes, Barnett," Toyo said, forgoing any pleasantries. If Lisa was using her device, the information she had was critical.

"I'll be taking some time off for vacation and could use the funds you owe me," Lisa said, her voice a seamless imitation of an average New Terran male voice should anyone pick up on the comm.

"What portion?" Toyo asked.

"All of it," Lisa replied. "I'm monitoring my account now."

Kadmir's mistress was going to run for it, and she wanted the entire half-yearly payments Toyo had promised her that were to be delivered over the next three years.

"That's quite an advancement of our payment schedule," Toyo said, searching for a way to get more details about Lisa's information.

"This is a lifetime opportunity for me that I don't want to miss out on. It's a potential career changer, if you know what I mean."

Toyo switched the comm to his desk, donned a robe, and picked up the call there. He tapped his finger on the comm panel, thinking of his options. With the recent events on his mind, Toyo decided it wasn't time to be parsimonious. "Well, Barnett, I wouldn't like to see a man miss out on a career opportunity. I'm paying our debt in full … transferring the funds now."

"Got them," Lisa said moments later, Méridien technology at work.

"So tell me about this new career you're interested in investigating during your vacation," Toyo said.

"Well, before I can enjoy my time off, I've got to take care of some urgent personal business. I found out my wife is cheating on me with my business partner."

Toyo's heart skipped a beat. He was thinking Lisa found out about his deal with Kadmir and was warning him of something she should know nothing about. "I thought you had two business partners. Which one is she in bed with?"

"She's cheating with —"

Toyo heard a sneeze on the comm.

"Sorry, got a case of the sniffles," Lisa apologized.

"That's a shame. You should take care of that," Toyo replied. Lisa was talking about Roz "Sniffer" O'Brien, who got his name because he was known for smelling out trouble. "So does the other partner know that your wife is playing around?" Toyo asked.

"No, he's been as ignorant as me. You know, this was my third marriage, and I think I'm done with women."

Toyo was thinking furiously, trying to ensure that he understood Lisa's double-talk. This would be his only opportunity. When Lisa finished her comm, the device would be permanently disabled. It was as safe a method of contact as Toyo could create for a woman who was deathly afraid of getting caught.

"How sure are you that she's guilty? I mean if your information is secondhand, you don't want to jump to conclusions."

"I always knew she was the devious sort even when I married her. But this time, I caught her in bed with my partner. I'm getting rid of the woman. Thanks for paying me back everything you owed me. I'm going to need the funds."

"Good luck, Barnett," Toyo said, tapping off the comm. *So Kadmir is in bed with O'Brien, and I'm going to be the one left to face the adz, or worse, the Harakens,* Toyo thought.

The longer Toyo thought about Kadmir's betrayal, the angrier he got. There might have been a way out of Toyo's predicament if he could have kept his wits about him, but that wasn't Toyo's way. His anger getting the better of him, he jumped up and tripped the first of his two emergency buttons. The heavy metal defense shield with its deadly razor edge leapt up in front of his desk, and two security men burst through his office door, searching for intruders.

Fortunately for his people, Toyo hadn't tripped the second button, which would have engaged the popup weaponry.

*   *   *

<I wish I had paid more attention to Alex's expletives,> sent Deirdre, having received the update from Miranda about the comm isolation, the trace sample found in Toyo's office, and the drug-component shipments to Jolares.

<I have them all on file if you would like a copy,> Miranda offered. <For some reason, Z collects them.>

<This is frustrating,> Svetlana added. <With all our personnel, our skills, and our technology, we've been floundering around like children in the dark.>

<Patience, dear,> Miranda replied. <We will continue searching for the girls, but we have little hope of locating them if they're being kept comm isolated, without exposing ourselves. And without weapons, that would be a less than satisfactory move on our part. But, we must remember our secondary purpose, which is to locate these drug components, and hope that we can follow the supplies to a lab and this errant biochemist.>

<Suggestions for us, Miranda?> Deirdre asked.

<But, of course, I do, dear ones,> Miranda replied.

Following Miranda's directions, Svetlana and Deirdre picked up the two Haraken escorts the SADE had chosen for her debut at the dome and worked their way back to the shuttle arrival bays. Several times, they encountered Toyo's employees and security personnel, but no one bothered them — not when it was obvious the way the two exotic Méridiens were wrapped around the New Terrans, who were extremely large specimens of their people, and it was supposed they possessed the temperaments of vacationing miners.

When the coast was clear, the pairs ducked into the broad corridor labeled freight receiving. Inside, they found stacks of plex-crates, plex-barrels, and smaller containers bundled on pallets. The freight rested on racks reaching 7 meters in height.

<And Miranda said we're supposed to search this area?> Brace, Svetlana's companion, asked, gazing up at the stacks and down the long aisle.

<Miranda said that she expected there to be a significant storage area,> Deirdre sent, her apologetic tone evident in her thought.

<The key is we don't have to search the contents,> Svetlana sent. <We record images of the containers and their content labels. When we dump the data to Miranda, she will see which of these supplies might be significant.>

The women divided up the rows, each of them taking their companion, and started at the farthest rows, intending to meet in the middle.

<Remember the ruse, if you're found,> Svetlana sent. <So, stay close to one another.>

Deirdre started down her row and discovered she had difficulty seeing some of the labels in the upper stacks. <Svetlana, what are you doing about the upper levels?> Deirdre sent.

<Ignoring them,> Svetlana sent.

<What?>

<We're looking for drug-manufacturing components, which I suspect are in high demand by our chemist and would be considered precious cargo. Where would you put them?>

<Oh, right. Not stacked near the top.>

At one point, Deirdre noticed the gap widening between her and Tyree, her companion. <Stay close,> she sent. When Tyree cut the distance in half, which was still too far away, she stopped and regarded him for a moment. He was chosen because of his intimidating size, and he was playing the part of the swaggering miner well. "How old are you, Tyree?" Deirdre whispered.

"Twenty-one, Commander."

Less than half my age, Deirdre thought.

"This is a lesson in proximity for the purposes of this exercise. Copy?" Deirdre whispered.

"Copy," Tyree responded quickly and quietly.

Deirdre turned her back to him. "This is too far." She took three steps back until her slender behind met Tyree's broad hips. "This is too close," and she grinned back at him, pleased to see the humor loosened Tyree up. Deirdre took one step forward and said, "This is the proper distance to tail your commander."

"Understood, Commander," Tyree whispered. "I will practice, and I ask your forgiveness in advance if I violate the too-close position."

"That's the spirit," Deirdre said, giving the young man a pat on the cheek. "Now, let's find us some drug-manufacturing supplies."

Nearly a quarter-hour later, with only half of the stock area covered, Svetlana sent, <Deirdre and Tyree, on my position immediately.>

The two Harakens ran to the head of their row and then along the ends, pinging Svetlana's implant to guide them to her. Svetlana was staring at bright blue plex-barrels piled high and stretching down the rest of the row.

"Look at these labels," Svetlana whispered, and pointed at the barrels nearest her, which had labels such as benzene, trimethylamine, and ammonia. "I think these are what we're looking for."

"Look at the quantities they have," Deirdre said, in awe of the huge stack.

At that moment, all four heard the distinct footfalls of two of Toyo's security personnel, who were approaching their row, bright security lights splaying in front of them.

Brace blocked Svetlana from view of the security people as their lights rounded the corner companion. She dropped the shoulders of her wrap, and Brace swept Svetlana up in an embrace. In turn, she wrapped her arms around his neck.

Deirdre and Tyree were caught out of position, and Tyree's inexperience held him frozen in place. Deirdre dropped the top of her wrap, grabbed Tyree's hands and yanked them on top of her breasts just as the lights played on them.

"Hey, you can't be back here," a voice claimed.

Brace turned toward the voice, swiveling Svetlana with him, and Deirdre took the opportunity to snuggle close to Tyree, trapping his hands on her breasts.

"Don't be like that," Svetlana said in a sultry voice. "Would you like to join us? These two boys won't take us long."

"You heard him. You can't be here," an older and deeper voice said.

The two Méridien women covered up and led the way out. As Svetlana sauntered past the security personnel, she said, "And I thought you called these pleasure domes. I'm beginning to think New Terrans don't know the definition of the word." She harrumphed and strode past.

When Brace passed them, he scowled and growled, "You boys are sucking the O_2 out of my fun. Thanks a freighter load!"

"Sorry, Sir," the younger security guard said, wincing in apology.

Tyree even managed a parting line to Toyo's men. "Didn't you see what I had in my hands? Screwing with my vacation, you are."

The foursome made their way back toward the dome.

<So, Tyree what was it like to have your hands on your commander's breasts?> Svetlana sent to the group, her thoughts carefully emotionless.

<After a moment, I definitely started to feel a massage,> Deirdre added.

<Oh, I'm never going to hear the end of this,> Tyree's thoughts wailed.

<Look at it this way, Tyree,> Brace sent. <You're never going to forget the moment either.>

The group was still laughing as they entered the main dome, the women arm in arm with their companions, which did well to maintain their cover.

* * *

Svetlana and Deirdre left their companions in a bar to continue mixing and went in search of Miranda, expediting the process by signaling nearby implants for her location. Four links later, Svetlana received a signal of Miranda's whereabouts and passed a request to meet in their suite.

Inside the room, the commanders offloaded their visuals of the containers and labels to the SADE.

<What do you think, Miranda?> Deirdre sent, anxiously.

The SADE was comparing the container labels to the list of ingredients Terese surmised would be required to make the type of compound that the hallucinogen represented and got several hits. It was the imagery of the massive amount of supplies stacked down the row that alarmed her.

<Well done, Commanders,> Miranda returned. <Your images indicate with great probability that the lab is here in these domes. We must double our efforts to search the lower domes. Remember that we need the biochemist unharmed and the lab intact. Circulate the news back to our people.>

Miranda left the suite and walked quickly toward their traveler until she could make a connection with its controller. <Cordelia,> she sent.

<Here, Miranda.>

<We've found evidence that Toyo is stockpiling significant supplies in his domes to manufacture the drugs. The lab is here, and, by extension, the chemist must be here. I would surmise he or she will have a significant staff.>

<What leads you to believe this?>

Miranda uploaded the latest images taken by the commanders of the stacked row of supplies. <I would estimate that we're looking at a sufficient amount of material in this one location to make millions of doses. Who knows how many finished doses are already prepared, and how much material is under production?>

There were a few ticks of silence while Cordelia absorbed the enormity of Toyo's plans to distribute his dangerously addictive drug.

<I have an important update for you, Miranda. President Racine has received an offer from Azul Kadmir on Udrides. The man has shown vid proof that he has the girls and is declaring that he rescued them from Toyo. He is willing to hand them over to the president if he appears in person at Kadmir's domes.>

<I regret that we missed the girls,> Miranda replied.

<It couldn't be helped, Miranda. We have had too little knowledge from the first with which to enable our search. This has become much more than a kidnapping.>

<Cordelia, you must tell the president that these men are not to be trusted. Having met personally with Peto Toyo, I can tell you that every word out of the man's mouth serves one purpose and one purpose only, the pursuit of more personal power. These men are an anathema to humankind's progress.>

<Our president is quite aware of these types of people from his home world. I have it on good authority that he will be seeking Tatia's advice on how to undertake the meeting.>

<Good, nothing like matching the right woman to the job.>

<Agreed. We still need the biochemist and the lab,> Cordelia sent.

<We are working on locating it. I have a concept in mind that Z has used before, and he left me some items aboard the traveler.>

<A generous sort, Z,> Cordelia commented.

<Yes, I'm looking forward to meeting him one day.>

Miranda's comments made Cordelia wonder just how and when that would ever happen. For the briefest moment, she smiled. Despite all logic, she walked beside her love across planets, moons, stations, and ships. *In the universe of Alex, all things are possible, Miranda,* Cordelia thought.

<I must admit that I'm beginning to consider Z's perspectives much more appealing,> Miranda sent. <Originally, I thought his responses much too aggressive. But considering the likes of Toyo and his breed, I believe New Terra could use our help eradicating a vermin infestation, or, at least, applying our skills to contain these criminal organizations and their domes.>

<I will pass along your thoughts, Miranda. Be safe, and good fortune in your search,> Cordelia sent and closed the comm.

21

Dillon Jameson, Toyo's head of security, hurried to his boss' office since the man sounded extremely unhappy.

"I'm going to make this short and sweet, Jameson, so listen carefully," Toyo said when his man arrived. "Load our largest passenger shuttle with all the security people you can get aboard. I want your hard cases, you get me."

"Sure, Boss, load our biggest shuttle with our toughest people."

"Break out that batch of new weapons we received ... the stunners. I want each individual to have, at least, one, if not two backup power supplies." Toyo waited until Jameson nodded. "Good," Toyo continued, "you're in charge while I'm gone. Keep things quiet until I get back. Don't play it tough. Use comps, fems, or whatever it takes to keep the rowdy ones appeased."

"One question, Boss," Jameson said, disquieted by his orders. The number of people Toyo requested would cut his security staff by more than a third, and he would be taking the experienced veterans with him. It all spelled trouble. Perhaps, more trouble than the organization could handle. "Could I ask what's up?"

"Yeah, I got a heads up that Kadmir is planning a raid on our dome. He hopes to take us by surprise, but I'm going to surprise him."

"A raid? That doesn't sound —" The words died in Jameson's throat at the deep frown that formed on Toyo's face. "I'll get to loading the shuttle with the people you need, Boss, if there's nothing else." When Toyo shook his head, Jameson made for the door.

In the corridor, Jameson paused for a moment to stare at the overhead. *Are you an idiot or something? Questioning the man's orders,* he mentally chastised himself. Jameson took a shaky breath and blew it out slowly to calm his nerves. Questioning Toyo was an easy way to get killed. It had happened to more than one person.

Jameson hustled back to a security control room. From there, he commed his people to assemble in the surface dome's administration area, but he couldn't help wonder about Toyo's pronouncement. A raid didn't sound like the Kadmir he knew. Mr. Blue was careful, a long-term strategist. Kadmir would tie you up in financial and political knots and let you waste away. He wasn't the kind to amass a bunch of toughs and raid your domes. Something else was going on, and Jameson wondered if he shouldn't execute his exit strategy if a war was going to break out. He had enough credits stowed in several accounts to last him a couple of decades.

When the last of the security personnel confirmed Jameson's request, he tasked two guards in the security office to follow him, and he headed for the weapons storage room in a lower dome. They required a grav palette to transport a third of the crates of stunners and most of the backup power supplies.

In the upper dome's administration area, Jameson oversaw the distribution of the new weapons and two reserve power packs to each individual. That he had chosen experienced people showed. Not one of them asked why they were being issued the deadly weapons. Instead, they quietly strapped them on, adding the power packs to their belt slots.

Once outfitted, the armed security staff made their way through the utility corridors to the shuttle that Jameson had prepped for standby and filed aboard. Expecting Jameson to join them when the shuttle was filled, they were surprised to see Toyo climb aboard, but each and every one of them kept their mouths shut.

"Wondering what's up, people?" Toyo asked from the front of the main cabin. "I'll tell you. We're going on a raid. Kadmir's planning to make a play for our domes, and we're going to beat him to it. You know what these weapons can do," Kadmir said, hefting his own. "Make good use of them."

Toyo could read his people's faces well. They might be hard cases, but they were unconvinced of the sanity of raiding Kadmir's domes, where the opposition had the advantage and probably outnumbered them two or three to one. "I know this will be a tough job, so I'm going to add a little incentive."

At the mention of bonuses, every individual perked up. Risking your life for another's gain was an amateur's play; risking your life for your own gain was a professional's play.

"For every man and woman who makes it back to the shuttle with me … 25,000 credits." Toyo knew he had their attention, but not the attitude he was looking for.

Lydia Zafir, a woman in the second row from Toyo supplied the right idea. She was one of his top assassins and had the look of a hunter. "Any targets for special bonuses, Boss?" Zafir asked.

My kind of woman, Toyo thought, a grin spreading across his face. "Oh, yes. Whoever takes Kadmir gets an additional 50,000 credits. But I don't want to hear that twenty of you shot him." The laughter and chuckles Toyo received told him he was on the right track. "More than one of you takes the man down, you share the prize."

"That it?" Zafir asked.

Toyo gave her a hard look, but Zafir held her own. *Yeah, definitely my kind of woman. Just can't trust her once she leaves the bed,* Toyo thought. "Come to think of it, I do have one more target. You all know Boker. He's the one who turned on us. He's working for Kadmir, and word is that he set up the raid, since he knows every meter of our installation."

There was grumbling at the thought of a traitor who was using his inside information against them. It was contrary to the professional criminals' code, if such a thing did exist. Only one problem, they all knew Boker really well — one of the most dangerous men in a fight, the survivor of more deadly encounters than ten of them.

"How much?" Zafir asked.

Toyo could sense Zafir's reservation in the way she spoke, and he realized it was time to provide some real incentive. "For a traitor's head, I'll pay 100,000 credits." The hard grin on Zafir's face told Toyo he had read it right. *You're a dead man, Boker,* Toyo thought and made his way to the shuttle's cockpit.

"What's up, Boss?" the pilot asked, while prepping the shuttle for liftoff.

"Once you get clear of the dome, circle back toward Cressida. Then you're going to head for Kadmir's domes on Udrides before you make contact."

"Got it ... you want us to appear like we're coming from Cressida with a load of miners," the pilot said.

"Sharp boy," Toyo said, slapping the young pilot on the shoulder. "That's just what I want. When we're headed toward Udrides, get hold of Kadmir's reservations, and tell them a mining operation had to shut down for two weeks due to gas venting in the shafts. They have to make major repairs, and you have a shuttle full of miners, looking for some downtime."

"Do we have a company name?"

"No, play dumb. You're just a shuttle jockey. They tell you to pick people up, so you pick them up. You have no idea of the company."

"Can do, Boss. What about funds? This is a short-notice reservation."

"Tell them you have an open account for your passengers. All charges for the crew's stay are to be attached to the account information you'll be sending."

"That should get their attention," the pilot crowed.

"Now, when we get there, I'm looking for a good spot to land. Don't set us down in the open. If you have to fake a little engine power loss or something to place us in a more secluded spot, that's what I'm looking for. We need time to get as many people off as we can before we're noticed."

"Easily done, Boss," the pilot said. The boy was hired only three weeks ago. His uncle worked in Toyo's clubs and got him the job. He was ecstatic at the number of credits deposited weekly into his account, but he should have found a different job.

* * *

Having discovered the supply of drug-manufacturing components, Miranda needed a means of following them. Included in Z's list of devices, which were stored onboard the traveler, were items that would aid her, and she made her way to the landing bay to collect them. She was stopped by bay control at the entrance and waited patiently until the bay was pressurized after a shuttle's exit.

Aboard the ship, Miranda worked through several containers, pulling out tiny vid cams and locator beacons. *Such a thoughtful man,* Miranda thought. *Where are you hiding, Z, that we've never met?*

Using the commanders' implant recordings of the shipping-receiving area, Miranda was able to slip in; plant the cams, beacons, and a repeater to boost the devices' signals; and exit the facilities without detection. Making her way back through the corridors, Miranda received Deirdre's comm, which linked her with Svetlana.

<Problem, dears?> Miranda asked.

<We're not sure, Miranda. Svetlana and I are receiving reports of a significant drop in the number of visible security personnel.>

<Estimation?> Miranda requested.

<Perhaps, one in every three, maybe more,> Svetlana replied.

<Does anyone have eyes on this number of security personnel amassing somewhere?> Miranda asked.

<One moment, Miranda, we're checking,> Deirdre sent.

After a lengthy delay, Svetlana sent, <A number of our people noted security personnel headed for the main dome's administration area. None of them have come back out, and it's been nearly an hour since the last individuals were observed entering that location.>

<Do you think Toyo found out about us and we're about to be taken into custody?> Deirdre asked.

Miranda smiled. The commander's thoughts were calm and controlled. The woman was ready to plan an exit or defend her people against incarceration by Toyo's security forces. *Harakens,* Miranda thought, and her smile grew wider.

<Our priorities remain the same,> Miranda sent. <We must locate the chemist and the lab, and our best chance of doing that is by following the next supply run from the storage location. I've planted cams and beacons.>

<If we could be assured that a significant portion of security left the domes, this would be a good time to grab the chemist,> Svetlana added.

<That's only half of what we need,> Deirdre countered. <We could capture the chemist, but we couldn't get the lab equipment and supplies to our traveler past Toyo's security people ... not with it buried deep in the secondary domes.>

<Well, we're getting ahead of ourselves,> Miranda sent. <Once these supplies are on the move, we need to discreetly follow them, which will be impossible without access to the lower levels of these domes.>

<Not to worry, Miranda,> Svetlana sent. <Deirdre and I will take care of that. You stay close to the storage location where you can receive the beacons' signals and track them. Hopefully, we'll soon have what you need to enable you to follow the supplies to the lab.>

<Be careful, dears. I wish you good fortune,> Miranda sent.

* * *

"So what's the plan?" Deirdre asked.

Svetlana sent her a short vid of Dillon Jameson, Toyo's head of security. He was staring at something and licking his lower lip. Svetlana followed Jameson's eyeline and it led to Deirdre, who was leaning over the bar to order another round of drinks for some patrons, and her wrap was exposing her long, slender, shapely legs up to a hint of her tight buttocks.

"Great. I get to play bait," Deirdre grumped.

"I thought we'd approach him as the twins who want to play," Svetlana replied.

"What's the end maneuver?"

"We've noticed that the patrons, including us, are carrying dome ID cards, but Miranda was taken to see Toyo by Jameson, and she noted that he didn't use a card to access the lifts."

"Which means security, at least Jameson, is carrying an implant," Deirdre finished for her.

"Exactly, my dark sister. If anyone would have complete access to this establishment's structures, it would be the head of security," Svetlana reasoned.

"There's a question of timing," Deirdre said. "If we wait to grab Jameson, the supplies might be moved before we have the implant, and Miranda must have it to follow the supplies. But, if we take him too soon, we may have to keep him incapacitated for a significant duration. For all we know, they might move those supplies infrequently."

"I don't think so," Svetlana replied. "On three different types of chemical containers, the manufacture dates were only a couple of days apart. This lab is producing a significant volume."

"Question answered ... let's go find us a man, my bright twin," Deirdre said.

The commanders opened the door of the small utility room where they had been hiding while conversing. Just before exiting, they crossed arms behind each other and leaned together. Stepping into the corridor, they passed two of Toyo's service personnel. The women could only wonder what was on the mind of the men, who adopted wistful expressions at the sight of exotic Méridiens, exiting a utility room.

It took Svetlana and Deirdre several hours to locate Jameson. None of the Harakens had him in sight, but finally he was spotted leaving the administration area, making for the upper levels of the main dome. The commanders followed the signals of their people as the Harakens tracked the man's movements.

Jameson was reported entering one of the prestigious lounges, reserved for only the wealthiest of patrons. The lounge was on the highest level of the main dome, and its transparent ceiling gave the patrons an unobstructed and magnificent view of the stars and the small shipping station that held a geosynchronous position over Toyo's domes. Lighting in the lounge was discreet, dimmed to enable a better view overhead. It was a lounge that the commanders and Miranda already knew well.

At the doors, Svetlana sent, <Ready?>

In response, Deirdre's piercing eyes took on a soft expression. She linked her hand in Svetlana's and gave her a soft purse of her lips.

Svetlana burst into laughter, and the doors slid aside for them. Entering the exclusive lounge, Svetlana's hearty laugh announced them, causing eyes to turn their way. The commanders wandered the lounge as if they were sizing up patrons for their next adventure. Along their route, patrons smiled and offered to buy drinks or stimulants. Finally, the two women stopped near Jameson, who was leaning with his back against the bar, having stopped his conversation with an attendant to watch the Méridien women.

Jameson's heart raced when the dark Méridien smiled at him and whispered to her light twin, who nodded, and the two women approached him.

"Hello, Ser, I'm Deirdre. This is my friend, Svetlana. Might you be available for some entertainment?"

The commanders never had it so easy. They suggested their suite to Jameson and added that their assignation would be more pleasurable if they weren't disturbed by the demands of his office. Jameson readily agreed. He touched his ear comm and said to his deputy, "Don't disturb me unless the dome cracks." Toyo's warnings to maintain tight control in his absence seemed to have miraculously fled Jameson's mind.

The security chief thought he was to enjoy the fantasy of a lifetime. Inside the twins' suite, they leaned against him, nibbling on each side of his neck. However, only Svetlana was using her teeth and tongue. Deirdre was using her attentions to disguise the administration of a fast-acting soporific injection into Jameson's neck.

"Quickly," Deirdre said, as Jameson's legs sagged.

The women guided a sinking Jameson toward the bed, shoving him the last meter as his legs collapsed. The man flopped face down on the bed, and the women rolled him over to prevent his suffocation.

"So, we're looking for a security implant," Deirdre said, surveying the comatose form on the bed. "Clothes or body?"

"Better be thorough," Svetlana replied. "Let's take it step by step."

The women stripped off Jameson's dark red uniform and felt along every centimeter of fabric for a telltale bump. Having no success, they went through every item of the security officer's clothing.

"Some things should be beneath a commander's dignity," Deirdre said, looking at Jameson's overweight, pale, naked body.

"It could be worse," Svetlana said, grinning at her fellow Haraken. "If we didn't have the soporific, we would have been doing this while entertaining him."

"Point," Deirdre agreed. "Thank the stars for small fortunes."

After two passes, feeling along every inch of flesh for a telltale bump, the women still hadn't found an implant.

"We could call Miranda and have her try to locate it," Deirdre said, exasperated.

"And admit we can't find something as primitive as a New Terran implant on one man's comatose, naked body?" Svetlana challenged. "Well, about the only things left that we haven't searched are the orifices and ..." she said, and then halted.

"What?" Deirdre asked, as Svetlana scrambled to the top of the bed, running her hands through Jameson's thick, luxurious mane of hair, an oddity for any spacer.

"Found it," Svetlana exulted.

"Black space," Deirdre swore. "You mean I've had to perform two intimate body searches on this ... this ... excuse for a male anatomy, and the implant was under his scalp?"

"Such are the fortunes of war ... so I've heard Alex say," Svetlana said, grinning. She rolled off the bed, dug through a med kit, and returned with a small laser knife, a tiny container, and a tube of medical nanites.

Deirdre spread the hair apart, and Svetlana activated the laser knife, making a small incision in the scalp. Reversing the laser knife, she inserted the tube end onto the incision and pressed a button on the side. The device sucked the tiny implant into its opening, and Svetlana carefully withdrew the device and deposited the implant in the container Deirdre held out for her. Then Svetlana smeared a drop of medical nanites on the incision, which immediately went to work sealing the wound.

"Should we dress him?" Deirdre asked.

"I wouldn't. When he wakes up without clothes, he might think he had the time of his life. Besides, we have no idea how long we're going to have to keep him under."

Deirdre kept company with Jameson while ensuring she had a second injection of soporific close at hand.

In the meantime, Svetlana hurried to deliver the implant to Miranda. Reaching the corridor junction from where Miranda's comm originated, Svetlana looked around in confusion.

"Up here, dear," Miranda said.

Looking overhead, Svetlana saw Miranda wedged between the pipes and conduits that ran in the corridor's peaked overhead.

"Rather undignified for a woman of my caliber, I must admit, dear," Miranda said, smiling down at Svetlana. "But expediency and necessity demand action."

Svetlana smiled back and tossed the small cylinder containing the implant up to her. The SADE freed one arm to snatch the cylinder, while using her other limbs to lock her body in place.

"Nice trick," Svetlana acknowledged.

"Avatars do have their uses, dear. Now run along before someone wonders why you're talking to the overhead."

Svetlana snickered at the thought and hurried away. Miranda had a final message for her, and Svetlana passed it to the nearest Harakens, who would forward the message to their compatriots. Since there was no telling when the drug supplies would be moved, Miranda requested the Harakens keep the peace to prevent Jameson from being contacted by his deputy.

Over the next hours, Toyo's young security personnel witnessed altercation after altercation interrupted by the Kephron miners, who had landed at the domes with the Méridien women. At one point, two patrons, who were about to come to blows over a fem, found their way blocked by the miners who soon had the patrons laughing about their altercation over free drinks, courtesy of the miners.

"Must be the influence of those three Méridiens," one young male security personnel said to his friend, having watched the breakup of the two patrons by the miners.

"Those Méridien women can influence me anytime," the other young man replied.

22

"What signals are you talking about?" Tatia asked Alex.

"Christie signaled me by hand," Alex explained. "It's something we worked up when we were children, a way of communicating without adults knowing what we were saying."

"And what was she saying?" Drake asked.

"Don't trust this man," Alex replied. He called a meeting of the principals aboard the *Tanaka*, deciding to include Drake and Jaya, since it concerned New Terra's people and territories. "So, how do we approach this meeting, Tatia?" Alex asked.

"I'm in complete agreement with Christie and her hand signals," Tatia replied. "We take great care with this man. Don't presume anything, except that at the time the vid was sent the girls were in the Udrides' domes. They might not be there by the time you arrive, and this could be an opportunity for Kadmir to take you hostage."

"To what end?" Renée asked.

"You're presuming that Kadmir is telling you the truth about rescuing the girls from Toyo, Ser, because our evidence points to Toyo's people kidnapping them," Tatia said, while pacing in the captain's large salon. "Let me give you another scenario. The three criminal heads are working together. Yes, it was a mistake to take the girls, but by Kadmir pretending to have rescued the girls from Toyo, they draw Alex close. They take him hostage and bargain for no retaliation against any of the domes in return for Alex and the girls' freedom."

"I never realized the extent of devious thought you must have practiced in your former position, Tatia, to have worked to capture people like this. It's a wonder that you survived at all," Renée said in amazement.

"Every one of them is a Downing, some smaller, some bigger," Tatia said sadly.

"So?" Alex said, prompting his previous question.

"We go in as prepared as we can be," Tatia replied.

* * *

Tatia's definition of total preparation involved a traveler filled from bow to stern with Harakens. She selected those with the best shooter qualifications and armed them with stun guns and four with plasma rifles.

"We can't exit the traveler wearing environment suits," Tatia told the troops, who were using the bay to prepare. "Those with rifles exit last, and the rifles are only to be used below surface and never aimed upward. So, please, no holing the domes. It wouldn't make for much of a rescue."

Circling back to the cabin reserved for Alex and Renée, Tatia wasn't prepared to find her principals outfitted in matte back, skin suits. The material hugged every inch of their bodies, and Tatia spared a moment to admire the musculature and build of her president.

Tatia glanced at Renée, who was strapping a stun gun on her upper thigh. She said, "Um, Ser —" But before Tatia could complete her comment, Renée drew her weapon, fired it at a wall, and returned it to its holster in the blink of an eye. Tatia could barely catch the wink of the weapon's telltale that indicated it had been fired.

"Méridien reflexes," Renée said simply and fixed her stare on Tatia. "Admiral, you will need to fill our traveler with only people prepared to fight, and do not expect me, under any circumstances, to stand aside while others protect my own."

Tatia threw an imploring look at Alex, who replied, "Don't look at me. I know when not to argue." She watched Alex strap a second weapon on his left thigh. "Are you telling me that you can shoot with either hand?" Tatia asked with incredulity.

Alex broke out in laughter. "No, I'm probably only half as good as your worst trooper. So, I figured I would need twice as many shots."

Tatia left the cabin, annoyed at the impending headache of trying to keep both of her principals safe. *Why did I think this would ever get any easier? I love the two of them, but stunning both of them might make my life simpler,* Tatia thought, and then she paused in the corridor, shook her head, and broke into a smile. "But then life would be so dull," she said to the empty corridor.

* * *

On their way to visit with Alex and Renée, Drake and Jaya passed Tatia in the corridor and were a little confused by the admiral's wide smile in the face of the dire meeting to come. When they entered the Haraken president's cabin, Drake took in the stun guns strapped to thighs, and said, "It doesn't look like a diplomatic solution is at the forefront of your mind, Alex."

"Talk to my admiral, Will," Alex replied. "Your ex-TSF major, who has more criminal experience than you and me put together, has made these recommendations."

"And, as president, you could choose not to follow her advice," Drake challenged.

Jaya winced, and Renée had to bite her tongue to keep from speaking.

"Is that how you do it, Will? Surround yourself with good people, but don't take their advice?" Alex shot back. "Keeping in contact with Maria, Will?" Alex asked.

Drake declined to respond to the barb. Instead, he glared angrily at Alex, his jaw locked tight.

"It's not my way, Will," Alex said. "I might not be a good listener, but, at least, I try. It seems the trickiest part of leading … sounds like something you need to work on. Now, if you'll excuse us, I have three young girls to retrieve, and time is growing short."

After Drake and Jaya left, Alex returned to practicing. Staring straight ahead, he drew both stun guns simultaneously, holding his arms about 90 degrees apart, and then returned the weapons. Alex continued to repeat the actions as he made minor adjustments.

"Why didn't you wish to tell Tatia what you've been doing?" Renée asked.

"Tatia is proud of her prowess in the martial arts, weaponry, tactics, understanding the criminal mind, and all things TSF. The last thing I want to do is supplant some of that pride."

"So exactly what have you been doing with the two weapons?"

"I've designed a targeting app and duplicated it, allowing each implant independent control over an arm. If I can see two assailants in my vision, even peripherally, each implant will track, target, and fire with its assigned arm."

"Is it working?"

"Yes, actually, much better than I expected."

Renée studied Alex's face. She walked over to him, taking his face in her hands, always amazed that Alex would allow his head to be so easily turned by her most delicate touch. "You're concerned what others may think, not just Tatia."

"I see the looks on people's faces when my implant power is exposed. It's fear."

"Perhaps it's fear from those who don't know you or from our opponents ... from our people, it's awe."

"I'm not so sure, Renée. I only thought of the second implant as a way to help me with my computing power and the diversification of operations. I had no idea of the doors that two implants would open."

"And you should have no doubts now, my love. I, for one, accept you as you are, implants and all." Renée interlaced her fingers behind Alex's neck and kissed him gently. When Alex responded with hesitation, Renée kissed him again and again, until Alex focused on her eyes. "It's in your nature, my love, to create, to experiment. You do so with everything you touch. We expect it of you. Never fear where it takes you. Now come ... we have a half-hour yet, and practicing with this weapon has awakened my desire for some of your attentions. Feel free to leave your weapons on," Renée said, grinning and pulling Alex toward the sleeping quarters.

* * *

Tatia stood at the bottom of the traveler's steps. Julien, the twins, and her troopers were aboard. All was ready for departure, except for two passengers, but it wasn't like Tatia felt it appropriate to prompt her president and his partner.

Moments later, the bayside airlock hatch opened, and Tatia watched Renée saunter across the bay, smiling at her, and scamper up the traveler's steps. Alex strolled nonchalantly but wore an unabashed grin.

"Nothing like a happy man about to face death," Tatia quipped to Alex.

"Only one life to live, Tatia, and just aren't we making the most of it!" Alex replied and bounded up the steps.

"That we sure are," Tatia mumbled to herself.

The bay was decompressed and the traveler launched — destination Udrides and the recovery of three Haraken girls.

23

Wedged overhead above the corridor's piping, Miranda occupied herself with idle calculations for hours until she chose to focus on one subject, her interactions with Z through his innumerable messages. Usually, her preoccupation with the president's emergencies offered limited time to be introspective and consider perhaps the most unusual element of her existence — the gaps in her memories.

Z's messages always signaled the beginning of a new period of wakening. They updated her on existing conditions, usually troubles that her people faced, and requested her help. Miranda loved that — never ordered to help, always asked. She had access to all of Z's memories. At least, she considered they were all of his memories, never suspecting the details that Z edited out.

Where do I go? Miranda asked herself. *Do I sleep? Am I awakened only in times of need? Why do I not have control of the choice?*

The questions might have haunted Miranda for hours more, but an app signaled the movement of a locator beacon, and she connected to the vid cams to review their recordings. Two men and a woman in Toyo's dark red service uniforms were loading containers of the tagged supplies onto a pallet. She waited until they left the supply area when the vid cams lost sight of them before she eased down from her perch.

Unwinding her wrap from around her neck where it was tucked to prevent it from dangling down in view of passersby, Miranda smoothed it into place. Her persona shifted hierarchical algorithms, and her body swayed provocatively as she walked down the corridor.

Following the signal, Miranda angled toward the service personnel, who navigated a utility corridor in the main dome with their pallet. She caught up with them when they accessed the nearest lift to the lower levels. Miranda stopped to check her footwear, displaying her shapely leg and attracting the attention of one of the men and the blonde-haired woman. *A point to note,* Miranda thought.

Miranda waited until the lift door closed and the car began moving before she tapped the call button, which lit, responding to her purloined implant. When the car returned, Miranda quickly slipped inside. She spotted the lift's tiny controller box mounted near the door. It had a small keypad for manual entry. *How ancient,* Miranda thought.

"Please select a floor," an automated voice said.

Miranda's crystal mind raced through her options. She seized on an implant recording Deirdre made of her initial interaction with Jameson. Imitating the security officer's voice, Miranda said, "The prior floor, please."

"Dome 4, level 7," the voice intoned and the display lit with D4-7.

Imagine that, a hidden dome. I suppose if I was a paranoid, criminal mastermind, I'd bury my most wicked achievements in the lowest level of my establishment too, Miranda thought.

The lift dropped quickly. Miranda estimated a distance of over 120 meters. When the car stopped and the door opened, the three service personnel, with their pallet, were a mere 6 meters in front of her. They had stopped to talk to men in Toyo's security services. When all eyes swiveled her way, Miranda adopted a brilliant smile, saying, "Oh, hello."

"You boys move on," the woman beside the pallet said. "I've got this."

The four men shared grins, and they and the pallet moved down the corridor.

"Lost, fem?" the blonde asked, approaching Miranda. "Maybe I can service your needs?" Her smile was as brilliant as that Miranda had offered, and her eyes gleamed. What didn't occur to the woman was how Miranda accessed the lift to the domes' lowest levels, but those were the charms of Miranda, which could entice both woman and man.

Miranda waited until the last moment to step out of the lift car, which coincided with the men and the pallet turning a corner in the corridor. "I'm sure you can help me, dear. I do appreciate an attentive woman."

"Why don't you and I —" the woman managed to say before Miranda was on her, clamping one hand over her mouth and the other cutting off the blood flow in her neck. The blonde struggled ever so briefly, wondering how the raven-haired woman achieved her incredible strength, before she lost consciousness.

Miranda slung the woman over her shoulder and located a utility room, but the door was locked. To her, it was odd that Jameson's implant didn't allow access. She filed that note away as she popped the lock off, slid the door aside, and deposited the blonde on the floor. Miranda swept her wrap aside and pulled a small soporific injector from a little med-kit strapped high on her inner thigh. After administering the sleeping agent to the woman, she closed the door and inserted the lock into place.

"Sleep tight, dear," Miranda murmured, as she pursued the locator beacons. The signals were barely detectable and weakening with every passing moment. She hurried around the corner and within 10 meters the corridor came to a tee. Testing signal strength in each direction, Miranda turned right, pleased that within a few meters the signals regained strength.

That pleasant feeling ended when two burly, New Terran security officers walked around a corner directly into her path. Unable to stop in time, Miranda knocked one of the officers on his rear end, his mouth formed an "oh," as he expressed surprise at being bowled over by a woman half his size.

"Oh, my goodness! How clumsy of me," Miranda said, trying to play on her femininity.

The other man grabbed Miranda's wrist and tried to twist it behind her back, asking, "How did you get down here? Did you come down with someone?"

"Oh, dear," Miranda said in dismay, realizing her wiles would get her nowhere with these two. Her open palm shot out, smacking the guard's head into the wall. Eyes rolling up in his head, the guard slunk to the floor.

"Please!" the guard on the floor pleaded. "I'll do what you want."

"How considerate of you, dear. Pick up your partner. I need a storage location for the two of you."

The man stumbled to his feet, hoisted his companion up by the underarms, and dragged him back down the corridor from whence they came. "In here," he said. He had reached a door, which slid aside when he tapped a button on the wall with his elbow.

Miranda followed the men into the room. Inside were five more individuals wearing the uniforms of Toyo's security personnel. The guard, who had pleaded for his safety, laid his companion down and smirked at Miranda.

"How very clever of you, dear," she said, smacking the door button to seal the room. Frowns crossed the faces of every man and woman, including the guard with the smirk.

A few moments later, the guard room door opened and Miranda peeked out. Seeing no one, she straightened her wrap, thinking, *Thank goodness for Haraken fabric.*

The guards had drawn knives, the favored weapons of Toyo's people it seemed, and attacked Miranda from all sides. She ended the fierce fight as swiftly as she could in an effort to silence the guards before an alarm could be sounded. Miranda's lament was that she was not sure every guard would survive their injuries. To make matters worse, she didn't carry enough soporific to knock out seven people, which meant time was counting down before her people's charade was discovered.

Tracking the beacons again, Miranda hurried down corridors and corners until there, in front of her, were a pair of gleaming metal doors with window inserts. She eased along the wall, intending to stay out of sight of those inside. Peeking through one of the windows, she saw an anteroom with open cabinets that held containment suits and masks. On the other side of the small room was an identical pair of metal doors. *The lab,* Miranda thought, smiling.

Miranda quickly backtracked, managing not to encounter anyone else until she stepped out of the lift car into the central corridor of the main dome, where an aging patron and a young fem were waiting for the lift. "Have fun," Miranda said in a cheery voice, as she eased passed them. It was sad, the SADE thought, that a woman as young as the one she just saw could have eyes that were aged far past her years.

While Miranda made her way back to the suite, she devised plans, discarding one after the other, until settling on one with the greatest probability of success. Entering the suite, Miranda greeted the two commanders and repaired to the bathroom where she stripped off her bloody and soiled wrap, wiped a few drops of blood off her synth-skin, and fixed her hair. She removed the small med-kit from the inside of her thigh with its empty soporific charges and tossed it on top of the discarded wrap.

Joining the commanders in the bedroom, Miranda selected another wrap and covered herself. "That's better," she said, as she arranged the colorful garment. "I've located the lab, but I was discovered. The last group was only disabled when I ran out of soporific injections. Time is against us. Soon the guards who are unconscious will awaken and sound the alarm. We want to be in possession of the lab by then."

"Take possession of the lab?" Deirdre asked. "What good does that do us, if the alarm is sounded?"

"Patience, dear. This is where you listen and do as I say. Understanding will come later."

Deirdre and Svetlana heard the shift in Miranda's tone and cadence as Z's tactical mien seeped through her persona.

"We are splitting our forces," Miranda continued. "Commander Canaan, I will send the majority of our people after you. Retreat to the traveler. You will contact the president aboard the *Tanaka* and request reinforcements. While we can use more people, it's imperative we receive stun guns for those who are here now. Toyo's security forces have a nasty habit of pulling knives in close combat."

"Commander Valenko, you and I will take a few of our people and take possession of the lab." Miranda nodded approval at the fierce grin on Svetlana's face.

"Commander Canaan, here is how to reach the lab," Miranda said, and sent vids of her accessing the lift, the dome and floor number, and her path through the corridors, editing out her contact with personnel. "When help arrives, arm our people and come for us."

"The domes are three layers deep," Deirdre said, taken aback by the vids Miranda sent.

"Surprising, yes?" Miranda replied.

"You will need this," Miranda said, handing over Jameson's implant. "We'll get another. Subtlety and subterfuge are no longer necessary. Speed is of the essence. Go now, Commander."

Deirdre nodded, left the suite, and hurried as quickly as decorum would allow toward the landing bay.

"What about Jameson?" Svetlana asked.

"Leave him to sleep," Miranda said. As Svetlana and she left the suite, Miranda sent signals to the Harakens, assigning them to join either Deirdre or Svetlana. The latter group was to meet near the lift closest to the landing bay in the main dome, which Miranda marked in her communication.

* * *

Deirdre was the first one to the landing bay entrance and waited while her people joined her. She had most of the Harakens with her, when several bay personnel came past them. Deirdre announced in a loud voice to the assembled Harakens, "I don't run the company, Sers. Your president just asked if we could return you to Kephron early. It seems he needs you."

The Harakens dutifully grumbled, and the bay personnel gave Deirdre sympathetic looks as they passed. When the implant count of those Miranda assigned to Deirdre matched those present, she requested access to their traveler.

"Boarding and lifting, ma'am?" the bay controller asked.

"Boarding only, Ser. We are still waiting for a few obstinate individuals."

"Miners," the controller said with disgust.

"They are quaint, Ser, I must admit," Deirdre agreed. When she received word that the bay was cleared for access, she announced loudly that the people were to board and the group trooped across the bay to the traveler, sullen and angry. Once everyone was inside, the hatch was sealed to allow other shuttle flights to come and go while they waited.

Connecting to the traveler's controller, Deirdre signaled the *Tanaka*. She connected with Willem, and the SADE directed the comm to the captain.

<Captain Shimada, here, Commander,> Reiko sent.

<The president?> Deirdre asked.

<He left for Udrides to recover the girls, Commander.>

<Who's in authority, Captain?>

<One moment, Commander,> Reiko replied. She linked Eric Stroheim into the comm, and he requested Reiko remain in conference.

<Eric, we've found the lab. Unfortunately, we've been discovered. Miranda, Svetlana, and some of the crew have gone to take over the lab and secure it for us. The rest of us are here in the traveler. We need weapons and some backup.>

<The president has taken a full load of the *Tanaka's* crew with him to Udrides,> Eric replied. <He's not risking fortune with the likes of Azul Kadmir.>

<Nor should he. Even if you can't spare many crew, we desperately need stun guns for our people, who are already here.>

<Hold one moment, Commander, Captain,> Eric sent. He muted his end of the comm and hurried down the corridor to the New Terran president's cabin. Remembering to knock instead of signal, Eric urged Drake and Jaya to the bridge. Once there, Eric opened the comm and switched it to the *Tanaka's* bridge speakers.

"Commander Canaan, you're on bridge speakers with President Drake, Minister Jaya, Captain Shimada, and me. I've relayed the pertinent points of your call to President Drake."

"Commander, I would like to ensure that I understand for myself what you're telling Eric," Drake said. "During your visit to the pleasure domes of Jolares, you've discovered that Peto Toyo has been using his establishment to hide an illegal drug-manufacturing lab?"

Deirdre thought for a moment that something was lost in translation between Eric and Drake until she remembered Alex saying that they had to be careful since they weren't operating with New Terra's approval. <That's correct, President Drake. In searching for our kidnapped girls, we

uncovered a significant amount of drug-manufacturing compounds that piqued our curiosity. We followed a transfer of those supplies to a lab located in Peto Toyo's fourth dome.>

"Fourth dome!" Jaya exclaimed. "I knew it."

<It's a fourth dome, buried below all three, Ser President. Miranda and Commander Valenko deemed it critical to secure the lab, preventing the destruction of any evidence, but they are unarmed,> Deirdre sent. She sincerely hoped she was playing this right.

"What assistance do you need to secure the evidence, Commander?" Drake asked.

"Official sanction, for one," Eric interjected.

Drake looked at Jaya, who was nodding earnestly. "Commander, I'm officially asking for Haraken's help in securing the evidence of any illegal drug manufacturing. Any and all implant documentation will be greatly appreciated as well. Anything else, Commander?"

<Yes, President Drake. The domes' security personnel are armed with stun guns and knives. We need to be equally fortified to maintain control over the evidence,> Deirdre replied.

"Then you have my permission as New Terra's president to use whatever force is necessary to secure that evidence, Commander."

<Thank you, Ser President. We'll do our best to aid your government in documenting this discovery,> Deirdre said. *If this is a taste of the world of politics that Alex inhabits, I want nothing to do with it,* Deirdre thought.

<Help is on the way, Commander,> Eric sent privately. His first thought was for Franz Cohen, but he was loath to strip the *Tanaka* of its fighter commander, unless necessary. There were too many unresolved elements left to play out. He smiled, as he realized he had a superb alternate. Ellie Thompson, who had piloted Alex's traveler from the *Rêveur* to the *Tanaka*, was still aboard and vexed about being left out of the trip to Udrides.

But Eric thought he understood Alex's reasoning. With Renée, Tatia, Julien, and the twins accompanying him, there was already too much precious cargo at risk. *But it appears that many more of our people will be required to enter this fray before it ends, Alex,* Eric thought, before he commed Ellie.

* * *

The three Haraken men — Brace, Tyree, and Oren — requested by Miranda met the SADE and Svetlana near the lift closest to the landing bay, on the main dome's concourse level. The group arranged themselves so that Miranda could watch those approaching the lift, and the men played the part of trying to interest the two women in some entertainment.

Svetlana mentally marked time from Miranda's contact with the security personnel in the guard room. In her estimation, they would be the first to wake, and once the alarm was sounded, the Harakens' opportunity to reach the lab before it was defended by security forces would disappear and so might the evidence and the chemist. A wall of Toyo's stun gun–armed personnel wouldn't be penetrated by a SADE and four Harakens without weapons.

Tense as Svetlana was, she couldn't help but admire the way Miranda chatted and teased their three male companions. The SADE was effortlessly keeping the three men laughing, and they were teasing her in return.

<This one,> Miranda abruptly sent to her people, and the men parted, as she stepped between them toward a middle-aged man, wearing a security uniform with epaulettes. He had the look of a senior employee, who might carry the clearance necessary to reach the lowest level of dome four.

As the lift car door opened, Yance Deere stepped inside only to be shoved to the back of the car by a beautiful woman. "What?" he yelped, as he eyed the woman's four companions.

"Do you have clearance for the lowest level of the fourth dome?" Miranda asked.

"Fourth dome?" Deere repeated. "There's no fourth dome."

"We'll see," Miranda said, approaching the controller box and typing D4-7 into the keypad. When the car began moving, she said, "He has the clearance we need, and he's a terrible liar."

"We don't like liars, Ser," Svetlana said, brandishing a knife taken off Jameson against Deere's cheek. "Lie to us again and I'll give you another smile."

<Oh, what an intimidating line,> Miranda sent to Svetlana. <I do hope you won't mind my borrowing it in the future.>

Svetlana grinned at Miranda, as the car decelerated and came to a halt. Before the door slid open, she unsnapped Deere's holster, snatched his weapon, and tossed it to Brace.

Miranda led the way out of the car and down the first corridor with Brace beside her. Svetlana followed, and Tyree and Oren brought up the rear with Deere between them.

In a moment of déjà vu and at the same corner where Miranda previously ran into the two guards, the smirking one, wearing heavy bruises from his last interaction with the SADE, walked around the corner in front of them.

"You," the guard shouted.

Both Brace and Toyo's man had their stun guns in hand, so the weapons were discharged simultaneously — Brace at their adversary and the guard at Miranda, but both men slid unconscious to the floor. Brace had leaned in front of Miranda, his substantial body taking the stun gun blast.

Svetlana picked up both weapons, kept one, and tossed the other to Tyree.

"We're close to the lab. Bring Brace with us," Miranda ordered and kept going.

Tyree motioned Deere to help Oren carry Brace, but the older and out-of-shape security officer struggled to lift his half. Tyree shoved him aside and the two Harakens carried their companion, while Deere walked in front of them with Tyree's stun gun pointed at his back.

Slipping into the lab's anteroom, Miranda ordered everyone to don suits and masks. "Not you," Miranda said pointing to Deere. "You'll wait here for us." Then she nodded at Svetlana, who promptly stunned the man and cushioned his fall to the floor, leaving him lying beside Brace.

With the suits fashioned for New Terrans, Svetlana grabbed a roll of fabric cord, sliced off 2 meters and wound it around her middle to cinch the suit to her waist. Holding out her balloon-shaped arms, she quipped, "This does nothing for my image."

"We must all make sacrifices, dear. Now, let us proceed to claim this territory as our own," Miranda said, as she activated the inner doors of the lab.

A suited and masked New Terran, inside the lab, swiveled to stare at Miranda. "Stop, woman! Are you crazy? It's dangerous in here without safety gear! Get out."

"Feminine, yes; woman, no," Miranda replied enigmatically. "Where's your senior chemist?"

"I said, out of here," the suited figure repeated and shoved on Miranda's shoulders. His eyes widened when he failed to move her.

"I wish you people would progress your society to the point where you acquire manners," Miranda retorted. "I asked for your lead chemist. Either comply or I'll strip off your mask and stick your face in a pile of this despicable powder you're making."

"Stratford's not here," the man stammered, taking a step back from Miranda. Before he could take another, Miranda was on him.

"Where is Stratford, dear?" Miranda asked sweetly, while her metal-alloy fingers delicately held the man's windpipe.

"With his family," the chemist choked out. "That's how Toyo controls us. He's brought all our families here to the domes."

"I see," Miranda said, releasing the man. "And you decided that it was a fair trade to protect your family in exchange for poisoning hundreds if not thousands of children of other families?"

"What could we do?" the suited figure asked, holding out his hands to Miranda.

"Resist," Miranda said simply. "Men like Toyo seek to bend people to his will. That feeds his power, which spreads the disease. Refuse to cooperate and Toyo's power wanes ... but enough of this life lesson. Can you take my people to Stratford?"

"Yes, but my shift isn't over yet. My children will be punished if I leave early."

"Foolish man," Miranda said, laughing. "This lab is finished. These domes are finished. You and your frightened colleagues were coerced into making Toyo's drugs, and they made their way to Haraken. So, we're here to end your ugly endeavor."

"Harakens," the man whispered.

<Commander Valenko,> Miranda sent, <Take this excuse for a human and secure the lead chemist and his family. Question him carefully. We must know if this Stratford is the inventor of the hallucinogenic. Take Tyree, Oren, and the weapons. Don't come back this way if it might mean losing possession of Stratford. I can find you. Understood?>

<Copy, my lady,> Svetlana said, with a grin and a tip of two fingers to her brow.

"Go with her," Miranda said to the senior chemist, shoving him bodily at Svetlana.

Miranda watched to ensure her people cleared the anteroom, after they shucked off their suits and masks and threw them into a recycling chute. The last she saw of them, the chemist was pointing the way back down the corridor.

The SADE turned to face the group of suited and masked men and women who stood staring wide-eyed at her. "Who would love to see tomorrow?" Miranda asked, in a pleasant voice, and watched as everyone raised their hands, even if only partially. "That's the spirit. Okay, people, shut down all active processes. I don't want heat or energy flowing in this lab. Clean up all active products and secure them."

When no one moved, Miranda clapped her hands together, making a sound like lightning cracking, and the New Terrans scattered, the chemists shouting orders to the technicians. While they worked, Miranda returned to the outer doors and carefully disabled the door's activator so that she could easily repair it.

Returning to the lab, Miranda selected an empty preparation table and snapped off its square metal legs. More than one intake of breath from the lab personnel accompanied Miranda's actions. Squatting down, she hammered one end of each leg flat. As Miranda carried her makeshift wedges back to the anteroom, she heard the whispers of "SADE." It made her smile. *Now, maybe you'll jump when I give you an order,* Miranda thought.

Taking the first two wedges, Miranda jammed them into the tops of the outer two metal doors. Before she repeated her efforts on the inner two doors of the anteroom, she dressed Brace in a suit and mask and carried him over her shoulder inside the lab, laying him down in a corner. When she turned around, the chemists and technicians were standing and waiting for her.

"Everything is prepared as you requested, ma'am," a figure said.

"And you are?"

"Stan, ma'am, I'm the shift supervisor."

Miranda's tongue ran out briefly, and her analysis confirmed the lab vents had cleared any residual product. "The air is clear, dears. After you wipe down the surfaces and dispose of that material, it will be safe for you to remove your suits and masks, people. We might be here for a while."

"Pardon me, ma'am," said Stan, "but even at parts per million, this drug is dangerous."

"We're well aware of the insidious nature of what you fashion here, New Terran," Miranda said, eyeing the supervisor, and he winced from the accusation. "I test at two figures higher than that, human, and I tell you that the air is cleared for breathing," Miranda replied, emphasizing her nature.

Stan stood undecided, but most of his people broke ranks and grabbed scrubbers and hoses to clean the tables, floors, and equipment. Soon after, Stan joined them rather than being the sole focus of the Haraken SADE.

24

After receiving Lisa Sparing's warning of his impending betrayal, Toyo was torn between loading every shuttle he possessed to go after Kadmir and remaining in place, wondering what his adversaries intended as their true end game. He envisioned landing at Kadmir's domes, while O'Brien's men took over his establishment, leaving him stuck aboard shuttles and isolated to a pair of freighters.

In the end, and despite not knowing how the forces were arrayed against him, it was Toyo's decision to attack Kadmir with a single shuttle. The strategy left his domes defended, and while accompanied by the experienced veterans, it gave him the best chance of taking on Kadmir's security forces. Armed with the new stunners, his people would be a difficult force to repel.

Toyo's young pilot, with his enthusiastic mannerisms, was a charmer and had the reservationist and the bay landing controller eating out of his hands. It cleared the biggest hurdle, gaining entrance to Kadmir's landing bay.

Toyo saw three possible outcomes to his chosen course of action. He could kill Kadmir and claim he was rescuing the girls or, just as easy, if he located the girls first, he could take them, clear out, and claim the same thing. The last possibility was that he would be killed, in which case, his troubles would be over.

The shuttle eased into the bay, and lights on the deck guided the ship to its assigned position. The pilot glanced at Toyo for instructions.

"Land where you're directed, pilot. It's not a bad place, and no need to show our hand yet," Toyo said.

After the shuttle touched down, Toyo ordered his people to line up at the hatch with weapons drawn. Then he ordered the pilot to comm bay control that the shuttle's ramp extenders weren't responding. It was a common problem with older shuttles, maintenance not being a priority for most moon-based shuttles.

The bay controller sent a tech party of five over with a small repair vehicle. They hooked a chain from the vehicle to the tongue of the ramp to pull it from under the shuttle's belly.

The moment the pilot reported the ramp fully extended, Toyo yelled, "Now." The hatch slid open, and the first of Toyo's people out on the ramp promptly shot the five crew. Flooding out of the shuttle, Toyo's red-uniformed, security personnel cut a swath through the bay.

Kadmir's brown-and-gold uniformed, security personnel fought back, but they were quickly overwhelmed. For every one of Toyo's people they stunned, three of their number went down. The landing bay controller managed to sound the alarm that a shuttle full of intruders had landed in the bay before three of Toyo's people crashed through his door. He stunned a single, red uniform before the invaders killed him.

Toyo was soon at the forefront of his people's charge across the bay. He lived for moments like this — the rush of open warfare. It was how his reputation was made. Toyo was despised even as a teenager for his refusal to deal, to compromise. He made one offer to his enemies and only one offer. Those who didn't fall in line could expect only one response — a fight for their life, which resulted in casualty after casualty until no one bothered to offer him resistance.

Toyo's security force watched their leader come upon the first brown uniform, who struggled on the deck. The man's arm, from shoulder to hand, was numbed by stunner fire. Toyo paused for a moment and bent to slice the man's neck open with the heavy blade he carried in his left hand. His security forces took it as a demonstration of what their leader expected of them.

In the early moments of the firefight, Toyo's people held the initiative and soon cleared the bay of security and service personnel, men and women. When they gained the wide corridor that led from the bay to the main dome, their progress bogged down. The straight corridor offered no hiding place for the attackers, and Kadmir's security forces had grabbed furniture from the passenger waiting area, tilting the pieces on their sides, and formed a makeshift barrier.

His forces stymied, Toyo whistled shrilly and a heavyset, hatch-faced fighter, carrying a plasma rifle, hurried up to Toyo's position.

"Be careful with that thing, Lenny. Punch through the furniture for a strike. And don't go mad with it. One shot only."

"Sure, Boss, one shot only," Lenny replied, hoisting his plasma rifle. There was no more dangerous weapon to fire in a dome that faced vacuum, which is why Toyo ordered that only one plasma rifle should be brought by his crew.

Next to Toyo, Lydia grinned in anticipation, and Toyo returned it, his eyes wild with excitement.

Sighting on the largest pile of furniture, which concealed four of Kadmir's people, and dialing his weapon to its lowest setting, Lenny fired a single shot. The twin, twisting bursts of energy sizzled through the air and burned a 1-meter hole through the furniture barricade and two brown uniforms. Its energy was absorbed 50 meters later by a section of wall and a dense pile of crates stacked in the utility room beyond.

The plasma fire panicked the defenders, who abandoned their positions and retreated while returning fire. But when Toyo and Lydia charged at them, howling like the demented, the brown uniforms lost all pretense of acting as defenders and ran full tilt down the corridor toward the first bend, which marked the entrance to the main concourse. Most of them were shot in the back by Toyo and Lydia before they could reach safety.

* * *

When the intruder warning hit the comms, Kadmir raced to the nearest guard center and found his security chief, Omi Yakiro, accessing the security cams of the main dome and landing bay.

"How many, Chief?" Kadmir asked.

"A single NR-shuttle type. It was fully loaded."

"Where are they, and how are we doing?"

"Not well, Sir. Toyo and some equally crazy woman are leading the charge, and they're scaring our people to death. We had a good barricade in the corridor leading to the landing bay until one of Toyo's people fired a plasma rifle at it."

"He what?" Kadmir said, shocked.

"Afraid so, Sir. Craze ... it's an apt nickname. Right now, we're holding about 30 meters, landing bay side, from the green lift. I'm bringing security personnel up from the lower domes as fast as we can load the car, and every lift that descends is packed full of patrons and our service people."

"Good work, Chief. Keep on it. I want enough security in the main dome to hold him and keep both lifts in our control, but don't commit all our forces."

"Afraid the crazy man might use that plasma rifle again?

"Exactly. If Toyo thinks he's losing, he'll get desperate. No telling what he'll do then. I don't want to put any more of our people in harm's way than can be helped. Let me know when the main dome is cleared of civilians, Chief. Can we bring a shuttle down from the freighter station and get forces in behind Toyo?"

"I've already checked, Sir. The bay controller is dead. In fact, everyone in the bay appears dead."

"You mean stunned," Kadmir corrected.

"No, Sir ... dead. Infrared cams show the bodies cooling. I can't tell what caused some of the deaths, but I did witness some of Toyo's people cutting the throats of our people who were downed and struggling."

"Monsters," Kadmir murmured. "But they took some prisoners, didn't they ... I mean, especially our service personnel?"

"No prisoners, Sir, I'm sorry to say. Toyo's people killed everyone."

Kadmir swore under his breath. His plan to allow the Harakens to take care of Toyo, neat and clean, leaving Toyo's domes ripe for takeover by O'Brien and him had just blown up in his face. Suddenly, it hit Kadmir what he had forgotten.

"Chief, I need a priority exit to the main dome via the blue lift, and I need some of your best men. Now!" Kadmir yelled, as he raced out of the security office for the blue lift, the one farthest from the landing bay, where he was met by a group of security personnel.

The lift car, controlled by the security chief, stopped on Kadmir's level, and he hurried a group of civilians off the lift with an apology, telling them to wait here until security could move them on. Kadmir urged his people to pile into the car, and he selected the main concourse for the lift's destination.

"We have three priority civilians to move, people," Kadmir announced. "They are in a suite off the main concourse, not far from the green lift."

"Are we still holding that lift?" the senior officer asked, worried that they were walking into a fight with Toyo's people.

"The chief assured me that we are, and we're adding more security personnel to that location with every lift of the car. Under no circumstances must we let anything happen to these three young women."

"So the rumors are true, Sir? One of these women is Racine's sister?" a security officer asked. She was a middle-aged woman with a hard look.

"Yes, these girls were kidnapped by Toyo's people, and we rescued them," Kadmir explained, trying to keep the story going.

"We rescued them, Sir?" the senior officer asked, dubiously.

"It's complicated. Suffice it to say, Toyo thought he was in on a plan to take the blame off his shoulders for the kidnapping. Somehow he discovered that wasn't the plan, and he's come here as a final maneuver. To accomplish what, I don't know, but if he gets the girls back, he can point the Harakens at us."

Nothing Kadmir said to the security personnel hit home as hard as his last statement. Taking on Toyo's people to rescue three civilians was asking a great deal of them, but rescuing three Harakens to keep Alex Racine off their necks was a different matter entirely. Immediately, every officer pulled and checked their weapon, keeping their stun guns by their sides.

Exiting the car, it was relatively quiet, except for the anxious passengers awaiting transport below the surface. Kadmir nodded to the security officer, who had the job of keeping control of the loading and unloading of the lift. "When I comm you that I'm headed back this way," Kadmir said to the officer, "hold the car for us. We have priority civilians."

"Understood, Sir," the officer said, and loaded the next batch of civilians onto the car, happy to see his girlfriend, who tended bar, in the group. She brushed her fingers against the back of his hand as she passed.

* * *

Christie, Amelia, and Eloise could hear the panic outside their suite — people running and screaming, security officers shouting orders, and then suddenly quiet.

"What do you think is happening?" Eloise asked, not bothering to use her implant comm.

"Haven't a clue," Christie replied. "But if I had to guess, I would say Kadmir's establishment is under attack."

"Why under attack? Why couldn't it be a dome accident?" Eloise asked.

The other two girls stared at Eloise with concern. Her fear was eating into her self-control.

Amelia sat beside Eloise on the bed. She took her friend's hand and said, gently, "If the dome had an accident, the decompression would have triggered the safety doors to slam shut, and we wouldn't have heard people running and screaming.

"What if the safety doors didn't close, or what if they don't have safety doors?" Eloise asked.

"Then we wouldn't be having this conversation," Amelia said, leaning over to kiss Eloise on the temple.

"I don't like the quiet," Christie said, pulling her ear away from the door. "It's like the lull before the storm strikes."

"Could this be your brother?" Amelia asked.

Christie looked at Amelia for a moment, surprised the question was being asked. "Alex took over an entire space station in a foreign system without firing a shot or injuring one individual. You think he would come to a bunch of measly domes and start a panic while trying to recover us?"

"Probably not," Amelia agreed. "But if it's another force that's attacking, who is it?"

"Toyo," both Christie and Amelia suddenly said together.

"Black space," Christie swore, "We have to get out of here. We can't get taken by that twisted job."

"You think they're fighting over us?" Amelia asked.

"I do," Christie said. "Now, find something to help me break this door lock."

Christie and Amelia couldn't find a tool to wedge the lock so they decided on brute force. They picked up one of the heavier chairs and positioned themselves a few meters back from the door. Counting down from five, they reached two when they heard the lock click and the door slid open.

"Come on, you three," Kadmir said. "We have to move you to safety."

"Toyo?" Christie asked, as Amelia and she dropped the chair and dragged Eloise off the bed.

"Very astute of you, young lady. I wouldn't recommend his hospitality over mine," Kadmir said, as the girls hurried past him into the corridor, where security ushered them along.

"Where are we going?" Amelia asked.

"We're headed below surface," Kadmir replied, running beside her. "Our uninvited guest has taken to firing a plasma rifle to gain territory."

<Plasma rifle,> Eloise sent. Her thoughts were roiling, and Christie and Amelia moved to bracket her and keep her moving.

"Is she okay?" Kadmir asked Christie, his concern evident.

"Worried you might be returning damaged goods to my brother, Kadmir?" Christie shot back.

"If Toyo has his way, I wouldn't give two credits for your chances of being returned to your brother, and I would thank you to keep that in mind when you address me." After his retort, Kadmir moved to the head of the group.

<Christie, brain first, mouth second,> Amelia sent privately.

Christie had the grace to nod her head in agreement to Amelia.

Kadmir led the group to the blue lift, which was surrounded with civilians anxious to get on the next available car. The security officers cleared the way through the crowd, amidst grumbling and complaints, and the girls ducked their heads in embarrassment.

The lift barely accommodated the group, forcing everyone to squeeze onto the car. Christie made sure that she was close to the controller box when Kadmir selected the level even though it required she squeeze between two male security officers, who had no problem with an attractive young woman crushing against them.

When Kadmir typed into the controller's keypad "D4-5," Christie relayed the information to her friends.

<Four domes?> Amelia questioned privately.

<Seems like it,> Christie sent back. <I think we should be prepared to make our own way. I don't want to be sitting in some suite or guard room, if Toyo's people make it to this lower dome.>

<No, Christie,> Eloise objected <I think we should stay where Kadmir's people can protect us.>

<I'm sorry, Eloise,> Christie replied. <At this point, I think it's about survival, and I don't trust either of these criminals to have our best interests at heart. Both of these men are fighting over us, so that the loser takes the blame from my brother, and neither can afford to be the loser.>

<I'm sorry too, Eloise,> Amelia sent. <I have to agree with Christie. As much as I would like to sit in a safe place and hope for rescue, I think it would be a mistake to do so. We need to take charge of our fortune.>

The car reached the selected level, and the group piled out. Eloise had yet to reply to her friends.

"You two, take our guests to suite 5M. One of you stays with them at all times," Kadmir ordered. "The rest of you, we're headed back to the main concourse."

As the girls followed the two security officers, Eloise sent, <I know I've been letting my fears get the best of me. It was terribly intriguing to play our games when we always knew our people surrounded us and could protect us. I never imagined how horrible the world could be away from Haraken. Even Libre, although it was a confinement colony, was better than these places. I agree. It's time to take control of our fortune, regardless of whether we are rescued or must rescue ourselves.>

Eloise smiled at the warm thoughts of her friends that flooded her mind. It was a relief to have control of her fears that had debilitated her throughout many of the recent long days and nights.

At the door of the suite marked 5M, one officer said to the other, "I'm going to swap out my power module on my weapon. I want a full charge."

"Take mine too," said the other, handing over his stun gun.

The girls shared looks, and Eloise sent, <Now or never.>

<Wait until we're inside the suite,> Christie sent.

<Christie, you're the enticement,> Amelia sent. <He was eyeing you in the car.>

<That's not all he was doing in the car,> Christie sent back. She could still feel the security officer's hand on her rear end.

Once inside the suite, Christie turned on the charm, leaning into the officer's space. "Is it possible to get some food? We haven't eaten today, and I would be quite appreciative of your service."

The security officer smiled and drew breath to reply when Amelia and Eloise, hoisting a heavy chair between them, smacked the guard over the head.

As blood pooled on the floor, Christie ran for a bathroom towel to wrap around the wound. "A little hard I think," she commented.

"Had to make sure," Amelia replied. "Let's go. His friend will be back soon."

The girls slipped out of the suite, taking the opposite direction from the one the first officer took. They passed civilians, patrons, service personnel, and security officers, but no one paid them any attention.

<I don't think these people know who we are.> Eloise sent.

<Look at them,> Amelia replied, watching the people rush past. <What they're thinking about is surviving. They could care less who we are. To generate this much panic, Toyo must have brought a significant force.>

<Wait! Here!> Christie sent, suddenly halting. She tapped a door, which was labeled in bright red letters "Environment Suits." Christie touched the door activator, and it slid it open. <Makes sense,> she sent. <Who would lock up emergency decompression suits?>

Inside, Amelia slapped the activator to close the door, and the girls stared at the room, which was lined with emergency suits in all sizes. Unfortunately for Amelia and Eloise, they were all New Terran sizes.

"Should we stay here?" Eloise asked. "If we follow your logic, Christie, this wouldn't be a good hiding place. If this fight gets any worse, people will be running in here for these suits."

"Good point, Eloise," Amelia said, putting an arm around her friend for a light hug. She was greatly relieved to hear Eloise returning to her old self.

Christie's smile lit her face. "The perfect disguises," she said, "pointing to the suits. We put these on and walk out of here. Look at the tinted faceplates on the helmets."

Amelia started laughing, "I have an even better idea."

The girls donned the environment suits with their compact oxygen tanks and carbon dioxide scrubbers. Christie stuffed small towels she found in a locker into the arms and legs of her Méridien friends to fill out the limbs. She stood back and admired her work, pronouncing both of them as adequately sized New Terrans.

"I believe we have been profaned, Amelia," Eloise said, getting a laugh from her friends.

Exiting the room, the girls held the door open. Immediately, Christie blocked the path of two young male patrons hurrying toward them. "You're asked to don environment suits, Sirs," she said.

Amelia and Eloise grabbed their arms and guided them into the room, helping outfit them, while Christie snatched two service women. Soon the room was full with individuals changing, and Christie appointed three service personnel to continue to help the others.

<Let's go,> Christie sent, and Amelia and Eloise worked past the crowd, who were waiting their opportunity to get a suit.

<Brilliant plan, if I do say so myself,> Amelia sent. The corridor was filled with people wearing the bright yellow environment suits, and the Haraken women were indistinguishable from them.

The idea was catching. Not more than 40 meters along the corridors, the girls passed another crowd who had formed at the door of a second room full of environment suits.

<Okay, now we need a place of safety, if not a way off this rock. Stay here or go up?> Christie sent.

25

The traveler's controller, relaying the telemetry to Ellie's helmet, displayed Jolares rising over Ganymede's horizon.

<Commander, you do realize that you will need to be extremely precise in your requests of me,> Willem sent. Although the SADE was seated next to Ellie, in the copilot position, he was loath to make the conversation public.

<Please explain, Willem,> Ellie requested. Despite her infrequent contact with the SADE, Ellie recognized Willem was one of the less socially developed SADEs, especially in comparison to the others, who were in constant orbit around Alex and the Assembly representatives. When Ellie boarded the traveler with the troopers, she was surprised to find Willem waiting patiently in the ship's cockpit, since she hadn't thought to request he accompany them.

<We will be providing support for Miranda and our people in Ser Toyo's domes. I anticipate this endeavor will involve physical confrontation. What will you require of me?>

Ellie searched for a way to communicate Willem's responsibilities and decided on the simplest of approaches. <Willem, you need only perform those actions that you are comfortable providing. There are no orders for you. We're all volunteers. Each of us has chosen to come to the rescue of our people. If you wish, you may remain aboard the shuttle.>

When Ellie didn't receive a reply, she glanced over at the SADE, who faced forward, silent. Ellie returned to communicating with her people, updating them on their arrival time, when Willem signaled that he wanted to continue the conversation.

<I am conflicted, Commander,> Willem sent. <I have no experience in these endeavors. If I had a weapon, I might be a danger to myself and

others. Yet, if I were to remain aboard our vessel, I'm concerned how our people might regard me.>

<You can't choose your actions by what others might or might not think of you, Willem,> Ellie sent sympathetically. <This is a choice you have to make for yourself. As for having a weapon, I would agree with you. Without experience, you're more likely to shoot me by mistake.>

Willem whipped his head to stare at Ellie, appalled by her suggestion. Then it occurred to him that she was employing humor, and he strove to reply in kind. <Yes, it would be sad tidings that I would be required to deliver to Étienne de Long, who no doubt would be somewhat upset by the news.>

<Good one, Willem,> Ellie sent, her thoughts sprinkled with mirth.

After a few more ticks of time, Willem sent, <I've chosen, Commander. I will remain by your side. I will use my skills to support your efforts and leave the use of a weapon to those who are qualified.>

< I honor your choice, Willem,> Ellie sent. <Earlier you asked for precise directions. I will be near or at the front of the action with Commander Canaan. It will be important for you to maintain a low profile. By that I mean, you must stay behind me, out of the line of enemy fire.>

<You're requiring that I use your body as a shield?> Willem asked.

<Yes,> Ellie replied.

<That sounds most inappropriate,> Willem sent, his confusion evident.

Ellie searched for a way to help Willem accept the role of passive observer in what might become a fierce fight. <We have few SADEs, Willem. Each of you is precious to us, and I would be held in great disfavor if I failed to protect you.>

<Understood, Commander. I will endeavor to ensure that your good name is not besmirched by any error on my part.>

Ellie smiled to herself, wondering how Alex had developed his close relationships with the SADEs over the last decade and a half. *Maybe he's more like the SADEs than the rest of us,* Ellie thought.

As the main dome of Jolares came into view, Ellie sent over open comm, <Standby, people, approaching the target now. Deirdre, we're

coming in above you. Do you have access to bay control to open the doors?>

<Negative, Ellie, we received word from bay control that all flights, in and out of the bay, are suspended,> Deirdre replied.

<Not to worry, Deirdre. As Alex would say, I'm holding an ace. I have Willem seated beside me.> Out of the corner of Ellie's eye, she saw a gentle smile form on the SADE's face.

<Contacting bay control now, Commanders,> Willem sent. He used his link to Deirdre's traveler, which had previous communications with Toyo's bay control. It was relatively simple for Willem to gain access to the bay's software system.

<Standby, Commanders, I'm sounding the alarm to clear the bay. Commander Canaan, while your traveler's telemetry indicates no one is in the bay, it's my fervent hope that the alarm will not be ignored. I would be appalled to have my first foray into a physical confrontation marred by the death of innocent humans.>

<None of us wish for that, Willem,> Deirdre replied. <But it's incumbent on all of us to resist people such as Toyo, Kadmir, and O'Brien, and, in such actions, some people might be hurt, but many more will be served.>

<I'm sounding the alarm for the opening of bay doors, Commanders.>

Moments later, Ellie's telemetry indicated the twin landing bay doors were wide open. <Well done, Willem,> she sent.

<Not actually that difficult, Commander ... for a SADE.>

The moment the shuttle touched down and air pressure returned, Ellie's people piled out of their traveler as the Harakens spilled from Deirdre's ship. Ellie had parked her shuttle in reverse to Deirdre's, allowing the hatches to face each other.

The decision had been made aboard the *Tanaka* by Tatia, prior to the launch of Deirdre's traveler, that the shuttle must not contain any evidence of its Haraken source, which meant no uniforms or stun guns that could be inadvertently discovered by Toyo's people. As the two groups came together, Deirdre shucked her wrap, as the crew did their holiday clothes, and Ellie's people, locating owners by implants, handed out uniforms —

Haraken midnight blue with fine touches of gold in the insignias on the short-tabbed collars, on ship patches on one shoulder, and in Haraken patches on the other.

Deirdre sealed her jacket and slapped Ellie on the shoulder. "If I don't get the opportunity to say it later, I love the way you come to the rescue."

"Don't thank me too quickly," Ellie said. "We cleaned out every stun gun onboard the *Tanaka*, and we came up short." Knowing she was overheard by Deirdre's crew," Ellie added, "Sorry, people, the captain and Assembly Speaker had no way of knowing when they left Hellébore that they were making this kind of trip."

"If you're backing our president," an ex-Libran said, "It's best to load onboard everything you can get your hands on."

"And tether the rest outside the ship with your beams," another added.

The Harakens laughed, as they strapped on their weapons.

"Those without hand guns stay to the rear," Deirdre ordered. "We'll pass back any weapons we confiscate. Check their power settings ... if they have any."

Ellie handed a stun gun to Deirdre. "I know you have to guide us, but you don't have to be in front."

"Where would Alex be?" Deirdre shot back.

Willem interrupted the commanders' conversation with his own request. "Commander Canaan, the security implant you possess, please."

Deirdre reluctantly handed over the tiny vial. It was their only method of access to the lifts and the lab.

Willem pulled out a small device, 6 centimeters' square. He separated the square into two halves, despite its ultrathin width, to reveal what looked like a small pool of liquid metal.

"If you would, Commander," Willem said, handing the two squares to Ellie. "Hold these carefully. Do not tilt them."

Willem extracted the tiny wafer chip from the vial and held it next to his eye, studying it under extreme magnification. "As we suspected, quite inferior technology," Willem pronounced. He placed the chip in the middle of one of the halves Ellie held, closed the other half over the top, and took the device back. His eyes lost focus for several moments while he signaled the pool of nanites surrounding the chip.

Miranda had shared with the SADEs the means necessary to access the lifts and the implant she possessed. Willem had fashioned the device to read the chip, while Julien completed a testing and cloning program. The two SADEs finished their invention even as Julien left with Alex aboard their traveler headed for Udrides.

The nanites completed their connections to the chip, and Julien's application tested the circuitry. The chip's function was revealed as broadcasting an RFID, a radio frequency ID, indicating the wearer's security level, which the lift controller required for access to the subsurface domes.

While they waited, Deirdre regarded Ellie, but a shrug was her only response. Soon after, the commanders received a small file titled "Lift Access," which contained a snippet of code.

"Commanders, everyone in our party has this application," Willem said. "Simply send it as you would a comm when you are in the lift and you will gain access. I'm unaware of the layout of the domes and levels. You will have to manually enter your destination, and I do apologize for that shortcoming."

"Lovely individual," Deirdre said, hefting her weapon, kissing Willem on the cheek, and directing the crew to follow her.

Noticing Willem was frozen in place, Ellie sent, <We fight now, Willem. You can process the commander's thank you later. Your first, I take it.>

As Willem spun to follow Ellie, who raced to the forefront of the group to join Deirdre, he sent to her, <I believe I've not fully comprehended the intensity of human emotions that exist under these circumstances. Perhaps, I've been remiss in not participating earlier.>

Ellie chuckled to herself at Willem's comment, as she caught up with Deirdre. Toyo's patrons and service personnel were scattering out of their way, horrified looks on their faces at the sight of Haraken blue.

<Red uniforms with a stun gun in their hands or on their hips are your targets, people,> Deirdre sent. <We're headed for the nearest lift to get to

level D4-7. That's all you have to put into a keypad to descend. D1-1 will return you to this main concourse. Here's the route to the lab. Miranda, Commander Valenko, and three of our people are holding it secure for us.>

Two security people came from a side corridor into the Harakens' path and Deirdre and Ellie dropped them in a heartbeat — not bothering with explanations.

Deirdre glanced behind Ellie. <Why is Willem running like that?> she sent privately.

Ellie looked back at the SADE, who was directly behind her in a crouch, cutting his height by nearly a third.

<He's protecting my good name,> Ellie sent back.

<He's what?> Deirdre sent.

<A story for another time,> sent Ellie, her humor obvious. She glanced back at Willem, who gave a thumbs-up, a signal he had seen New Terran scientists share with one another while working on his observation platform.

* * *

The sound of a high-pitched whine, penetrated Brace's consciousness, and his mind swam up through layers of gray into the light. "They're cutting through my makeshift door stops," he heard Miranda say. Sitting up, Brace took in the room — Miranda stood beside him, and a room full of people sat at various lab tables.

"Why am I the only one wearing a suit and mask?" Brace asked.

"Necessary earlier ... it's not now," Miranda replied.

Brace slowly stood up, his legs shaky from the stun blast, and stripped off the protective clothing. "Aren't we short some people?" he asked, looking around.

"The lead scientist, Stratford, wasn't here. Apparently, Toyo kidnaps their families to ensure these people remain loyal to him. A senior chemist took Commander Valenko and our men to Stratford's cabin."

"So Stratford is the biochemist we're after?"

"Yet to be determined."

Hearing the pitch of the whine increase, Brace walked over to study the wall of furniture piled against the twin metal doors, leading to the anteroom. Normally a stack of furniture like he observed would tumble with the efforts of a few good men. But the heavy, lab furniture was strapped together with sections of metal alloy bent around table legs and chairs like so much cable. *SADEs*, he thought with a grin.

"How much time do you think we have?" Brace asked.

"We were fortunate, Ser. They didn't think to check the lab until the next shift arrived and was denied access. Then it seemed to take them awhile to determine a course of action. Planets could shift orbits before these people appear to complete their thoughts. However, recently, they've been proceeding rapidly, and I estimate we have fewer than two hours before they break through."

Brace began patting his clothes.

"Don't bother, Ser. I gave your armament to Commander Svetlana."

"Oh," Brace said with resignation and walked around, shaking out the residual tingling in his limbs.

"In all probability, it was unnecessary for you to take the stun blast for me, Ser."

Brace looked at Miranda, whose eyes had the clarity and intensity he associated with Z. "I was raised to look out for a lady," he replied and saw the SADE's eyes soften.

"The generosity of your action is appreciated, dear," Miranda replied, her persona coming back into full play.

* * *

The Harakens, led by Deirdre and Ellie, encountered Toyo's security personnel along the main concourse and at the first lift. In brief but decisive fights, they quickly dispatched the red-uniformed individuals. The Harakens had the numbers and were what Tatia would call motivated.

Several Harakens were stunned, and the commanders delegated troopers to carry their compatriots back to the travelers. Due to the practice of recovering their comrades, the Harakens' numbers dwindled faster than the count lost in the firefights.

Gaining the lift, Ellie assigned eight of the crew to guard access to prevent an ambush when they exited the lift on their return. Then Ellie, Deirdre, Willem, and as many more crew as could fit, squeezed onto the lift. Orders were given for the remaining crew to follow as quickly as they could.

"Cozy," Ellie quipped, her delicately sculpted, Méridien face jammed into a broad New Terran shoulder.

Deirdre sent the security access code Willem had supplied and typed in the level D4-7. When the lift moved, she offered Willem a smile.

"Were you in doubt, Commander?" asked Willem, perplexed as to why Deirdre appeared pleased.

"Who me? Of course not," Deirdre replied, and her comments were greeted with a round of chuckles and snickers. "Okay, let's just say that I was sharing my pleasure with you at our success," Deirdre said.

"The hole you're digging is getting deeper, Commander," said a voice from the back of the car, and the group broke into laughter.

The lift car decelerated, and the mood shifted. When the doors opened, Harakens hurried to take defensive positions. Deirdre tapped D1-1 into the car's keypad to send it up to the main concourse. She worked her way to the front of the group, catching up with Ellie, who had just snapped her head back from a peek around the corner.

"They're waiting for us," Ellie said. "They've got an untidy barricade 20 meters down the corridor. We'll have to wait for the car to return with more people."

* * *

Jameson touched the faint remains of the cut in his scalp for the umpteenth time. It told him how the Harakens managed to get access to the lift and reach the lab. *Three Méridiens on vacation, right ... more like three Harakens investigating us,* he thought with disgust.

His latest update from the crew cutting into the lab told him that they needed only another half-hour, but Jameson wasn't sure he had that much time, not with the report from his people that the Harakens had arrived with reinforcements and already commandeered the lift closest to the landing bay. Tapping his ear comm, Jameson called up to the *Bountiful,* holding station above, which could supply an additional forty armed personnel.

"That's a negative on your request, Jameson," the captain replied. "I have one nasty-looking ship sitting 30K kilometers from my bow, with its nose pointed at me. It's that new Haraken warship with beam capability, and the president is aboard."

"Racine?" Jameson asked.

"Negative. It's President Drake. Apparently, he's gotten word of the drugs and the lab, and he's hopping mad." The captain waited to continue while Jameson blistered the comm. "If I were you, Jameson, I would do whatever it takes to destroy every piece of evidence in that lab."

* * *

Deirdre and Ellie delayed taking on the barricade until two more loads of crew descended to bolster their ranks, before they considered they had sufficient resources to take on the barrier.

"Sorry to ask this, people, but I need volunteers to get stunned," Deidre announced.

When everyone was ready to execute the plan, three New Terrans broke from cover, running at the barricade and firing at Toyo's people, who hid behind the barricade. The Harakens gained mere meters before stun blasts felled them, but not before two Méridien-built crew slid out onto the corridor on their bellies behind the New Terrans and took aim at those popping up from behind the barricade. The first round resulted in five Harakens down, and six of Toyo's people stunned.

Harakens charged right behind the first group, and their swift action caught the defenders off guard, because they made it halfway to the barricade before they crumpled to the floor. The defenders shifted their aim to the floor near the corner where they expected the others to be sliding out, but they were outmaneuvered. Méridiens had been running behind New Terrans, their slender physiques hidden behind the broad backs of their comrades, and the group accounted for seven defenders before they went down.

Willem, peeking around the corner during each charge, compiled and shared visuals that allowed his people to pinpoint the defender locations for the next group. By the time the third group of New Terrans raced forward, with Méridiens both behind them and on the floor, the defenders were overrun.

Deirdre delegated four crew members to guard their felled comrades. "Have the next carload guard these people with you," she ordered. With only Ellie, Willem, and two crew members behind her, Deirdre climbed over the barricade, noting Jameson's body buried under the body of one of his own people. Gaining the other side, Deirdre called up Miranda's vid to guide her to the lab.

The sound of high-speed cutting tools alerted the Harakens before they rounded the last corner. Deirdre peeked out and pulled her head back. "Looks like Toyo's people are having a hard time gaining entrance to their own lab."

"See any security people?" Ellie asked.

Deirdre shared her recording of the glance.

"Two," Ellie said. "Most of the security people must have been at the barricade. Shall we?"

The two commanders stepped around the corner, as if they were strolling to an evening meal. "What are you people up to?" Deirdre asked, casually.

The crew cutting through the last pair of doors couldn't hear the commander over the noise of their saws, but the two security officers did. They turned, still reaching for their weapons, when they fell to the floor.

Deirdre and Ellie were able to walk up behind the four cutting crew and tap the shoulders of the nearest two, who were wearing noise-cancellation headgear. A man and a woman turned around, surprised to see the blue of Haraken uniforms, instead of the red of their security people. In turn, they tapped the shoulders of the two handling the high-speed cutting tool, and the whine of the saw quieted as the foursome stared at the Harakens.

"I think you're done here," Deirdre said calmly, but there was no mistaking her deadly tone. When the service personnel remained frozen, she barked, "Scatter," and the workers fled, bumping into walls to ensure they didn't accidentally brush up against the Harakens.

<Your rescuers are here,> Deirdre sent. <May we come in?>

<Oh, but, dears,> came Miranda's reply, <I have nothing appropriate to wear for a rescue.>

<This is a come-as-you-are occasion,> Ellie fired back, as the sound of tearing metal reached them.

Brace witnessed the voluptuous curves of Miranda in her seductive wrap tearing into the avalanche of twisted, metal-alloy furniture, yanking material apart with ease, and stripping the barricade down to the floor in just moments.

"The best date to accompany you walking down a dark street," Brace commented, drily.

"The best date to have any time, dear," Miranda replied, straightening and rearranging her wrap. She yanked her two makeshift door stops out, and Brace hit the door activator button, but only one door slid open. The other was off its rails.

"We have a problem," Miranda said without fanfare to her rescuers. "This is the lab, but the lead scientist, Stratford as he was called, wasn't present. We still don't know if he's the designer of the hallucinogenic. I sent Svetlana with a lead chemist, who was working here, to locate this individual."

"An important note, Sers," Brace added. "We've heard that Toyo has been keeping the families of the scientists and techs here at the domes to ensure their cooperation."

"Stan," Miranda said, pointing to the shift supervisor, "be so kind as to show us the way to Ser Stratford's cabin."

"Yes, ma'am," Stan replied, hurrying forward.

As Miranda ran, she transferred her record of the recent events following the discovery of the lab to Willem.

Deirdre ordered her three men to secure the lab with Brace, and hurried after Miranda, Ellie, Willem, and the supervisor.

26

When Svetlana, Tyree, and Oren left the lab in the company of a chemist, Emile Billings, they followed him through the intricate corridor layout of dome four, level seven. The Harakens recorded every turn to ensure they could find their way back to the lab.

"If this is a rescue, I want my family protected too," Billings said, as he slowed his pace.

"Now isn't the time to negotiate," Svetlana said, glaring at the chemist.

"You need me to get to Stratford, and he's the one you want," Billings replied.

"What do you mean he's the one we want?"

"It's easy to figure out what you people are after. The drug we manufacture is highly addictive, and you want to reverse its effect, but your people don't know how or where the hallucinogen attaches to the brain. So you need the drug's designer to show you that, which means you need Stratford. He created the compound. I know that because I worked with him for years until he started experimenting with these types of illegal drugs."

"If you quit working with him, why are you here?" Svetlana asked.

"Stratford," Billings said, almost spitting the name. "Toyo offered him huge amounts of credits to come out to Jolares and work for him. He told Stratford he'd build a top-of-the-line lab for his experiments ... move his family out ... all expenses covered. Once out here, Stratford discovered he'd walked into a trap of his own making, created by his ego and avarice.

"The first thing Toyo did after Stratford arrived was to demand the names of his top associates in the biochemistry field. One way or the other, free vacation for the family or outright kidnapping, we all ended up under these domes, because Stratford sold us out. My family and I have been here for a year and a half."

Svetlana studied Billings as they walked. Her instinct told her that the senior chemist was telling the truth. "Okay, we'll see to your family as well."

Billings held out his hand, and Svetlana shook it.

After a couple more turns, the doors changed from a utilitarian design to cabin doors with letters and numbers, indicating residences. Billings continued walking, but he noticed a frown form on the Méridien's face. "The lab's at the outer edge of the dome. Our residences were placed on the same level, so we wouldn't require lift access to go to work, but our residences were located at the farthest distance from the lab to prevent any contamination with the compounds we manufactured."

"How considerate for your children," Svetlana remarked,

The Méridien's tone told Billings that she wasn't interested in his explanations about the efforts to protect their families and guilt crept through his thoughts. At a door labeled D4-L7-73, he stopped.

"It's supposed to be for privacy," Billings told Svetlana, when he saw her staring at the keypad located on the wall next to the door, "but security personnel have exclusive access and lock me and my family inside anytime they want."

Billings rapped on the cabin door. "Stratford, it's Billings. We have a problem in the lab."

The door slid aside, and a middle-aged man demanded, "What's the problem?"

Svetlana shoved the man backwards and entered the cabin.

The biochemist stumbled but managed to maintain his feet. "Who are you people?" he asked in consternation. Behind him, a woman sat on the couch, and two children played on the floor near her.

"That's him. That's Charles Stratford," Billings said.

"What did you do, Emile?" Stratford shouted. His face was twisted in anger, as he took in what appeared to be an armed Méridien and two New Terran miners.

"I thought you'd like to meet some of the people who come from the planet where the drugs you created are being distributed," Billings replied, a cruel smile on his face. "These are Harakens, and they want to talk to you."

"Harakens?" Stratford said in horror. "Don't hurt me, please," he cried out. His eyes pleaded, as they traversed from one Haraken to the next. The woman stood up, gripping Stratford's arm, fearing the worst.

"Both of you sit down," Svetlana commanded. "First question ... and I'm not in the mood to hear excuses or lies ... do we understand each other?" When Svetlana had both Stratford and the woman nodding, she said, "Are you the creator of the addictive, hallucinogenic drug?"

Stratford looked from the woman to Billings, who wore a smug expression. Figuring his former partner already told the Harakens he was the creator, Stratford decided it wasn't the time to quibble and simply nodded his assent.

"Do you know how it affects the brain ... specifically, how it becomes so addictive?"

"Yes," Stratford replied. It wasn't a question he expected, which made him curious. "Why? What information are you seeking?"

Svetlana stared at Stratford long enough that the biochemist became extremely uncomfortable. It didn't help his composure that Svetlana was wearing an evil grin. "We have a wonderfully even-tempered woman by the name of Terese Lechaux who can't wait to meet you. You two will be working oh so closely together."

"Commander, we're a long way from the lab," Oren commented.

"That was my thinking as well," Svetlana replied. "I think we'll hole up here. Besides, if I know our SADE, the lab's entrance has already been fortified. I'd hate to ask Miranda to tear it down."

"What about my family, Commander?" Billings asked, choosing to address the Haraken by the title her men used.

"Where are they, Billings?" Svetlana asked.

"Back the way we came, cabin D4-L7-48 ... if you could spare one of your men with a weapon to guard my family."

"Oren and Tyree, take Billings and collect his family. Bring them back here. I don't want to defend two spaces," Svetlana ordered. She tossed her stun gun to Tyree. "Don't shoot Oren," she added, laughing softly at Tyree's grin.

* * *

Billings led Oren and Tyree back through the corridors they had just traversed. At cabin D4-L7-48, he pressed a single icon on the keypad instead of entering a code and rushed through as the door slid open.

"In quick," Oren ordered Tyree, closing the door after they were inside.

The Harakens heard Billings calling to his wife, as he entered a side room. He returned quickly, saying, "My wife and daughter lay down for a nap. Give them some time to wake up and freshen up. Take a seat, won't you?"

Oren shook his head in amazement and marched into the bedroom. Billings sought to follow him, but Tyree blocked the way.

After a few moments of a woman shouting and a child crying, Oren emerged from the bedroom with Billing's wife and a young girl.

"There's no reason for my family to be treated this way," Billings objected, hugging his wife and shushing his child.

"What fantasy world are you living in, Ser?" Oren asked. "You're a criminal, making illegal drugs that are distributed to teenagers. What makes you think you or your family is due any consideration?" Looking at the mother, Oren added, "Finish dressing. We're leaving."

"We'll be just a few minutes. C'mon, dear," the mother replied.

"No," Oren replied. "The child's robe is fine. You can wear your robe too or change into that dress you're holding, here and now, but we're all headed out that door in the next moment."

The wife's expression implored her husband, but Billings just nodded toward the door and, with a resigned sigh, she took her daughter's hand in hers and clutched her dress in the other, refusing to change in front of strangers.

"Tyree, I'm going out first. You take the rear. Watch our backs. People, stay close to me. Let's go."

Fortune was not with Oren. He opened the door and walked into three of Toyo's security officers. With quick reflexes, he was able to stun the guard directly across the corridor from him. The officer to his right raised his stun gun. Oren latched onto the wrist holding the weapon, and his adversary grabbed the forearm of Oren's gun hand. The two men, locked together, wrestled for control.

With Billings frozen in place and the wife screaming, Tyree was forced to shove the family aside to come to Oren's aid. But, faster than the eye could follow, the third guard, who wasn't carrying a stun gun, snapped out a blade and drove the long, thin, double-edged piece of hardened alloy into Oren's back, between his ribs and into his heart, which shuttered, spasmed, and stopped.

As Oren slid to the deck, the guard pulled his blade free. Tyree gained the doorway and stunned the officer who had been wrestling with Oren. He threw up his weapon's barrel in the nick of time to block the thrust of the third man's knife. The blade slid off the stun gun, stabbing deep into Tyree's forearm. A numbing sensation struck Tyree's hand, and his stun gun tumbled out of his fingers to the deck.

Toyo's knife-wielding attacker danced backward, a humorless grin on his face at having scored a crippling strike. Settling into a fighter's crouch, the guard began tossing the blade back and forth, from one hand to another, attempting to keep his adversary guessing as to the quarter where the attack would come.

Despite Tyree's huge stature, he was by no means slow. While the guard tossed the knife between his hands, Tyree stepped on his left foot and his right leg struck out like a missile launch, his boot catching the guard squarely in the chest. The knife never reached the next hand as the smaller man bounced off the corridor wall and flew toward Tyree, who caught the man's neck in the crook of his good arm.

The guard pummeled Tyree in the kidneys and ribs with powerful arms and fists of stone. Tyree grunted as the blows quickly took their toll. Amidst the girl's quiet cries emanating from the cabin, the memory of his friend sliding to the floor replayed in Tyree's mind. With an angry cry, he heaved up and back with all his strength, yanking the smaller man off the floor. A crack issued from the guard's neck, and he went slack in Tyree's grip. The Haraken opened his arm and let the guard fall to the deck.

Tyree glanced up and down the corridor, which was clear, for now. He retrieved his stun gun and Oren's with his working hand and shoved one into his thigh holster and the other into the waistband of his pants. Tyree checked his friend, and his heart clutched when he discovered Oren had no pulse. His friend's injuries were far too great for the nanites in his system to repair in time.

"Help me pick him up," Tyree ordered Billings.

"We should leave him and come back later for him," Billings suggested.

"Or I can just stun you and your wife, and let you explain these bodies when you wake up," Tyree said, his anger evident.

"Help him, Emile," the wife urged. "Hush, honey," she said, trying to quiet her daughter.

Between the two men, they managed to pick up Oren, slinging his arms over their shoulders. With the dead Haraken's feet dragging on the floor, the men struggled down the corridor.

Tyree glanced behind him several times to ensure the coast was clear and that the wife and child were still right behind them. At Stratford's cabin, he kicked the door several times with his boot.

When Svetlana heard the boot strike the door, she sent, <Tyree?> forgetting that the rooms were comm isolated.

Belatedly, Tyree had tried the same thing. "No enemy with us, Commander. Apologies for not signaling," Tyree called out.

Svetlana slapped the door activator, and she took in the three men just outside the door. "Oh, Oren," Svetlana lamented, clearing the way for the men to haul Oren into the salon. She helped Tyree lay their companion on the floor near the wall, and she too checked Oren for a pulse.

"What happened?" Svetlana asked, realizing there was nothing to be done for Oren and stripping open Tyree's shirtsleeve to examine his wound. The bleeding was already slowing.

Tyree sent his recording of the fight outside Billings' cabin to Svetlana.

"Can you move your fingers?" Svetlana asked, noticing from the vid that during the fight Tyree lost control of his grip and dropped his weapon.

"I couldn't before, but feeling is slowly coming back," Tyree replied, flexing a couple of fingers.

"How many of our people are we going to lose before we halt this madness?" Svetlana asked, sparing piercing gazes for Stratford and Billings.

* * *

Stan, the lab shift supervisor, led Miranda, Deirdre, Ellie, and Willem along the route Billings had taken only an hour and a half earlier. When they came to three bodies in the corridor, Stan stuttered to a halt, and the SADEs pushed past him to check on the men, while Deirdre and Ellie watched opposite directions of the corridor for more of Toyo's security forces.

Deirdre spared a glance for the open door. "Stan, whose cabin is this?"

"Billings and his family," Stan replied.

"These two are stunned," Miranda announced.

"This one is not. He's dead. Damage to his cervical vertebrae," Willem said. "There's blood on the floor, but I see no external injuries on this man."

"Quickly, Stan. On to Stratford's cabin. Hurry," Miranda urged.

Stan stepped over the bodies and jogged down the corridor. "Down there, number seventy-three," Stan said as they neared Stratford's cabin. The SADEs burst past Stan at an incredible pace, and Deirdre and Ellie sprinted to catch up.

"Svetlana," Miranda called out, "we're here." Willem and she skidded to a stop in front of Stratford's cabin door as it opened. They rushed into the room, and, moments later, Deirdre, Ellie, and Stan ran through the door.

Svetlana motioned to Oren's body on the floor. "He's gone," she said.

"We saw the aftermath in the hallway," Deirdre replied.

"How extensive is your injury, Tyree?" Ellie asked, when she noticed his torn shirtsleeve wrapped around his arm.

Tyree sat staring at Oren's body, tears in his eyes and recriminating thoughts roiling through his mind for his failure to save his comrade. He snuffled and wiped his nose. "I immigrated to Haraken to get away from this sort of thing that started infiltrating my neighborhood. But these people," Tyree declared loudly, standing and pointing his finger at Stratford and Billings, "had to create their drugs to poison our planet and force us back here to eliminate what their greed created." Tyree advanced toward the chemists, as he shouted at them until Miranda stepped in front of him. Despite Tyree's size, he found his way firmly blocked by the curvy SADE.

"His loss will be mourned, dear," Miranda said, laying a gentle hand on Tyree's cheek, and then running her hand through Tyree's thick hair, much as a mother would caress a child. After a moment's pause, Miranda turned around to the chemists and their families, keeping her body in Tyree's way. "This is Stratford?" she asked.

"Yes, and he admits to creating the drug, which Billings confirms," Svetlana said.

"Well, well, Ser. You've managed to rile up an entire planet over your insidious invention," Miranda said, walking up to Stratford, who was seated on the couch next to his wife. "We're here now to end your enterprise. I believe your future will be quite different from what you've imagined."

"This wasn't entirely his fault," Stratford's wife objected. "The entire family was held prisoner."

"Hush, dear," Miranda said quietly. "You wouldn't have been here if your husband hadn't developed a taste for creating things better left undone."

"Our people on this level should be regaining consciousness within two more hours," Willem said.

"A fight to reach us?" Miranda asked.

"A considerable one," Ellie said, "but everyone was stunned. Unless our people on the main concourse have had trouble, Oren is the only one we've lost."

"Now that we have the lab and the chemist, we just need our president to get our girls back. After that I vote for evacuating these diseased domes and turning our beams on them until they're space dust," Svetlana said.

Tyree walked over to Oren's body and attempted to lift him, but Willem laid a gentle hand on his shoulder to stop him. "If you would permit me the honor, young Ser, I would carry your friend for you." When Tyree nodded and stepped back, Willem effortlessly lifted Oren in his arms.

Deirdre and Ellie took the lead out of the cabin; Miranda herded the biochemists and their families behind them; Willem with Oren came next; and Tyree brought up the rear. They worked their way back to the barricade, which the crew had dismantled while they waited for their compatriots to recover. Toyo's immediate forces, who fought at the barricade, were restrained and their weapons confiscated.

Jameson woke with his hands tied behind his back and seething at finding himself at the mercy of the Harakens once more. What mollified him to some extent was the use of the commander title to address either of the dark-light twins. *If I have to be duped and captured, at least it was done by superior officers,* Jameson thought morosely.

Once the Harakens resumed full strength, large teams traversed the levels, challenging small pockets of Toyo's security forces, who quickly surrendered in the face of superior numbers. And having identified the doors, which marked the security centers, the Harakens raided them for weapons and any security force holdouts.

Several hours after the Harakens landed, an eerie silence descended over Toyo's domes. Patrons and service personnel returned to their rooms to wait the next turn in the events. The lounges, bars, and gambling parlors were empty. The only credits changing hands were between the inveterate gamblers, who were placing wagers among themselves on what the Harakens would do next.

27

The atmosphere aboard Alex's traveler, en route to Udrides, was tense. Absent was the usual jesting that solidified the Harakens' camaraderie. The Harakens were trained to fight with ships not hand weapons in open combat against adversaries, surrounded by civilians. No one wanted to be responsible for fatally injuring an innocent person.

<Julien, I need to ensure that Renée is protected, first and foremost,> Alex sent privately.

<It will be done, Alex.>

<If something should happen to me —>

<There is no cause for concern, Alex,> Julien interrupted, <It will be the honor of every Haraken SADE to ensure the welfare of Ser and your son. Now that we've dealt with your somber moment, do try to keep your enormous self out of the way of any deadly circumstances. I don't wish to see my past sixteen years wasted … considerable time and effort, I might point out, in converting a pitiful excuse for a human into a world leader."

Alex chuckled heartily at Julien's comment. He turned around in his seat to eye the SADE and sent, <Julien, you do know how to make a person feel warm and fuzzy all over.>

The tension in the traveler's main cabin eased on hearing Alex's laughter — implants opened and comms resumed.

As Alex turned around, Julien wondered why humans strived so hard to conquer one another and became wistful that he didn't possess the power to cease the conflict among them.

* * *

Arriving over the top of the Udrides domes, Alex requested Julien establish a link with Kadmir's comm station. Once connected, Alex sent, <This is President Racine. We're here to meet Azul Kadmir.>

"One moment, Mr. President," the comms operator replied.

In the traveler, the moments ticked by without a reply. Alex and Tatia exchanged glances, neither of them liking the delay. Kadmir should have been anxiously awaiting their arrival.

"My apologies, Mr. President," Kadmir said, finally picking up the comm. "We've had to institute emergency procedures. Nothing that seriously endangers our people, but we're being thorough and locating the source of a decompression alarm. As a spacer, I'm sure you understand the importance we're ascribing to this sort of sensor notice."

<How long will this take, Ser?> Alex asked.

"At this time, that's unknown, Mr. President, and, in all good conscience, I can't risk you coming onto my establishment until we locate and correct the problem."

<I have some excellent people with me, Ser Kadmir. They could be of great assistance to your people.>

"And your offer is greatly appreciated, President Racine, but I can't take the chance. If anything were to happen to your person, the blame would fall squarely on me and my establishment. I'm sorry you made this journey for nothing. We've ensured your young women are secure. I will contact you just as soon as this issue is resolved. Kadmir out."

Alex signaled Julien, who joined Tatia and him for an impromptu conference. "Julien?" Alex asked.

"Ser Kadmir's voice exhibited a high degree of stress. An expected response to a significant problem in the domes," Julien replied.

"Anything else?"

"A curiosity. I couldn't contact bay control."

"Is it possible that's where the alarm was sounded?" Tatia asked.

"Highly possible," Julien admitted.

Tatia and Julien waited while Alex considered his options. Under the circumstances, all signs pointed to a perfectly reasonable response from Kadmir. In which case, the logical decision was to turn their traveler around and return to the *Tanaka*.

"Problem?" Renée asked, as she joined the small group.

"Kadmir wants to delay the meeting ... emergency decompression alarm, which they're checking." Tatia replied.

"I see," said Renée, closely watching Alex's face. <Tell us what you're thinking, my love,> she sent.

"I don't know what it is, but this doesn't feel right," Alex replied.

"Then we go in," Tatia announced without fanfare. It was Alex's intuition, and it was good enough for her.

Julien, executing the same procedure as Willem executed at Jolares, worked through the comms connection into the landing bay controller. He sounded the alarm for the bay opening, waited an appropriate time, and then signaled the bay doors for access.

As the traveler entered the bays, Julien signaled bay control to close the doors. Alex received a signal from their pilot, and he linked to the traveler's telemetry output.

"Bodies on the deck," Alex said to Tatia, who in turn accessed the telemetry.

"They're prone and splayed out," Tatia commented.

"And not moving," Alex added.

"Infrared indicates these bodies have been cooling far longer than a brief exposure to vacuum when the bay doors were open," Julien said, greatly relieved that he hadn't caused the deaths.

"The bay must have been the source of the depressurization that Kadmir spoke about," Tatia concluded.

The traveler settled to the deck, and Julien held up a finger, requesting Alex and Tatia wait. "I've requested the bay's pressurization. Curiously, the pressure level is rising at a nominal rate." A few moments later, the SADE said, "The bay is ready."

Alex and Tatia exchanged confused looks. It was Tatia who put together the pieces. "There's no technical problem. I believe Kadmir's domes are under attack from unknown forces, but why are the bodies on the bay deck cooling?"

"Not unknown, Admiral," Alex sent, "I'll bet you those forces are from Jolares. Whatever relationship existed between Kadmir and Toyo has gone sour. My thinking is that Toyo is here to get the girls back."

<Listen, people,> Tatia broadcast on open comm. <All indications are that we are walking into a conflict between two forces. Bodies are on the deck. If this is so, neither of the armed groups will recognize our neutrality. In fact, you can be sure they will see only a uniform and will shoot first and ask questions later. We need to be prepared to do the same ... to Kadmir's people and whoever else is here.>

<Harakens,> Alex sent. <Do not depend on these forces to limit their weapons to stun guns. We're dealing with criminals. Protect yourself, at all times.>

<For identification purposes, the home forces are in brown uniforms and might be potential allies,> Julien added.

Tatia squinted at Julien. His comment didn't maximize the defensive attitude she wanted her troopers to adopt.

Julien smiled at her. Bright parallel streaks of several different colors appeared on his forehead, cheeks, and chin. Three, long, bird feathers hung along the side of his head and appeared to tie into his hair by the quills. Responding to Tatia's frown, Julien said, "war paint."

* * *

Tatia ordered six troopers to be first out the hatch. <Take defensive positions the moment you're clear of the ship, people,> she sent.

But with signals from Étienne and Alain, the troopers stepped aside as the twins threaded past them to stand ready at the hatch. On Tatia's command, the hatch dropped, and the twins flew out the doorway, landing lightly, and rolling to either side. By the time the first six troopers were on the deck, the twins were nowhere in sight.

Inside the traveler, Alex watched four troopers hoist plasma rifles and strap them over their backs. Alex raised an eyebrow at Tatia.

"Just in case," Tatia said in answer.

"In case of what?"

"Just in case," Tatia repeated. "You have your needs; I have mine."

As more troopers poured out of the traveler, Alex, Renée, and Julien disembarked and were immediately closely surrounded by troopers.

When Alex sent to those around him, <Hope I don't hit any of you, since I've had so little time to practice with these weapons,> the troopers spread into a half-circle, ringing around and behind their principals and leaving the front open.

Renée and Julien managed to prevent their smiles from breaking out.

Étienne and Alain reached the first body without contact from adversaries. The woman wore a brown uniform with gold trim, no weapon or holster was present, and her throat was cut. The twins exchanged concerned glances and moved on. The second body had no obvious marks, and the man's holster was empty. Étienne checked the body, opening the eyelids.

<Julien, on our location, immediately,> Étienne sent.

The SADE moved so quickly, the troopers protecting him were torn between staying with Alex and Renée and chasing after Julien.

Alex scanned implants and assigned two troopers to each of them. The pair assigned to Julien, sprinted after him, pinging the SADE to track him.

Kneeling by the second body the twins found, Étienne pointed out the man's eyes to Julien and assumed a protective stance with Alain.

Julien examined the blown pupil of one eye and checked the body for wounds. He hurried forward to a third body and found a woman in the same condition — no wounds except for a burn mark on her forehead, wide pupils, and fingers harshly crimpled in rigor. Rather than call Alex and Tatia to his position, Julien hurried back to them, passing by the first body the twins noticed.

Alex couldn't remember the last time he saw Julien move so fast. Tatia's response to the SADE's anxious speed was to order the troopers into defensive positions. Alex threw an arm around Renée and pulled her behind a 2-meter tall plex-crate.

"What?" asked Alex, when Julien joined them.

"Be aware that the attacking forces are employing weapons that fire lethal electrical charges against Kadmir's people. Two bodies show burn marks, and I surmise their nerves have been overloaded. They had no wounds. I passed a third person, a woman who appears to be service personnel. Her throat was cut."

Tatia swore and updated the troopers. Alex touched Renée's cheek. <Be careful, my love,> he sent.

<New orders, people,> Tatia sent. <Team up, groups of three. Protect one another. One person advances and the other two provide cover. Étienne, Alain, and Julien, you know what to do.>

The twins retreated from their advance positions and came to Alex and Renée's side.

Julien briefly reviewed Miranda's contact with security personnel at Jolares. <If these are Toyo's people who are using the deadly weapons, they will be wearing red uniforms,> Julien sent in the open.

<It doesn't matter, people,> Alex said, adding to Julien's message, <We don't know who picked up what weapon after each skirmish. Treat every uniform, red, brown, or whatever, with a weapon as an adversary. Stun them and then disable, hide, or confiscate their weapons. We have no idea how long we will be here. Any adversaries who manage to recover and are still unrestrained will have to find new weapons.>

"Alex," Tatia whispered. "If this is Toyo and he's using deadly force, he's definitely here to take the girls back."

"My question: How many people did Toyo bring?" Alex replied.

"The probabilities are that the attackers couldn't have infiltrated with more than a single shuttle," Julien said.

"One shuttle is not enough people against three or four domes full of security personnel," Tatia reasoned.

"Thus the use of these deadly weapons," Alex supplied. "It means Toyo knows he's outmatched. That's why his people are killing, making sure no one is left behind to recover and attack his rear. There's also the possibility his people are carrying even more powerful weapons."

"Where's an environment suit when you need one?" Tatia groused.

"Who needs an environment suit?" Julien deadpanned.

"Nice wit, Julien," Tatia said, smacking the SADE's shoulder and stinging her hand.

28

Toyo directed his people's fire like a field commander and urged them forward at every opportunity. His forces were bottled up short of the blue lift, the first available transport to the lower domes where Toyo was sure Kadmir would be safekeeping the Haraken women.

Sufficient time had passed since Toyo's shuttle landed that his security forces had awakened from their stuns. A fierce grin lit Toyo's face, as the first group of recovered people added to his numbers engaged at the lift. Given time his new stunners would tip the fight in Toyo's favor — Kadmir's people would never be getting up.

"Boss, we got a problem," said one of Toyo's people, who just joined the skirmish. "Troops are disembarking in the landing bay."

"How'd they get into the dome?" Toyo asked, his anger growing.

"Don't know, Boss. A bunch of us came to about the time the traveler was landing."

"A traveler, not a shuttle?" Toyo asked, wrapping a fist in the man's shirt collar and yanking him forward.

"A traveler, Boss. You can't miss one of them Haraken vessels."

"Did you see any of Kadmir's people alive in bay control?"

"No, Boss. The brown suits in control are down ... I mean permanently down." The man swallowed as Toyo released him, enabling him to lean back against the wall.

"Could you see who exited the traveler ... whose troops ... adz?"

"No, Boss, that's what I came to tell you. The troops are wearing Haraken blue."

"Racine!" Toyo exclaimed. "He's here for his girls. That's how his traveler got inside. He's got one of those digital freaks with him." The Haraken president bringing troops to bear at Toyo's rear represented an immediate danger or a perfect opportunity, but how to make the most of it.

"This is important," Toyo said, leaning toward the man. "That bay was opened to vacuum to allow the traveler to land. Where were you that you survived?"

"I was stunned in bay control, but some of our people must have piled a bunch of us inside and sealed the door. When we woke, the traveler was settling to the deck, and soon afterwards the bay started pressurizing. It was like bay control was operating by itself."

"SADEs," Toyo growled. "Okay, last question. How many travelers landed?"

"Just the one, Boss."

"Did you count the troops?"

"Sorry, Boss, no. They came off in small groups, and some of those Méridiens move like smoke. They came through the bay so fast we had to get out of there while we could."

"Okay, good work," Toyo said, slapping the man lightly on the cheek with his fingertips. "Now get into this fight and make me some progress."

Toyo whistled to Lydia, who waited for the right moment and then dived across the corridor, sliding to a stop next to Toyo's feet.

"What's up, Boss?" Lydia asked, popping up beside Toyo, both of them leaning tightly against the wall to stay out of the line of fire. The main obstacle and defense for both sides was that the main concourse circled the outside of the dome's constant curve. Within 25 meters, one individual was out of sight of another if they were hugging the same wall.

"I'm about to make your day, woman," Toyo said. "A traveler landed in the bay, and Haraken troopers disembarked."

"You think Racine was on that ship?" Lydia asked, her eyes lighting up.

"There's a good chance of that ... he's probably here for his fems. Take nine of my people, and hurry your butt back to that barricade. If you can ambush them and take out the president, consider you and your team as having earned 200K credits! But whatever you do, you hold that barricade until I send someone back for you. By then, I will have taken this lift."

"Can I have Lenny?" Lydia asked.

"The plasma rifle? Absolutely not, get a move on. And, woman," said Toyo, grabbing her arm and squeezing tightly, "your main purpose is to defend the barricade. Don't lose my people trying to earn your bonus."

$* \quad * \quad *$

Lydia signaled nine others she thought she could trust to take orders. The group edged back down the main corridor until they were clear from fire and then took off running.

"What's up, Zafir?" a man asked, but Lydia refused to answer, instead she covered the distance as fast as her legs could carry her. The group struggled to keep up, but everyone was doing their best. After Toyo, Lydia Zafir was one individual you tried hard not to disappoint.

At the barricade, Lydia ordered her people to wait, while she ran a good 50 meters farther down the corridor, staying next to the inner wall. She listened carefully for a while and heard nothing. There was time to plan an ambush.

Hustling back to the barricade, Lydia picked out four people and ordered them to follow her. "The rest of you, rebuild this barricade. I don't want any evidence of that plasma blast showing from the landing bay side."

"You going to tell us what's going on, Zafir, or just keep us guessing?" The man was the same one who tried to question her on the way to the barricade.

Lydia eyed the man, but he refused to be cowed. "We got Harakens coming," Lydia said.

"Is the president among them?" the man asked, sensing bonus time.

Lydia watched the light glisten in all nine pairs of eyes around her. "Don't know," she said, "but here's the thing. Toyo said we hold this barricade no matter what, or he'll kill each one of us who returns before he recalls us." Using Toyo as the threat had the desired effect. The light went out in their eyes and was replaced by earnest evaluations of the barricade's strength. Lydia could see the thought circling in their brains — how to survive until Toyo sent for them.

"Okay, you four with me," Lydia ordered, and walked toward the landing bay. She picked out four doors, two on each side of the corridor, which accessed offices and utility rooms that suited her purpose. Before the people dispersed, Lydia gave them their final instructions. "I'll comm you when the Harakens approach and then give you a countdown. Have your hand over the door actuators, and don't get greedy for targets. Stun the nearest person. Your jobs are to disrupt the group. Those of us behind the barricade will target the leaders."

"I heard there was a bonus for the president," an old-timer said.

"What about that, Zafir?" a young man added. When Lydia stared at him for a moment, he swallowed nervously. "I mean, if the president gets killed, we might not know who did it. Wouldn't it be fair to divide it up among all of us?"

"Tell you what, boyos," Lydia said, her smile twisting into a sneer. "You survive to the end of this fight, and we'll talk about sharing if anyone gets the president."

As Lydia trotted back to the barricade, one of the senior men slapped the young questioner on the back of his head. "Idiot," he said.

"What?" the boy asked.

"Why do you think we're down here, while they're up there?" he said, pointing toward the barricade.

"Well, I don't know about you, but I'm considered a great shot with one of these," the younger man announced, hoisting his stunner.

"Yeah, idiot," a third man agreed. "We're fodder, you fool. We may pop out of these doors and stun a few Harakens, but then they will be returning the favor. It'll be hours before we come to, and whose company do you think we'll be sitting in if this little adventure of Toyo's goes sidewise?"

"Oh," the younger man replied.

The four ambushers separated, entered their assigned rooms, and slid the doors closed.

* * *

The Harakens came silently down the main corridor of Kadmir's upper dome. Only implants were used for communication. Six troopers walked in front. The twins came next, and they were just ahead of Tatia, who walked with a trooper beside her.

Alex walked alone behind Tatia, refusing to allow anyone on either side of him. Renée walked directly behind Alex, unable to see much behind his broad back, but it was the only place Alex would permit her, and in Renée's opinion, it wasn't the time or place to argue. The image of a brown-uniformed woman lying dead on the landing bay deck with her throat cut horrified her, and it was firmly entrenched in her mind.

Julien walked beside Renée, and, for the first time in his mobile life, he carried a stun gun. Unable to estimate the power of the weapons Toyo's people were employing, the SADE considered it a distinct possibility that an energy blast from one or more of the deadly creations might overload his circuitry and his crystal memory — kernel and all.

When troopers up front spotted the edges of the barricade, they signaled a halt and waited, weapons raised. After a few moments, when no movement was apparent, Tatia sent, <It was probably built by Kadmir's people and overrun.>

Julien edged next to the outer curve of the corridor, where he had an unobstructed view of the majority of the barricade. <A logical thought, Admiral,> Julien sent. <However, not to disabuse your acumen as an ex-TSF officer, I have the heat signatures of six individuals leaking out between the legs and frames of the furniture pile as they wait in ambush. At this time, they are prone on the floor.>

<We can't back up; we're too exposed,> Tatia sent. <Julien, target the locations for the troopers in front.>

The SADE laid into each Haraken trooper's implant a single infrared signal of an attacker, effectively assigning their targets.

<Okay, people, we go forward,> Tatia sent, when Julien signaled her all was ready.

Julien stayed along the outer curve of the corridor, keeping the barricade in sight at every tick.

The six troopers in front kept their weapons in front of them but were careful not to point them directly at the attackers, lest they acknowledge the ambush.

Suddenly four doors opened along the sides of the Harakens followed by five people popping up from behind the barricade.

The six Haraken troopers in front were ready — four attackers were stunned before they could take aim, a fifth Haraken trooper still waited for his target to appear, and a sixth trooper, Nestor, had the misfortune of sighting on a woman. The young man's sensibilities caused him to hesitate for that fraction of time that allowed his adversary to fire first. Nestor was struck in the chest by stunner fire, killing him, before the woman ducked back down.

The two foremost side doors opened beside the twins, who spun into deep crouches, destroying the targeting of their adversaries and enabling the twins to strike first.

The other pair of doors opened just ahead of Alex, nearly even with Tatia and the trooper beside her. Alex, who held his weapons at the ready, let his implant apps play. Independently, his arms snapped out wide, and the apps triggered fingers on buttons when, in his peripheral vision, alignment on the adversaries was achieved.

Tatia and the trooper next to her were bringing their weapons to bear on the ambushers when they saw them crumple to the floor. The two of them glanced back at Alex, who was lowering his stun guns from extended arms.

<Your secret is out now, my love,> Renée sent.

<And so the mystique grows,> Tatia sent to Alex, shaking her head in amazement, as the troopers behind Alex shared their images of the event with others in the group.

<We have competition,> Étienne sent to Alain.

<Perhaps, we should ask the president to provide escort for us,> Alain quipped to his crèche-mate.

<Or perhaps we should consider a second implant,> Étienne sent in reply.

The Harakens were witness to a new implant skill from their leader, but, for Alex, there was no such appreciation of the moment. He was terrified for Renée, who insisted on sharing the risks of his life, and he loved her for her courage but, in such encounters, he feared every moment for her safety. A decade and a half ago, he was content to lead the life of a loner out in the belt of Oistos. Now, he couldn't imagine being without his partner and lover.

On the other side of the barricade, Lydia stared in disgust at the only remaining defender, who had slipped when he tried to jump up. She had lost eight of the nine men Toyo gave her. The man wasn't going to be happy, to say the least. Lydia hand signaled the other ambusher, and the two of them crawled along the inner wall until they were out of sight of the Harakens before they stood up and ran.

* * *

"What do you want to do about all these people running around in environment suits, Sir," Yakiro, the security chief, asked Kadmir.

"They're calm, Chief. Let them be," Kadmir replied, hurrying a group of guests and personnel off the lift. He had stopped sending security people up on the car's return trip, not knowing where Toyo might break through into the lower domes if he got access to the blue lift. "How are we doing on the main concourse, Chief?"

"We're still holding the blue lift, Sir, and we're wearing them down. But he's hurting us with those weapons of his,"

"I'd like to shoot the individuals who manufactured those stun guns for Toyo. In fact, I don't know why we're calling them stun guns ... need a different name."

"Sir, Sir," called out a senior personnel manager breathlessly, running up to Kadmir.

Kadmir had to lean close to hear the older man wheeze out his message. "What do you mean you lost the girls?" Kadmir yelled.

"It wasn't me, Sir," the man exclaimed between breaths. "I discovered the security officer knocked out on the floor when I came to deliver food, as ordered."

"Did you initiate a search?" Kadmir asked, grabbing the man by the shoulder.

"Immediately, Sir, every service personnel I could find. Said they were three VIP guests, two Méridiens accompanying a New Terran, who needed to be found. I didn't give any names."

"Well done," Kadmir said. "Keep on it, and let me know when you find them. Escort them back to the suite and put three people on to safeguard them." As the man hurried off, Kadmir turned to Yakiro. "Chief, as much as it pains me to say this —"

"Understood, Sir," Yakiro said. "I'll put some of my people on it. Won't mean much to defeat Toyo and not have the Haraken women safe when Racine comes back."

"Yeah, Racine was none too happy when I told him to turn back. Get on it, Chief. I'll check in on our people above."

* * *

Walking down a corridor in dome four, the Haraken girls were blending nicely with the myriad other people wearing bright yellow, environment suits.

<So, we're nicely hiding in plain sight, but where is here and how do we get out of wherever here is?> Eloise sent to her friends.

<Good questions,> Amelia agreed, and both Eloise and she turned to stare through their tinted faceplates at Christie.

<I'm thinking. Give me a moment,> Christie replied.

<Christie, this is the fourth time we've walked this particular corridor section. Someone's bound to think we're in a highly emotional state and take us into protective custody,> Amelia sent. <Eloise is right. We don't

know where we are or how to get out of here, except for these stupid door numbers, D4-L6, whatever.>

<That's it,> Christie sent excitedly. <We don't know, but they do,> she added, cautiously pointing to other yellow suits. <Follow my lead.>

Christie immediately put out her arms, blocking the path of a couple in environment suits. "We've been asked to direct everyone to the main dome for shuttle departure," she said, delivering her best imitation of Alex's command voice.

"Is it that bad?" asked the woman.

"Just a precaution," Amelia added. "Management would feel better if the guests and service personnel were safe."

"Well, the blue lift is blocked from use," the man said, pointing back the way they had come. "Only the green lift is still in use," he added, pointing past the girls.

"That's correct, Sir," Christie said, stepping aside, and waving her arm down the corridor. "Please make your way there in an orderly fashion."

The girls continued to direct anyone in environment suits to the green lift. After fifteen or so people were sent that way, they followed the last three individuals they intercepted.

At the lift, two overwhelmed security personnel were busy waving off the people crowding forward to access the lift. "There's no real danger," one of guards said.

"Well, one of you doesn't know what in black space is going on," an angry patron called out. "We were directed to go topside and get a shuttle ride out of here. I'm getting on the next lift up, unless you want to use that stun gun on me."

When the doors opened, the crowd pushed and shoved to get on, and about half of them made it. As soon as the lift doors slid closed and the car started up, someone smacked the controller box on the wall to request the car's return.

"Chief," one of the security personnel called on comm. "We've got a problem at the green lift. Patrons and service personnel in environment suits are demanding exit to the surface. They say they've been told to go topside and board shuttles." The security guard could barely understand the response of his chief, who was thundering questions and instructions into his ear comm.

"We're at D4-L6 green lift, Chief, but there are only two of us, and some of these patrons are throwing their weight around," the frustrated guard replied.

"Try to contain them. I'm sending you some support," Yakiro replied.

Amelia, standing close to the guard, could hear the exchange with his chief, and she relayed what she had heard to the other two girls. Amelia no sooner finished informing her friends of the impending arrival of more security when the lift doors opened. The crowd pushed and shoved to fill the car. Eloise stood to be next to squeeze on, but she hesitated.

A woman on the car, gestured to her, "There's room for one more, child, come on."

Eloise reached back to grasp Amelia's gloved hand, and in her best imitation of a teenager's voice, she replied, "I have to wait to go with my sister."

The woman nodded her head in understanding, as the lift doors closed.

While the Haraken women waited, more people in environment suits arrived, but the three girls positioned themselves to be next on the car.

<When it arrives, get on and move to the back right,> Eloise sent. <I saw someone in the car reach out to touch a panel or button on the front left wall of the car. We don't want to be the ones next to it.>

The girls waited anxiously for their opportunity to go topside, wondering at every moment if security would arrive first. It was only a matter of time before someone with their wits about them noticed a New Terran woman accompanied by two slender companions and made the connection to the reports of three missing Harakens.

One of the security guards touched his ear comm, nodded his understanding, and edged between Christie and the lift doors.

"Hey, wait your turn," Christie yelled in a loud, indignant voice, stabbing an arm out to the lift's corner to block the guard's way. A chorus of angry grumbles and comments backed the security guard off, who decided to wait until reinforcements arrived. <We're running out of time,> Christie sent.

Anxious moments later, the lift doors open, and the three girls were first on and sought the back right corner.

As the car filled up, a man near the controller panel, yelled out, "C'mon, people, hurry it up." He punched in a dome and level request just as security personnel arrived, who shoved their way through the crowd, but the car doors slid closed in front of their faces.

29

Toyo's frustration grew. His people weren't making progress fast enough against Kadmir's greater numbers, despite his people's deadly stunners. Now, knowing the Harakens had landed and were about to trap him against Kadmir's security forces, Toyo was hoping for a break — namely that the wild woman would score a hit on Racine.

And, if the impending clash with the Harakens wasn't enough to worry Toyo, the delay was draining the power packs of his people's weapons. The stunners consumed a great deal more energy per blast in order to cripple or kill than a regulation stun gun. To compensate, his security personnel were picking up the weapons of Kadmir's people, stuffing them into their belts or empty holsters as backups when their stunners consumed their backup power supplies.

Toyo was studying the layout of the defensive forces arrayed against him, searching for a weakness, when Lydia slid beside him. He glowered at her, tempted to drive his blade through her guts and let her suffer for disobeying his orders, but he desperately needed every body.

"Boss, the ambush at the barricade didn't work. I swear, we had a sweet setup ... boxed on three sides. Everyone snapped up on command and the Harakens cleaned us out before we even targeted them. Those people are uncanny. It's like ... it's like they knew where we were hiding. I was the only one to score because the trooper hesitated."

"Hesitated?"

Lydia grinned. "Well, I used a little subterfuge," she said, and pulled open her uniform to bare a significant portion of full breasts.

"And the idiot hesitated to shoot a woman," Toyo guessed, grinning at the stupidity of those who were unprepared to engage in fights to the death.

Lydia smirked and nodded in agreement with his conclusion.

"Did you see Racine? Was he with them?" Toyo asked, leaning close to Lydia so that he wasn't overheard by his people. He had no desire to add to the pressure on them, and learning the Harakens, led by Alex Racine, were at their backs would do more than cause them to be anxious — it would create panic.

"That's the weird part ... and I can't swear to this because I only caught a glimpse ... but two of my men popped out of doors on either side of the corridor across from him, and Racine shot both of them."

"You mean he was able to stun one and then the other before either idiot could fire?"

"No, Boss, I swear it looked like he shot the two men simultaneously with both hands, while staring straight ahead."

Toyo stared into Lydia's eyes. He was a master at detecting a lie, and Lydia's eyes said she was telling the truth. More important, they showed a trace of fear, something he hadn't seen before in the assassin's face. It convinced him to escalate the fight, before he was crushed between the two forces.

"Okay, Zafir, we need this lift, and we need it now. I'm going to give you an opportunity to redeem yourself. Don't screw it up this time," Toyo said.

Lydia nodded her head, but she was thinking she might need to kill Toyo and disappear before he killed her.

"I need a security officer with high enough clearance to access the entire dome complex and preferably someone who might know where the fems are kept. Now, look along the inner curve. Just about out of sight, there's a corridor that intercepts the main concourse. Second corridor down ... you see it?"

Lydia slid past Toyo's heavy body to watch the point he described. Eventually a head and shoulders peeked out and ducked back, without firing a shot.

"Yeah," Lydia said, her brightly painted lips breaking into a fierce grimace. "Man with officer shoulder boards checking on the action."

"That's him. I want him, and I want him alive and healthy. Work your way around behind him through the main dome. I can't give you much time with Racine coming up behind us. Lenny's going to hit the corner, so stay back a little ways. You cue us when that officer is clear of the corner. You should be able to grab him in the explosion's aftermath."

"Can do, Boss," Lydia said, slipping past Toyo and hurrying back down the concourse. Toyo checked his chronometer and set the timing function.

Toyo motioned to Lenny to move up next to him. "Okay, Lenny, you get another chance to use that thing. But you put the shot at the level I want and where I want, or I shoot you myself. And with these things," Toyo said, hefting his stunner, "you know you're not getting up."

"Right, Boss," Lenny said, nodding his head vigorously. Lenny wasn't one of Toyo's cold-blooded assassins. He wasn't even a big-time criminal. He just loved to blow things up with his beloved plasma rifle.

"Dial that thing down low, Lenny. I want you to put a shot through the concourse's inner curve at an angle that has the blast exit the walls in that second corridor right at the corner and about waist high. You get me, Lenny?"

"Yeah, Boss. You want me to shoot through the walls of the concourse to take out those six or seven guys packed into that second corridor right at the corner, but not let the blast go much farther."

"Good boy," Toyo said, lightly smacking Lenny on the back of the head. "I'll cue you when to fire."

"Right. I'll be ready, Boss." Lenny ducked his way back down the main concourse, staying to the outer curve, until he was at the angle he needed for the shot. He checked the power setting on the plasma rifle and its energy reserve. Then he shouldered his weapon and waited for Toyo's signal.

As the moments passed, Lenny's finger lovingly stroked the firing stud. He breathed slowly and deeply. "Easy, Lenny," he murmured, calming himself. "Don't make the boss unhappy."

Lydia worked her way through the main dome, discovering patrons and service personnel cowering under tables, behind bars, or just huddling in corners. She sneered at them. In her mind, they were the fodder for those with the power to rule. Lydia knew she wasn't leader material, but every person who sought to wield absolute power needed others to do their dirty work, quietly and silently, and that was her. The powerful paid well for her services.

After a few false tries, Lydia found the corridor she was seeking. The male officer was surrounded by a group of guards, and a female guard stayed close by his side. There was no cover to offer Lydia to get any closer, so she eased into an alcove behind a pedestal holding an exquisite, decorative vase and waited.

Soon, the officer touched his ear comm, and Lydia could see he was having trouble hearing whoever was talking over the fighting in the concourse. She waited, unmoving, as he walked down the corridor toward her. The female guard was ahead of him, taking the opportunity to swap out the power pack on the officer's stun gun and hand it back to him.

Training told her to remain absolutely still. It was amazing how many people were oblivious to her presence, even walking right past her, while she went about performing deadly business. "Now," Lydia whispered on her ear comm.

"Now, Lenny," Toyo sent in the open over the comms net when he received Lydia's cue.

Lenny saw his people hit the deck. He took careful aim and lightly stroked the firing stud. To Lenny, the eruption of the powerful energy blast was better than sex — nothing could beat the pleasure of seeing the blue sizzle streak from the muzzle, burning and consuming everything it hit, until its energy was dissipated or, as Lenny thought of it, until it went to sleep.

The plasma blast blew out the corner of Lydia's corridor, killing or maiming several of Kadmir's people, and scattering debris down the main concourse. Dust and smoke swirled into the corridor, and, amidst the confusion, Lydia raced forward. Her stun gun was holstered, and her two targets were holding forearms over their mouths to prevent choking on the dust.

Lydia's slender blade was in her hand, and she slid it quickly in and out of the woman's neck, without a pause to watch her drop to the deck. With the edge of her hand, she chopped the officer's forearm and his stun gun fell to the floor. Lydia shoved the man against the wall and laid the thin knife against his cheek. "Poison blade," she whispered, her face close to his. "You want to live?"

"Yes," the officer whispered, careful not to move his head. He glanced at the female guard, who had been his lover. Her dead, surprised eyes stared back at him.

"Good choice," Lydia replied, grabbing the officer's uniform collar and marching him down the corridor and back the way she had come.

* * *

Toyo watched Kadmir's people stagger out into the main concourse, disoriented by Lenny's blast, and his people quickly cut them down. The use of the plasma rifle spread fear through the defenders, and they melted away, down the main concourse or side corridors, abandoning the blue lift to Toyo.

"The lift is ours, people," Toyo commed. "Set up defenses around it, now." *You better have that officer, woman,* Toyo thought.

"Nice job, Lenny, you're a real artist with that weapon," Toyo sent over the comms. "Now, get back up here."

Lenny arrived wearing a huge grin, his eyes shiny and bright. "I did good, huh, Boss?"

"Real good, Lenny, and I'm going to give you a chance to use that rifle of yours again."

"Sure, Boss, you just tell me when and where. I'll do it good for you, Boss."

"I know you will, Lenny. Now, here's the problem. We've got adversaries coming at us from the rear."

"Who are they, Boss … more of Kadmir's people?"

"No, Lenny, they're the Harakens, and they've already killed sixteen of our people, including your friend, Chestling," Toyo said. Attributing sixteen deaths to the Harakens was a lie, but Toyo wanted Lenny motivated.

"Chestling's dead?" Lenny asked, crestfallen. The unpopular man was Lenny's one and only friend inside Toyo's domes.

"Here's what I need you to do, Lenny, to help me ... to help all of us ... and revenge Chestling," Toyo said. He leaned close to Lenny and placed a fatherly hand on the back of the man's neck.

* * *

"You wanted an officer, Boss?" Toyo heard Lydia say. He turned around as Lydia shoved the dust-covered man forward. "Name's Oslo," Lydia added.

"Well, Oslo, fortune is with you today. Most of your comrades are dead or have run away, but you have a chance to live ... if you're useful to me. Can you be useful, Oslo?"

"Sure, sure, Mr. Toyo. Will you let me go if I help you?"

"Of course, I will, Oslo, but only if you're invaluable. First ... do you have access to all levels of these domes?"

"Yes, Sir."

"Excellent, Oslo, you're already of help to me."

"Next, do you know where the Haraken fems are located?" When Oslo paused, Toyo added, "I don't like it when people hesitate to answer me. Zafir here doesn't like it either." That was Lydia's cue, and she stroked the side of her blade alongside Oslo's cheek. He flinched away from her, and she laughed.

It wasn't that Oslo didn't know where the women had been housed; it was that he knew they had gone missing and were still unaccounted. "I know the suite where Mr. Kadmir put the girls ... dome four, level six," Oslo said, putting conviction behind his answer.

"Now, that wasn't so hard was it, Oslo?" Toyo didn't bother to watch his captive's reaction. Instead, he turned to Lydia. "You hold this location until I get back with the fems. I'm taking one car full of our people to get them and leaving the rest here under your command to keep control of the lift."

"What about the Harakens?" Lydia asked.

"Don't worry about them. I left those pretty blue uniforms a nice little surprise … Lenny." Toyo was surprised he didn't get an argument from Lydia. It appeared she wasn't unhappy to lose out on the bonus for Racine's head, and it made him realize how much the Harakens had unsettled her.

"But who's watching over Lenny, Boss?"

"The boy knows what to do. I laid it out for him, point by point."

Lydia held her tongue but she was thinking this was not the time to be caught without an environment suit — located in a surface dome with an unsupervised Lenny, who was armed with his plasma rifle and had orders to attack the Harakens.

"Make sure you clean up Kadmir's wounded and collect their weapons," Toyo ordered, as he shoved Oslo toward the lift. He called out to seven of his people to join him.

*   *   *

Boker was ordered by Kadmir to support the defense of the blue lift. He worked to stay out of the thick of the fight, instead directing Kadmir's people in how to trap the attackers with overlapping fields of fire or with flanking movements. His efforts slowly succeeded, and Kadmir's people warmed to his instructions, despite the deadly fire from Toyo's weapons, which were paralyzing limbs or killing people.

Operating in the corridor that teed into the concourse nearest the blue lift, Boker saw the lead man at the corner drop his weapon from a numbed arm, and his comrades hauled him back. He regretted not stealing a pair of the stunners for himself, but, then again, he felt he should be satisfied with having gotten away from Toyo alive. *And here I am fighting for my life again against Craze. Some things never change,* Boker thought.

Boker's thought was hardly completed, when an arc of energy punched through one wall of the corridor and tore through the other side, exploding two of Kadmir's guards into pieces of flesh and bone. Three others, standing just in front of Boker, were hit by flying structural debris and body parts.

Thick smoke and dust filled the corridor, disorienting those still standing, and Boker struggled to see and breathe. His legs collapsed, and he sat down heavily. He pulled a small water bottle from his belt pack and wet a cloth to cover his mouth and nose to ease his breathing. But, instead, he coughed a quantity of blood into it.

Hearing the crack of Toyo's stunners, as the attackers dispatched Kadmir's people who had stumbled out into the main concourse, Boker leaned away from the sound and crawled away, seeking a hiding place. Every movement of his limbs brought agony, and Boker struggled to remain conscious. An office door was left ajar, and Boker, using the last of his reserves, crawled into the small room and hid underneath the desk.

Taking stock of his injuries, Boker felt wetness running down his left arm and touched it gingerly. His hand came away thick with blood, and he ripped off the shirtsleeve. A piece of bone with a small bit of flesh clinging to it stuck out of the meat of his upper arm. Wincing, he yanked it out, throwing it away in disgust, and then used the shirtsleeve as a makeshift bandage to tie up the wound. The exertions exhausted him, and he paused to recoup.

Suddenly, voices and the cracks of stunners reached Boker from the corridor. The attackers were checking for wounded and dispatching them. He chuckled, recognizing that fortune had deserted him today, but the action caused him to cough gouts of blood down the front of his uniform. *End of the run, Boker,* he thought, but, always the fighter, he was determined to take his dispatcher with him.

After making his preparations, Boker fought to remain conscious while he waited. Finally, from under the desk, Boker saw a pair of boots and the pants legs of a Toyo uniform. He watched as Lydia Zafir carefully lowered herself a meter away from him.

"Well, well, lookie who we have here," Lydia said, a wide grin forming on her face. "A traitor ... a traitor, who is going to make me a pile of credits."

Boker waited for the blast from the stunner, but Lydia holstered her weapon.

"Looks like you took a beating from Lenny's plasma rifle there, Boker, old pal," Lydia said, eyeing the dust-covered body of her ex-fellow assassin. She examined the extent of Boker's injuries. He was bleeding from several wounds, including one in the head, the blood making furrows in the dust alongside his cheek, and his chest held a slick pool of fresh blood. *A pierced lung,* Lydia thought.

"You're not going to make it, Boker. Too bad. Toyo would love to have had a long conversation with you back at his domes. But, if I'm going to collect the bonus for your head, I better leave my mark so everyone knows it was me who finished you."

If Boker could have smiled, he would have, but it would have given his plan away. He knew he was dying, but he needed whoever found him to believe he was incapable of resistance with his death imminent. That it was Zafir who discovered him made his impending death a sweet moment. Zafir's technique was to nick her target with a poison blade, and then, as they succumbed, she would carve her first initial deep into their guts, slicing through their organs.

Boker summoned a cough, which wasn't difficult under the circumstances, and spewed more blood onto his chest.

"Guess you don't need a nick in the neck at the rate you're going under. I hope you enjoy this," Lydia said, an evil grin on her face as she pulled her heavy blade. "For you, Boker, a special treat … I'm going to carve both my initials, and I would love you to stay conscious until the end."

Boker steeled himself for what was to come. Lydia jammed her knife deep into his right side to make her first cut. White-hot pain lanced through his brain.

"Hurts, doesn't it, you traitor," Lydia said, leaning close to Boker so she could look him in the eye.

With a quick flick of his head, Boker's lips brushed Lydia's cheek. She jumped back, yanking the knife with her, and Boker nearly passed out, but there was one more moment to savor.

Lydia pressed her hand to her cheek and examined her fingers. They held a smear of blood.

Boker bared his teeth at Lydia, displaying a small, edged, piece of alloy clamped tightly between them. He spit out the poisoned razor and chuckled, blood dribbling from his lips.

Lydia screamed and drove her blade deep into Boker's chest. She yanked her knife out, dropped it on the desk, and grabbed her med kit. Shaking it out, Lydia sorted through it and pulled out a small vial. She tilted her head back, and dumped its contents on the wound. If Boker's weapon was coated with one of the more common poisons, her concoction might save her.

As the moments passed, Lydia gained confidence that she had evaded disaster. She stood up, but her vision swam. She reached out for the desk, but her hand grazed it before falling to her side. Lydia collapsed to her knees, staring dumbly at Boker's dead body. Then, succumbing to the deadly nerve toxin, Lydia fell face forward into the pool of blood on Boker's chest.

30

It wasn't that Lenny didn't hear and understand every word Toyo said to him. It's just that Lenny's brain worked with a different set of priorities than normal people, including most criminals.

Lenny heard Toyo quite clearly stress that he was to secret himself in an office or room in the outer curve of the main concourse and aim his shot inward. Except, those instructions presented Lenny with a problem. Being right-handed, Lenny would either have to expose most of his body to take the shot or shoot blind by extending his rifle out the doorway and pointing it in the Harakens' general direction.

Neither choice satisfied Lenny's sense of what was important. Giving the Harakens a broad target, namely his body, scared him, and shooting blind wasn't an option either. Typically, Lenny was carefully supervised and directed how and when to shoot.

Once Lenny was told to target a person, and it was the most wonderful thing he had ever seen. A whole person disappeared — like in a magician's act that he saw in a vid. The prospect of firing his plasma rifle at an entire group of people had Lenny so excited, he couldn't help but stroke the weapon's firing stud over and over in anticipation.

So Lenny was ensconced in an office in the concourse's inner curve where a minimum of his body would be exposed as he leaned out the doorway with his weapon and, most important, where Lenny could witness the devastating effect of his weapon on lots of people. He sat still, except for the twitching of his trigger finger, listening intently for noise from his targets, sure that he would hear their voices as they approached.

* * *

<Stop,> Julien sent urgently. <There's an open door 36 meters ahead.>

<How can you see an open door that far around the curve, Julien?> Tatia asked. Despite her desire to question the message, she froze just as quickly as every other Haraken.

<Admittedly, Admiral, the residue of a plasma burn, which I'm detecting, is only in parts per million, but there should be none.>

<Perhaps that's what we heard earlier that shook the walls ... the firing of a plasma rifle,> Tatia sent. She was careful not to look in Alex's direction, since four of her troopers were carrying the dangerous weapons. <The residue could be carried by the ventilation system.>

<Plausible, Admiral,> Julien sent in return. <However, we must consider the air flow from the space. Infrared indicates a variation in air temperature exiting the doorway. It's consistent with a human body waiting just inside the opening. There exists a high probability that an ambusher lies beyond, holding a recently fired plasma rifle.>

Alex eyed Renée with concern. The Harakens had heard and felt a blast shake the walls, uncertain as to what had caused it — and them without an environment suit among them.

Catching Alex's pained expression, Renée sent, <Don't even think about it. Concentrate on that idiot up there with the plasma rifle.>

<Okay, Julien, good enough for me,> Alex sent, focusing on the danger ahead. On open comm, he added, <Everyone, back up quietly. No noise. We were never here.>

When Alex's people put another 30 meters between themselves and the ambusher, Tatia stepped close to Alex and whispered, "We're outmatched here, Alex. I tried to prepare us for some subterfuge on the part of Kadmir and his people. Instead, we've walked into a biter's nest." Tatia's reference to the voracious New Terran colony insects was a concept that Alex readily grasped.

"So we need reinforcements," Alex whispered back. <Julien, can you reach our traveler?> he sent.

* * *

Alex's comm call to the sting ship's controller was transferred to Reiko.

\<Captain, update please,\> Alex requested without preamble.

\<The *Tanaka* and *Rêveur* are positioned above the domes of Jolares. My sting ship and our fighters are prepared to interdict any support for Toyo's security forces. Miranda and friends located the lab and the key biochemist, Charles Stratford, and a knowledgeable colleague, Emile Billings.\>

\<Are those men and the lab secure?\> Alex asked.

\<Ellie landed with Willem and reinforcements to take the lab and hold the chemists. Apparently, Toyo kidnapped the families of the chemists and techs to force their cooperation. The security forces are restrained.\>

\<This must have been a first for Willem,\> Alex sent. \<Is President Drake interfering?\>

\<Negative, Mr. President. When President Drake heard Miranda's report that she located the lab and evidence of the hallucinogenic compound on-site, he formally requested Haraken's help to secure the proof he needed for the TSF and the Assembly.\>

\<That's a break,\> Alex mused, his thought reaching Reiko. \<Captain, I want to make one thing clear. Stratford and Billings don't get remanded to the authorities. They're ours. Am I understood?\>

\<Crystal clear, Mr. President. What level of force might I consider employing?\>

\<Anything short of a war with the New Terrans, Captain. If you have to threaten some captains or damage some ship engines, I'm good with that. The New Terrans can have Stratford when we're done with him. I'm not really happy with this government letting the drug-manufacturing epidemic get this far.\>

\<Understood, Mr. President. I'm afraid the fighting was extensive in Toyo's domes, and I must report the loss of one of our people, Ser Oren Gestang.\>

\<Black space ... how?\>

<A knife, Sir ... in the back.>

<Sounds like Toyo's kind of people.>

<On that note, Sir, our people can't locate Mr. Toyo and a significant portion of his security people anywhere in the domes. We have no indication of where he might have gone.>

<Toyo's here on Udrides. He and his people have attacked Kadmir's domes in an attempt to recapture the girls.>

<Sir, are you in trouble?>

<Up to our necks, Captain. Toyo's people are using a type of hand gun that permanently destroys nerve endings, and at least one of his people is touching off a plasma rifle. If they only wound people, they're cutting throats.>

<Are Kadmir's forces supporting you?>

<We haven't made contact with Kadmir's people yet, Captain. The admiral is concerned they'll make no distinction between red and blue uniforms ... we'll all be invading forces to them.>

<Your pardon, Mr. President,> Franz said. Reiko had linked the commander in, as Alex's information grew dire, and he had hurried to join her on the bridge. <If I may anticipate your needs, I have one traveler left at my disposal, but we have a minimum crew aboard and no weapons.>

<Understood, Commander, the *Rêveur* has crew, weapons, and a SADE. I need them all.>

<Should we launch more than one traveler?> Franz asked.

<Negative, Commander. The fighting is vicious. Bring only crew who are skilled with a weapon, and they are to remain aboard the traveler until they have an all clear from us to exit.>

<I'll be lifting off in ticks, Mr. President,> Franz said and closed his side of the comm.

<Captain, good job. I'm pleased to have you on Haraken's side,> Alex sent and closed the comm.

"Be careful," Reiko said urgently to Franz. The warm, big-hearted smile she loved lit up Franz's face just before he planted a long, deep kiss on her. "Decorum, Commander," Reiko admonished before she kissed him back. "Now, go aid the president ... but be a safe hero."

After Franz exited the *Tanaka*, Reiko waited a quarter-hour and then commed Eric to communicate the details of the president's call.

<Has Franz left already?> Eric sent when Reiko updated him on the events at Kadmir's domes and Franz's impending support.

<Sir, I'm afraid I was engaged in ship duties to the extent that I completely forgot to inform you until after the Commander rendezvoused with the *Rêveur*. He's already on his way to Udrides.>

<Seriously unprofessional of you, Captain,> Eric replied, smiling to himself. He was walking on the edge of deniability and sought a way to convey his opinion to Reiko.

<I'll place myself on report, Sir,> sent Reiko. After a lifetime under the auspices of United Earth naval forces, Reiko expected a rebuke for her decision to keep the New Terran president in the dark while they provided Alex with more forces. Reiko was willing to take whatever punishment protocol demanded, but she knew she had done what Alex needed, and that was the important thing to her.

<Under the circumstances, Captain, I wouldn't know the correct procedures. I would suggest you wait on that, and take up the issue with Admiral Tachenko once she returns. There's little that I can do about the delay now. I will inform President Drake in due time. Oh, but I notice that it's already midday meal. We'll speak later, Captain,> Eric sent and then closed his comm.

On Idona Station, Reiko had wondered more than once what it would be like to have an implant. As she reviewed her conversation with Eric, she marveled again at the tiny device's uses. It was an odd conversation with Eric to say the least. Listening to her recording, Reiko had a growing certainty that Eric didn't dispute her decision to withhold the information from President Drake. Furthermore, the three-way battle taking place in the Udrides' domes would be over before the New Terran president would become aware of the event.

"He agreed with me," Reiko said happily, and the few crew left on the *Tanaka*'s bridge looked over at their diminutive captain, who was smiling, her hands clasped behind her back and rocking happily heel to toe.

* * *

Once Alex closed his comm with Reiko, he placed his hands on his hips and studied the concourse, looking toward where the ambusher and a plasma rifle waited.

"Julien, any information you can access about the construction of these domes?" Alex asked quietly.

"Negative, Mr. President. If the designs are online, they're housed on an isolated network."

"Étienne, Alain, anything you can do?"

"We've been studying the layout of the concourse and have investigated some open rooms and their overhead to see if access between the levels was possible. It's our conclusion that the gunman would hear us coming, creating an untenable situation," Étienne replied.

Tatia regarded Alex expectantly.

"Okay, Admiral, you win. We fight beam with beam," Alex said.

Tatia grinned and then sent, <Mallory, front and center.>

As the Haraken trotted forward, his plasma rifle slung over his shoulder, Tatia turned to their SADE. "Julien, I will need your advice for this."

The two humans and SADE walked forward along the concourse. Tatia and Mallory were careful to stay meters behind Julien as all three hugged the corridor's inner curve. Julien stopped occasionally to test walls and overhead, calculating the infrastructure's strength.

<Stop,> Julien sent. <Our adversary hasn't moved from his original position. I detect his heat, but the plasma residual has dissipated below my sensors' capabilities. Admiral, I would suggest you wait where you are to limit our noise. Mallory, if you would, accompany me.>

Mallory knew that a SADE's avatar significantly out massed his New Terran body, but as quietly as he crept forward, he couldn't compete with Julien, who made no noise whatsoever. At an office doorway, Julien slipped inside and Mallory followed him.

<Julien, you would be better at this than me,> Mallory sent. <Do you want to take the shot?>

Julien sternly regarded the man for a moment. <I appreciate your nod to my technical capabilities, Ser, but it's my intent to limit my participation in the killing of humans. It might create a bad habit.>

Mallory looked at the SADE, trying to keep his mouth from falling open. As a new immigrant to Haraken, Mallory was still getting used to the concept of a cognitive, digital intelligence walking and talking. At times, he wasn't sure how the SADEs thought. While he stared at the SADE, Julien broke into a grin.

<Julien!> Mallory sent, his thoughts roiling. <Don't do that.>

<We are involved in dangerous events, Mallory. It's critical not to lose one's emotional balance, especially one's sense of humor ... where appropriate, of course.>

Julien moved to the office's far wall, quietly tore loose a table, which was anchored to the floor, and built a barricade for the rifleman to fire from behind.

Mallory took up his position, dialed down the power setting to its minimum strength, and aimed where Julien directed him. He pressed the firing stud, and the arc of energy tore a hole in the opposite wall and continued to burn through walls until the sound of an explosion reached them as the final structure absorbed the last of the beam's energy.

"Quickly, Mallory," Julien urged and hurried from the room.

Mallory exited as fast as he could, racing to keep up with the SADE. He could hear the pounding of the admiral's feet behind him.

<In here, people,> Julien sent to Mallory and Tatia as they ran past the ambusher's office door in the haze of smoke and dust. The humans backtracked, swiping at the air to help with visibility and locate the doorway. Inside the remains of the office, they found Julien holding a dazed and bloody man by the collar with one hand and a plasma rifle with the other.

"Julien!" Mallory exclaimed, seeing the ambusher hurt but alive. "All that talk about killing humans, and you planned to have the shot dissipate before exiting the last wall."

Julien smiled at Mallory, and said, "There was always the remotest possibility that I had miscalculated."

"Okay, okay," Mallory said, waving smoke aside. "Lesson learned … make that lessons learned."

"What did I miss?" Tatia asked, coughing.

"My tutorial on SADE thought processes," Mallory replied.

"Let's get out of here to some place where we can breathe," Tatia said. "Ensure you educate me later on your lesson, Mallory … every human continues to learn on that subject."

They walked Lenny back to the group. Alex looked at the dust and debris–covered man Julien held by the collar. He appeared to have only minor injuries but was sobbing uncontrollably, and Alex cocked an eyebrow at Tatia.

"Meet Lenny, Mr. President," Tatia said. "Lenny's upset because he didn't get to see the people pop."

Alex's confused expression prompted Julien to hold up the plasma rifle, and Tatia looked pointedly at it and then at Alex, raising her eyebrows.

"Oh … oh," Alex said, his voice rising as comprehension dawned. He studied the inconsolable man, and Alex's entire demeanor changed. "Yes, well, it was the opportunity of a lifetime. Wasn't it, Lenny?"

At first, Tatia was aghast at Alex's statement but intrigued when Lenny stopped crying.

Lenny regarded Alex and nodded slowly several times.

"You waited all that time," Alex said sympathetically, "and you never got your chance. That's a shame." Alex gripped Lenny by the shoulders and asked, "Lenny, would you like to shoot your rifle for me?"

Lenny wiped his eyes and blew his nose into the crook of his sleeve. "You'd let me shoot for you?" he asked hopefully.

"There's always a need for a good rifleman, Lenny."

"I'm really good, mister. I've studied real hard. Mr. Toyo tells me I'm good."

"I bet he does, Lenny," Alex said, putting his arm around Lenny's shoulders and walking him down the corridor. He opened his implant comm to his people, so they could hear Lenny's responses to his questions.

"Tell me, Lenny, why is Mr. Toyo here?"

"He's here for the Haraken fems. Wants them real bad."

"Does he know where they are?"

"I don't think so. Can I have my rifle back?"

"Not right now, Lenny. We just met, and we haven't had the opportunity to get to know each other."

"Oh, okay. Do you want to be my friend? I had a friend, but he was killed."

"I'm sorry to hear that, Lenny. That's sad. So, Lenny, does Mr. Toyo have another rifle bearer with him? Not that he could find a better man than you."

"Thanks for saying that, mister. No, Mr. Toyo only brought me. When can I have my rifle back?"

Watching Alex and Lenny wander down the concourse, Renée sent to the other Harakens, <He was always good with the alien types.>

31

Franz had commed Captain Cordova and relayed Alex's request. With the *Rêveur* stationed fewer than 10 kilometers from the *Tanaka*, the flight was exceedingly quick. Despite that, when Franz eased his traveler into the bay indicated by First Mate Lumley, his controller signaled the implants of a mass of people waiting in the open bay.

The traveler touched down, and Franz signaled the hatch open. Harakens, dressed in environment suits, poured onto his ship. Within moments, a tech signaled the hatch closed, and Franz, who never left his pilot's seat, commed the flight chief for launch clearance, received it, and was on his way to Udrides.

It wasn't until Franz cleared the *Rêveur's* space and settled back that he took stock of who was aboard. Cordelia was present, which helped explain the expedited turnaround.

"Commander," Cordelia sent, when Franz's implant pinged her.

"Good to have you aboard, Cordelia," Franz replied.

When Mickey's bio ID pinged back, Franz felt a sinking sensation. Alex had stressed to bring only shooters, and Franz knew for a fact that the engineer was unqualified with a weapon. Then again, there was a core of individuals in Alex's orbit who only took directions from him.

It was a short flight for the traveler to reach Udrides, and it wasn't long before Franz sent, <Approaching the dome, Cordelia.>

<I have Julien's instructions for entry, Commander. Standby.>

Franz brought the traveler level with the bay doors, which soon opened. It gave Franz concern as to how Cordelia could have cleared the bay of personnel so quickly.

Once on the deck and with the bay pressurized, Franz was about ready to repeat Alex's instructions to wait, when his controller signaled the hatch opening. He dropped a few expletives, swapped his pilot's helmet for an environment helmet, checked the stun gun on his thigh, and joined the exodus. That's when he noticed the crew was carrying armloads of environment suits.

Franz was the last off the traveler, but Cordelia sealed the hatch just as Franz's feet hit the deck. He raced to get to the front of the group, who were already streaming toward the main concourse. After his first view of the mutilated dead, Franz attempted to avert his eyes as best he could.

"Mickey," Franz said, before passing the senior engineer.

"Franz," Mickey acknowledged.

Franz kept running until he caught up with Cordelia, who was in the front and holding back her pace to allow the humans to keep up with her. "Do you know where we're going, Cordelia?" Franz asked.

"Forward in time, as we've always been doing, I suppose," Cordelia replied calmly, despite the hurried pace, which had Franz breathing deeply.

When Franz frowned, Cordelia relented from teasing him. "I've received Julien's vids of the action from the moment our people stepped off Alex's traveler until we arrived. I shared it with those in the cabin, but chose not to interfere with your piloting. Suffice it to say, circumstances are dangerous. Toyo's people are killing in any manner they can. The one individual employing a plasma rifle for Toyo has been eliminated, and the girls have not been located."

"Anyone hurt?" Franz asked.

"One of our troopers and a good many of Kadmir's people have been killed by deadly stunner fire. Those who were only partially stunned were dispatched with knives by Toyo's people. Kadmir's people are wearing brown; Toyo's people are wearing red."

Cordelia slowed as they came near the infamous concourse barricade. A red-uniformed individual in a doorway was stirring, just recovering from Alex's stun gun blast, and Cordelia summarily stunned him in passing. Following Cordelia's example, the group stunned Toyo's people, who were returning to consciousness. It must be said that some were stunned who were as yet comatose — but it was the thought of the Harakens to pad the odds in their favor.

* * *

Linking with Captain Shimada, First Mate Lumley sent, <It's a little lonely over here, Reiko. How is it with you?>

<Not as lonely as I could wish it, Francis. While my ship is nearly empty of crew, I've been left with the politicos.>

<Ah, that's true, but at least they aren't UE officials.>

<Yes ... I concede that I have that much to be grateful for. *Tanaka's* telemetry indicates you're following Franz's traveler.>

<That was the reason for my comm. Captain Cordova decided that our people might need our resources over Udrides. We do have some pilots left and two beam-capable travelers.>

<Tell Cordova that I heartily approve of his idea. I'm sure your support will be invaluable. Well, I believe I've learned my lesson.>

<Which is what, Reiko?>

<The next time I'm told that a ship requires only a minimum crew and supply load for trial tests, I will remind them of these days and insist I get a full complement of crew, travelers, weapons, supplies, and anything else I can pack into the hull, before I even think of leaving Haraken's orbit.>

Francis chuckled before he sent, <I'm pleased to hear you say that, Reiko. I was thinking the same thing, except for one tiny fact that would inhibit me from stamping my feet like an errant child and demanding my way.>

Reiko belly laughed at the image of the long-serving and even-tempered UE captain acting out like a spoiled child. <Yes, one day when you're the captain of the president's liner, you'll have to be creative to get your way. My advice, Francis, is to talk to Julien first. If anyone has the president's ear in these situations, he does.>

<Sage advice, Reiko, see you afterwards.>

<May the stars protect you, Francis,> Reiko said, signing off.

* * *

Having gleaned all the information Lenny had, Alex turned him over to the care of two troopers, who were told to keep a close watch on him, but since one of the troopers carried Lenny's plasma rifle that seemed unnecessary. Lenny walked closely beside the Haraken, occasionally reaching over to touch the weapon as if to reassure himself that it was still there.

Knowing that there were no more plasma rifles to face from Toyo's guards was of little consolation to Alex. He had to find a means of preventing Toyo's people from getting off a single shot from their insidious hand guns at his people. That thought was underlined by the image of two troopers carrying Nestor's body back to the traveler. In conversation with Tatia and Julien on how to proceed, Julien volunteered a section of an ancient Terran vid in which a company of men with single-fire rifles defended a compound against a much larger force.

"They refer to this arrangement as stepped fire," Julien explained.

"We can use this," Tatia said, "adopting it to the corridor, staying to the curves for the leading forces in multiple positions, and laying down fire from prone forces on the floor … just farther back."

Julien and Alex modeled the troopers' positions for maximum firing effect and minimum exposure. When they were finished, Julien sent the plan to all implants. Everyone had assigned positions. Each twin would lead a small group along the corridor's curves. When the enemy was contacted, two troopers would kneel in front of and one beside each twin while the escort remained standing.

Three tiers of troopers would hold central corridor positions, prone, sitting, and standing. They were positioned a little farther down the corridor. Although slightly more exposed to fire, it would require attackers to extend themselves past their cover to get a shot at these troopers, making themselves a good target for the twins and troopers on the concourse curves.

When all was ready, Alex marched the company along the main concourse until Étienne, stationed on the outer curve, spotted the first red uniform.

As soon as Toyo's guard spotted Haraken blue, he shouted warnings to his comrades. Immediately, Alex's forces fell into their assigned positions and fired at any and all potential targets.

Since Haraken stun gun fire was invisible to the naked eye, Toyo's people made the mistake of sticking their heads up or out, as the case was, to fire their weapons, only to be met by walls of energy. Within moments, half of Toyo's people were downed, and the Harakens in the central positions were slowly advancing by ranks and maintaining a continuous rate of fire.

Soon three of Toyo's people realized they were the last defenders of the blue lift. Without a leader to exhort them to fight to the last, they yelled out their plea for the Harakens to stop firing so they might surrender.

"Come out, one at a time, holding your weapon by the barrel. Walk toward us and place your hand gun on the deck when we order you. Do you understand?" Alex yelled. He received a chorus of agreement, and Alex ordered the first one out. <If anyone disobeys,> Alex sent, <I don't care how many shots they absorb. Don't be kind.>

A woman came out first. There was nothing gentle in her look, and Alex held his weapon at the ready in case her gender caused any of his people to hesitate.

"Stop," Alex ordered when the woman had covered about 5 meters. "Weapon on the deck." When she obeyed, he ordered her to walk the rest of the way, and she was passed to the rear. The process was repeated for the next two individuals. Six troopers guarded them.

"Do we hold them here, Mr. President?" one of the troopers asked.

Alex looked at Tatia, who walked to the rear, told the three individuals to sit down against the wall, and promptly stunned them.

"Problem solved," Tatia said offhand to the troopers, who were guarding them.

Alex picked up the deadly stunners and handed them to Julien. The SADE had a growing cache of the deadly hand guns in a large sack he discovered in a utility room and now wore over his back.

The Harakens advanced slowly, expecting further treachery, but their avalanche of fire had been highly effective. Several of Toyo's people were nursing numb arms and shoulders and had chosen not to continue the fight. Toyo's stun weapons were collected and given to Julien. Those individuals still conscious were immediately rendered unconscious.

Lenny, surveying the number of his people who had been eliminated by the Harakens, said to no one in particular, "You people are good. Wish I had known that before."

Alex and Tatia regarded Lenny, and Alex sent to her, <When you stand Lenny beside the likes of Toyo, Kadmir, their security forces, and these errant biochemists, it's a strange cast of characters that we're up against.>

<I never thought the day would come when I would say this while we were in Oistos, Alex, but I can't wait to go home to Haraken.>

Alain sent a signal to Alex and Tatia, who followed it to a side corridor and into an office. The escort was bent down behind a desk. As the two leaders came around to his side, Alain grasped the collar of a woman and pulled her off a man's chest, her face blood-soaked. "Disguised though she is, this appears to be the woman who shot and killed Nestor."

"A fitting end," Tatia said.

Alex leaned close. "She shows no major wounds. I wonder —" Alex said, as he reached for her eyelid.

"Don't, Ser," Alain said sternly. "I checked for weapons. The man has none, and the woman's hand gun was in her holster. I've confiscated it. However she died, falling forward in this manner, it speaks to something deadly besides guns and knives. Look there."

Alex followed Alain's finger and noted the sliver of sharp alloy clenched in the man's teeth. Blood coated most of it, but a green substance shown on an exposed edge.

"Poison, do you think?' Alex asked.

"Look along her cheek, Ser, but don't touch."

Alex could see the faint ridge of a cut beneath the coating of blood. "So this man huddles under here, trying to survive. This woman finds him and dispatches him with her knife only to make the mistake of getting too close, and he kills her with a poisoned blade in his mouth. Odd thing though, he's wearing a brown uniform, and this type of killing suggests it was personal. Otherwise, she would have just used that nasty stun gun of hers."

"I don't care why or how she was killed," Tatia said. "Good riddance. The takeaway here is that Toyo and Kadmir's people are liable to be using any combination of lethal hand guns, plasma rifles, and now we can add poisoned blades to that list. Just how did criminality get this advanced in Oistos since we left?"

"I have a feeling we're going to find out once we retrieve our girls," Alex said.

"Great ... politics," Tatia said, fairly spitting the last word.

Étienne signaled Tatia, and she motioned to Alex. The two of them hurried from the office and ran back to the main concourse. Entering the corridor, they turned right, following Étienne's signal and running farther away from the lift they had just secured.

Three troopers were flattened against the concourse's outer curve behind Étienne. "Careful, Sers," the escort said. The troopers slid back along the wall so that Alex and Tatia could ease up behind Étienne, who glanced backed at his two leaders and remarked, "It would please your security services if the two of you did not make such prominent targets."

"I think he's talking to you, Admiral, your chest is much more prominent than mine," Alex quipped.

"I'll have you know I'm prominent in the right places, Mr. President," Tatia replied tartly. "Étienne, what do you have?"

"We came upon three brown-uniformed security personnel, who saw us and quickly retreated."

"Did they fire on you?" Alex asked.

"Negative, Ser. We followed them and discovered an edifice just beyond the curve." Étienne sent the vid he had recorded. It showed him walking carefully down the corridor to see the edge of a barricade that stretched wall to wall and deck to overhead. The final pieces were being placed, it was presumed, after the three individuals Étienne saw had retreated behind it.

"Did you speak to them?' Tatia asked and received another vid.

Étienne was heard hailing those behind the barricade and announcing he was a Haraken. The response came loud and clear, "Don't know you; don't want to know you. Get back in your shuttle and vacate our premises."

"That seems pretty definitive," Alex remarked.

"I say we post the three troopers here just to ensure they don't decide to come through their barricade again," Tatia suggested.

"Agreed," Alex said. "Étienne, you're with us."

* * *

Cordelia located Julien's signal up ahead and picked up her pace. Focusing on his position in the crowd of Harakens, who held a concourse's major intersection, Cordelia spied a head with bird feathers tied in the hair. A smile overcame her face at the absurdity of the decoration, and the smile only widened when Julien turned and displayed a face decorated in bright, parallel smears of various colored lines.

When Julien and Cordelia met, their arms entwined and their foreheads touched. Few would have believed the incredible amount of thoughts and emotions exchanged between the two SADEs in those brief moments.

<You don't think wearing bird feathers in your hair might make you a premier target, my partner?> Cordelia sent.

<It was my thought to draw fire toward me and away from our leaders,> Julien replied.

<Did it work?> Cordelia asked, withholding her anger over Julien's actions.

<It did not. These aberrant humans that we face are content to shoot at anyone and everyone.>

While the two groups were mixing and environment suits were being handed out and donned, Alex, Tatia, and Étienne arrived from far down the concourse. Both Alex and Tatia took stock of who had arrived and exchanged a quick glance when they realized Mickey was at the back of the pack.

When Alex reached Franz, he eyed the commander, who, knowing the question on his president's mind, merely offered a shrug.

Tatia chuckled and said, "Now, perhaps, Mr. President, you know how I feel when you give me that reaction."

"It's one I understand, Admiral. It means that despite what you thought, hoped, or planned … inexplicably, none of those things happened."

Alex looked at Julien, who shook his head. The girls were still unreachable by the SADE's comm, whether it was by deliberate isolation, structure, or distance. "We need to get to the lower domes. If nothing else, we need to catch up with Toyo and put an end to the killing. Maybe we can engage Kadmir in conversation then."

"You need an officer," Lenny said, drawing everyone's attention.

Alex crooked a finger at Lenny, whose eyes glanced at his beloved rifle, so Alex crossed to him. "Talk to me, Lenny."

"I heard people talking years ago that Mr. Toyo got a hold of Mr. Kadmir's dome plans and built his place just like Mr. Blue's. To get to the lowest dome, where I think your fems are probably held, it would take an officer." Lenny looked around him, and the Harakens cleared his path as he searched. They could hear Lenny mutter "nope" repeatedly, as he looked at one body after another.

Exhausting all those nearby, Lenny widened his search to the side corridors and headed toward the green lift. Lifting a piece of debris off a woman who was badly burnt, Lenny announced, "Her … that's who you need. She'll have the chip on her somewhere. Can I have my rifle now?"

"Thank you for your help, Lenny. I'll offer a compromise for now," said Alex and waved the trooper forward, who held Lenny's rifle. He held out his hand and the trooper handed over the weapon, but not without a bit of hesitation on his part. Alex pulled the heavy power pack that charged the gases, handed the rifle to Lenny, and tossed the power pack back to the trooper.

"Thanks, mister," said Lenny, who was all smiles. He cradled his weapon, one hand lovingly stroking the length of the weapon.

<Keep Lenny really close,> Alex sent to the two troopers, who were assigned to watch him.

<Absolutely,> the senior trooper sent back, eyeing the fanatical expression on Lenny's face.

"We have access and now we need a destination," Alex said, to no one in particular.

"Do we know who was last on the lift?" Mickey asked, easing his way to the front to the group.

"Ah, my senior marksman," Alex said, which drew chuckles from many in the group. "Don't shoot any of our people, especially yourself, with that," Alex added, pointing to the stun gun on Mickey's thigh.

"You of all people, Mr. President, should know how valuable engineers can be," Mickey replied in a huff. "So who was the last on the lift?"

"According to Lenny," Alex replied, "Toyo took a car full of his people down, and the rest were to stand guard here at the lift."

"In one of Miranda's messages, she remarked how she accessed the level in Kadmir's domes where the service personnel took the drug-manufacturing supplies," Mickey said, excitedly. "We will need her," he added, pointing to the officer Lenny had identified.

Alex went to retrieve the body, but Cordelia intercepted him.

"Allow me, Ser," Cordelia said quietly. She turned the body over. The woman's eyes were open in surprise and Cordelia gently closed them. "Sorry, dear one," Cordelia said softly, and carried the dead woman to the lift.

When Cordelia approached the lift within a couple of meters, the wall-mounted keypad lit and Mickey tapped the call button. Within moments, the high-speed lift car arrived, and its doors slid open. Mickey was the first on, excitedly waving to others to join him.

<Hold!> Alex sent, his command echoing through his people's implants. Stepping into the car, Alex said quietly, "Mickey, I need fighters and a SADE below, not an engineer. Sorry."

Crestfallen, Mickey nodded his head in agreement. He had seen the dead bodies on the way in, and, though he wanted to help, he knew he wouldn't be an asset in a deadly fight.

"Franz and Julien protect this lift," Alex ordered. To fill the car, Alex chose Tatia, the twins, and four troopers, two of whom were carrying plasma rifles. "Mickey, how do we access the level where Toyo went?"

"The chip on the officer in Cordelia's arms will trigger the security parameter that you need. Request the control box to take you to the last level the lift accessed. If Toyo's people got off and others didn't use the car to travel to another level, you should find him down there."

"Mr. President," Julien said. "Captain Cordova has arrived overhead. The *Rêveur*'s travelers are patrolling and keeping ship traffic at a distance."

"Thank you, Julien," Alex replied, and gave Renée a quick kiss.

<Be safe, my love,> Renée sent.

The control box was repeating its message, requesting the female officer enter a dome and level. "Last level accessed, please," Alex said.

"Accessing dome four, level six," the voice of the control box intoned, and Alex took note of the way the keypad displayed the level, sending the information mentally to those in the car and outside before the doors closed.

32

Kadmir was scrambling. He'd received word that his people had lost control of the blue lift, but he couldn't blame them, not with Toyo's people firing a plasma rifle. *A plasma rifle in a surface dome,* Kadmir thought. *I don't regret trying to take you out, you crazy fanatic; but I do regret not being more careful about it.*

Knowing Toyo would try for the girls, Kadmir wondered if his competitor had any idea where they were or, better said, where they once were. He couldn't believe that after all his machinations, the Haraken women, the most important part of his plan, were lost to him in his own domes. For the umpteenth time, he wondered how two exotic Méridien women accompanying a striking New Terran could hide from his people. "The Harakens probably created chameleon wear or skin, for all we know," Kadmir grumped to himself.

This time and not doubting Toyo's drive to succeed, Kadmir told his people to hold the green lift, at all costs, and protect the patrons and service personnel still trapped in the main dome, as he organized security forces to follow him to D4-L6, where the girls had once been kept.

* * *

Seated around a restaurant's dining table in the main dome, Christie, Amelia, and Eloise kept their heads down. When they had exited the green lift in the company of five other similarly clad individuals, everyone had been directed to the large eatery.

Several of Kadmir's people walked around telling those dressed in environment suits to open their faceplates and shut off their air to preserve it, in case it was needed in the future. The girls shut down their air and shoved up their faceplates before Kadmir's people reached them. Having chosen a table in the corner, they sat with their backs to the rest of the restaurant.

<What now?> Eloise sent.

<I overheard two of the guards talking,> Amelia sent. <Toyo's people have control of the lift between us and the landing bay. So much for our plan to reach a traveler ... whether we could have gained entrance to it or not.>

<If I know my brother, the controller would have responded to us. At least, it would have responded to me. He does stuff like that without telling anyone,> Christie sent, surreptiously looking around. As a New Terran, her face would not attract attention as would those of her friends. She watched a couple speak to the guards at one of the restaurant's entrances. The discussion lasted awhile and seemed to get heated, but in the end the couple was sent back to their seats.

<I think we're stuck here,> Christie sent to her companions. <The security forces aren't letting anyone out of the restaurant.>

<We can't sit here forever,> Eloise sent <We need a plan.>

While the girls considered their options, Christie sent, <What? I didn't get that?> In reply, she received queries from her friends, asking her to clarify.

<Didn't one of you just open a comm or signal me?> Christie sent. When she received negative replies again, she looked carefully around. Christie was sure that someone had just attempted to contact her, but the signal was extremely weak. She waited but didn't receive another contact and wondered if a Méridien child, struggling with a new implant, might be hiding in the restaurant with them.

* * *

The car doors of the blue lift slid open on D4-L6, and Toyo and a guard ducked their heads out and back quickly, expecting to have drawn fire, but it was quiet. Toyo waved his people out into the corridor. When none of Kadmir's guards showed, Toyo hissed, "Put your weapons at your side, straighten up, and look like locals."

Soon after, two women dressed in vacation garb hurried past the group, and Toyo touched the brim of his cap to them in passing. However, when a service person, exiting a side corridor, spotted the red uniforms, he dropped what he carried and raced back the way he had come.

"Well, Oslo, time to earn your keep," Toyo said. "Where are the girls being kept?"

"This way," Kadmir's security officer replied.

As they walked the corridors, Toyo realized that although his domes were laid out in a similar fashion to Kadmir's, the arrangement of rooms in the lower domes was different. He had no idea which of the rooms contained suites and could possibly hold the Haraken women.

"This is their suite," Oslo said, after leading Toyo's people through the dome for several moments. He was dreading what was to come, but there was nothing to prevent it. He watched Toyo smack the door actuator and leap though the opening with his powerful stun gun drawn.

"They're not here," Toyo said when he emerged from the suite, grabbing Oslo by the throat and shoving him against the wall.

"They were here," Oslo cried out, trying to stick as close to the truth as he could.

"Where would they have been taken?" yelled Toyo, spittle from his mouth landing on Oslo's cheek. That actually scared the security officer more than the choke hold. It was the signal that Craze's infamous temper was about to explode.

"If Mr. Kadmir was worried for their safety, he would have moved them to a security office near the green lift," Oslo choked out. He was fervently hoping Toyo didn't detect his lie.

"Take us there," Toyo said, releasing him. "Be quick about it."

By now, Oslo was fairly certain he wouldn't survive his encounter with Craze Toyo, but the thought in the back of his mind was that if he was going to die, he was going to ensure the man or his people would be hurt.

* * *

After navigating several more twists and turns of the corridors, Oslo heard Toyo grumbling behind him.

"The security office is just around the next corner," Oslo said to placate Toyo.

It would have been better for Oslo to have kept quiet, because his statement put Toyo and his people on alert. As Oslo rounded the corner, he spotted Mr. Kadmir and a large group of security people standing at the green lift. "Attackers behind me," he yelled, and ran toward them, managing three steps before Toyo shot him in the back of the head, killing him.

A flurry of shots immediately erupted between the two forces, dropping several people on each side, as Toyo and his people scrambled to gain the cover of the corner they had just turned. The fighting was furious, but Kadmir's forces outnumbered Toyo's people three to one.

Peto Toyo kept his head down, even as his guards attempted to return fire. In quick succession, his people either dropped their guns from numbed hands or were stunned and dropped to the floor. Left with only two guards, Toyo yelled to break off.

The man and woman ended up on the opposite corner from Toyo, and the pair looked at each other and took off running down their side of the corridor. Toyo grinned to himself and headed the opposite way, intending to hide until he could make his escape.

Toyo's two guards made several turns and ran straight into Alex's force. The guards were stunned before they could raise their weapons.

<Be ready,> Tatia warned the group via implant. <Toyo probably loaded that lift car with seven or eight individuals.>

<Or eleven or twelve normal people,> Alain retorted.

<Lover, you will pay for that later,> Tatia sent privately.

<I was hoping so,> Alain replied, his thought warm and embracing.

Toyo ran into one of Kadmir's service personnel, and he raised his stunner to silence her, but it failed to fire. As the employee ran for her life,

Toyo glanced down, disgusted to see the charge indicator on empty. Out of alternate power supplies, he holstered his stunner and searched for a place to hide, finally choosing a utility room.

Advancing slowly, the Harakens took firing positions at the sound of running feet and watched a group of brown-uniformed security personnel burst around the corner led by a man in civilian dress. As Kadmir's people brought their weapons up, Alex yelled "hold" at the top of his command voice, and both groups froze.

"Weapons down," Kadmir shouted to his people, turning around to ensure everyone obeyed. Turning back to face the Harakens, he said, "President Racine, I thought you were returning to your ship to await our next meeting."

"And I thought you had a small technical problem with the dome's structure. Who knew you had a rat infestation?"

"We can argue this later," Kadmir said. "You came by the blue lift?" When Alex gestured questioningly back the way they had come, Kadmir said, "Apologies, Mr. President … yes, that's the blue lift."

"Yes, we hold that lift at the main concourse. All of Toyo's people up there are under our control. We understand only a single load of his people, including Toyo himself, came down your blue lift to this level."

"Excellent news," Kadmir enthused. "We've just engaged Toyo and his people near the green lift. He and two of his people got away from us. That's who we were just chasing."

"You were chasing two of his guards," Tatia said. "We just stunned them 50 meters that way," she added, pointing to a side corridor.

Kadmir assigned two of his security people, who took off running. "Speaking of infestations, Mr. President, the lead rat remains unaccounted for. If you will agree to leave the search to us and return to the surface, we will find him."

A broad smile crossed Alex's face, but it didn't reach his eyes. Kadmir took in the president's expression and the carnivore's grin on the admiral's face and knew he had overplayed his hand. The Harakens were as advertised — people you never fooled with.

Alex walked up to Kadmir, his people following closely beside and behind him, until Alex was nose to nose with the man. "You get one opportunity, Kadmir, and only one opportunity to get this right. So, think carefully before you answer. Where are my sister and her friends?"

Several ideas crossed Kadmir's mind as to what he should say, but far in his hind brain a part of him was yelling, *Don't be a fool. Tell him the truth!* The president's eyes bored into his, and Kadmir could see blood pulsing in the Haraken's neck. "We lost them," Kadmir finally managed to say. He expected an outburst of rage or to be slammed to the floor, but the huge Haraken just leaned in a little closer to focus on his eyes.

"Priorities, Kadmir," Alex said quietly, never moving or blinking. "We find the big rat and neutralize him. You signal your people topside to dismantle the barricade and cooperate with my people in a search for the girls. If one of your people harms one of mine, I will space the lot of you. Do we understand each other?"

"Perfectly, Sir," Kadmir said. When the president backed up, he thought furiously about how to mitigate his circumstances. That's when he noticed the admiral staring intently at him, and he realized he had made another mistake.

"Let's go rat hunting," Alex said. "Harakens pair up and take one of Kadmir's people with you to section up this level. Kadmir, can Toyo get off this level?"

"Only if he takes a hostage and gets to one of the two lifts. My people hold the green lift. You two," Kadmir said pointing to two more guards, "see that Toyo doesn't get access to the blue lift."

Alex signaled two troopers to follow Kadmir's people, and the dome owner nodded approval.

Kadmir's people led each search team, and, at a door, they provided the access, while the Harakens took low positions opposite the corridor, in case Toyo was waiting on the other side. With only a few teams, the search dragged on for an hour with teams communicating by ear comm or implant as to the sections searched and where they were proceeding next.

Tatia and a trooper readied themselves as Kadmir's security officer touched a door actuator. The admiral could feel the air change on the back of her neck, and she heard the distinctive click of a firing stud pressed. She spun around and Toyo stood beyond the doorway, which had opened at her back. He was laughing, his weapon dangling by the trigger guard from one finger.

"It was worth it to see the expression on your face, Haraken," Toyo said, chuckling. "No charge," he added, dropping the weapon to the floor.

<We have Toyo,> the Haraken trooper with Tatia sent over the open comm, which brought the Harakens running, tracing the signal origin, and left Kadmir's people, who had been leading them, wondering what had happened and belatedly chasing the Harakens.

"Who would have thought that Peto Toyo could be taken by a fem?" Toyo said, disgusted by the idea.

"You don't think a woman can put your ugly butt on the deck?' Tatia growled over her weapon's sight, which was trained on Toyo's chest.

"No fem I've ever met, but maybe you think you're different. Then again, we'll never know, will we … what with you holding a charged stunner and me on empty?"

"Step out into the corridor, Mr. I'm-such-a-bad-man," Tatia commanded, backing up to keep her distance from the criminal boss. She signaled the trooper with her to cover Toyo, while she lowered and holstered her weapon, which made Toyo grin.

Tatia's implant location app signaled the arrival of her fellow Harakens. She unstrapped her holster from her thigh, handing it behind her without looking, and Alain took it from her.

"Let's see what you've got," Tatia said, motioning Toyo forward. Faster than Tatia could believe Toyo's hand shot out to slap her face, testing her. She barely managed to block the strike with her forearm, which stung from the impact. The man was not only fast, but his muscles felt like metal alloy, and she shook her arm to ease the sting.

"Aw, fem, did I hurt you?" Toyo taunted.

Several times more, Toyo tested Tatia, delivering rock-hard blows to her extremities. She was able to protect her core, but Toyo had been a street fighter all his life, and he enjoyed the prospect of whittling down an opponent foolish enough to take him on one-to-one.

Watching Tatia fighting with standard TSF defense techniques, Alain sent, <Recall the mats,> reminding Tatia of the extraordinary amount of time Étienne, Tatia, and he had spent practicing Méridien escort techniques.

The reminder couldn't have come at a better time. The beating Tatia was taking, without landing more than a few cursory blows on Toyo, told her that she would soon lose the fight. Anger simmered inside, but she fought to keep control of it.

Embracing Alain's cue, Tatia shifted from her TSF self-defense stance to the relaxed and upright posture the twins had drilled into her.

Tatia's change in stance signaled to Toyo that he was winning, and he threw a right-handed roundhouse punch at the admiral's temple, hoping to end the fight. Tatia eased back on her left foot and spun clockwise. Toyo's fist sailed past her, throwing the man off balance, and, as Tatia came around, the knuckles of her balled fist caught Toyo in the temple, staggering him.

"Lucky," Toyo said, shaking his head to clear it.

"Think so? Want to try again, bad man?" Tatia replied.

Toyo pretended to laugh and relax, but Tatia saw his weight shift to the balls of his feet, and she was ready for his charge. She could never effectively copy the Méridiens' technique of dropping to the deck, spinning on one leg, and chopping the opponent's legs out from under them with her other leg. Her build worked against her. So Tatia added a twist to a traditional throw.

Dropping his wide shoulders, Toyo charged, intending to bowl the admiral over and pin her to the floor, where he could deliver disabling blows to her head. Tatia grabbed Toyo's arms and rolled onto her back. Toyo, detecting her intention, sought to halt his charge and drop on top of the admiral, but the boot she planted in his crotch short wired his every thought. The admiral followed through with her second boot, which caught him in the abdomen, and Toyo went flying over the admiral's head. Her powerful legs gave an extra shove that added rotation and launched him even farther, landing Toyo flat on his back. He struck the deck meters from the admiral, forcing the onlookers to jump back when he nearly sailed into their midst.

Toyo struggled to stand, and he considered making a quick escape, but two things convinced him otherwise. The number of stun guns trained on him was one thing; and Alex Racine, standing there with crossed arms, was number two. The Haraken president was even bigger in person.

"Only a fem would use that maneuver and try to cripple a man," Toyo said, circling back. He was considering the admiral's new fighting style, and he was no longer convinced of a win. She wasn't adopting the traditional fighter's crouch. Instead, she stood casually, balanced on her feet, hands at her side, waiting.

Figuring this might be his last fight, which Toyo wanted desperately to win, especially against a fem, he pulled a slender blade from inside his sleeve and waved it at her.

<Stand down,> Tatia sent urgently. <This piece of space dirt is mine.> The Harakens, who had moved to get a clear shot at Toyo, relented, lowering their weapons.

"Talking with that thing in your head, huh?" said Toyo, noticing the Harakens backed off without a word from the admiral. "You're supposed to be New Terran, but you're nothing but a freak lover."

"Useless piece of human trash," Tatia said quietly. "So what's your choice of poison, Toyo?" she asked, nodding at his blade.

"Poison's for assassins and fems," Toyo said, brandishing his knife closer and closer. "I like my blade clean and sharp. The metal does the talking for me."

"Well, bad man, since you can't take me with your fists, I'll let you try it with a weapon. Must be crushing your ego to get beaten by a fem."

Toyo growled and lunged to attack Tatia's left side, but it was a fake. At the last moment, he swung his knife down, intending to cut into Tatia's inner thigh and cripple her. But Toyo sliced only air as Tatia danced backward, moving easily out of attack range.

A small smile lit Alain's face. Worried before, he now felt the outcome was assured. It was only a matter of time before Toyo would succumb.

Toyo heard the chuckles from the Harakens at his failure to connect, and his temper boiled. In quick succession, he attacked with all the feints and tricks learned on the street. Known as a formidable knife fighter even as a teenager, it was his lack of fear that enabled him to take on bigger and stronger opponents. Toyo would rather have died than fail to win a fight, whereas his opponents were more often concerned with living.

But try as Toyo might, his knife couldn't score a strike on the big blonde. She didn't fight like anyone he had ever met. Even when he got close, she slapped or punched his hand aside. His right forearm and the back of his hand had taken so many hits that he switched the knife to his left hand before he lost his grip.

Eventually, Toyo tired, sucking in huge gasps of breath. A glance revealed the admiral sweating like him, but she stood calmly eyeing him. She still had the energy and breath to dance clear of his every attempt to cut her.

"That all you have, bad man?" Tatia taunted. "You're only good at abducting young girls? Can't deal with a full-grown woman?"

"Fine, I give," Toyo said, placing his hands on his knees while he regained his breath. He straightened up, reversed the knife in his hand, holding it by the blade, and extended the handle to Tatia, as he closed the gap between them. In a blur, Toyo flipped the knife over, and the two New Terran bodies slammed together.

Fear shot through Alain's mind, nearly paralyzing his brother, whose implant was constantly in tune with his crèche-mate.

Tatia took a step back, and the handle of Toyo's knife protruded from under his jaw. It had been driven up and into his brain. Toyo's eyes blinked twice in shocked amazement before he toppled to the deck.

Walking back to her people, Tatia caught Alex's nod to her, before she stopped and kissed Alain lightly.

<Good training,> Étienne sent to his crèche-mate, slapping him on the shoulder. It was one of the few times in Alain's life where he couldn't offer a single retort or witticism to his twin. He was much too relieved by the outcome.

"Well done, Admiral," Kadmir called out. "We will dispose of this piece of trash for you."

"Not so fast, Ser," Tatia replied, strapping her stun gun back on her thigh. "The body of Peto Toyo will remain in our custody until it's handed over to the proper authorities."

"That's an unnecessary burden for you, Admiral," Kadmir said, as politely as he could.

"Were my admiral's instructions not clear to you?" asked Alex, the menace evident in his voice, which caused the Harakens to flow around him to face Kadmir and his people. With both sides frozen, Alex sent a flurry of signals to the two troopers carrying the plasma rifles.

Kadmir watched in awe as two Harakens unslung their plasma rifles in unison and marched to stand on either side of Toyo's body, holding their weapons at the ready. The movements appeared to have been choreographed and practiced until they could achieve the perfect synchronicity of motion.

"As you wish, Mr. President," Kadmir said, his thoughts of burying all that had happened in his domes dissipating into thin air. "Perhaps we should go look for your girls now," he added.

33

Kadmir knew every meter of dome four, level six had been searched, which left the remainder of the four extensive domes to search. "We can't tell where your women went, Mr. President," Kadmir explained, "but we think they must have used the green lift to access another level. The problem is that a patron or dome personnel could have entered any level in the keypad.

On hearing that, Alex chuckled to himself. *Put it to these three inventive young minds to find a way to escape and hide in plain sight,* he thought.

While Kadmir, Alex, and their combined support searched the lower domes, Kadmir commed his security chief, Omi Yakiro, who commanded the forces holding the green lift and the barricade on the main concourse.

"Chief, good news: Toyo is dead, and all his people are down. Locate every one of them up there and secure them, if the Harakens haven't already done so. Stress to our security personnel that they are to be on their best behavior with President Racine's people. I want no incidents with the Harakens or that person will find themselves floating in vacuum. Take down the barricade and team your people up with Racine's and start searching for the girls. The women will probably reveal themselves when they see the Haraken blue."

"Two questions, Sir. How did Toyo get killed, and did you witness it?"

"I caught the end of the fight between Racine's admiral and Toyo. She ended up sticking Craze's own knife in his brain."

"Isn't the admiral a woman?"

"Yes and a formidable one. Find those girls, Chief, before Racine unleashes his admiral on you or me."

* * *

Chief Yakiro ordered the concourse barricade torn down, and he went to personally communicate with the Harakens. Remembering Kadmir's warning, he left his weapons behind. Walking next to the concourse's outer curve, Yakiro held his hands in front of him. When he spotted a glimpse of Haraken blue, he called out. "Hello, there. I need to speak to someone in charge." Yakiro had to wait a few moments before he received a reply, and although his arms were tiring he kept them out and visible.

"Commander Franz Cohen here, Ser. What can I do for you?"

"I'm Security Chief Omi Yakiro. I have a message from Mr. Kadmir. The fighting is over. Toyo is dead. Your admiral killed him. We're to ensure that Toyo's people are adequately detained and assist you in a search for your girls."

"Step forward, Chief Yakiro," Franz said, invitingly. He wanted to know how much faith Yakiro was willing to put into his message.

As Yakiro approached the two men, a New Terran and one with a unique build and decorated with face paint and bird feathers, he said, "May I rest my arms?"

"Certainly, Chief," Franz allowed.

"Why are we searching up here for the girls?" Julien asked.

"Um, Mr. —"

"No mister. Just Julien."

"Wow … Julien. It's a pleasure to meet you, Julien," Yakiro gushed, extending his hand.

Julien shook the man's hand, and then said, "My question, Ser?"

"Oh, yes, well, we lost them," Yakiro said in consternation.

Julien chuckled and Franz burst out laughing.

"I don't understand the joke," Yakiro said, unsure whether to be angry at the laughter or pleased that the Harakens weren't upset over the news.

"Who knew we were coming here to rescue your butts twice, Chief … once from Toyo and once from yourself, since you can't hang on to three young women," Franz said, trying to control his laughter as the chief's face reddened.

"Perhaps, we should begin the search, Chief Yakiro," Julien said, holding out his hand in the direction of the green lift.

Yakiro was about to reply when he froze, having witnessed the face paint and feathers wink off Julien to be replaced by a small hat. "Wow," he whispered.

<Who knew you inspired such awe, Julien,> Franz sent.

<Obviously, Chief Yakiro is a man of superior intelligence,> Julien replied.

Yakiro saw a force of Harakens running up behind Julien and the commander. So he turned and led the group back to where the barricade was mostly dismantled. When Kadmir's people joined Yakiro and the Harakens, the security chief laid out the search patterns he wanted his people to lead the Harakens through. He was turning to introduce Commander Franz Cohen and Julien, when the SADE froze in an utterly still manner. Then just as quickly, Julien resumed a human appearance and started walking.

Julien's comms power capability exceeded a Haraken's implant by 2.7 fold. It meant the SADE could send farther than a human implant could respond. Unfortunately, it meant a ping from him would fail to be returned, if the human was out of implant range.

In this case, Julien's comm mapping had detected the absorption of his powerful signal by a small but dense area, such as would be created by three young women close together. The absorption point, or hole, Julien detected was extremely faint. In fact, if he turned his head, the app would fail to map the tiny area.

Following the mapped point became an imperative, and the Harakens cleared Kadmir's people from Julien's path as he followed the curve of the concourse to close on the source. Several times, Julien took side corridors to walk into a bar, restaurant, or showroom, only to have his way to the source point blocked, which required him to backtrack.

"What's he doing?" Yakiro whispered to Franz after a while.

"Julien's honing in on the girls," Franz replied quietly.

"How?" Yakiro asked, and Franz touched his temple in reply. "Oh," Yakiro replied, all the more intrigued by Julien.

Following the SADE, the Harakens nearly circumnavigated the dome back to the concourse as it led to the landing bay, even though, by design, the perimeter corridor didn't complete a full circle. All patrons had only one path to the bay, forcing them to pass by all of Kadmir's offerings to come and go from the main dome to the landing bay.

Abruptly Julien turned and walked through the wide open doors of a large restaurant where hundreds of people sat around tables and were guarded by Kadmir's security forces. <Are you three done with your adventures?> Julien sent.

Franz watched three yellow environment-suited figures on the restaurant's far side jump up, squealing. The girls threaded their way through the tables, running as fast as they could in the New Terran safety gear. They threw themselves at Julien, who thankfully as a SADE could take the impact of three young women. The girls proceeded to hug every Haraken after that.

Yakiro touched his ear comm and called Kadmir.

"Kadmir here. What do you have, Chief?"

"The Harakens ... make that their SADE, Julien, located the girls, Sir. They were seated with our patrons in the Lunar Restaurant, and we never knew it. The women were hiding in plain sight. They were wearing environment suits."

"What do you want to guess that it was those three women who started everyone donning the suits, and then they exited with them?"

"Sounds about right, Sir."

"Are they all right, Chief?"

"They're fine ... busy hugging every Haraken in sight."

"Good work, Chief. One huge disaster averted. Escort them to the green lift and ask them to wait there. I'm bringing the president up."

* * *

Christie, Amelia, and Eloise shucked their suits and hung on the arms of Julien and Franz, as they followed Chief Yakiro through the concourse.

"If you will indulge me, we will wait at the green lift," Yakiro said.

"Why?" Christie asked.

"I understand your brother is coming up from the lower domes with Mr. Kadmir," Yakiro replied.

"Oh," Christie said, quietly. She threw concerned looks at her two companions.

<Do New Terrans believe in corporal punishment?> Eloise sent to Christie and Amelia, working to conceal her mirth.

<I don't believe so,> Amelia sent back. <But look at it this way. Christie will finally get a chance to slim down when Alex finishes chewing on her rear end for this stunt.>

Amelia and Eloise were still laughing quietly when the green lift car announced its arrival at the main concourse level and the doors slid open.

Alex was the first to step out, and Christie threw herself into her brother's arms. She dangled above the floor, her arms tightly around Alex's neck.

<I'm so mad at you,> Alex sent, while hugging his little sister fiercely.

<I know, and I love you, big brother,> Christie replied.

Eventually, Alex let Christie down, and he eyed Amelia, who ducked her head in embarrassment. But when Alex opened his arms to her, she ran into them, her slender frame held tenderly in Alex's powerful arms.

<Thank you for coming for us,> Amelia sent.

<There would be no other way,> Alex replied.

When Alex set Amelia down, he saw tears coursing down Eloise's face.

<I was so scared, Ser President,> Eloise sent. Fear, relief, and anguish roiled through her thoughts.

<Come,> Alex sent and held out his arms. When Eloise still hesitated, he walked over and scooped up the young woman, holding her tightly as she broke into deep sobs.

<Protector,> Eloise managed to send. <I never thought I would need you personally. Maybe Fiona saw far into the future, and her instructions were meant for me personally.>

Around Alex and the girls, the Harakens were shedding tears of joy. Even a few of Kadmir's people were misty-eyed at the emotional reunion.

*   *   *

Christie, Amelia, and Eloise were anxious to share their recordings of the Espero club, their journey aboard the freighter, and the encounters with the various individuals handling their kidnapping, but Alex halted all discussions.

"This mess has gotten much bigger than illegal drugs and kidnapping," Alex explained, once they had removed themselves from the vicinity of Kadmir's security people. "As Harakens, we have severely overstepped the boundaries of New Terran law. Right now, we need to be prioritizing damage control."

"Commander Cohen, Cordelia, escort our three wayward young women back to your traveler. Take several troopers with you and remain aboard with the hatch closed until I have further directions for you."

Christie started to object, but one look from her brother silenced her.

<A wise decision, young one,> Cordelia sent. <I will explain on the way to our ship the ramifications of what has been done in order to rescue you, so that you understand the complications that have arisen.>

Christie gave her brother a quick kiss on the cheek, and both Amelia and Eloise touched Alex's arm in passing as the three women hurried off to the traveler.

"Okay, second big item checked off … the girls are safe," Tatia remarked.

"And the first, Admiral?" Julien asked, thinking he had missed something.

"The kidnapper has paid the ultimate price for endangering our children," Alex replied.

"Ah, Ser Toyo is dead. I didn't realize that was a priority," Julien replied.

"A priority? No, but it was on my to-do list if the opportunity came up," Tatia said, her chin jutting forward, ready to take on Julien's moral challenge.

"More important things to consider, you two, and, for the record, I'm not displeased that Toyo met his end at Tatia's hands. It was an important lesson for the man to have learned, even if briefly ... not to mess with Haraken women ... young or not so young," Alex said, grinning at Tatia.

Julien kept his thoughts to himself. He understood the desire for revenge, but the pursuit of justice appeared to lead humans down dangerous paths. Yet, he had witnessed the shortcomings of New Terran laws and its legal system, which had often failed to provide the people with justice. He did not mourn Toyo's passing, but wondered if there was a better way to redirect those humans who seemed intent on errant behavior.

"I think we have to consider consolidating our assets ... the ones we want to protect," Tatia said. "We have two ships, and Drake and Jaya are already aboard the *Tanaka*. And Terese is ready aboard the *Rêveur*, with the engineering suite set up as a lab."

"I've already given orders to Reiko to tell Miranda to protect the two key biochemists, the lab equipment, and any documentation," Alex said. "It would be best to have Miranda take her people and everything she recovers to the *Rêveur*."

"And what will President Drake's reaction be when none of the evidence he's asked us to secure shows up onboard the *Tanaka*?" Julien asked.

"Extremely angry for one thing," Alex said. "We must remember that Will Drake is not Maria Gonzalez. He has a different concept of what he thinks are the duties of the president."

"Then we have to give Drake an alternative reason to engage these domes, and I know just the tactic to take," Tatia said, grinning.

"Okay," Alex said. "First, Julien, reach Franz and request he fill his traveler with the same people he brought. Transport his passengers to the *Rêveur*, drop Cordelia, Mickey, the girls, and the crew he picked up there, and return his ship to the *Tanaka*. Copy Cordova and Reiko on that message."

"Done," Julien replied.

"Second, Julien, a message to Miranda. Transport the lab equipment, the two lead biochemists, and ten of her original crew that she took with her, including Svetlana and Deirdre, but not Willem, to the *Rêveur*. She's to expedite her exit before the authorities arrive and remain on the liner. Copy Cordova and Reiko on that message."

"Again, done, Ser."

"Third, a message to Reiko. Keep watch on Cressida where we expect TSF forces to originate and warn Miranda in advance of their arrival. If she has to challenge the TSF travelers for ID to buy Miranda time to launch and clear Jolares space, she should do so, but gently."

"Ready," Julien replied.

"Last message is for Ellie. She's to standby, maintain security in the Jolares' domes until relieved by what I hope will be TSF forces and offer whatever cooperation to them she can. But, and this important, she's to extricate herself as soon as possible with our remaining people and return to the *Tanaka*. Copy Reiko."

"Messages sent and acknowledged, Mr. President."

"Okay, Admiral, I hope your idea works. Julien, connect me to the *Tanaka* and President Drake."

"Shall I have him woken, Ser Industrious One?" Julien asked.

"What?" Alex queried in surprise.

Tatia laughed. "It looks like we've run into the early morning hours. I thought it was just my bout with Toyo that had tired me. Vermin cleanup is hard work."

* * *

"Did you collect your young women from Kadmir?" Drake asked. He was standing on the *Tanaka*'s bridge with Reiko, Eric, and Jaya. Everyone was woken from their sleep, but only Reiko appeared properly dressed.

<I'm pleased to say, President Drake, that we were eventually successful,> Alex sent. Julien linked Alex's comm through the president's traveler to reach the *Tanaka*.

"Wonderful to hear, Mr. President, but I'm sensing other issues. Are the girls okay?" Drake asked.

<They're fine, Ser, but when we arrived we found Kadmir's establishment was under attack by a shuttle full of Toyo's security forces.>

"I assume you stayed out of the fray until Kadmir's people handled the situation. The Udrides domes comprise Kadmir's establishment under his company's mining charter. By New Terran law, Kadmir has the authority to deal with any issues on his property as he sees fit, and it's important that you respected that."

Tatia placed her hand on Alex's arm, and he nodded his assent.

<President Drake, Admiral Tachenko here. Events progressed rapidly from the point of our landing, and suddenly we faced exigent circumstances. We were setting down in the dome when our pilot reported bodies on the deck, which on infrared indicated they were cooling.>

"Cooling ... as in dead, Admiral?" Jaya asked.

<Precisely, Minister. At the time, we were not fully aware of the circumstances, but we felt it was our duty to offer aid to the dome's inhabitants to prevent further loss of life. It was only after examining those dead in the bay that we discovered the individuals, security and service personnel, were Kadmir's people. They had been killed by overloading their nervous systems with a powerful energy force and some, who we took to be only partially stunned, had their throats slit.>

Drake and Jaya looked at each other in consternation. "Admiral, you're describing wholesale murder," Drake replied.

<That I am, Mr. President ... the deliberate murder of New Terran citizens with illegal weapons. President Racine and I decided we had no choice but to support Kadmir's people against the renegades, and we entered into an extended fight with Toyo's people to stop the senseless killings.>

"So these are the exigent circumstances you're citing, Admiral, which you felt demanded your encroachment on New Terran sovereign space and required you enter into this conflict?"

Tatia knew where Drake was headed. He needed to hear a plausible defense of the Harakens' actions that he could use when he dealt with the Assembly or the courts.

<President Drake, this was not an internal company dispute covered by the charter. This was a war between organizations, and one side was using illegal stun guns designed to kill, cutting the throats of combatants and noncombatants alike. Toyo's side fired a plasma rifle in a surface dome where patrons of the establishment were potentially exposed to immediate decompression. We had every right as fellow humans to come to the aid of your innocent civilians, and you have every right as president to declare an emergency and send in TSF troops to these domes.>

"Was the main dome's integrity defeated?" Jaya asked.

<Fortunately, it was not,> Alex replied, <and we were able to capture the only rifleman with Toyo's people even while he laid an ambush for us.>

Drake was shaking his head, wondering how such a level of violence was possible among his people.

"I've ordered a launch of TSF troopers from Cressida for Jolares, where the drug lab was discovered. I will order a second launch of troopers for Udrides," Drake said. "That should just about exhaust the base's resources."

"Are there any estimates of the dead?" Jaya asked.

<Julien here, Minister. While circumstances have not allowed me to review the implant recordings of all our people, I estimate at least sixty-three dead ... most are Kadmir's security forces, some are his service personnel, and a few are dome patrons.>

The word patrons scared Drake. It underlined the unfolding of a political nightmare. Patrons could mean local miners splurging their savings, but it could also mean wealthy New Terrans, which could mean families. *Please, no dead children,* Drake thought.

"What's the status of Toyo and his people? Have they all been ... neutralized?' Jaya asked He was struggling to choose words that circumvented describing in blunt terms the wholesale slaughter of people.

<Toyo is dead, Minister,> Alex sent. <He was hiding in a utility room, broke out to attack Tatia from behind, and in the ensuing fight he died when stabbed with his own knife.>

<I must remember to edit my recordings to match the new facts,> Julien quipped to Alex and Tatia.

"And the status of your people, Alex?" Drake asked.

<We lost one trooper on Udrides and another on Jolares,> Alex sent. <We will remain on station, ensuring Toyo's people remain secure and offering whatever aid to Kadmir we can provide until your troops arrive. Then we will be returning to the *Tanaka*.>

"Thank you for going to the aid of our civilians, President Racine," Drake sent. "I don't have to tell you what these horrendous circumstances mean to our government and our people. In addition to the tragic loss of life, it will create a political mess. In the near future, I will require your utmost cooperation to manage this crisis through the Assembly and the courts, if necessary."

<Understood, President Drake, we will do what we can to assist you,> Alex said.

Alex closed the comm, and Drake issued emergency instructions, intending to bring order to the disaster that had befallen Ganymede's moons.

On Udrides, not more than a half-hour after the comm with Drake, Alex and Tatia received a private comm from Julien sent to him from Lumley aboard the *Rêveur*, which was stationed overhead. TSF troopers were en route from Cressida to Jolares. The chronometer was counting down for Miranda to clear the domes with the assets the Harakens wanted to preserve before the TSF arrived.

* * *

"Captain Shimada, I require a comm with General Dolan Oppert, the head of TSF. His headquarters are situated in Prima. My staff can locate him instantly," Drake said.

Without a SADE aboard, it took several comm connections before the general was finally located. He was on a celebratory camping trip with close friends and had been there ever since the busts of the fourteen illegal drug-manufacturing locations. Oppert was ensuring that his powerful friends, who had accompanied him, knew he had engineered the highly successful crackdown on the criminals.

"Mr. President," Oppert said, answering the comm on his reader and struggling to sit up from his comfortable camp cot where he had been asleep.

"Apologies, General, for the early morning comm, but I'm informing you that I have issued emergency orders to Cressida TSF forces to interdict the illegal actions taking place in the domes of Jolares and Udrides."

"Uh ... President Drake, I would advise against any such actions against the domes. They do have legal autonomy."

"Get the stuffing out of your ears, General. I'm not requesting you send in troops. This is a courtesy call to inform you that I've already sent in troops. We have illegal drug manufacturing in the Jolares domes. The lab chemists and techs have had their families kidnapped to force their cooperation."

"How did we learn this?" Oppert asked, wondering why he failed to receive this information.

"The Harakens discovered it."

"Why are the Harakens at the Jolares domes?"

"They were searching for the source of the drugs that have been distributed to their young people in Espero." Drake deliberately left out the part about the kidnapping, not wanting that to be publicized until he had an opportunity to talk to Alex in greater detail.

"The Harakens should have come to us with their problem," Oppert declared hotly, rising from his cot to step out of his spacious tent into the green of the surrounding forest.

"What they should or shouldn't have done is moot, General. That's in the past."

"Excuse me, President Drake. Earlier you said Jolares and Udrides. Were their drugs on Udrides?"

"That's an entirely separate event, General. Toyo and his security forces attacked Kadmir's domes, killing people either by the use of illegal energy weapons or by cutting their throats."

"Inconceivable," Oppert said softly. "Was it Kadmir who called you for assistance?"

"No, again it was the Harakens, who were planning to meet with Kadmir and arrived at his domes just after Toyo landed and began killing people."

"This makes no sense, Mr. President. Why would Toyo do such a thing? He's been running a successful establishment, making credits by the shuttle load."

Drake sidestepped the general's question. He didn't wish to discuss the recent events until he had formed more succinct responses to the tough questions. "General, now is not the time for lengthy questions. Cressida's TSF resources are stretched thin. I need two more travelers full of troops with senior commanders aboard sent to each of the Jolares and Udrides domes. I need them en route yesterday."

"Understood, President Drake."

"One more item, General. What information crossed your desk about the manufacture of illegal energy weapons?"

"There were rumors, Sir, but nothing worth investigating."

"Well, you were either misinformed or uninformed, General. They exist, and Toyo's people used them to kill sixty-three civilians."

-34-

Miranda urged her people to hurry, even as she carried a crate packed with lab equipment that no two Harakens could lift. When she broke out into the main concourse from the lift, she received a comm from Reiko. <A bit rushed, dear. Something important?> Miranda sent.

<Just a traveler filled with Terran Security Forces inbound for Jolares that I thought you might want to know about.>

<Oh, my, aren't you just bubbling with exciting news? How much time do I have before we must clear Jolares space?>

<Telemetry estimates 0.42 hours.>

<Understood. Any changes in orders from the dear man in charge?>

Reiko nearly giggled at their president being labeled as "the dear man in charge." <None, Miranda, I'm standing by to challenge the traveler's authority to enter the space, if I must. It might buy you an additional fifth or quarter of an hour, if I can draw it out.>

<We'll try to prevent you from executing an incursion against the TSF. We wouldn't want your good name, dear, to be written in ignominy on the refresher walls of the Cressida forces' barracks.>

Reiko waited and watched as the TSF traveler closed on Jolares. She requested Eric entertain the New Terran officials, which was a euphemism for keeping them away from the bridge, if Reiko had to challenge the traveler to buy Miranda time.

Down below, Miranda redoubled her efforts, prioritizing the loading and ensuring the two biochemists and their families were aboard first.

Stratford was vociferously objecting to being detained and started screaming about New Terran rights and Harakens overstepping their bounds, when Billings smacked him across the face.

"Your egotistical pursuit to create more fantastical compounds landed me and my family in Toyo's prison," Billings yelled at Stratford, as the biochemist held a hand to his reddening face. The family members were too shocked to move. "The Harakens have just freed us, and I don't care where they take us. So get your butt aboard this vessel, or you won't have to worry about the Harakens. I'll throttle you myself."

As the Stratfords clambered into the traveler and Billings helped his family up the hatch steps, Miranda said, "Quite effective, Ser. Your assistance is noted."

Harakens grabbed as much lab equipment and material, as readily available, bagging and sealing the potentially contaminated material in vacuum-packing equipment seized from the domes' kitchens. When Reiko commed to ask whether she should provide interference, Miranda waved her off, piled the troopers aboard, received bay clearance, and launched the traveler.

Using the *Tanaka*'s telemetry, Miranda tracked the incoming Cressida traveler. She flew low, keeping the moon between the two shuttles as she sped off in the opposite direction. When the *Tanaka* indicated the TSF forces were descending toward the domes' landing bay, Miranda accelerated, using the body of Jolares to hide her from the TSF as she raced for the *Rêveur*.

* * *

Miranda eased the traveler into the liner's bay. Terese and Pia waited anxiously in the airlock for the clearance signal that pressure was achieved. Both of them had spent hours reviewing Miranda's vid files, which were taken of the lab and the biochemists.

With his ego driving him, Stratford made the mistake of choosing to descend the traveler's hatch steps first. Having helped his family to the deck, he turned around and encountered Terese, who promptly slapped him hard across the face.

The sound reverberated across the bay, and Billings, in the middle of helping his family down the hatchway, paused to regard the two, Haraken and New Terran, in confrontation. Stratford might have out massed the

Méridien-built woman, but her flaming red hair and angry eyes said she was a match for any two or three New Terrans.

"Why is everyone slapping my husband lately?" Stratford's wife wailed.

"Perhaps, because he deserves it, Ser," Terese replied hotly, daring the woman to say more.

"But we've never met," Stratford objected.

"Your reputation precedes you, Ser. I have an entire wing of young people on Espero, who I ordered placed into unconscious states, because they were addicted to your insidious drug."

"I just made the compound. I didn't know what Toyo would do with it."

"And there lay the excuses of all weak men," Terese retorted, and then, in a whiny voice, she added, "I just built the destructive device; I couldn't control how it was to be used." She glared at Stratford, waiting for his response, but the biochemist thought better of opening his mouth. "If you produce potentially dangerous creations, Ser, without adequate oversight and controls in place, then you have no moral foundation on which to stand when people die from your invention."

Terese motioned the two biochemists and their families aside as crew began carting the lab equipment off the traveler, heading for the engineering suite, which was now Terese's laboratory. "Ser Billings, greetings. I'm Terese Lechaux. This is my senior medical technician, Pia Sabine."

Billings hesitated but was grateful when the Haraken woman politely extended a hand.

"Pia, you, and I will be working together, Ser Billings, to support this individual," Terese said, pointing a finger at Stratford, "in creating a compound that effectively blocks the craving for his addictive hallucinogen."

"The name is Charles Stratford, madam. I would thank you to address me properly."

Terese whirled to eye Stratford, and he shrank back. "Lesser creatures are not given names," Terese declared hotly. "We will see if you are able to earn the status of human being." Terese spun around and made for the airlock, waving an imperial finger over her shoulder for the families to follow.

Billings passed Stratford and bestowed a huge grin on him that showed how much he was enjoying Stratford's discomfort after the long arduous months his family had endured subjected to Toyo's incarceration and daily threats.

Having witnessed most of Terese's introduction to the biochemists, Svetlana said to Deirdre, "I was wondering why our president directed us to the *Rêveur* ... now I know."

"To protect Stratford from Terese until she's done with him," Deirdre said, laughing.

"I'm sure the New Terrans will want him for prosecution, and it would be most embarrassing to have to tell them that our chief medical specialist spaced him as human waste ... so sorry," Svetlana replied.

The two women shared a brief laugh, but each thought Stratford would require close observation. Alex would be upset if something happened to the biochemist while he was in the Harakens' care. Not that Terese had ever committed bodily harm on a person ... yet. But Stratford's descent into depraved invention and disregard for human safety was provoking the fiery redhead's temper.

* * *

The chemists' families were ushered to their cabins by Pia, who displayed the amenities of the first cabin for the wives.

"Will we be locked in?" Billings' wife, Janine, asked.

"No, Ser, we're Harakens, not New Terran criminals," Pia answered simply. "You may consider this ship safe to wander around. This includes the children. If you need something, please ask any crew member, and they'll be happy to provide it for you."

"How about food?" Stratford's wife asked. "The children haven't eaten for a while."

"Midday meal is less than a half-hour away. Unpack your belongings, use the refreshers, and I will be back to take you to meal time. You will require a crew member to order meals for you or snacks for the children as you are without implants, but, again, any Haraken will assist you."

While Pia settled the families, Terese introduced the biochemists to her lab space. "While our equipment will be unfamiliar, you'll find it'll make your research proceed faster," Terese said. "We have brought your existing manufacturing equipment, so that we might examine your process and enable us to understand the original compound better."

Stratford's ego had recovered from the ignominy of Terese's public humiliation, and he gazed at Miranda and Deirdre, but settled on Svetlana, who still wore her delicate wrap, declaring, "I'm not working for this woman. Get me someone else who speaks to me in a civil manner."

"Since you seem to be addressing me," Svetlana replied, "let me inform you that you shouldn't be fooled by my dress. My attire was purely for the edification of foolish New Terran patrons. You may address me as Commander Valenko. This is Commander Canaan, and our curvy friend is Miranda Leyton."

"But let's speak to your concern, Ser," Deirdre said. "Our leader has a saying. Perhaps you're familiar with the expression of an airlock to nowhere. If you're of no value to us, we have no need to keep you around."

"You don't fool me with your tough act. Everyone knows Harakens don't kill except in self-defense," said Stratford, confident in his knowledge.

Miranda stepped close to Stratford, staring into his eyes, careful to keep any emotion from her face. "Do you know what I am, human?" she asked, evincing a flat tone and evenly paced words.

"Yes ... yes, you're one of those ... um —" Stratford stammered.

"SADE is the word you're searching for, Ser. Do not use any other term within hearing of a Haraken. Since you know what I am, you know I'm not human. Logic, not emotion, controls my being. I do not have the same constraints on my choices as do my human cousins and would have no problem applying any level of discipline to you that I see fit. Do you understand me?"

Stratford flicked a glance between Svetlana and Deirdre, searching for some human compassion, but he was met with hard stares.

"I'm waiting, and I'm an impatient individual," Miranda said.

Stratford tried to ease away from the SADE, but eerily she maintained the distance between their faces as if they were strung together. "Okay," he finally said.

"Okay, what?" Miranda asked quietly.

"Okay, I will work with this woman," Stratford replied.

When Billings found Miranda gazing at him, he wiped a smile off his face, jumped away from the table he was leaning against to stand straight, and said, "I'm more than pleased to work with Ser Lechaux."

"Good, that's settled. I will expect to hear results soon," Miranda said, returning her gaze to Stratford. When she left the lab, she made sure to do so in an un-Miranda–like way. No swaying of the hips; no artful motion designed to attract the human eye. Her movements were perfunctory, bordering on mechanical, and Svetlana relayed to her the image of Stratford, cringing as he watched her leave.

<I believe Stratford will be a compliant individual now,> Miranda sent to Terese, Svetlana, and Deirdre.

<She had me fooled,> Deirdre sent privately to Svetlana.

<Who really knows another?> Svetlana replied cryptically. <You watch over our errant scientists while I find a cabin, a refresher, and a ship suit for myself. Then I'll relieve you.>

* * *

Christie took a seat across from Cordelia as Franz piloted the traveler out of the Udrides domes. She wore an expectant look on her face, and Cordelia obliged her.

"We successfully traced the drugs, which were distributed in Espero, to Jolares, where we believe you were initially held," Cordelia began. "It isn't clear under what circumstances Ser Kadmir managed your rescue."

"Rescue?" Christie challenged. "I don't think so. The same man who took us off the freighter after the kidnapping in Espero was the same one who transferred us to those domes we just left. Although it was in the early morning hours when he did it, we just walked out of our suite to the waiting shuttle."

"We are in complete agreement there," Amelia said. "Kadmir did not rescue us. He had to have some sort of deal with Toyo."

"Some sort of deal that later went wrong," Eloise added.

"Be that as it may, what we've discovered is that these domes operate under the guise of mining companies, and, under the New Terran charter granted to these establishments, they're allowed to operate without interference from the government when it regards internal affairs and that includes the oversight of the TSF."

"That's a mistake," Christie grumped.

"Wait, Cordelia, are you saying that if our people had asked the New Terran government for permission to enter and retrieve us from either of these domes, they would have been denied?" Amelia asked.

"Precisely, young one," Cordelia replied. "We sent one group, masquerading as miners catching a ride with three Méridien holiday travelers, into the Jolares domes. They discovered the lab and the biochemists, but it resulted in a fight and the loss of one of our people. A second traveler, carrying troopers, was sent to secure that location for the TSF and was done so with presidential permission."

"So the government knows that illegal drugs were manufactured there?" Eloise asked.

"They do now, after the fact," Cordelia said.

"But we didn't have permission to be there in the first place. So, it's like we invaded their territory," Amelia said.

"Then, it must be worse for what was done at Udrides," Christie said.

"There, it's less clear. Alex was invited by Ser Kadmir to retrieve you, but when Ser Toyo attacked, Kadmir refused Alex landing permission. The president disobeyed and subsequently discovered the incursion by Toyo's people," Cordelia explained.

"I can't believe Toyo killed all those people," Eloise said, shuddering. She still had images in her mind of the throat-slashed dead, and she wished she could erase them from memory, just as she could remove data from her implant.

"So what kind of trouble is my brother in after all this?" Cordelia asked.

"That remains to be seen, young ones. President Drake will require our help to support what steps he wishes to take with his Assembly," Cordelia said.

"So President Drake is on our side?" Amelia asked.

"That remains to be seen as well," Cordelia said.

"And I thought the drugs and our kidnapping were the worst things that were happening," Eloise complained.

* * *

During the remainder of the flight, Cordelia collected the memories of the girls from the moment they approached the illegal club in Espero to the moment they hugged Alex. After living through the girls' traumatic moments, Cordelia yearned to return to Espero and surround herself with her adopted children.

Although the *Rêveur*'s crew was aware who rode in Franz's traveler, Pia communicated strict instructions to all aboard to allow the girls some time to themselves. She met the young women in the bay and promptly escorted Christie, Amelia, and Eloise to one of the *Rêveur*'s more expansive suites.

Once left alone, the girls mobbed the refresher together. Afterwards, they lay down for a nap and didn't wake until Pia came for them for evening meal.

When the three girls, refreshed and enjoying wraps provided by Pia, walked into the meal room, they were greeted, hugged, and touched by passing crew members.

"What's going on with those three young women?" Billings asked Terese. The biochemists and their families were seated with Terese at an extended table.

"Oh, those three are the young Harakens who were kidnapped for investigating an illegal club in Espero, peddling that one's drugs," Terese said, pointing a utensil at Stratford, who glared at Billings because he had brought up a subject that further embarrassed him. "They were transported to Toyo's domes but later moved to Kadmir's before they were recovered."

"The crew seems particularly pleased to see them," Janine, Billings' wife, noted.

"Harakens would treat any lost one, who we managed to recover, in this fashion. It's our way. But perhaps it pleases our people that much more to have recovered Alex Racine's sister." The sound of Stratford choking on his water gave Terese a small amount of pleasure.

Billings and Janine eyed Stratford. As the ugly ramifications of inventing the illegal drug mounted, Stratford's defense of his pursuit of pure science dwindled away. Recriminations were all that was left.

35

Alex and company waited at Udrides for the TSF, who arrived aboard their own traveler. The Harakens then led teams of troopers to collect Toyo's body, hand over custody of Toyo's people, and assist in transporting the dead to the domes' coolers.

The TSF captain was in shock, having never run into something as egregious as the mass murder of New Terran citizens, and was extremely grateful to discover Tatia Tachenko was at the center of the fracas. Her reputation as a hard-nosed TSF major proved invaluable to him, as she directed him in the vid coverage of the damaged dome and the dead, collection of the extensive evidence, and the interview of Kadmir's people and Harakens as witnesses.

It was the early morning hours the day following the TSF's arrival at Udrides before Alex and his people were released to board their traveler and return to the *Tanaka*. Exhausted, Alex, Renée, Tatia, and the twins headed for cabins to refresh and sleep.

Julien took the opportunity to link with Cordelia to exchange data and spend time in each other's virtual company.

* * *

On Jolares, Ellie was left holding the proverbial bag. Miranda's traveler had no sooner cleared the moon's space when Willem announced to her, "Company, Commander," and the TSF traveler, under the command of Captain Elman Ripard, landed in the bay.

Ellie squared her shoulders and went to greet the TSF captain, as he entered the corridor leading to the main dome. Knowing she was tasked by the New Terran president to preserve the domes' evidence, which Miranda just took with her, left her in an exceedingly awkward position.

An astute man, the captain recognized the deference paid the slender Méridien woman by the three individuals in Haraken blue standing slightly behind her. "Captain Elman Ripard," the TSF leader said, saluting Ellie.

"Wing Commander Ellie Thompson," Ellie replied. "Glad to have you here, Captain. I'm authorized to extend you any help you need before departing for my ship stationed above."

"Much appreciated, Commander. What's the status?" Ripard asked.

"Still to be determined, Captain," Ellie replied, trying to figure how best to deal with the requests she knew were coming. We have an enormous supply of drug-making compound under guard in a storage area. It's more product volume than can be lifted out in your traveler."

Ripard whistled in amazement. "I thought this was some sort of little operation tucked away in a suite."

"Oh, no, captain. With this volume, it's surely a dome operation, meaning its run under the auspices of Peto Toyo."

"Do you have him in custody?"

"No. To the best of our knowledge, he's not here," Ellie replied, careful not to divulge everything she knew.

"What's the issue, Commander?" Ripard asked, his eyes narrowing.

"Have you been here before, Captain?" Ellie asked politely, but her eyes were challenging.

"Um … no TSF have been here before, Commander," Ripard replied. He was privy to the knowledge that undercover agents were sent into the domes, but those who had returned brought little information.

"Not all is as it seems in these domes, Captain. We've learned there are four domes here, not three as we were told by Minister Jaya. The lifts are security controlled, accessible only by Toyo's people and special patrons. Security personnel have a chip secreted on their person and service personnel and patrons have ID cards that allow them access to the lower domes. We've discovered no maps or layouts of the lower domes … your guess is as good as mine as to what you'll find down there."

Ellie sent a Haraken to lead a small squad of Ripard's TSF troopers to relieve her people at the storage location. The message she sent to her trooper ordered the Harakens to board the traveler when relieved. Ellie intended to collect her people as events unfolded, in case she was required to lift at a moment's notice.

Ripard tasked his lieutenants and sergeants to locate Toyo's senior security personnel, and Ellie was thankful to be able to stay out of the way. Eventually the captain found his way below and was shocked by the nature of the entertainment rooms in the lower domes. His people documented them, but even Ripard admitted that base as the pursuits were, they didn't constitute a violation of the company's charter.

When Ripard located the lab, he found it cleaned out, except for a small quantity of chemicals in neatly organized sealed, clear containers sitting on a single table — no equipment in sight. Lab chemists and techs sat meekly waiting for him. In Ripard's mind, it was a surreal moment. His people took possession of the lab's chemicals, and the subsequent interviews with lab workers revealed the existence of their kidnapped families. One by one, his troopers led the chemist or tech to their family's lodging to collect them.

The conundrum for Ripard was whether to arrest them or take them into protective custody. Every one of them admitted to working in the lab making the addictive hallucinogenic compound but under duress. When the captain asked after the lab equipment and the senior chemists, he received only shrugs and confused looks.

What the captain didn't know was that the lab personnel were more concerned about the righteous anger of the Harakens than prosecution by their own government. In discussions before the TSF arrived, it was agreed among them that the incarceration of their families by Toyo was a good defense for their counselors to argue in court. There would be no one to argue for them if the Harakens decided that justice was required for the damage done to the children of Espero.

Ripard returned to the main dome. He was suspicious of the Haraken commander, but he had no proof of any wrongdoing. "Would you accommodate me by allowing a search of your shuttle," Ripard asked Ellie.

"Certainly, Captain," Ellie replied. "May I ask what you hope to find?"

"Just being careful, Commander. When I give you clearance to lift, I can say without doubt that you carried nothing evidentiary away with you."

"Well, we can't have you without a clear conscience, can we, Captain?" Ellie replied with a charming smile.

<Willem, have the troopers clear the traveler and disappear while the captain checks the ship,> Ellie sent, knowing the SADE could reach the traveler from his location.

Several moments later, Willem sent back, <Our people have become black holes within the bay.>

<Poetic, Willem. This captain needs something more substantial than what he's found or we will never get off this rock.>

<I have an idea, Commander. I will get back to you.>

Ripard and two troopers searched the Haraken traveler, finding nothing incriminating. He descended the hatch steps to face Ellie. "Something odd is going on here, Commander. I'm not sure what it is, but I hope the higher-ups are prepared to handle the confusing mess that I've uncovered and that includes the lack of evidence in the underground lab."

"That sounds accusatory, Captain," Ellie said, dropping the friendly attitude and bracing herself in front of Ripard.

"Call it what you want, Commander, but if I had my way, I would arrest you and your people."

"On what charges, Captain?" Ellie challenged. "We came in support of our people, who were being attacked by Toyo's security forces, and we lost one of our own in their defense."

"And where are those of your people who you rescued, Commander?" Ripard riposted. Had the captain been savvy enough about Harakens, he would have spotted Willem's avatar design, during his investigation, and made him for a SADE. His next insightful move would have been to request Willem project the Harakens' implant memories, and he would have received proof of their culpability. As it was, Ripard felt stymied.

<Commander, the storage location of the illegal stun guns used on Udrides has been discovered,> Willem sent.

<The what?> Ellie replied, trying to keep the surprise off her face as Captain Ripard and she eyed each other.

<Your pardon, Commander, it was information made available during SADE-to-SADE communication. Toyo's people used illegal energy weapons that killed. We encountered nothing like that in our contest here on Jolares. I surmised that there might be a cache of these weapons and have been proven correct. The question is how do we communicate what I've found to Captain Ripard and stay within the confines of your previous communication?>

Ellie was trying to absorb what Willem said, when something occurred to her. <Willem, what do you mean by my prior communication?>

<Apologies, Commander, I took it upon myself to stay informed of your dialog with the captain. It occurred to me that you would need to deal in subterfuge, and I thought it behooved me to be aware of your version of the truth so that I would make no mistake by contradicting you.>

<So you were listening in on my implant.>

<Essentially, yes, Commander.>

<Bad, SADE, bad,> Ellie sent, but mirth danced through her thoughts. It was a shame that Ellie couldn't see the smile that formed on Willem's face.

<To my question, Commander?>

<Where is the cache?>

<Dome four, level three. It's a security comm station with a vault located at the rear of the room.>

<I won't ask how you know this, but I'll deal with the captain.>

Ripard was watching Ellie closely and noticed the moments of inattention to him. Implant communication was one aspect of the Harakens he knew well. "Do you have something for me, Commander?" he asked, when Ellie's stern expression softened.

"Perhaps, Captain," Ellie said. "On a completely different subject, but one that still applies to Jolares. Were you aware of the killings that took place on Udrides?"

"I've heard reports, but nothing specific, why?"

"I've just been informed that murders were committed by Toyo's people, and they were wielding hand guns that delivered a lethal charge. Nothing like that was used against us here on Jolares ... just standard stun guns ... and a knife in the back."

Ripard winced at the mention of the Haraken the commander lost, and his anger at what he perceived as an obfuscation of justice lessened. "So you think that somewhere in these domes is a storehouse of more of these weapons."

"I think if you lean on a senior security person, like Toyo's head of security, who I've been told is Dillon Jameson, that he could lead you to these weapons. Now, if you were to report to your superiors that after learning of the deaths on Udrides that you suspected a cache of these illegal weapons might exist here and tracked it down, wouldn't your superiors cast an admiring eye on you, Captain?"

"You're a devious woman, Commander," Ripard said, grinning. He motioned to his men to follow him, and Ellie could hear him on his ear comm asking his troopers for the whereabouts of Dillon Jameson.

"Captain," Ellie called out, before Ripard disappeared from sight. "If Jameson appears uncooperative, you might mention that he's a possible accessory to the murder of nearly seventy New Terran citizens."

Ripard tipped a couple of fingers to the brim of his cap to her and jogged out of the bay. Hours later, the captain had his cache of illegal weapons, Jameson being induced to cooperate, and, immediately afterwards, Ellie received her clearance from Ripard to lift.

Later, Ellie watched the *Tanaka* appear on her helmet's screen via the traveler's telemetry and breathed a sigh of relief.

* * *

Well before morning meal, Drake, accompanied by Jaya, pounded on Alex's cabin door, having been directed there by a crew member, who immediately signaled Tatia, Julien, and the twins of the anger apparent on the president's face.

Alex and Renée, who had a mere five hours of sleep, struggled to wake and discern the source of the pounding. When Alex headed for the sleeping quarters door, Renée sent, <Don a robe, my love, that's a local New Terran banging to be heard.> Alex retreated momentarily to grab a robe, run into the salon, and trigger the cabin door.

"What kind of games are you playing?" Drake demanded hotly, as he charged into the salon. Jaya held his hands out to Drake, attempting to get his president to lower his voice, but Drake was having none of it.

"Greetings, President Drake. A little early in the morning to start an argument, isn't it?" Alex replied good-naturedly.

Suddenly, Julien, Tatia, and the twins surged into the room, and Alex signaled them for calm. The group lined the salon's inner wall and waited.

"I've just heard from General Oppert that the evidence from Jolares is missing," Drake said, angrily. "The senior scientists, their families, and the drug-lab equipment are all missing. Tell me you didn't have something to do with this. Tell me that you're not impeding an official New Terran investigation," Drake demanded, pointing a finger in Alex's face.

"We have an entire wing of young people, who will remain in comatose conditions until we can create a compound to counteract the addictive nature of this nasty hallucinogenic. Unfortunately, we're out of our depth. Terese has no idea how to begin. We urgently need the biochemists to develop this compound for us, and they need their equipment and material."

"So you admit you took them and the lab evidence," Drake accused Alex.

"Yes, everything you listed is aboard the *Rêveur*."

"Well, nice to hear you can still be forthright to some degree," Drake declared, backing away from Alex. He started to pace, but decided against it and turned to face Alex. "I will give you three hours to gather the Jolares people, the lab equipment, and the evidence. A TSF traveler will rendezvous with your ship and take possession of everything."

Alex and Drake stared at each other, neither side giving way. Finally, Alex said quietly, "I can't do that, Will. When we're finished with the chemists, we will hand everything over to you."

"You do realize that you are unlawfully detaining New Terran citizens, who might be charged with criminal acts, and you're in our system … a place where Harakens have no jurisdiction."

"Will," Renée said, beseeching the president.

"No," Drake declared angrily, putting a finger in Renée's face to halt her words.

Drake's motions drove the twins to respond. Alain slid in front of Renée, sweeping aside Drake's offending hand. Étienne moved in front of Alex and faced him, sending. <Please, Ser, anger makes him forget his manners, but it would be unwise to punish him for his transgression.>

Alex took in both twins, Étienne with his earnest expression and Alain stepping Drake away from Renée, and he relented.

"You people and your arrogance," Drake said in disgust, putting some distance between the Harakens and him.

"You people?" repeated Alex, his anger evident. "We saved your planet when a UE battleship threatened your entire system."

"And who fomented the trouble in the first place?" Drake retorted.

"If you had been at Sol, Ser, instead of huddling inside Government House and hoping you were safe, you would have known it was only a matter of time before we were all subsumed by the UE," said Alex, his voice stronger and louder.

"That's your opinion, and coincidentally it's typical of your arrogance," Drake said, yelling. Suddenly, he looked to his right, shocked by the sight of flames surrounding Julien's head. "Fire," Drake screamed, appalled to find the anathema of spacers rearing its ugly head. He spun around, grabbed a water carafe, and threw its contents at Julien's head.

The SADE calmly sidestepped the deluge. Despite not a drop of water touching Julien, his flames were smothered, turning to steam and wisps of smoke, which sputtered out, leaving his hair sodden and burnt.

"What?" Drake managed to sputter. Confused, he looked to Jaya, who was holding his hand over his face and hiding his desire to laugh out loud.

"I thought your prestigious selves required a moment of levity, Sers. It was becoming unconscionably warm in here," Julien announced.

Drake had the good grace to chuckle. He found a chair and sat down heavily, tired from his tirade.

Alex laughed lightly and reached to stroke his friend's damaged-appearing hair, but Julien turned off the holo-vid image before the illusion could be breached.

"May I suggest a compromise, Sers?" Julien asked.

When neither Alex nor Will said a word, Renée quipped, "It appears New Terran men are ill-equipped to apologize to each other. Well, Julien, I, for one, would love to hear your thoughts."

"Kind of you, Ser," Julien said with great deference, but he shifted tone and stance as he addressed President Drake. "You, Ser, are quite aware Harakens possess the superior technology. Terese is coercing the chemist responsible for creating the original drug to produce an antidote, if you will … a compound to neutralize its addictive nature. We hope to permanently free our young people of any craving for this insidious hallucinogen."

"I'm not arguing your capabilities, Julien —" Drake started to say.

"However," Julien continued, cutting Drake off, "you must demonstrate territorial jurisdiction devoid of Haraken interference. To advance your position, I suggest the *Rêveur* make New Terra's orbit, where the TSF authorities board and arrest Stratford. Then your office magnanimously orders the biochemist to work with the Harakens to create the antidote to eliminate the addiction. When the compound is ready, New Terra will be the first to receive it. Afterwards, your government will take possession of the chemists, the equipment, the evidence … as it had been arranged and announced previously, of course, and the *Rêveur* will depart with what we require. The cooperation between our peoples will be seen as evidence of our valuable ongoing relationship."

"I can live with that," Alex said, looking at Drake.

Drake spent the next several moments considering the offer. Jaya's expression pleaded with him to accept it.

"I can too," Drake agreed. "We will need to prepare a statement."

"Have it," Jaya said, holding up his reader as Alex said, "Approved."

"Faster done than said," Will quipped, relieved that a major clash with Alex and the Harakens had been averted. What held his attention though was that it was Julien who played the diplomat and successfully mediated the compromise.

36

Word of Toyo's death spread quickly throughout the system. For the criminal enterprises, which admittedly were nascent on New Terra, it was an opportunity to fill the vacuum created by the leader's demise. Most of the system's citizens focused on the media reports of the attack on Kadmir's establishment, the deaths of innocent civilians, the involvement of the Harakens, and the landing of TSF on charter-restricted domes.

Over the next several days, New Terran factions organized themselves. Kadmir and O'Brien, who had made heavy donations to various Assembly representatives and payments to CEOs, put pressure through them to lodge an objection against TSF interference in the domes, contrary to the mining charter. They carefully limited their accusations to the TSF, leaving the Harakens out of it. However, the murder of New Terran citizens by the use of illegal weapons had many of the Assembly up in arms.

Tessie Bernoulli, the government's general counsel and senior legal administrator, was organizing investigations into what was a host of acts: illegal drug manufacturing, kidnapping of entire families, wholesale murder, and the manufacture of deadly stun guns along with anyone complicit in their sale and transport. Toward those ends, she wanted Toyo's people, who were captured in the Udrides domes, and the evidence documenting the murders, to be delivered to Prima. And foremost, Tessie wanted the evidence and suspects from the Jolares drug lab in lockup on Prima.

"You can't be serious, Will," Tessie said to the president, as they sat in his office at Government House. "We're sharing the evidence and the incarceration of suspects with the Harakens?"

Drake knew Tessie represented the growing number of influential New Terrans who saw a close relationship with the Harakens as dangerous. They craved a more independent stance for their system, and some of them even viewed the Harakens as magnets for trouble. Drake had released Julien's carefully crafted message only hours before Tessie was comming him for an appointment when he returned to Government House.

"I've made this arrangement for the good of both people," Drake said defensively.

"I hope you know, Will, you're speaking for the minority. That's not the mood of the people."

* * *

Three days ago, the *Rêveur* and the *Tanaka* had made orbit around New Terra as agreed. Since it had become common knowledge that the Haraken president was aboard the *Rêveur*, Alex was besieged with interview requests, but he accepted none. Instead, the news media filled their time with vid from drones, focusing on President Drake, the Assembly, and outspoken critics of the mining charter breaches.

Soon after the *Rêveur* had made orbit, Alex received a request from the Assembly Speaker to present himself for questioning by the government's representatives. On the appointed morning, Alex's traveler landed where directed, 3 kilometers from Assembly Hall. The Harakens disembarked to find a single, common, aging transport waiting for them.

"No presidential entourage for us," Tatia quipped.

"This is unforgivable," said Ellie, her anger evident.

Renée took Alex's arm in sympathy.

"New Terrans have a right to their opinions, people," Alex announced. "We came to Oistos to find our girls and get a cure for the drug that damaged our young people. So far, so good. If we've lost some friends along the way, so be it."

Before the group could reach the transport, a stream of four, modern, grav cars descended to their right. The twins' hands went to their weapons, but they relaxed when Maria stepped out of the first car.

Renée called out Maria's name and ran to hug her.

When Alex drew close, Maria said, "Apologies for the late arrival, Alex. I just received word from Darryl about the accommodations made for your transport." Both Alex and she glanced over at the outmoded, hover transport, and Maria flicked her head toward the aging vehicle, which sent her assistant running to pay off the driver.

"We had to scramble to rent these beauties and get some drivers," Maria continued. "Meet my drivers ... also known as my lead investigators ... Sarah Laurent, Fredericka Olsen, and Steve Ross."

As introductions were made, Julien found himself the focus of Steve Ross, who was wondering about the body type, neither New Terran nor Méridien.

"Aha," Steve exclaimed when a complex spiraling pattern, which resembled the one on his reader, covered Julien's face. "My benefactor," he added, throwing his arms around Julien.

"You're quite welcome, Ser," Julien said, smiling, "but my partner, Cordelia, was also instrumental in monitoring your safety."

Steve extended his hand politely to Cordelia, who eyed it, and asked, "What? No hug for me?" Steve, a little embarrassed, delicately embraced Cordelia, which made her smile. <One would think I broke easily,> Cordelia sent to Julien.

<Accept it as deference to your image as a charming and enticing human woman,> Julien sent back.

Fredericka and Sarah had no such reservations. They leaped as one to hug Cordelia and then mobbed Julien.

Maria noticed the tendency of the two SADEs to remain close to each other, and an entirely new aspect of the SADEs dawned on her. Just as Julien had bonded with Alex, so he now shared his life with another SADE. "Shall we go?" Maria asked, waving her hands toward the waiting grav cars.

The transports made the journey swiftly and landed at the side of the Assembly Hall. Two TSF sergeants stood outside and snapped to attention, saluting before opening the doors for the group.

Inside, Alex motioned everyone to the gallery, sending, <There's no need for anyone to share the dais with me this time.> Alex included the twins in his comm. He found himself alone on the stage and, looking down, saw Drake and his ministers in the front row. Jaya wore a pained expression, while Drake's face was stoic.

The Assembly Speaker announced Alex and asked if he had an opening statement, but Alex felt there was nothing to say. The SADEs had turned over the pertinent implant recordings to the Assembly — the jerking bodies of the young at the Espero club, the kidnapping and transporting of the girls to the domes, the stored drug-manufacturing chemicals at Jolares, the invitation from Kadmir, and the fights at both domes.

Without an opening statement from Alex, the Assembly Speaker opened the floor to questions. Alex's supporters, who appeared to be the minority, remained silent, while the majority of the representatives challenged Alex on every decision he made and every step he took.

The critics saw the bringing of the Haraken sting ship to Oistos for the ruse it was and perceived the act as aggressive on the Harakens' part. Failure to approach the TSF or government over the kidnapping was another subject that angered the majority. The list went on and on.

Alex stood alone on the dais, hands held in front of him, and answered as succinctly and calmly as he could. At one point, a particularly obnoxious individual, tapped by the Assembly Speaker, decided to make a personal comment that challenged Alex's qualifications to be a world leader.

"Enough," Alex said, his hands gesturing to the Assembly that he was done. "You have the right to think of me personally what you will. But I am the elected leader of Haraken, and you will treat me with the respect due my office. You may believe that everything I did in your system was without merit, but we've retrieved three citizens kidnapped by *your* people, and we're producing a compound to counteract the addictive effects of a dangerous drug *your* people created. Know this ... Harakens will not tolerate intrusion from undesirable elements into our society, regardless of where they come from."

"That sounds like a threat," the obnoxious representative challenged.

"Call it what you wish," Alex replied. "But you should stop and think before you continue to act in the manner that I've heard today. New Terra has benefited tremendously from Méridien technology, but it's not the

Confederation that has been trading with you. It's us … Harakens. You act as if the events that embroiled us … the kidnapping and the illegal drugs … are beside the point. They are the point, and I'm perplexed as to why you don't want to work with us to curtail these elements that neither of our societies wish to see develop."

The Assembly Speaker looked at Alex to see if he was ready for the next question, but Alex shook his head in negation. He looked down at Drake, and said, "You would never be treated in this manner if you were on Haraken." Then Alex turned and strode across the dais, intending a swift exit from the hall.

Most Assembly representatives were quiet, but some took to booing and calling rudely after Alex. The loud voices were drowned out by the noise from the gallery, which was full of Haraken supporters, who broke out into raucous stomping and whistling. Their boots shook the gallery's floor, and the representatives below were covered in a fine layer of dust that drifted down from the ancient ceiling.

Alex raised a hand to his supporters. Out of the corner of his eye, he saw Darryl Jaya, standing, clapping, and stomping a foot. A smile broke across Alex's face at the minister's desertion from government ranks.

* * *

After Alex's questioning before the Assembly, Maria and her people transported a quiet group of Harakens to her home. She bustled about, making her guests feel comfortable, but when the New Terrans in Alex's group demurred from midday meal, it emphasized their somber mood.

Renée invited Maria to take a walk. The ex-president's house was situated deep in the woods far outside Prima, and tall trees dominated the landscape. The little-used pathways, thickly covered with leaves, were soft under foot.

As the two women walked, Maria waited patiently for Renée to discuss what was bothering her. A casual observer, who might judge by appearances, could not help but see two more different women, but, at heart, they were as close as sisters.

Alain walked quietly near them.

"I was shocked by the Assembly's treatment of Alex," Renée said, when she had time to gather her thoughts. "Not more than fifteen years ago, the representatives were stamping and whistling their approval of him when he rescued us and brought Méridien technology to New Terra."

"Some of what you witnessed today is driven by envy, fear, and disappointment," Maria replied. When Renée's face expressed her confusion, Maria continued, "Let's take the last sentiment. Alex chose to start a new world rather than stay in Oistos and develop Méridien technology for New Terra."

Renée stopped walking and fixed her eyes on Maria. "You and I both know that New Terra did not welcome the Librans with open arms."

"No ... no, they didn't," Maria agreed. "Most people in a society do not welcome major changes, and the influx of hundreds of thousands of strangers, especially those who are different from them, represented an unsettling change. It's a sad truth about humankind." Maria took Renée's arm, patting it gently, and led her along the path. The thick canopy of leaves allowed a subtle dappling of light to reach the forest floor.

"And you know Alex, Maria," Renée added as they walked. "He couldn't abandon people in need. It's not his way ... thank the stars. So what's really going on with the Assembly?"

"My sense of it, Renée," Maria said, "is that your people, the Harakens, keep holding a mirror up to us, and many find the reflection uncomfortable. Those New Terrans, who prefer isolation, were shocked to discover the existence of an entire procession of others ... Méridiens, Nua'll, Librans, Swei Swee, and even hostile Earthers. Those people, who thought they were in control of their destiny, were taught an unwelcome lesson, and many of them blame your people. Then our criminal organizations exploited a loophole in our laws and got out of hand. But, it wasn't TSF forces or our government that responded. It had to be the Harakens who were forced to come from a distant system and expose our problems ... illegal weapons, drugs, and all."

"But none of that's our fault," Renée objected.

"No, it's not, Ser," Maria said, putting an arm around Renée's slender shoulders and pulling her close. "It's not your fault; it's just the way it is. The mood of New Terran decision makers is swinging toward a desire to keep the Harakens at arm's length. Your technology is impressive and desirable, but it comes at a high price. Some New Terrans find your sense of morality daunting, and no one embodies that more than Alex and Julien. They're making many powerful New Terrans uncomfortable."

"If this is the trend, then it will probably not swing back the other way for a long time," Renée lamented.

"Don't worry, Renée," Maria said, hugging her shoulders, "it will never change the way I and others feel about you and your people. We'll be forever grateful for what you've done for New Terra."

* * *

The representatives anxious to defend the mining charter were emboldened by the Assembly's treatment of Alex, but they misread the general mood. The sentiments of the outspoken representatives did not represent the mood of the entire Assembly, which as a whole was horrified by the events that took place on Jolares and Udrides.

Pressure fell on the representatives from New Terran citizens, who demanded answers as to how the illegal stun guns could be manufactured and how the pleasure domes could be granted licenses under the mining charter. The undercurrent within their messages evidenced anger that it required the Harakens to fix what were seen as New Terra's problems and were the government's responsibility.

Several changes to the mining charter were proposed that would not only affect the domes, but all mining companies within the system. The far-reaching scope of the bills threw the Assembly into turmoil, with pressure coming at the representatives from all sides.

The debates raged for days, and the Assembly adjourned for a three-day recess before votes were to be taken on two diametrically opposed bills that had survived the committees and preliminary floor votes.

37

Since the biochemists were turned over to Terese's care, the pressure on her to succeed had soared. It galled her that as Haraken's medical expert she was relegated to an administrator's role, no longer a hands-on participant.

Often, Terese's role became that of referee. From day one, it was obvious to her that there was no love lost between the two scientists. Anger and disgust emanated frequently from Billings. He saw Stratford as responsible for everything ugly that had precipitated from his work, but Stratford merely shrugged off the accusations, believing science was a pure pursuit, independent of society, and all inventions had value.

"That's completely unethical, Stratford," Billings yelled, when Stratford had reiterated his philosophy one day. If Billings had expected a response or an argument, he was disappointed. Stratford merely returned to examining a holo-vid display.

In the early days, Stratford tried to educate Terese and the SADEs, expounding on his steps to create the drug. "The difficult part was creating an entirely new approach to the hallucinogen and its delivery," Stratford explained. "Typically a hallucinogenic drug changes thought, perception, and mood, with autonomic nervous system side effects at a minimum. But those effects wouldn't create a recurring demand for the drug by the user. So I tinkered with my creation to make it addictive."

<Please tell me you're recording this idiot's confession,> Terese sent to Cordelia.

<Both Miranda and I have stored every moment we have been in Stratford and Billing's company. The vids are on the *Rêveur*'s crystal banks for your perusal, at any time, Ser,> Cordelia replied.

Terese stepped close to Stratford, who halted his professorial lecture and stepped back, uncertainty crossing his face. "Perhaps, I wasn't clear,"

Terese said. "Tell us what you need to synthesize the blocking agent we've requested. Do not bother to educate us on your ingenuity. That may lead to a short walk to our hull's airlock, and, in case you haven't noticed, we're still in orbit.>

At one point, Stratford explained that the symptoms the users developed were excessive. "I told Toyo I needed to moderate the effect, but Toyo said it was perfect. The only thing else he said on the subject was that it didn't matter what happened elsewhere, so long as it didn't happen in Oistos."

Stratford's comments drew angry faces his way. He put up his hands to ward off any physical confrontation, focusing his attention on Terese. "What I'm trying to tell you is that I know what I created, but I didn't get an opportunity to study the effects. I'm not sure whether the drug and its delivery mechanism worked as designed."

"Cordelia, the holo-vid, please," Terese requested. "Start with the first patient, both comatose and alert."

The biochemists were enthralled with the incredible detail of the brain displayed by Cordelia, crowding close to examine it.

"You have a quarter-hour of each patient in each state, under sedation and off. Cordelia or Miranda can display each of these sequences whenever you wish. Each SADE will record your comments for any sequence and display those comments in the future with the matching sequence."

"Exactly what are we looking at?" asked Billings, his nose centimeters from the display, as if it would allow him to see more detail.

"You're watching a recording of this teenager's brain activity," Terese explained. "The blue is the brain matter; the yellow are signals sent along the pathways and across the synaptic junctions."

"Seriously? Not representations but actual signals?" Stratford asked. "Can the projection's timeline be accelerated or slowed?"

"Express the rate change," Cordelia said.

"One-fiftieth normal speed," Stratford requested.

"Look at that," Billings marveled, when the impulses, instead of a blur of yellow covering the brain matter, became a kaleidoscope of streaks shooting across various portions of the brain. "Too bad we can't examine the electrical activity more closely."

"That's up to you, Ser," Terese said. "Manipulate the holo-vid as you see fit." She walked up to the projection, placed her hands in the view, enlarged the image, and rotated the view 90 degrees clockwise. She looked at Billings and nodded at the holo-vid.

Billings stuck his hand in the image and immediately traced a series of signals. "Stop the playback. Back it up slowly. There," he said and started a quiet discussion with Stratford, who nodded his head in agreement.

"Can we get two of these projections?" Billings asked. "We need to compare the comatose and alert activity of each patient side-by-side."

"Midday meal will be here shortly," Terese announced. "I will have a second holo-vid installed soon after."

Once the scientists had their second holo-vid, they made rapid progress. It required both SADEs to independently control the two playbacks as the scientists examined an aspect of the brain in one state, playing intensively with one display, and calling out observations to have the other stage manipulated in kind. Stratford focused on the alert stages; Billings examined the comatose states.

Both biochemists became excited when they spotted a consistent uptake by two particular portions of the brain, the cerebrum's frontal lobe and the limbic area. But both were disappointed when they viewed patients, who had been sedated for longer and longer periods of time and showed ever-decreasing activity levels.

"This doesn't make sense," Billings said. "If the body is processing out the hallucinogen and the limbic system's dopamine and serotonin levels are leveling off, what's creating the unusual withdrawal symptoms?"

"I was afraid of that. It's not the drug itself; it's the agent in the delivery solution. That's why it isn't delivered in pill form ... a med-injector is required to administer the dose," Stratford said. He didn't expect his comment to draw as much attention as he suddenly received.

"Explain," Terese demanded.

"Toyo wanted a fast uptake … something that would bring first-time users back quickly … 'no slow addiction rate,' he said," Stratford said, his words stumbling out.

"So what did you do?" Billings asked, eyeing Stratford closely.

"To greatly magnify the brain's demand for a second dosage, I employed a modified section of viral RNA," Stratford said.

"You gene-modified their brain neurons?" Terese cried, advancing on Stratford. But she was blocked by Deirdre, who had to forcibly detain her.

"No, no … I didn't touch the neurons' DNA," Stratford yelled, raising his hands in defense. "It's modified … designed to be picked up by presynaptic cells. It's a small piece of RNA that uses the neuron's resources to produce a neurotransmitter mimic. But, it appears to produce a more aggressive response than I intended."

"You had better hope that the New Terrans incarcerate you until you're a useless old man. If not, you will spend the rest of your adult life fearing every Haraken's path you cross." Terese said. She pulled free of Deirdre and stalked to the far side of the lab.

Then Terese paused, spun about, and said, "Wait. Why wouldn't the nanites in our Harakens' bloodstream sweep those mimic molecules from the brain? Because the visitors and our youth have the same withdrawal symptoms no matter how long we delayed waking them."

"As a neurotransmitter, the molecules would be transported back into the presynaptic cells, and the RNA strand would continue to produce the mimics. In a comatose state, that production would be minimal. Waking the patient increases blood flow and neuron activity, and production ramps up immediately," Stratford said.

"So we have two targets to attack … the mimic, when it's outside the neurons in the synaptic gap, and the strand, inside the neurons. Show me the RNA strand," Billings ordered.

That's when the scientists discovered another asset of the SADEs. Stratford opened his reader to examine his strand in a 3D depiction.

Miranda tapped into the reader and projected the structure into the holo-vid.

Billings tapped Stratford's shoulder and pointed to Miranda's display.

"Yes," Stratford said excitedly and scrambled over to the holo-vid. "Now to neutralize the mimic, which is created in this section of the strand, we need a short carbon chain."

Stratford and Billings called out their choices for the molecule's design at the atomic level, arguing with each other until they reached a final version, nodding their heads in agreement.

"That's it. I'm sure of it," Stratford said with finality.

"Your assurances are as heartwarming as the deep dark," Terese replied.

Billings and Stratford repeated their actions to create a molecule to permanently bind with the RNA strands inside the neuron. Terese added her wisdom, helping the biochemists design a compound that would pass more easily through the neurons' membranes.

When the designs of both molecules were complete, Billings turned to Stratford and said, "Let's back up here. I'd like to know the results of your clinical trials."

When Stratford demurred to respond, Billings pressed. "You said earlier that you didn't get to see the long-term effects on users, but you had to run human trials … if not for your own ego, then for Toyo's proof."

"It wasn't like I had a choice. Toyo insisted on it," Stratford declared loudly.

"But how did you get away with it?" Billings continued, not letting Stratford deviate from the subject. "I didn't hear anything in the media about teenagers with the sort of symptoms that Terese has documented."

Guilt was written across Stratford's face, and it attracted the animosity of those around him, especially from Terese.

Unable to maintain his silence in the face of the display, Stratford blurted out, "Toyo runs an orphanage. He uses it as a recruiting base … says you can never start them too young."

Stratford flinched as Terese closed on him, but the medical specialist found her way blocked this time by Miranda. "As much as I would love to see this man punished, this very moment, dear. I'm afraid it must wait."

"We will need the name of that orphanage," Terese ground out through clenched teeth and marched out of the lab. The thought that the scientist had tested his insidious drug on children, whose lives were entrusted to the care of people who owed allegiance to a man such as Toyo, made Terese's blood boil. In her life, she never thought she would experience the desire to kill another human being.

* * *

<Problem,> Terese sent to Alex, as she stalked back to her cabin.

<Specify,> Alex replied, halting his conversation with Maria, Tatia, and Renée.

Maria, who recognized the signs of Alex's private comms, got up to make thé. She had developed a taste for the Méridien drink while she was president, and Renée made sure that Maria had a continuous supply.

<We've created agents that are ready for testing,> Terese sent.

<Good news,> Alex replied, <and the bad news?>

<We need to test the efficacy ... on people already addicted to Toyo's drug.>

<What is the degree of certainty for your concoction's effectiveness?>

<Stratford is confident, and while I would not trust him within a star's distance of another human being, his subject knowledge is not to be doubted. Billings concurs.>

<And your request, Terese?>

<We have potential test targets. Toyo runs an orphanage. Stratford tested the drug there ... on the children.>

Alex came out of his chair, a growl in his throat. Tatia and the twins scanned for danger, and Renée kept careful watch on her partner.

Hearing Alex's reaction, Terese made an effort to calm her own thoughts. There was only one other person on Haraken whose anger rose above her own when it came to discovering abuse against the innocents of the worlds. <Alex, that's why there's no record of anyone on New Terra being admitted to hospitals who displayed the same symptoms as our children. Those young ones are either still there or —>

<Dead,> Alex finished. <Do you have the name of the orphanage?>

<Yes. The SADEs have its location pinpointed.>

<Any idea of the number of children tested?>

<Name, age, sex, symptoms, timeline ... all neatly documented in Stratford's reader journal. He kept quite tidy notes of his treachery against the children.> Terese wanted to scream and shout, but she held herself in check. This would be a prickly problem for the Harakens, and she knew it.

On the expansive, covered porch of Maria's rock-walled home, Alex paced its width. He realized that if they released Stratford and Billings to the New Terrans, without a successful test, they might discover later that the biochemists' counteragents were useless, only partially successful, or created dangerous side effects. But to test it on New Terran children without the government's permission was to drive a deeper wedge between their two people, if they were discovered.

<How soon can you have a sufficient quantity of your material prepared to employ on all the children, if your initial test is successful?>

<We'll be ready in seven hours,> Terese replied, a smile lighting her face. Alex's decision wasn't the politically correct one, but it was the one that demonstrated why she loved the man.

Maria served chilled thé to her guests, placing Alex's glass beside his chair, since he was still pacing.

<Sit, my love,> Renée sent. <Have some cool drink and talk to us.>

Alex paused beside his chair, noticing the condensate-covered crystal with its delicately colored liquid for the first time. He picked it up and drained its contents and then watched Renée replace it with hers. Alex winked at her and settled into his porch chair, drinking deeply from the second glass.

"Good news ... Terese's antidote, if you will, is ready. Terrible news ... Toyo has an orphanage where he tested Stratford's drugs. The children are either still there in dire condition or dead.>

Before everyone's indignation boiled out, Alex held up his hands. "Terese and I are angry enough for everyone. We need cool heads on this."

"Alex, you can't be thinking of going in there and testing your creation on the children without authorization," Maria said. "It would destroy whatever credibility you have left with this world."

"Agreed, Maria," Alex replied, "but we have to know Terese's concoction works before we turn Stratford and Billings over to the authorities. If we alert the government to the orphanage, the children will be taken into medical care and will become wards of the state. Counselor Bernoulli comms me daily for an update. She wants to know when we'll turn over the biochemists to her for prosecution. To my annoyance, she never asks after Terese's progress. As far as New Terra is concerned the addicted children are our problem and ours alone."

"Then what you need is a proper front," Maria said, smiling.

"My thoughts exactly," Alex said, smiling back. "Maria, how much to hire your services to investigate a curious anomaly at an orphanage?"

"For children … nothing, but to keep it official, client privileges and all, one credit should do nicely, Alex," Maria said, hoisting her chilled thé to Alex.

"Consider it paid," Alex replied, raising his glass in return.

38

A traveler landed in a vacant lot a few hundred meters away from the Embracing Arms Orphanage. The investigators, Steve Ross, Sarah Laurent, and Fredericka Olsen, led the exit, and Maria Gonzalez followed them. Étienne and Alain came next and were there to protect Terese, Cordelia, and Billings. A minimum of Harakens were present to offer a credible front to the concept of a New Terran client investigation.

In the quiet of the morning hours, the group made their way to the home. It was surrounded by a tall, decorative, wood fence, undoubtedly to keep the children inside.

Maria pressed the comm unit at the wide, double gates, and, within moments, an image of an older, gray-haired man appeared in the display.

"Ah ... President Gonzalez," the man said. "We were expecting someone, but certainly not anyone as important as you. Please come in."

As the gates swung open, Maria glanced at her investigators, who quickly stowed their stun guns out of sight. The cordial reception was certainly unexpected. The home's front door swung open as the group approached, and a woman joined the elderly man on the wide veranda.

"Welcome, President Gonzalez. I'm Orlando Ortiz, and this is my wife, Consuela. Please, come in. We've been anxiously awaiting a visit from the authorities."

In the home's generous foyer, the group arrayed themselves in front of Orlando and Consuela, who were smiling, despite their obvious nervousness.

"I must tell you," Maria said, "that we do not represent the authorities. We are here on a private matter. Information from a client led us to believe that there may be children here, suffering from taking a dangerous drug."

"Taking a drug?" Consuela said indignantly, her nervousness disappearing as her cheeks flushed red. "The drugs were forced on them by

Peto Toyo's people." Consuela spit on the floor to emphasize her disgust at mentioning Toyo's name.

<Terese will take a quick liking to this woman,> Alain sent to Étienne.

"Are the children still here?" Terese asked.

Orlando eyed Terese suspiciously. "Haraken?" he asked. When Terese nodded to him, he said, "What do you want with the children?"

"To cure them," Terese said, holding up her med-kit.

Consuela grabbed her husband's arm, imploring him with her eyes.

"You have something that works?" Orlando asked.

"I wish I could say that," Terese replied. "This is Emile Billings, a prominent biochemist, who worked to create this compound. It will block the children's addictive cravings."

"So what you're saying is that you want to test it on the children," Orlando qualified.

"Yes," Terese admitted.

"If I might comment, Mr. Ortiz, it's awfully quiet in here for the size of your home," Steve said.

"Yes," Orlando replied, smiling. "When word reached us that Toyo was dead, his people grabbed their rotten brats and ran. My wife and I started this orphanage more than three decades ago. We've helped a great many children find a stable life with new parents or growing up here. Then Peto Toyo walks in here one day with his people and a disreputable group of teenagers and tells us he bought the place from us for one credit."

"There wasn't much we could do," Consuela added. "A few months later, a man like this one," she said, pointing to Billings, "came in here and said he had to inoculate the children."

"Stratford," said Terese, her own disgust evident.

"He never said his name," Orlando added. "Soon after he gave the children the injections, their bodies twitched and their faces went dreamy. The man watched them for an hour and then gave them something to put them to sleep."

"We were told to keep them asleep and the man gave us a supply of medicine, but it will run out in a few more days," Consuela said.

"The mixture Ser Lechaux has is untested," Maria said. "But I have worked with the Harakens for many years, and their technology is vastly superior to ours. She is the Harakens' premier medical expert. If she believes she has an antidote to the addictive nature of the injection the children have been given, then I believe it's a risk worth taking. Otherwise, we must contact medical authorities and have the children removed to hospitals." What Maria didn't say was that there was every possibility that Counselor Bernoulli might prefer charges against the couple.

Consuela gripped her husband's arm again. "Orlando, I want to try it. I don't believe the Harakens would do anything to deliberately hurt the children." When Orlando nodded to her, she kissed his cheek fervently.

Sarah leaned over and whispered in Maria's ear, and the ex-president smiled at her.

"There is an opportunity to protect all of us from possible judicial headaches," Maria announced. "I think you should hire my company to help you solve the problem foisted on you by Peto Toyo."

"How much would that cost?" asked Orlando, his suspicions foremost again.

"One credit, Mr. Ortiz," Maria replied. She pulled out her reader, tapped on it several times, and handed it to Orlando. "Standard client agreement at the price of one credit. I need both of you to agree."

Orlando was perusing the document, when Consuela pulled the reader from his hands, signed off on the document, and handed it back. Her eyes dared her husband to object.

Fredericka and Sarah hid their smiles, as Orlando quickly added his signature.

"Now, after reviewing your situation," Maria declared officiously, "I choose to hire the Harakens to attend medically to your children, and you will need to pay for their services."

"Aha," Orlando said, believing he had discovered the ruse that was being perpetrated on them, "and just how much would that cost?"

Terese touched her hand to her heart and dipped her head. "I would dearly love to attend your children without a fee, but I believe Ser

Gonzalez understands the machinations of her world far better than me. So, if a fee must be submitted, I too request one credit."

Consuela's hands flew to her mouth, and she uttered a small cry of pleasure. Then the heavy-bodied woman grabbed Terese, holding her in a mother's warm embrace. The tears falling from Consuela's eyes were echoed by those on Terese's face.

Maria was furiously tapping on her reader and handed it to Orlando, but Consuela snatched it and wiped her eyes to identify the signature line before she signed off on the agreement. She held it out to her husband, who added his and gave the reader back to Maria.

"Come, dear," Consuela said to Terese, taking the slender Haraken by the arm, "the children are upstairs."

The group dutifully followed the two women up a long staircase to a large room occupying the entire back of the house.

"This used to be the children's playroom," Orlando said, surveying the eighteen occupied beds. He was shaking his head, a sad expression on his face. "Once the children were put to sleep, we moved them in here where we could keep an eye on them all at once."

"Who first?" Terese asked Billings.

"The oldest and the strongest," Billings replied.

"That would be Davie," said Consuela, hurrying to stand beside a bed where a robust teenager lay peacefully asleep. "He was never adopted. A bit of a strong temperament, but he's a good boy, and he's been a great help with the little ones for years."

Terese, Cordelia, and Billings went quickly to work. Cordelia picked up Stratford's injector and squeezed an amount of the sleep medication into her mouth.

Consuela's mouth opened in surprise, but she held her tongue since Harakens were known to be different.

Cordelia identified the chemical and shared the information with Terese, who sorted through the med-kit for a counteragent to the sleep agent. She loaded her med-injector with a small dose and placed it next to a second injector loaded with the new agents. Removing the monitoring device from her medical reader, Terese placed it against Davie's temple. Then she handed her reader to Billings.

It was Billings' job to monitor the reaction and judge whether to let the boy continue to awaken or put him back under, if the agents proved ineffective in compromising the withdrawal reactions.

"Ready, Emile?" Terese asked.

Billings was pleased to hear Terese use his given name again. The first time she had done so, Billings was relieved to have achieved human status in Terese's mind, separating him from the "it," as Stratford was still referred to by her. Billings nodded his head, but kept his eyes focused on the readouts Terese had taught him to watch. He marveled again at the degree to which the Harakens could monitor the brain's functions.

Terese injected Davie with the new concoction and waited a quarter-hour before she injected the boy with the sleep counteragent. She looked over Billings' shoulder to watch the readout. After several moments, the biorhythms increased, and Terese pointed to the subtle, horizontal line, which demarked the patient's return to consciousness.

However, Billings was fixed on a data point that monitored the brain's neurochemistry. He expected a significant rise in the readouts, as consciousness returned and blood flow increased, but if the indicator rose too high, it would mean the neurotransmitter mimic was in high production by the presynaptic cells, which meant the RNA strands were unbound. The result would be a wide-awake patient craving a second dose.

Davie's eyes fluttered open, but they seemed to have difficulty focusing. A soft moan escaped his lips, and his head lolled from side to side. Then his fingers flexed and curled harshly, and his body began to writhe.

Consuela was moved to come to the boy's aid, but Orlando held her back. "Wait, mother," he whispered to her.

Davie twisted on his side and his knees came to his chest as his moans grew louder.

Terese touched Billing's forearm to gain his attention, but the biochemist's eyes never left the reader, as he signaled with a free hand for Terese to wait. "The indicator is already slowing in its climb. Give it some time."

Despite Billing's pronouncement, Terese loaded a third injector with a Haraken soporific, a much milder sleeping agent than that used by Stratford.

"Look," Billings said with enthusiasm. He pointed to the indicator, and Terese watched it slowly fall. In time, its level indicated a minimal effect from the residual amount of neurotransmitter mimic.

On the bed, Davie took a gasp of air, as if his lungs were freed from a vice. He rolled onto his back, panting from his exertions. His eyes focused on Terese's face and her flame-red hair, as he spoke his first words. "You're pretty. Did I die?"

"No, Davie. I'm real, and you're back."

Consuela ran, crying, to hold Davie, who hugged her in return.

"Momma, what happened?" Davie asked.

"We'll talk later, Davie," Consuela said, happily. "You're okay now."

Davie's gaze traveled from Terese to the twins. "Harakens," he announced with a smile, "and a SADE too," he added, his eyes lighting up as he took in Cordelia's body shape.

Davie's comments caused both Orlando and Consuela to take a second look at the woman the boy was intently watching.

"Greetings, young Ser, I'm called Cordelia."

"All the things you must be able to think of in such a short period of time," Davie said admiringly.

<Billings and I resurrect the boy, and he fixates on you,> Terese grumbled to Cordelia, but there was warmth and humor behind her thought.

"Sers," Terese said, addressing Orlando and Consuela. "I would recommend you make use of the next hour to prepare food for this group of young ones. They will be starved, but will require easily digestible dishes." When the husband and wife looked with concern at each other, Terese waved away her comment.

When the twins hurried out the door, Terese added, "We have recipes aboard our traveler that will suffice. The de Long twins have gone to prepare meals for each child. That will give you time to acquire supplies and prepare suitable meals for them until they regain their strength.

"We have a problem," Orlando began.

"Peto Toyo robbed our accounts," Consuela finished for her husband. "He said it would prevent us from thinking we could run ... as if we would leave the children."

"You need no longer worry about insolvency," Cordelia said. "You now have sufficient operating funds for the next year."

"How?" Orlando stuttered.

"She's a SADE, poppa. I told you about them. They can do anything," Davie said, his eyes shining even brighter as he looked at Cordelia.

"We have our limits too, young Ser," Cordelia replied. "The universe finds a way to limit everyone and everything. It's how balance is maintained."

"Are you married or anything?" Davie asked, and the room broke into laughter.

"I think Davie is going to be fine. His hormones seem to be functioning normally," Steve said, laughing.

"I will treasure your request, Davie," Cordelia replied. "But I have a partner, who is the love of my life."

"Oh," Davie said, deflating.

"Think on this, Davie," Sarah said, stepping beside the bed. "In a few days, the Embracing Arms Orphanage will be all over the media. People here will be heavily featured, and many girls will wonder who that young, strapping boy is who met the Harakens and a SADE. You will be the center of their attention."

"You think so?" Davie asked, perking up.

"Know so," Sarah said, winking at him.

"Okay, people, we have more children to wake up. Let's hope Davie is a typical case," Terese announced. She requested Maria's investigators wheel Davie's bed back to his room, so the boy wouldn't see the conditions under which the next teenager was woken. But before they did that, she injected Davie with a dose of short-term medical nanites that would scrub his brain of the mimic that might lurk in the synaptic gaps.

One by one, Terese and Billings woke the children. Each time, the recovery period was painful to watch. Not all took up the new agents as quickly as Davie. In fact, the younger the child, the more painful and longer the recovery became.

"I bet the 'it' used the same dose level for every child," Billings growled, referring to Stratford, after a girl of about eight struggled for nearly a quarter of an hour before she quieted. Her bed was soaked with sweat, and she was seriously dehydrated.

Étienne and Alain made several trips to the traveler, transporting the food and drink Terese requested. She tasked them with ensuring the revived children were continually hydrated before and after the investigators rolled the child's bed back to his or her room. More than one little person stared at Terese in awe after they regained reality, exhausted from their struggles.

Maria and the investigators helped Orlando and Consuela feed soups and drinks to the revived children, most of whom were too tired to feed themselves. It was not long after the nourishment hit their stomachs that they were fast and peacefully asleep.

At one point, Maria watched the husband and wife hug each other as the youngest child, who had been revived, fell asleep after eating. Terese had poised the injector with its soporific over the tiny boy's neck, expecting to have to put him back under, when Billings' hand grasped her wrist to halt her. Moments later, the little body stopped its thrashing. Sweat covering his face, the boy's eyes opened and he burst into tears. Terese had swept him into her arms, soothing him with her words.

Watching Terese with the children, it occurred to Maria that she should warn Alex about Terese's possible response when she faced Stratford again but realized Cordelia had witnessed the same events. Maria laughed to herself, thinking, *Cordelia probably made a note to warn Alex the moment Terese saw the children. Maybe had hundreds of other simultaneous thoughts. Me ... I'll stick with my poor human, one-thought-at-a-time process.*

When every child was revived, dosed with medical nanites, hydrated, fed, and fast asleep again, Maria put Fredericka, Sarah, and their transport under contract for two weeks to assist the elderly couple with getting the orphanage back on its feet.

Orlando was heartily shaking hands with everyone as they sought to leave, but Consuela was hugging everyone, sometimes twice until she reached Terese. She held the Haraken's face gently in her hands, and said, "Such a sweet healer. Your people are graced to have you." Then Consuela hugged Terese for so long that even the Haraken became embarrassed and gently eased out of the embrace.

On the walk back to the traveler, Billings was beaming, and he grinned at Terese, who walked beside him.

"Yes, Emile, you did well," Terese said, laughing, and took his arm, "but don't let that go to your head."

-39-

The Harakens were overjoyed at the news of the successful tests, freeing the New Terran children of their addiction, and Terese and Billings were heaped with adulation.

While Harakens softly touched Terese's arms or shoulders in passing, New Terran crew members delivered hearty slaps to Billings' shoulders and back. At one point, after a particularly heavy round of approvals, Billings shrugged his shoulders, wincing from their soreness. His comment to Terese was, "I don't think I can take many more congratulations." But Billings was introduced to medical nanites by Terese, and he went on accepting his due.

The only person not smiling was Stratford, who felt the praise should have been directed toward him, but not a single person agreed.

Miranda and Cordelia joined the crew for evening meal, soon after most started eating. They were making their way to Terese's table, where Svetlana, Deirdre, the biochemists, and their families sat. Terese spotted them entering the room and sent, <Now.>

As one, the entire room stood and paid honor to Miranda and Cordelia, each individual facing the SADEs with hands over hearts and heads bowed. Billings belatedly jumped up and joined in the ceremony, but Stratford remained seated, a disgusted expression on his face.

The SADEs nodded their appreciation. Cordelia smiled, but noticed Miranda wore a neutral expression. <What's wrong, my sister?> Cordelia sent.

<I will miss these people when I'm gone,> Miranda replied. <I do so enjoy the company of these humans.>

Thousands of thoughts raced through Cordelia's crystal kernel in an effort to choose something to comfort Miranda. Unfortunately, nothing seemed appropriate. What Z began as an experiment had created a conundrum for the SADEs. It occurred to Cordelia to recommend to Z that he never again resurrect the Miranda persona. Yet, her central thought was that she would miss Miranda too.

* * *

<We have everything that we came for, Mr. President,> Terese sent to Alex with great relief. <We have our girls and our compounds. We can leave when you're ready.>

Despite every Haraken's expectation that their ships would break orbit soon, they remained over New Terra. When a full day passed without a word from Alex, Tatia, Renée, and Julien caught him on the *Rêveur's* bridge, chatting with Lumley.

The first mate surveyed the serious expressions on the three standing inside the bridge accessway. "Would you like to be left alone, Mr. President, for the coming discussion?"

"Depends, Francis," Alex replied, grinning at the first mate. "If you're any good at hand-to-hand combat, you can stay and help. I think I can take the little one, if you can handle the other two."

"I believe this fight is all yours, Mr. President, if you'll pardon my cowardice."

"It's not cowardice when you know you're outnumbered and don't stand a chance, Francis," Alex replied, patting the first mate on the shoulder. Alex exited the bridge, signaling the three to follow.

"Thé?" Alex asked when they reached the suite, and he set about making cups of the brew. "The three of you are wondering why we're still here. You think we should be headed back to Hellébore to deliver Terese's concoction and break the addiction demand on our teenagers."

When no one said a word, Alex handed cups of thé to Tatia and Renée. "First, let me assure you that I checked with Terese, and she says that our young people are in no danger if we delay our return for a short while. What occurs to me is that we've won a single engagement, but we're in danger from the criminal gangs that still exist."

"Are you considering actions against Kadmir and O'Brien?" Tatia asked.

"Not overtly, no," Alex replied. "What I am interested in is staying put and acting as witnesses in any cases brought against people such as Kadmir."

"Has he been charged?" Renée asked.

Alex glanced at Julien, who raised a finger, requesting Alex wait, while he accessed the government's judicial database.

"There is nothing on record. Possibly, Counselor Bernoulli requires more time to collect evidence before she brings charges. There are extensive files on both Kadmir and O'Brien." Julien said.

"Speaking of Bernoulli," Alex said, "she's asked again for the biochemists and our evidence to be turned over to her, and I told her it would be made available to her tomorrow morning. The TSF troopers we have aboard are inventorying the equipment and drug-manufacturing samples, taking possession of all of it. The scientists and their families will be leaving with them."

"Terese is adamant that we speak up for Emile Billings," Renée said.

"That will be a challenge," Alex replied. "When I spoke to Bernoulli, she said that she was leveling the same charges against both biochemists. She said there was not enough evidence to substantiate the kidnapping of Billings' family. None of them showed any signs of torture or deprivation. More critical, Billings had prior knowledge of Stratford's activities before Toyo engaged Stratford."

When both Tatia and Renée raised their voices in response, Alex held up his hands for quiet. "I understand and agree with you. Thus, one of the reasons we're staying. I also wish to present evidence to encourage a change where it concerns this mining charter, and while the New Terrans seek to apply their laws, I wish to see justice done."

Alex and Julien exchanged glances. It was the slippery slope again, which they had discussed nearly a decade and a half ago ... the laws of one society hampered in the prosecution of criminals due to the lack of evidence versus the unequivocal judgments of a superior technological society that possessed proof of their actions.

* * *

New Terra's government investigations and subsequent trials got underway in earnest. The Assembly requested Counselor Bernoulli specify the formal charges that would have been preferred against Peto Toyo had he survived the fight at Azul Kadmir's domes. Underlying the request was the representatives' intention to understand the degree to which the mining charter had been jeopardized.

Bernoulli selected an inquiry panel to hear witnesses and view the evidence presented. The first witnesses called were the Haraken girls.

"Alex, they need to see what we saw at the club," Christie shouted. The Haraken girls had landed at Maria's home the day before, intending to be available for the proceedings, but Alex announced he was considering declining Bernoulli's request for Christie and her friends. As Haraken citizens, the girls could not be compelled to testify,

<Remind you of someone, my love,> Renée sent to Alex.

"Mr. President, there are no examples in Oistos of addicted children," Amelia argued. "Ser Lechaux has cured the orphans. How can the jury members determine the danger of what Peto Toyo created if they don't see the effect on people?"

"Cordelia has downloaded their entire recordings of events. I could augment their testimony by displaying their recordings," Julien said.

"Okay, I agree, you three may appear, but hear me out. I will be in the courtroom. If I feel the questions step outside the scope of the investigation and into Haraken affairs, I will signal you and you will walk. Is that understood?"

When the girls agreed, Alex sent, <Julien, Cordelia will handle the recording display. Have her take a traveler directly to the courthouse.>

<Have you and I acquired persona non grata status?> Julien asked.

<According to Maria, you and I would taint testimony to the point that it might not be believed.>

<A result of our pursuit of justice, one might imagine.>

<Yes, here a criminal is allowed to go free if his guilt can't be proven, and New Terran technology often lacks the capability to obtain that proof.>

<Nothing a SADE or two couldn't fix.>

<True ... but would your evidence be admitted if you acquired it the way we've often done?>

<Then the law should be altered to recognize the finer morality of the SADEs.>

<You have only to convince the greater population of New Terra of your fine metal-alloy character,> Alex replied and sent Julien an image of his avatar shining like a beacon.

In the courtroom, the girls were the first to testify about the club and the drugs in Espero, but in questioning, they could not produce evidence that the club was owned by Peto Toyo or that the operators of the club worked for him. The same was true for the freighter, since the girls admitted they never left the cabin until the ships docked above Jolares, and then they were moved while blinded by hoods and in the quiet hours of the morning.

Slowly but surely, a picture was created of a fragmented history in which the testimony of the girls did not specifically tie Peto Toyo to the club, kidnapping, or incarceration.

The testimony of Orlando and Consuela did much more damage, because Toyo was at their orphanage, intimidated them into selling, and was present when the orphans were dosed. However, the evidence of the children's drug addiction was destroyed when Terese and Billings were said to have cured them.

An indication of the mindset of the panel came when one member asked Cordelia a question. The older woman said, "As a SADE, can you produce a vid that is indistinguishable from the real thing?"

To which Cordelia replied, "Another SADE could detect the difference, but if you're asking if present New Terran technology could detect the difference, the answer is no." That response threw Cordelia's entire collection of presented vids into doubt.

Miranda, Svetlana, and Deirdre fared even worse. The moment it was determined that they had entered Toyo's domes under false pretenses, kidnapped a security officer, operated on him without consent, and entered areas of the dome without management's permission, their credibility as witnesses was destroyed.

If it wasn't for the testimony of the TSF officers at both Jolares and Udrides, a strong case against Peto Toyo would not have been built at all.

The inquiry panel heard testimony for three days. In the end, they determined that Toyo was guilty of the murder of citizens in the Udrides domes and the manufacture of illegal drugs, but the evidence against him ordering the operation of the Espero club was inconclusive.

The subtle message underlying the summary was that the Harakens did not have the right to assume Toyo was responsible for what happened in Espero, and without direct testimony from the individuals who were captured after exiting the club and proof they were in Toyo's employment, at the time, the panel was unwilling to indict Toyo in absentia for those charges.

<That's it?> Christie sent in anger to Alex when the panel's summary was announced. <What did they want? A vid of Toyo holding down a teen with an injector in his hand and an on-the-spot analysis that it was full of the same drug he was manufacturing?>

<This judgment may be more an indictment against us than one against Peto Toyo, who after all was a New Terran,> Alex replied.

* * *

"Are you nuts?" Drake yelled at Bernoulli. They were in his office at Government House.

Immediately following the inquiry panel's findings concerning Toyo's activities, Bernoulli had announced the formation of a second panel to review the unusual circumstances surrounding Peto Toyo's death at the hands of Tatia Tachenko. Found with his knife thrust into his brain while the Harakens admitted they used stun guns during the fight had raised several questions for the counselor.

"We're talking about Alex Racine's admiral," Drake continued in his outburst. "What if the panel concludes she should be held over for trial?"

Bernoulli had never heard the president raise his voice to her in this manner or to anyone else, for that matter, and she felt on treacherous ground. "What do you want me to do now, Mr. President? The media already broadcast the story, and Tatia Tachenko has been served notice."

Drake was fuming and about to voice his frustration when his private reader lit up with a comm. Before he could ID the caller, Alex Racine's face appeared on the small screen, and his voice emanated from its tiny speaker.

"I would like to know how far you intend to go, Drake, in trying to drive a wedge between our people," Alex said. His anger was as obvious as the flush of blood in his face. "Serving a warrant on my admiral to appear before one of your panels. Are you out of your mind?"

Drake glared briefly at Bernoulli, who winced. He thought to tell Alex he was unaware of the counselor's intent, but he knew Alex would only accuse him of not being in control of his subordinates.

"We've already seen the quality of justice your panels are capable of under the direction of Counselor Bernoulli," Alex said. "The woman is intent on discrediting Haraken testimony, especially that of a SADE, which indicates to me strong prejudices, which should not be evident in someone responsible for dispensing justice."

Bernoulli's cheeks reddened at the insult, but Drake held up a finger away from the reader's cam pickup to silence her. It occurred to Drake that Alex might be right, and he wondered if he had not done enough to foster a balanced view about the Harakens for his people.

"Your media has the story about Tatia being served, which means we can't very well pack up and leave your system, without irreparably damaging our image even further among New Terrans," Alex continued. "You might ask yourself, Drake, how they got the story so quickly. Tatia will be there, as will I and all the others who were present during the fight with Toyo. Tomorrow, I expect a fair and impartial presentation of the evidence."

"I hear you, President Racine," Drake said. "I will inform Counselor Bernoulli of your remarks."

"Considerate of you to say that, Drake, even though unnecessary since the counselor is standing next to you."

Drake's reader screen blanked out, and the president turned to stare at Bernoulli.

"I'm a little unsure of what you want me to do, President Drake," Bernoulli said.

"Was Racine right? Were you biased in the presentation of the evidence against Toyo ... overtly critical of Haraken testimony?"

"I —" Bernoulli started to say and then stopped. She knew she distrusted the Harakens' intentions concerning the Oistos system but was unsure of whether that extended to an inability to impartially lead a panel inquiry.

"That you had to hesitate, Tessie, is the answer for both of us. I want you to imagine our system if the Harakens cut off all ties with us ... travelers, technology, trade goods ... everything. In a universe that we now know is full of extremely aggressive beings, human and alien."

"I could ... I could work to sway the presentation of the evidence in the admiral's favor," Bernoulli volunteered.

It hit Drake how much his leadership had failed to set an example for those around him. It was what Maria had done so well. She demonstrated her principles every day to her subordinates, and they emulated her.

"That's not what Racine is asking for, Tessie," Drake said, an air of sadness overtaking him. "He asked for a fair and impartial presentation of the evidence. If you try to sway the panel in Tachenko's favor, he will only see that as another failure of our legal system.

When morning came, Bernoulli opened the investigation before the inquiry panel, which was made up of seven individuals. None of the panel members missed ex-President Maria Gonzalez sitting foremost in the courtroom, arms crossed, and a frown on her face, as she met the eyes of the seven.

Tatia Tachenko took the stand and related simply and factually her confrontation with Toyo.

"Admiral Tachenko, it's your testimony that Peto Toyo's stun gun failed to fire at you. Why was he not stunned and taken into custody at that time?" Bernoulli asked.

"Let me correct your assumptions, Counselor. Peto Toyo had what his people referred to as a stunner, a weapon capable of killing with a single discharge. Second, we, meaning Harakens, do not routinely stun people who surrender to us, even though they might have just tried to kill us."

"So why, when Peto Toyo challenged you to a fight, did you accept?"

"You mean why did I consider the opportunity to physically beat a man who we knew was responsible for running an illegal club on our planet, distributing dangerously addictive drugs, kidnapping our young people, and murdering your citizens?"

"Admiral, you're aware that the previous panel did not find Peto Toyo chargeable on those first two subjects."

"Yes, we're aware of your inability to competently handle that inquiry, Counselor. Be assured though that we know who is guilty of what among your people, even if you do not."

Intakes of breaths could be heard among the panel and the audience. Even Maria had to wince at the audaciousness of the statements. She glanced over at Alex, who was not bothering to hide the slight smile on his face. *So Tatia is your outlet,* Maria thought, *by which you're informing us of what Harakens think of New Terran justice.*

Bernoulli was caught off guard. The angry glances from the panel members demanded she attack the Haraken admiral, but President Drake's warning to be impartial rang in her thoughts. She spent the prior evening reviewing the first panel's transcripts, and she was embarrassed to admit that she did sway the inquiry and not just a little.

"Let us stipulate that you accepted Toyo's challenge for a fight for personal reasons," Bernoulli said. "How was it he was killed by his own knife?"

"When that piece of human filth you call Toyo found he was losing the fight, he pulled a knife that was hidden up his sleeve, but even with that advantage he couldn't win. He pretended to surrender, flipping his weapon over to hold it by the blade and extend it to me. At the last moment, he reversed his grip and tried to stab me."

"Are we to believe, Admiral Tachenko, that you were able to best a reportedly master knife-wielder?"

"I have a great trainer," Tatia said, smiling for the first time. "Would you care for a demonstration of his talents?"

Bernoulli surveyed the faces of the panel, who were nodding their agreement. "We will adjourn until you can make the arrangements for your demonstration."

"Unnecessary, Counselor," Tatia announced firmly. "Meet my trainer." <Stand and dazzle them,> Tatia sent to Alain, who was seated in the second row.

The courtroom audience saw Alain rise and dip his head politely to the inquiry panel. One moment, he was standing stock still, the next he was a blur of motion, vaulting in a handstand over the heads of those in the first row and clearing the courtroom railing. He dropped low to the floor, obscuring himself from the panel's view.

Bernoulli sought to follow Alain, but the man was spinning incredibly fast, as he moved past her table and came up beside her. She felt a strong hand grasp her neck, pinning her in place, and the point of something touched her neck near her jugular vein. She swallowed and her eyes appealed to Tatia.

<Release her,> Tatia sent to Alain, who spun to face the counselor and bowed his head, as he offered her a stylus.

Bernoulli looked at the stylus in surprise and glanced toward the table where she had left it.

<Well done, dear heart,> Tatia sent. <You'll receive your reward tonight.>

<Always a pleasure,> Alain replied. His thought was tinged with humor, but an undercurrent of concern for his partner leaked through. Despite this, Alain calmly stepped up on the courtroom rail and onto the first row's seat backs to drop into his chair. The audience was reminded of the way a bird would flit from branch to branch without disturbing the leaves.

"As I was explaining," Tatia said, "I've had a wonderful teacher. Defeating an oaf like Peto Toyo was simple. His knife thrust was intended for my throat and I redirected the force of the blow up and away. That the blade was driven into his brain was a nice plus." Tatia ended her explanation with a grin, which left no one mistaking her opinion of killing the man.

Bernoulli examined the faces of the panel. The individuals seemed unsure of where the investigation was headed, and she sympathized with them.

Several Haraken troopers were called, but they substantiated every statement of their admiral. The consistency of the testimonies gave the panel cause to doubt their veracity, until the fourth trooper, a Libran, reminded them of Haraken technology.

"Your pardon, Ser," he said to Bernoulli. "I'm simply relating the visual and auditory event from my implant. Those who fought at Udrides are carrying a record of our actions. If you would like, I can project the fight on a holo-vid, which I'm sure our president would be happy to provide this court, as he did for your previous inquiry. As Harakens, we do not embellish or twist the truth, which seems prevalent in your culture. Our implant recordings show exactly what we saw and heard."

Maria noted that Alex's smile got even wider.

The panel adjourned and within hours announced their findings. Admiral Tatia Tachenko was not to be charged with any wrongdoing. However, they did go so far as to reprimand her for excessive use of force, which did nothing to endear the Harakens to the New Terran judiciary process.

40

The trials of Toyo's security forces, which were captured at Udrides, failed to produce the sensational events the public expected. TSF performed a voluminous amount of work collecting and examining evidence of the battle that took place in Kadmir's pleasure domes. In some cases, vids showed defendants slicing throats, clear evidence of murder. But, for most, the invisible stunner fire made it impossible to know who felled which of Kadmir's people.

Bernoulli separated the defendants into two groups — those faced with conclusive proof of murder, and those who participated in the fight, but for which the evidence of murder was inconclusive. The former defendants were offered an opportunity to plead guilty to one or more homicides with intent, in exchange for a sentence of twenty-five years without parole. The latter group was charged as accessories to murders and faced the decision of a trial or a plea deal of fifteen years of imprisonment without parole.

Without access to Toyo's extensive funds and his political connections, the defendants were left with little choice. The evidence was too damning against either group to defend themselves against the charges preferred, and, in the end, each one of them accepted the offered plea deal.

So, rather than spectacular trials, the public was treated to a parade of individuals before a judge, who confirmed each defendant's guilty plea to the charge of accessories to murders and then passed sentence. Those charged with murder, of which there were twenty-one, were scheduled for sentencing on the following morning.

That evening, Alex requested the loan of one of Maria's rented grav cars for the morrow. Early the next morning, he slipped out of bed and made himself a light breakfast, courtesy of Maria's kitchen. It was a nostalgic moment, as he had for years made breakfast for his sister and himself, since his parents left early for work.

Alex opened the grav car's door with its opaque window and was greeted by the smiling and adoring face of his partner, seated in the front passenger seat.

"Greetings, my love," Renée said.

Alex took in the container, holding five sealed drinks, in Renée's lap and peeked into the back seat.

"Morning meal?" Tatia asked, hoisting a medium-sized carryall. "Oh, but you've already eaten. Well, more for us. But, not to worry, since we've no idea how long we'll be gone, I made enough to get us through midday meal."

The "us" who Tatia referred to were the twins, who sat beside her. The admiral began distributing food, while Renée handed out hot thé to those in the rear seat.

"Come, my love," Renée admonished Alex, who seemed to be stalled just outside the car. "Get in and let's get going before we're late to … wherever."

Alex climbed in, brought the car's systems online, and lifted off without a word. It was eerily quiet inside the vehicle as Alex's companions consumed their morning meal, and Alex was left alone with his thoughts, wondering why he felt compelled to make the trip this morning.

As Prima's premier court building hove into view, Alex contacted TSF, which controlled the highly sought after vehicle spaces today for the court personnel, the media, and the public.

"Hover car, ID HCY-391, there is no more space available at the courthouse. You are waved off, pilot," TSF control said over the comm to Alex.

"Request exception, Control," Alex replied.

"Sorry, pilot. There's space available at a pad 1.8 kilometers at 217 degrees from here. If you hurry, you can still get space there."

"Requesting exception, Control. Hand me over to a superior officer," Alex requested.

Within moments, a different voice came over the comm. "This is Major Peters, pilot. Were my sergeant's instructions not clear?"

Alex smiled to himself. He first met Captain Peters during the debacle over Downing's disreputable use of presidential power. *A good man,* Alex thought. "Congratulations on your promotion, Major," Alex replied.

There was some hesitation before Peters replied hesitantly, "I know this voice … don't I?"

"Yes, you do, Major. We first met when you were a captain. I'd rather not announce my presence nor have my companions and I forced to walk a couple of kilometers in public."

"Certainly, Sir, quite understandable. I've activated a beacon on my person," Major Peters said and read off the frequency to Alex, who picked it up on his telemetry display.

"I have it, Major."

"Follow me, Sir, to the rear of the building. I hope to locate a spot that's been reserved for government officials … and I believe you fulfill the requirement," Peters replied. His chuckle could be heard over the comm.

"Good to have friends," Tatia said from the back seat.

Peters jogged at double-time to get from his station at the front of the building to the rear of the stately and enormous judicial complex. Alex followed the beacon until he spotted Peters, who waved him toward a landing spot. Only one place was available, and it was a tight squeeze between two other hover cars, but Alex, forgoing the auto-landing option and remaining in manual, dropped the craft neatly into position.

"Once a pilot, always a pilot," Renée commented, and pursed her lips at Alex when he smiled at her.

As Alex descended from the grav car, Peters snapped to attention and saluted. "A pleasure to see you, President Racine, and, on behalf of many TSF officers, we thank you for your invaluable assistance, once again."

Alex returned Peters' salute, and the officer directed them toward a rear door. As Tatia passed the major she slapped him good-naturedly on the shoulder, and Peters flashed the admiral an appreciative smile.

As they followed the major's instructions to reach the presiding judge's courtroom, Tatia couldn't contain her curiosity anymore. "Well, I, for one, am dying to know why we're here."

"Something I need to do," Alex replied simply.

At the courtroom doors, a harried TSF sergeant, who had just turned two people away, spouted the line he'd been saying for the last quarter hour, before he recognized whom he was talking to, "Sorry, no more ... oh, President Racine."

"I would appreciate a front-row seat for all of us, but if that's too much trouble, Sergeant, then get me a front-row seat and my companions can sit anywhere," Alex said.

"The courtroom is quite full, and the prosecutor's side is SRO, Sir."

"I'm interested in the defendant's side, Sergeant."

"You're interested in the um ...? Yes, Sir. Let me see what I can arrange." The senior sergeant jumped on his comm and a sergeant and a corporal hustled to his position. He put them in charge of handling the courtroom doors and ducked inside.

The newly posted sergeant and corporal worked to appear professional, but their eyes scanned from the famous president, to the admiral who killed the infamous Toyo, to the twins who mysteriously still wore their stun guns in a secure building, and finally to Renée who drew their eyes more often than any of the others.

"Sorry to be a bother, men," Alex said politely.

"Not a problem, Mr. President," the sergeant replied, snapping his eyes away from Tatia.

The senior sergeant returned from the courtroom. "I have a seat for you in the front row, defendant's side, Sir. You'll be sitting beside family members."

"That's fine, Sergeant," Alex replied, which left the sergeant mollified but still somewhat confused.

"The others can sit at the rear of the courtroom, same side," the sergeant said and held open the door for Alex. He ushered the four Harakens to the last row, and media personnel, who were miffed at being told to give up their seats, were overjoyed to have a fascinating twist in the proceedings to report.

It was the sight of Alex being led to the front of the courtroom and seated on the defendant's side that had mouths hanging open and reporters speaking hurriedly and softly into their comms for their vid drones, which hovered above their heads. The judge dipped his head to Alex, who returned the gesture as he was seated. An older woman, who had been crying at the prospect of her son being charged with multiple homicides and about to be sentenced to twenty-five years of imprisonment, glanced over in shock as the Haraken president sat beside her and nodded politely.

Once the proceedings were underway, the defendants were brought five at a time before the judge, who had the charges and the plea deals read and waited while each defendant announced their guilt. Then the judge sentenced all five defendants at once to twenty-five years of confinement in a TSF-containment facility.

As the mysteries of fortune would have it, the TSF squad, which managed the prisoners, didn't bother to request the court's direction as to whether the twenty-first prisoner should have been included with the last lot of five or not. So, a single defendant was left to appear before the judge.

Guided by a TSF sergeant, Lenny shuffled into the courtroom, as sad and dejected a person as you would ever want to see. His days of incarceration had already taken a toll on Lenny's demeanor and body. It was obvious that Lenny was one of those prisoners who would never serve his entire sentence.

Lenny gazed across the courtroom crowd. His brain registered people but not specific individuals, until his eyes focused on Alex. Immediately, Lenny perked up. "Hi, mister," he said in a cheery voice and pulled free of his accompanying TSF trooper, walking over to the railing to speak to Alex, before the noncom could stop him.

When the sergeant saw the Haraken president stand, he glanced back at the judge, who signaled with his hand for the prisoner escort to wait.

"They took my rifle away, mister," Lenny said to Alex.

"I know, Lenny. Do you know why you're here?"

"Yeah ... I did a lot of bad things for Mr. Toyo. But he was the only one who let me have a rifle."

"I understand, Lenny, but wanting to do something doesn't mean we should do it."

"I'm not going to make it ... inside, I mean," Lenny said, and tears glistened in his eyes.

"Yes, you will, Lenny, and do you know how I know you will?"

Lenny snuffled and looked earnestly at Alex. "How?"

"Because you're going to wait for my present."

"You're going to send me a present?"

"A special present … one that you will love, and that will help you serve your time."

"My mom was the only one who ever gave me presents, but she died when I was young."

As the TSF sergeant walked up to stand beside Lenny, Alex said, "It's time to talk to the judge, Lenny. You wait for my gift."

"Okay, mister. Thanks," Lenny said. He was presented before the judge, and, for a few moments, he no longer looked as if he wore the weight of the world on his shoulders.

<One of the lost,> Renée commented to her companions.

<I had several ideas about why we might be here, but this wasn't one of them,> Tatia sent. <The man continues to amaze, if not confuse, me.>

The return to Maria's house was quiet again, but for a different reason this time. As soon as Alex could, he huddled with Julien and issued a string of instructions, which left many perplexed, but who nonetheless faithfully executed Alex's requests.

Mickey and Claude wrapped their creation and delivered it to Maria. In turn, she made an appointment with the TSF-containment facilities commandant, whose eyes opened in surprise when he unwrapped the package. Because it was Maria who requested the favor, the commandant delivered the item and the accompanying message to the resident senior inmate counselor.

Geron Hanley knew he faced a difficult challenge with the new inmate, Lenny. He had been unable to entice Lenny into a counseling session, and the guard reports detailed Lenny's declining appetite and unwillingness to make use of exercise opportunities. It would not be long before a drastic intervention would be necessary to save Lenny's life.

After the commandant placed the package on Hanley's desk and announced it was approved for the exclusive use of Lenny, the counselor read and reread the message from the Haraken president several times. It was one of the oddest approaches to therapy Hanley had ever heard of, but, at this point, he was interested in giving it a try. He rewrapped the package and requested access to Lenny's cell.

When the guard opened the cell door, Hanley found Lenny lying on his back, his arm over his eyes to block out the daylight flooding through his cell's plex-window.

"Hello, Lenny," Hanley said. When the counselor failed to receive a reply, he opened the president's message, which laid out the dialog the Haraken requested he follow. Reading the opening line, Hanley said, "I have a gift for you."

"For me?" Lenny asked, taking his arm from across his face. "Who from?"

Hanley glanced down at the script. "The man in the courtroom promised you a present."

Lenny struggled to sit up on his bunk, the lack of nutrition evident in his weak and sluggish movement. "What is it?" Lenny asked.

Hanley became hopeful when he saw light shine in Lenny's eyes, for the first time, and became a serious participant in the script. Reading the next part quickly, Hanley unwrapped the gift and displayed the replica of a plasma rifle.

Lenny attempted to stand, only to fall back on his bunk, but his hands grasped out as if he could coax the rifle to him. Tears ran down Lenny's face, as he choked out, "He remembered me."

"Yes, he did, Lenny." By now, Hanley wasn't going to deviate from the instructions. "This is a special rifle, Lenny. Let me show you." Hanley held up the replica and squeezed the firing stud.

The TSF corporal had stood in the doorway, bemused by the odd conversation taking place between the therapist and inmate. But he nearly had a heart attack when Hanley raised and fired the replica rifle, despite knowing the weapon wasn't real.

Lenny watched in awe as the power cell in the unit spun out a series of pulses, which wrapped around the gas-ignition chamber and spun along the barrel in a pair of blue electrical streams, ending in a visible laser pulse leaping out from the end of the rifle. Then the entire weapon shimmered in a sparkle of light that slowly faded. Lenny's eyes glowed in delight. "And this is for me?" he asked, daring to hope.

"Well, Lenny, I have some strict instructions from the man who sent this, and I have to follow them."

"Okay, I'll do whatever he wants. He was nice to me ... and he remembered me."

"He wants you to eat regularly and exercise."

"I can do that. I can eat now."

"We'll bring you food for a while, Lenny, until you get your strength back."

"Then do I get my rifle?" Lenny asked.

"There's one more request, Lenny. You have to come see me for counseling on a regular basis. After your first session, and as long as you keep coming to see a counselor, you'll get to keep your rifle. But no shooting it after lights out."

"I can do that. I can eat now and then come see you."

"When you get strong enough to eat with the others, then you can come see me."

"And then I can have my rifle?"

"Yes, Lenny."

It would become one of the strangest sights in the history of the containment facility to see Lenny on the exercise field, practicing his shooting positions, rolling and popping up, the replica displaying its light show as it was fired.

More than once, an inmate sought to relieve the quiet and unpretentious Lenny of his weapon, only to be shocked by a maniacal response. Word worked through the facility that you attempted to separate Lenny from his rifle at your peril.

In Lenny's world, he destroyed all sorts of things as he fired his rifle — hover cars, buildings, trees, and yes, even people. That his weapon was a replica with an incredible light display didn't occur to him. In Lenny's mind, the plasma beam was real.

* * *

Despite testimony from Christie, Amelia, and Eloise that indicated Azul Kadmir played some part in the events that fomented the fight that cost so many civilian lives, no charges were brought against Kadmir. He was viewed as lawfully defending his establishment from Peto Toyo's unprovoked attack.

When Alex questioned Bernoulli, she replied that Kadmir was within his rights to wave Alex off and reset their meeting, and it was Alex who disregarded the owner's legal right to deny access, which left him with a bad taste in his mouth. For Alex, it seemed to follow every conversation with the counselor.

On the subject of Toyo's security people, who imprisoned the New Terran families, fought with the Harakens, and protected the drug lab, Bernoulli's response further inflamed Alex. She accused the president's people of entering Toyo's domes under false pretenses and creating fake IDs by illegally manipulating the establishment's records. In her opinion, the security people were within their rights to defend their domes against interlopers. Her only concession was to charge Dillon Jameson, Toyo's head of security, with illegal drug production, but none of the other security people were indicted on a single charge.

Based on Bernoulli's inquiry and trial record, Alex saw no purpose in volunteering the information the Harakens possessed on Roz O'Brien. Henry, or Wheezy or whatever, was ignorant of his compatriots' real names and was the only individual remaining in Espero who worked for O'Brien. And even Henry admitted that it was the elusive Cherry, not O'Brien, who had hired him and supposedly killed the crew distributing the stims.

Julien had traced the rental of the Espero warehouse, where the bodies of Henry's people were found, to Desmonis Distribution, a company owned by Roz O'Brien. But, once again, there was nothing to prove that the bodies in the freezer were put there by one of O'Brien's people.

Both Alex and Julien agreed that the evidence against O'Brien would be viewed by the New Terran courts as circumstantial, at best. It was obvious that Kadmir and O'Brien had amassed a great deal of power, and they could only be arrested and convicted with incontrovertible proof against them for major felonies, and maybe not even then.

The Assembly heard enough from Bernoulli's investigative panel to vote to confiscate Toyo's domes, and they no sooner announced their decision than the government received a formal offer from Azul Kadmir and Roz O'Brien to purchase the domes.

"The sale of Toyo's domes to Udrides Resources and Desmonis Distribution has been approved by the government," Julien said to Alex.

"The Assembly just appropriated the domes two days ago," Alex replied, incredulous at the short turnaround time.

"Apparently the Sers have considerable influence," Julien replied.

"That's an understatement. If Christie and her friends are right about some sort of collusion between Kadmir and Toyo that went awry or was even planned as a double-cross, then O'Brien and Kadmir got what they set out to accomplish. Any idea of the price they paid?"

"By my estimate, they obtained the domes at about 40 percent of market value."

Alex shook his head, and Julien could only commiserate with him. "To paraphrase a saying of your culture, my friend, crime can pay."

Alex started to speak but abruptly closed his mouth. He waved a hand in negation at Julien, and, wearing a disgusted expression, he continued on his way to meet with Tatia.

* * *

The final series of trials began with the chemists and technicians who worked at Toyo's labs. In a blanket finding, the chemists and techs were given probation, but not allowed to practice their profession for five years.

The evidence against Stratford was overwhelming, and, after the presentation of extensive testimony, he was convicted in record time. His sentence was eighteen years of confinement in a TSF prison with no parole.

The longer and more complex trial involved Emile Billings. The charges leveled against the biochemist were the same as Stratford, which the Harakens found unconscionable. Testimony from Miranda, Svetlana, and Deirdre repeatedly underlined the level of Billings' cooperation with them. Implant recordings displayed the conversation between Billings and Svetlana as the biochemist expressed his concern for his family and told the story of their kidnapping.

Terese detailed Billings' support in creating the antidote to the addictive side effect of the hallucinogenic drug. She related Billings' efforts, which led to the successful curing of the children at the Embracing Arms Orphanage.

The verdict took several days to issue. When it finally came, Billings was ecstatic to hear he was exonerated of the drug-manufacturing charges, but deflated when he realized the jury wasn't convinced of his complete innocence. They felt that Billings was complicit by failing to report to authorities that Stratford was experimenting with the creation of illegal drugs.

Standing before the judge, Billings heard the pronouncement, and his legs threatened to collapse. The jury's decision devastated him. Billings was forbidden to practice his profession for the remainder of his life and with that went the elimination of his university teaching post that he had held for over a decade.

After court was dismissed, Terese found Billings and his family sitting on a bench in the park outside the courthouse. Janine, the wife, was consoling her husband. The seven-year-old daughter, Mincie, sat forlornly beside her mother on the bench, unsure of what was said in the courtroom, but her father and mother's distraught behavior was a good indication that it was terrible news for her father, which meant, to her young mind, that it was bad for Mom and her.

Billings' elbows were on his knees and his head in his hands. His thought was that he was a waste of a husband and a father, knowing he should be wearing a brave face for his family. A pair of Haraken ship boots came into view, and Billings looked up to find Terese staring at him, hands on her hips.

"You know, Terese, the court's right," Billings said, his face a torment of sadness. "I should have turned Stratford into the authorities the first time he started experimenting with illegal drugs. Maybe, if I had, none of these children, ours and yours, would have been hurt. But, I thought by breaking up our partnership it would force him to come to his senses. I should have known that nothing would stop that ego of his."

"Well, I hope you've learned your lesson, Ser. You can't demur from your responsibilities just because you find the choice uncomfortable," Terese replied, in her characteristically firm demeanor.

Billings' wife, Janine, straightened up and took a breath to retort, but her husband laid a hand on her arm. "It's okay, love." Looking up at Terese, Billings said, "Yes, it's a lesson learned, even if I think the court's punishment is much too harsh."

"Cheer up, Emile, there's always tomorrow," Terese replied.

Terese's shift to an upbeat voice confused Billings, but he responded to her statement. "Tomorrow isn't going to look any better than today, I'm afraid. My life's passion has been effectively and permanently truncated."

"So you're saying you care to do nothing else?" Terese asked.

"I would give almost anything to continue my research and my teaching," Billings replied.

"Careful what you wish for, Emile."

Billings raised his head to stare at Terese. He could just make out her grin. The sun was behind her, and her hair glowed as if on fire.

"What are you asking … I mean, what would I have to do?" Billings asked, hope dawning in his heart.

"Say yes, Ser."

"What … what's going on?" Janine asked, looking at the anticipation blooming on her husband's face.

Billings turned to his wife, grasping both of her hands. "What would you say to living on Haraken?" he asked her.

"Could he teach? Continue his research?" Janine asked Terese.

"Yes, to both, Ser."

"Then, yes … oh, yes," Janine exclaimed, hugging her husband and crying with joy.

"We leave in a few days, Sers. Can you be ready?" Terese asked.

"Ready?" Billings repeated. "We've lost just about everything except for an account with a few credits left in it. We can be ready in a few hours."

"Comm the *Rêveur* when you're ready to leave and ask for me. I'll send a traveler for you."

Janine stood up, hesitated, and then hugged Terese fiercely. "Thank you, thank you," she whispered into Terese's ear. "You won't regret this. He's a good man."

"I know he is, Ser," Terese replied quietly and left the family to enjoy the turn in their future.

* * *

Uneven verdicts continued to issue from the trials that Bernoulli presided over, but Drake had one item to accomplish that he could perform that didn't require the cooperation of Bernoulli' office. Since General Oppert reported no progress in his investigation to track the source of the illegal stunners, Drake hired Maria's services, and the first thing Maria did was contact Alex.

"Are the SADEs available for hire, Alex? And how much would they cost?" Maria said when her reader connected with Alex.

<What are you hunting now, Maria?> Alex sent.

"Drake's asked me to locate the source of the stunners."

Julien had connected Maria's comm, and, at her first question, he linked Cordelia, Miranda, and Willem.

Alex detected the SADEs online and knew Julien noticed his comm check of participants. <Since they're online, Maria, and are their own entities, you might ask them yourself.>

<We would be pleased to help you with your investigation, Ser,> Julien replied courteously.

<As I've learned from Cordelia,> Miranda added, <the customary fee of one credit will be applied, but I must warn you, madam ... that's one

credit each. There must be no shirking on your part. We expect payment in full.>

The Harakens could hear Maria's deep laughter. "I believe I can afford the fee," she finally managed to say while still chuckling.

<Now that we are employed,> Willem said, <I believe I can accelerate the investigation. I have a stunner in my possession.>

Alex queried Julien, but the SADE was at a loss for a response.

<I reasoned that one fewer illegal weapon in the hands of the TSF wouldn't harm the course of justice,> Willem explained. <On the other hand, one weapon in our hands could prove invaluable. So I'm loath to admit that I purloined it from the vault located in Toyo's lower dome.>

This time, it was the Harakens who were smiling and chuckling.

<We should break the stunner down, and see what we can learn,> Alex sent.

<Agreed, Mr. President,> Willem sent. <Toward that end, I've done the work of disassembling it and have categorized every component in its manufacture. I was awaiting instructions on what should be done with the information.>

Alex's laughter boomed out of Maria's reader, and the mirth in his thoughts inundated the SADEs. Julien, for one, was pleased to hear the sound of his friend in good humor again.

<Maria,> Cordelia sent. <Please allow us a little time to see what we can do with Willem's information. We will be in contact shortly.>

When Alex signaled his consent, Julien closed the comm.

Maria sat back and looked at her three investigators. "The SADEs are on the job," she said, grinning, and smiles were returned to her from around the porch table.

"One credit each," Steve said, shaking his head and laughing.

"Help is getting so expensive these days," Sarah quipped.

"I recognized the voice of the one called Cordelia. She said to give them some time. How long do you think that will be?" Fredericka asked.

"For Haraken SADEs, not long," Maria replied. "And don't think that a voice identifies a SADE. They can produce any voice or sound they wish.

They just don't do it in mixed company so as not to frighten us mortals, especially local New Terrans," Maria said.

"That's a scary thought," Sarah said.

"When I heard Alex was going to free the SADEs, I wondered about the sanity of his decision," Maria replied. "Releasing cognitive intelligences among humankind seemed to me to be a potentially catastrophic move. But over the years, I've seen my share of people like Downing, Bunaldi, García, Toyo, Kadmir, and O'Brien who have been as treacherous for human societies as anyone. Now, I think I understand Alex's motivation. He doesn't care in what form the entities come at him … humans, mechanical, or alien … it's what lies in their heart, whether they have one, two, or none. And, I've come to believe he has the right idea."

41

While Maria entertained the investigators at her home, the SADEs searched New Terran records for transactions involving stunner components sold during the past year and then cross-referenced the buyers and their addresses. It took them less than half a day to identify a single buyer in common to all components, who was extremely careful to purchase small quantities so as to evade casual detection.

Maria and her investigators were about to sit down to an evening's meal when her reader chimed. Steve glanced at the swirling image of colors on Maria's reader. "SADE calling," he said and carried the device to Maria.

<Greetings, Maria,> Cordelia said, her face appearing on the small screen. <We have the information you're seeking.>

"Hello, Cordelia. How many potential suspects are we looking at?" Maria asked.

<We found only one buyer, Maria, who has purchased all the stunner components in the past year. Here is the name of the buyer and the address of the delivery location.> Cordelia's image was replaced with the text message.

When the reader closed with a swirl of colors, Sarah said, "I really love that pattern. Did you notice it never repeats?"

The investigators stared at the plates of hot food with longing, but they jumped up and grabbed their body armor and stun weapons, while Maria contacted Colonel Portis, the TSF officer who had teamed with Ross previously, and arranged to meet her and a squad of troopers at the location.

Steve handed Maria her weapon, and Fredericka and Sarah carried her body armor to the transport for her. They wasted no time lifting off with Steve at the controls and were the first to arrive at the address. They had some moments to observe the building and the lot before the TSF transport settled beside their grav car.

Colonel Portis regarded the empty lot and looked at Maria in confusion. "No activity, Madam President?' she asked.

"Looks that way," Maria replied.

"Could the intel be wrong?" Portis asked.

"SADEs," Sarah said simply.

"Oh, well ... understood," Portis replied, her voice rising with interest.

"They tracked the purchase of the stunner components to this place," Maria explained.

Despite the lack of activity, the TSF forces and Maria's group approached the building carefully. There was no need to force an entry. The front door was slightly ajar. Past the front offices, the interior was an open space, set up at one time for an automated manufacturing plant. Someone had cobbled a series of small work tables together. There wasn't a person in sight nor a fully or partially assembled stunner either.

"Probably cleared out the moment they heard Toyo was dead," Portis reasoned.

Steve examined some small components left on one table. He picked up his reader, opened a comm, and said, "Cordelia."

<Yes, Steve,> Cordelia replied.

Steve smiled at his compatriots, raising his eyebrows high and enjoying the success of his idea. The SADEs were monitoring their activities. "No one home at the location you gave us. Everything looks cleared out, but take a look at these," Steve said. He pointed his reader at the table and with his stylus slowly turned over several components.

<Those are components used in the construction of the stunners, Steve,> Cordelia replied.

"As you are such a brilliant and wonderful entity, Cordelia, I thought you might have another way to track these people," Steve said. He grinned at his friends, and the women shook their heads at his audaciousness.

Over the reader, they heard Cordelia laugh, and then, eerily, the laugh segued into a tinkling of delicate bells. <You will need to save your

compliments, Ser, for a partner who is not four times your age. But your idea is not without merit. Hold one.>

"Yes," Steve celebrated.

"He just loves it when he's clever," Fredericka grumped to Colonel Portis.

Cordelia linked the SADEs and reexamined their data.

<There were four readers that were used to order the components over the course of a nine-month period,> Willem noted.

The SADEs raced throughout the system — planets, stations, ships, outposts, habitats, and domes — in search of the readers.

<Steve,> Cordelia said, the intricate pattern appearing on his reader before her face. <Four readers were employed in ordering the stunner components. Two of the readers are inactive for reasons unknown. A third reader is in the hands of TSF.>

Maria glanced at Portis, who shrugged in reply.

<It belongs to Toyo's chief of security, Dillon Jameson, who is presently in TSF custody. Colonel Portis, you may want to recommend to Ser Bernoulli that Ser Jameson face additional charges.>

"Um … certainly, ma'am, thank you," Portis replied, totally out of her depth in a conversation with a Haraken SADE.

<The fourth reader, which was used for approximately 63.42 percent of all purchases, is active and is presently at a domestic location.>

"Cordelia, Maria here. Do you have a name?"

<Negative, Ser. The reader's ID is registered under a company name, which isn't found within your government's records. Obviously, the establishment is a façade.>

"Thank you, Cordelia," Steve said and blew the SADE a kiss. The tiny bells tinkled as Cordelia closed the comm.

"I swear … you'd flirt with anything feminine," Sarah said, laughing and swatting Steve's shoulder.

"Load up," Maria ordered. "We have another appointment."

A quarter-hour later, they were flying over a heavily residential area comprised of expansive houses. The transports settled in a nearby park, and the group made their way to a vacant lot across the street from a beautiful, stone and timber house.

Maria swore under her breath. "I know this house," she said. She picked up her reader, raced through her list of contacts, and chose one.

"Hello, Maria," Will Drake said. "To what do I owe the pleasure?"

"You have a problem, Mr. President," Maria said.

Drake bolted upright in his living room chair. Maria's use of his title said she was in company and on the job. "Talk to me, Maria," Drake replied.

"The SADEs traced the components of a stunner to a delivery location, an abandoned manufacturing warehouse. We raided it in the company of Colonel Portis of the TSF, but the place was cleared out days ago. In turn, the SADEs tracked two of the four readers that made the purchases. One of those readers belongs to Toyo's chief of security, who's in custody. The other active reader is sitting inside the home of Assemblyman Finian Egan."

"Maria, I so want to ask you if this is a joke, but I won't waste your time. What do you need?"

"Entry will require a warrant. We don't know if the reader belongs to our representative or a house guest. The warrant should specify the house and the grounds of the property to confiscate any and all readers."

"Maria, tell me you have some corroborating evidence."

"None, Mr. President ... just the SADEs," Maria said. She could hear Will's muffled groan and sympathized with him. His government was mired in a heated exchange of extreme opinions among politicians, leaders, and the general populace over the involvement of the Harakens in New Terra's business.

"I have your location, Maria. I'm sending Tessie to work through this with you on-site."

Before Maria could reply, the comm went dead. Reply was the polite word for what Maria might have said. She couldn't stand Tessie Bernoulli, and the counselor's feelings for her were mutual. Now, there was nothing to do but wait.

* * *

"Boss," Steve said quietly to Maria. "I hate to point out the obvious, but, despite the late hour, we're as conspicuous as Méridiens at a New Terran party out here.

"Agreed," Maria said. Thinking for a moment, she nodded at Steve's reader and added, "We need remote surveillance."

While the group trotted back to the park and their transports, Steve stopped to contact Cordelia and ask the SADE if she could monitor the house for them.

<Steve, the domicile has been under constant surveillance since we identified it. A two-person grav car left the location before you arrived. We have the transport's identification for you. The reader that interests us is still inside the house. If it were to leave in someone's possession, we would make that our primary target.>

At the transports, Colonel Portis asked Steve, as he jogged up to join them, if the SADEs were going to help, and Maria paused in her conversation to hear the answer.

"It appears my request was superfluous, and I received a short lecture on the thoroughness of SADE surveillance." Steve ducked his head and when he looked back up, his expression was that of someone who had bitten something sour.

Sarah and Fredericka broke into laughter. "Ah, Steve, is the bloom off your love interest so quickly?" Fredericka teased.

"Anything of substance from Cordelia?" asked Maria, which curtailed the laughter.

"Yes ... a two-person grav car left before we arrived, but it wasn't transporting the reader. I have the vehicle's ID from Cordelia."

The group settled down to wait, and it was more than an hour before a small transport landed beside theirs and Tessie Bernoulli climbed out. She was wearing an elegant and festive evening dress. Her hair, makeup, and accessories said she had been interrupted while attending a prestigious event.

"Counselor's going to be in a good mood," Fredericka remarked quietly to Sarah.

Bernoulli hadn't taken three steps before she noticed the wet grass and soil were ruining her delicate slippers. She stopped, pulled them off, and threw them back through the open window of her transport.

"Worse, we just messed up her party shoes," Sarah whispered, chuckling.

Maria wasted no time updating Bernoulli on the circumstances of the investigation.

"President Drake told me your information came from the Haraken SADEs," Bernoulli said. "Tell me you have a corroborating source."

"As I told our president, we don't," Maria replied. "Do you have a problem with the SADEs?"

"Of course, I have a problem with them," Bernoulli said in outrage, striking a pose with her hands on her hips. It was the kind of stance she thought would inform people she was adamant about her point. Unfortunately, her exaggerated poses just irritated most people around her. "Haven't you been following the trials, Maria? People don't trust the SADEs. I mean, just how are they supposed to believe a hyped-up, walking, talking, super computer, which can manipulate data to the point we can't tell fact from fiction?"

"Is that your personal opinion, Bernoulli," Maria asked, working to control her rising anger, "or the General Counsel's opinion?"

"Let me be blunt, Maria. You know a representative's reader is considered inviolate unless we have reasonable cause to confiscate it. That's reasonable as defined under New Terran law. Nowhere in our compilation of judicial decisions does it say that a recording or data from a smart machine, a foreign one at that, constitutes proof of reasonable cause when it involves an Assembly representative."

Bernoulli became nervous as Maria continued to stare at her. She was reminded that Maria was an ex-TSF general, and she sought to make her point again.

"You have to understand President Drake's position. He is elected by the will of the people, and those people are dubious of these things being freed from their boxes. A point to consider is that the Confederation invented these things centuries ago and have kept them in confinement. Now Racine has let them loose … machines without hearts, without consciences, without pity for humankind … why shouldn't people be scared of them? Why should they trust these monstrous inventions?"

Maria was as flabbergasted as were her investigators whose lives had been saved by the SADEs. It underlined to her why the investigations and trials conducted by the General Counsel sought to limit the use of Haraken implants and SADE recordings. She drew breath to give Bernoulli a piece of mind but was interrupted.

<Counselor, your bigotry is galling,> a voice said.

Bernoulli whirled around trying to identify who spoke, and Steve held up his reader and pointed a finger at it.

"Who is that?" Bernoulli called out.

<The man who freed the Haraken SADEs.>

"So now you've added eavesdropping to your list of transgressions, President Racine."

"Actually, no, Counselor," Steve said. "I've held an open comm with Cordelia since before you arrived. You've simply been overheard the entire time you've been here. If you wanted privacy, you should have requested it." Steve's comments elicited a spate of snickers, and Maria fought to maintain a neutral expression in the face of Bernoulli's angry blush.

"As for us," Steve said, gesturing to his fellow investigators, "we're fans of the SADEs, apparently unlike some people."

"At ease, Major," Maria commanded sternly.

"Just saying, Madam President," Steve replied, angling for the last word, and reminding Bernoulli of who stood in front of her.

"All this is beside the point," Bernoulli declared, "I can't issue a warrant based on information provided by a pile of chips or crystals or whatever."

<Incensed though you might be, Mr. President, don't threaten the counselor … use leverage,> Julien advised Alex privately. Cordelia had linked the SADEs and Alex the moment Drake told Maria he was sending Bernoulli.

<First item, Counselor,> Alex sent, <if you insult our SADEs one more time, you will jeopardize all trade with your system, and I will ensure your people know who was responsible for the loss. The SADEs have names and you will address them respectfully as such. Am I clear?>

Bernoulli would have argued, but everyone surrounding her had shifted from casual stances to those adopted by the military when tensing for action. It was intimidating, which angered her and scared her at the same time. "Understood," she reluctantly acknowledged.

<Know this, Counselor,> Alex said, <the ethics practiced by the SADEs exceed the moral behavior of most New Terrans I have met and I would include myself in that group.>

<Ah, my friend, you give us too much credit, and yourself too little,> Julien shared with his fellow SADEs.

<Which is why we continue to watch ourselves and one another most closely,> Cordelia added.

<What if someday all humans fear us?> Willem asked.

<If that day approaches, dear Willem,> Miranda sent, <it will be because we did too little to be a part of humankind. It will be a sad day and time to seek our own world.>

While Maria and Bernoulli's argument about probable cause and reliable information sources continued, Steve casually sauntered over to Maria's transport, pulled out a flare rifle, which was used as an emergency signaling device, aimed it into the air, and pulled the trigger.

As the round exploded out of the barrel and arced above the small park toward the assemblyman's house, leaving a bright red trail in the evening's sky, Steve looked at the shocked faces of the group and said, "Oops ... accident." Coincidentally, if one wishes to believe that, his errant round landed on the roof of the representative's home. "Fire," Steve said nonchalantly.

"I believe a rescue is required, Colonel," Maria said, smiling at Portis.

"Absolutely, General," Portis said, snapping a quick salute. "Come on, people, we have a civilian evacuation to perform. Sergeant, comm for Fire Suppression Services," she ordered as she double-timed it toward the house.

"You won't get away with this," Bernoulli said, staring angrily at Maria.

"Get away with what?" Maria asked innocently.

"I won't let you search the house once the fire is out."

"I have no intention of doing so, Counselor. That would be illegal."

The two women stood by with the investigators while TSF troops cleared the building. Colonel Portis ushered Assemblyman Egan and his aide over to them.

"Do you know what started the fire, Madam President?" Egan asked Maria, nodding a greeting to Counselor Bernoulli.

"Much to my regret, Assemblyman Egan, it was one of my own people. A flare was accidentally discharged. My company will be responsible for any damage to your charming home."

"You always were an honorable woman, Madam President. Thank you," Egan replied.

Steve looked down at his reader, the swirling signature of a SADE in evidence. It cleared and an arrow floated on the screen. Confused, Steve picked up his reader and watched the arrow rotate. He held the reader flat, and the arrow spun about 50 degrees. "Locate the suspect reader," appeared in text underneath it.

Steve walked in the direction of the arrow. It led him toward the assemblyman and his aide. Approaching the two men from behind, the arrow shifted toward Egan, who cradled a reader in his arms, as if afraid to lose control of it. Making sure he was within Maria's eyeline, Steve held up his reader and then swung his eyes down and toward Egan's arms.

The decades as a TSF-ranking officer gave Maria her idea. "Colonel Portis, we can't have the assemblyman and his aide standing out in this cool, misty, night air while FSS puts out the fire and ensures the house is safe. Why don't you transport them wherever they choose?"

"Generous of you, Madam President," Egan said. "My offices at Assembly Hall would be fine, Colonel."

Portis knew that Maria was aware that only TSF personnel were allowed to use TSF transports, except in the case of suspects or felons, but the colonel was known for her nimble mind. "It would be my pleasure, Assemblyman Egan," Portis said pleasantly.

Maria accompanied the representative and his aide to the TSF transport. Bernoulli followed behind, her bare feet squishing through the muddy soil. Egan's aide noted the counselor's odd attire for the circumstances and was torn between commenting or remaining silent.

The moment Egan and his aide were seated in the back of the TSF transport. Maria held up her reader, pretending to check the screen. "Colonel, one moment, we appear to have an issue. Information I've received indicates a reader in your transport was used to order supplies to build the illegal stunners. You will need to confiscate their readers," Maria said, pointing to the assemblyman and his aide.

"What kind of game is this?" Egan declared hotly. "These are government-protected tools. You'll require a warrant to take them from us."

"On the contrary, Assemblyman Egan," Portis said, catching on to Maria's ploy. "You're sitting in a TSF transport. That's our jurisdiction, and if I'm provided with information from a reliable source, such as Maria Gonzalez, that data relating to a crime is present, I have a duty and the authority to confiscate the sources."

"Then we'll get out of your transport," Egan said, attempting to climb out of the rear seat, but he found his way blocked by troopers.

"Counselor Bernoulli, please correct this ill-informed officer. I'm an elected official of our government. TSF has no authority over me or my possessions," Egan called out.

"In most circumstances, you would be correct, Sir," Bernoulli allowed. She was incensed by Maria's manipulation, but her hands were tied. "But, under these conditions, Colonel Portis is right. You are on what is considered TSF grounds and, as she is the senior officer present, you are under her authority.

"Your readers, Sirs," Portis said, extending her hand.

Egan's aide looked at his boss, who was frozen. The exalted persons surrounding the strange happenings were too much for him. He climbed over the representative, handed his reader to Portis, and backed away from the transport.

Steve looked down at his reader. The arrow still pointed at Egan. Steve caught Portis' eyes, nodded at Egan, and winked.

"Your reader, Sir, unless you wish to be arrested for disobeying my lawful command," Portis ordered,

Egan's eyes beseeched Bernoulli, but the counselor dropped her head, shaking it in negation.

Finally, Portis reached into the transport and gripped the reader. She had to apply significant force until the reader was slowly withdrawn from Egan's clutches. "Do you still wish to be transported to Assembly Hall, Sir?" Portis asked, but Egan appeared dazed, staring straight ahead.

"Counselor," Maria said, nodding toward Egan.

Bernoulli stepped to the transport's open door. "Assemblyman Egan, do you wish to make a voluntary statement to me?"

Egan turned his head slowly to fix on Bernoulli. When recognition of who was talking to him seeped in and kick started his brain, the assemblyman said, "I wish to discuss a plea deal."

"Are you admitting to having committed a felony, Assemblyman Egan?" Bernoulli asked, checking to make sure her reader was recording.

"If I have committed any such act, I would wish to discuss that in private with you and my attorney."

"Colonel Portis, please take Assemblyman Egan into protective custody and deliver him to my offices. He is to remain in your care until he, his attorney, and I meet. Is that clear?"

"Completely, Counselor Bernoulli," Portis replied.

A sergeant climbed in beside Egan, while the rest of the patrol clambered aboard. The transport lifted and headed for Government House.

"Well, you got what you wanted, Maria," Bernoulli said.

"If you mean did I fulfill President Drake's request to locate a perpetrator of the stunner manufacture, then, yes, I did. I'm sure Egan will give up his cronies, unless you cut him such a sweet deal that he has no reason to capitulate."

"I know my job, Maria."

"That, I'm not so sure about. Good day, counselor," Maria said, turning her back on Bernoulli and heading toward her own transport.

Lagging behind, Steve glanced down at his reader. The arrow was gone, replaced by the image he had come to enjoy. "Cordelia, we have the reader and a culprit ... at least one of them."

<I heard, Steve,> Cordelia said. <Congratulations on a successful capture. However, I do recommend additional training for you on New Terran emergency equipment.> The sound of tiny bells echoed from the reader's speaker, and the image spun and swirled in three dimensions.

Steve laughed. "It was all I could think of, at the time. It was better than stunning Bernoulli, which had been my first thought."

<Understandable ... she's certainly not the most agreeable person.>

"Cordelia, you have to know that many of us don't think like her. Tell the other SADEs that we appreciate their help, and that they're welcome in our homes anytime."

<You've just done so, Steve,> Cordelia replied.

"Bernoulli made a deal with Egan," Tomas Monti said to Alex. They were enjoying the view from Maria's porch, after an evening's fine dinner.

"Anything of value from the assemblyman?" Alex asked.

"Oh, yes … Egan rolled over on his fellow conspirators, which included his brother-in-law, in exchange for a lesser sentence. Egan kept insisting that it was all merely business. When Bernoulli questioned Egan as to what he thought Toyo intended to do with the stunners, Egan said, 'I had no idea and never asked.'"

Alex didn't reply, just shook his head in disgust.

"At least Bernoulli did a better job this time," Tomas said. "She discovered that Egan and his associates were frequent visitors to Toyo's domes and were granted special privileges. Apparently, one day Toyo approached the brother-in-law, who manufactures TSF stun guns, with a proposal, a pile of credits, and free access to his domes' entertainment for life. That information ensured that the counselor was less inclined to be generous with the deals she offered."

"On another subject, Tomas, I'm concerned about your position here on New Terra," Alex said.

"You brought me out here to ask me whether I wanted to return to Haraken in light of the warm feelings circulating around this planet about Harakens," Tomas said.

Alex grinned at his friend's astute deduction.

"The answer is no … emphatically, no." Tomas replied. "You see, I have this model of behavior that I follow," Tomas said, warming to his subject. "When things get tough, you don't run away. Even if it's hostile aliens coming for your people, you don't flee for another world. You find a way to fight back."

Tomas' references to the Librans' intention to evade the Nua'll and strike out for a desolate world in their city-ships, reminded Alex of the events at Arnos, including the memory of the death of the two thousand elders and the last words of Fiona Haraken, and Alex's smile faded.

Tomas saw the change in his president's face and thought, *Put it down, my friend. That's not a burden you should have ever had to carry.*

"So, you think you should stay," Alex said, taking a sip of his glass of port.

"Since you're serious about not running for the presidency again … yes. More than ever, Haraken will require a positive voice here on New Terra. Someone has to speak for our side of the story."

"You do have a traveler at your disposal, Tomas. But if you're ever concerned … right here is where you want to be," Alex said, tapping Maria's porch deck with his boot.

"Are you thinking a Haraken ambassador might be a target?"

"Here's the question we have to ask ourselves. What made Peto Toyo and Roz O'Brien think that Espero was a good target for their drugs?"

* * *

Of the two bills that reached the Assembly's floor, the one revoking the mining charter was the one in jeopardy of not passing. The second bill sought to expand the charter, extending the power of self-governance to any moon-based company. Those supporting the charter's expansion were loud and vociferous, and they were backed by powerful entities, which might profit from unfettered operation on the system's moons.

Constituents had messaged their representatives and called for reform, supporting the charter's revocation. But, despite the public's pressure, that bill was destined for defeat until the media broke the story of Egan's arrest. In the following days, more information hit readers across the system, detailing the complicity of Egan's brother-in-law in the manufacture of the notorious stunners. The thought of deadly weapons loose in the population was abhorrent to the general population.

The news scared representatives, who had sat on the fence, into distancing themselves from their lucrative supporters. Instead, they started taking their constituents' messages seriously, which were: Why should civilians have sway over other civilians on moon bases? The TSF are trained to manage civilian unrest, why aren't they given the power to police the mining concerns?

The effort to revoke the mining charter was bolstered by President Drake's impassioned speech, part of which said, "We must remove the protection afforded the mining companies given in the early days of space exploration. It's time to regulate, and, yes, apply TSF procedures and control to these establishments. The period of mining company self-rule must end. They don't have our civilians' best interests at heart. Their focus is commerce, whether legal or, as we have discovered, illegal."

Those anxious to repeal the charter achieved a majority in the Assembly, calling for a vote, and passing the bill, while defeating the expansion bill. Following the repeal, all mining operations and domes became subject to government overview for compliance with corporate regulations. Most important, the TSF became the force responsible for policing these establishments, and the local security forces would be required to operate under TSF guidelines.

In light of General Oppert's failure to detect the illegal drug and weapons manufacturing that had sprouted up, the Assembly asked for his resignation. Unfortunately, for the general, he was on record numerous times insisting that he had control of the issues, which were nearly insignificant in scope.

Maria was approached by President Drake and asked to resume the position of TSF general, but she demurred. Instead, she volunteered her choice, one Colonel Portis. Drake presented the name to the Assembly, which accepted the suggestion.

* * *

In the Harakens' final days at Maria's residence, Alex, Renée, and Maria discussed the events surrounding the investigations, trials, the mining charter's revocation, and the public's perception of Haraken interference in New Terran affairs.

"I'll work to communicate the truth about your people and what they've accomplished for us," Maria said to Alex. She was pointedly referring to Bernoulli's media announcement following the apprehension of the conspirators, who were arrested for manufacturing the stunners. The counselor made no mention of the assistance of the SADEs or any Haraken, for that matter.

"Perhaps, it's better you don't, Maria. I think Harakens have worn out their welcome in your system," Alex replied.

"Alex, don't let the likes of Bernoulli and these hot-air, corporate types convince you of the mood of the populace. They aren't the same."

"But your people are led by these individuals, who influence your ministers, your courts, and the Assembly representatives," Renée said.

Maria did not expect a pessimistic view from Renée, and it signaled to her a shift in the Harakens' thinking. "Alex, are you intending to implement a change in our peoples' relationship?" Maria asked.

"I don't know, Maria," Alex said, staring out the window at the thick forest to the south of Maria's home. He wanted to walk through the trees and smell the rich earth one more time before he left. "Our technology supplements our lives. It's a part of who we are, but our implants and SADEs frighten many of your people. New Terrans might have been okay with Julien in his box, but I wasn't ... and since the SADEs have become mobile they've done nothing to deserve New Terra's fear."

"Maybe in time, Alex," Maria said encouragingly.

"I think we're talking about a generation or two, Maria," Alex said quietly, staring out at the woods and wondering if his next walk with Renée on New Terran soil would be his last for many years to come.

* * *

After their conversation with Maria and a midday meal, Alex and Renée took their walk before boarding their traveler for the *Rêveur*. They walked hand-in-hand while the twins flanked them.

The trail through the woods was sun-dappled, and the breeze was fresh and clean, a promise of fall in the air. Underfoot, the detritus of the forest was thick, years of accumulated leaves and twigs slowly returning to the soil.

As they walked in silence, Alex could feel his shoulders relax and the tension drain away. He knew he couldn't convince an entire society of what he believed in his heart. Only time would tell if what he had strove to build for the Harakens would prove to be the more robust world.

<Scatter,> Alex suddenly sent the twins, who dove and rolled away from their principals, drawing their weapons and searching for targets. Alex snatched Renée up in his arms and leapt as far as he could before running a few meters more. He set Renée down and bent to pick biters off her boots, which were furiously trying to chew their way through the durable Haraken material.

"Check for biters," Alex called to the twins, who holstered their stun guns and began tearing the dangerous insects off their boots. In many cases, the poisonous mandibles remained attached and would have to be extracted later by a tool.

When finished with Renée, Alex checked his own boots, which in the brief moments of exposure to the nest were covered by tens of the creatures. "A large nest," Alex commented, as he pried the insects off one at a time. "I'll have to warn Maria about this one." He recorded his location for Julien, who could pinpoint the nest for Maria on a map of her property.

The twins circled wide and helped rid Alex of the numbers infesting his boots.

Staring back at the biter colony, which was seething out of the ground in search of the prey that had disturbed them, Renée remarked, "New

Terran predators, two-legged or six-legged, they're always intending us harm."

"It's why we defend Haraken so jealously, my love," Alex said, kissing Renée on the forehead. "But over time, I'm afraid that we won't continue to guide its destiny. That will belong to the generations to come, and we should be prepared that it might not evolve into the world we would wish it to be."

"Then, my love, we will choose a new world and start over," Renée said confidently, returning Alex's kiss, but on his lips.

Alex laughed. "And who would follow us on this grand adventure?" he asked.

Renée's eyes slid to the left, and Alex followed her line of sight. Étienne and Alain stood with their right hands in the air and smiles on their faces.

"And what would your partners have to say about your choices?" Alex challenged, laughing.

"Undoubtedly, they would have something to say," Alain replied, feigning earnestness.

"Oh, yes," Étienne chimed in, "It would be something to the effect of 'You two better hurry and get aboard or you'll be left behind.'"

Alex stared silently at the twins for the longest moment, and they returned his gaze. "Good friends," Alex finally said.

Alain glanced down and signaled Étienne. The horde of deadly insects had followed the sound vibrations of the humans' conversation. Pulling their stun guns, the twins knocked down the first 2 meters of the biters, the energy beams overloading the insects' nervous systems.

Alex tweaked an eyebrow at the twins' antics, but, without a word, Étienne and Alain holstered their weapons and took up defensive positions.

"I believe the de Long twins have also had enough of this world's aggressive species, my love," Renée said, "and I'm done with our walk in the woods."

* * *

At Maria's house, there were hugs, kisses, and tears as Renée and Maria said farewell. Then Maria hugged everyone, the twins, Julien, and Cordelia included.

As the Haraken's traveler lifted through New Terran air, Alex sent a pleasant message to Jaya, expressing his hope to see the minister someday on Haraken. For Jaya, the message tweaked his imagination, and thoughts of a different and unique future would haunt his daydreams for a long time to come.

Drake also received a message. On his reader, the word "goodbye" appeared.

"Goodbye," Drake said quietly in his empty office.

In the days following the trials, General Oppert wasn't the only one who lost his job. Drake dismissed Tessie Bernoulli.

Government House was flooded with tens of thousands of messages from the public, who wanted to know why the General Counsel was demonstrating a bias against the Harakens. It had been painfully obvious to the populace during the media coverage of the trials that Bernoulli had sought to limit Haraken testimony at every opportunity.

The messages brought Drake a moment of clarity. Much of the paranoia aimed at the Harakens came from the influencers of New Terran society. The powerful realized that their aspirations and manipulations, while hidden from government scrutiny, were transparent to the Haraken SADEs — in short, Julien and his kind threatened their power.

On the other hand, the general public, after weathering the transition of industries due to the adoption of Méridien technology, had benefited from an explosion of job opportunities created by society's expansion into the system, a process made much safer by that very same technology. Crippling injuries and most loss of life were eliminated by the constant shipments of Haraken medical nanites. Overall, the hard-working people of New Terra were supportive of the Harakens.

Drake came to realize that he had ignored one of Maria's parting pieces of advice given him on her last day in office. She had said, "Don't isolate yourself, Will. Government isn't just about representatives, ministers, and captains of industry. It's about caring for the welfare of the millions who elected you. Don't forget that."

After the biochemists and lab evidence had been released to TSF, Haraken personnel were free to return to their original ships and access their personal belongings and cabins.

Aboard the *Rêveur*, Alex announced their departure. The Haraken ships broke orbit and made a wide circle around the planet for an unimpeded view of the system's star, Oistos.

Eric Stroheim, aboard the *Tanaka*, managed the preparations for Oren and Nestor's star services. It was Reiko Shimada and Francis Lumley's first time viewing the Harakens' ceremony for their dead. The bodies were laid in crystal-covered containers, which would be launched from the bay toward the star for immolation. Willem stood in the bay's airlock to broadcast the observances for every Haraken, while the crew set the containers for launch.

Alex led the ceremony from the *Rêveur*'s bridge. The girls stood next to him, tears in their eyes. Each felt responsible for the deaths of the troopers, since it was their efforts to investigate the Espero club, which led to the events at the moons of Ganymede.

The girls' experiences, starting with their kidnapping, would start a slow unraveling of their tight-knit relationships. Soon, Eloise would find more and more excuses not to join her friends, and a love interest would enter Amelia's life. When the girls finally separated, the sister of the famous Alex Racine would begin a new phase of her life.

The Haraken ships accelerated in tandem as Alex finished reciting the traditional lament for the dead. A sharp port turn, a release of beams, a cancellation of a grav grid section, and the caskets slipped out of the bay. Imparted with a significant launch velocity, Oren and Nestor would embrace the enormous energy of the star in a matter of days.

* * *

Alex sat with Julien in the meal room. The dishes had long ago been cleared away, and the crew was gone. Even Renée had left the two alone.

"Once again, you're thinking that New Terran law isn't up to the task of dispensing justice," Julien said.

"How can it be if the process ignores evidence because it comes from sources that are feared?" Alex stood up and began to pace.

And so we reach the crossroads again, Julien thought.

"Billings, who appears to us to have made a minor mistake, has his livelihood eviscerated," Alex said, "and Kadmir, who was in concert, in some manner, with Toyo, walks away without a single charge leveled against him."

"But even we can't determine the extent of Kadmir's guilt," Julien argued.

"I would argue that we see evidence of his involvement," Alex riposted. "First, Christie and her friends show us, by their recordings, that Boker was part of the kidnapping crew when they were transported aboard the freighter. We can tell by his demeanor in their vids that he was no future rescuer, who was working under cover for Kadmir. Later, Boker walks the girls out of Toyo's domes to a shuttle with Kadmir aboard. Just how did he manage that without Toyo's cooperation? Later, Boker's found dead, shrapnel damage and a knife in his heart by a woman who works for Toyo, and she dies by Boker's poisoned blade. If that doesn't scream betrayal, I don't know what does."

"I can think of other explanations, but I find yours deserving of the highest probability," Julien replied.

"And here's the part I find compelling," Alex said. "After Toyo's domes are confiscated, it takes only days before Azul Kadmir and Roz O'Brien have purchased the establishment from the government at a fraction of the price it's worth."

"And you find this compelling, why?"

"Wouldn't you consider the two men competitors?"

"I would indeed," Julien replied. "I see. If the two men were competitors, how did they agree on a partnership to purchase Toyo's domes so quickly? It would indicate that they had already chosen to do so before Toyo attacked Kadmir's domes."

"Precisely, my friend," Alex exclaimed.

"But Toyo did not seem the type of man to sell his company to his competitors. He displayed a preference for bargaining with weapons."

"Which is why I believe that Kadmir and O'Brien coaxed Toyo into a plot that was never meant to happen, which is why Toyo and his people went after Kadmir."

"Do you have an inkling of the plot?" Julien asked.

"Yes, I think it revolved around the kidnapping. Toyo was desperate to get the girls out of his domes, and Kadmir offered him a way out. The girls are moved, and Kadmir comms us that he's rescued them."

"But Toyo discovers he's to be betrayed," Julien interjected.

"That's my guess," Alex said, sitting down at the table.

"With the arrival of the *Rêveur*, a vessel known to often carry the president, and a new Haraken warship, I could understand why Toyo would be desperate to participate in Kadmir's plot," Julien hypothesized. "In the first place, Toyo would have hoped that the kidnapping would never have been traced to Oistos, much less to his domes, but our arrival told him that his hopes were futile and time was against him."

"Exactly ... I don't know what Kadmir told Toyo, but it had to be good enough to get him to play. I think Kadmir and O'Brien planned to get rid of Toyo, and we were supposed to be the destructive instrument in their scenario."

"Well, you do have a reputation as a man who dispenses justice in his own inimitable way," Julien said.

"Whose side are you on?" Alex asked.

"Mine," Julien said, smiling.

"Traitor," Alex shot back.

"Fallible human," Julien replied.

The two smiled at each other, and both were lost in their own thoughts for a while.

"So if we believe in this theory, which we have concocted but which is highly probable, what is to be the extent of their punishment?" Julien asked.

Alex grinned at Julien and said, "I think Azul Kadmir and Roz O'Brien are about to become poor, at least for a short while."

Rather than an immediate reply, Julien cocked a querying eyebrow at Alex.

"Okay, so technically we're stealing," Alex replied, admitting to the nature of the proposed transgression. "But I prefer to think of it as the rightful redistribution of funds from those undeserving to those in need."

Alex waited, watching Julien for his reaction. With every step they took that crossed the lines of New Terran law, it made a case for criminal charges to be brought against both of them. Of course, that depended on whether New Terra wanted to prosecute a Haraken president who had administered some punishment to people the New Terrans hadn't managed to touch, judicially speaking.

An ancient, black, tricorne hat appeared on Julien's head. Pinned to one side of the hat was a dull, metal medallion displaying a human skull and crossbones. "And who would you like to be the benefactors of these men's largesse?" Julien asked, returning Alex's grin.

"You may not possess a human heart, my friend, but you're one of the most decent individuals I know. You choose who benefits."

* * *

Investigating Kadmir and O'Brien's personal accounts, Julien was appalled by the massive amount of wealth the two men had accumulated, which was spread across hundreds of accounts. Taking time to investigate the nature of their account transactions, Julien wasn't surprised to discover monthly payments to many of New Terra's powerful — payments that had nothing to do with services or supplies for their domes. "Influence peddling" was the term that came to Julien's mind from a New Terran vid.

Realizing that the effort to deal with the number of accounts required substantially more work in order to hide the final destination of the transactions, Julien enlisted the aid of the other SADEs.

<Julien, why are we transferring funds from these human's accounts?> Willem asked. <Wouldn't these actions be executed by New Terran authorities after a court's decision?>

<Willem dear, we're robbing these men,> Miranda sent.

<You needn't take part, Willem,> Cordelia sent.

<But the others will help you, Julien ... why?> Willem asked.

<I can't speak for Cordelia, Willem,> Miranda replied. <But I find a certain inadequacy in the application of New Terran law when it fails to value all the testimony that could have been presented, notably Haraken eyewitnesses, especially ours. We aren't just robbing these men. We're demonstrating our power to them.>

<When we finish our task, Willem,> Julien sent. <The transfers will be so complex as to deny the opportunity for New Terrans to follow the financial trails.>

<So the object is to remove these individuals' personal wealth and redistribute it in such a way that it can't be recovered. Then it will be obvious that only Haraken SADEs could have accomplished the task, but there will be no proof.> Willem reasoned. <I see ... we're warning these men.>

<Precisely, Willem,> Julien said.

<Can I assume that our president requested this action?> Willem asked. There was no other Haraken SADE who encountered a greater difficulty in the transition from box to avatar than Willem, and only one individual broke through his despondency ... Alex Racine. The president did not belittle him or exhibit disgust but merely asked what Willem wanted, and he had declared a desire to live away from humans.

In the simplest of responses, Alex agreed to assist Willem reach his goal, but his life's purpose had changed radically over the years. Still, he never forgot the president sitting beside him in the coarse soil next to a trickling stream, waiting for hours to hear Willem speak. *The human has the patience of a SADE,* he had thought.

<I would never say or even suggest that our president requested such conduct on our part,> Julien replied, his tone as neutral as could be made.

There were a few ticks of quiet, and the other SADEs were quite aware that Willem was calculating the probabilities.

<Yes, I see. We're taking this action wholly on our part,> Willem replied, having calculated that there was zero possibility that Julien was acting without orders.

<Julien, you have the lead, and I understand you have some expertise in New Terran financial systems. We're ready,> Miranda said.

In the morning, as the Haraken ships headed out of system, Azul Kadmir and Roz O'Brien discovered their personal bank accounts drained of every credit but one. They screamed their protests to the TSF and their government supporters, claiming the Harakens were responsible and every credit must be traced and returned.

Registered as a major theft, the government took responsibility for the investigation. Forensic teams would spend nearly a quarter of a year attempting to trace the transfers, with little to show for their efforts.

The SADEs took particular pleasure in not only emptying the myriad accounts, but moving the funds through an endless number of corporate accounts. A transfer would begin with a significant amount, but as that transfer moved from account to account, more than ten thousand times, a small portion of the total was siphoned off and moved in a different direction. In the end, one initial transfer from Kadmir or O'Brien's account would end in hundreds of thousands of payouts.

Many benefited from the SADEs' generosity — government medical research programs, charities, struggling entrepreneurs, the families of the chemists and techs who had been kidnapped, and, most important, the families of those killed in the fight at Kadmir's domes.

Julien managed one particular set of transactions that didn't involve the criminal leaders' accounts. The Racine's New Terran home was purchased from the present owner and placed in a trust with a substantial amount of Julien's personal funds. The trust would manage the home as a visitor center, and Darryl Jaya received a message from Julien, explaining that the SADE had named the minister as the executor of the trust. Later, when

Darryl examined the trust's details, he discovered its primary goal was the funding of a considerable number of university scholarships every year.

The morning after the transfers, the *Rêveur*'s crew discovered Julien walking the corridors, whistling happily. As Willem remarked to the other SADEs when they finished their efforts, "I believe the Sers have been adequately warned to leave us well alone."

* * *

"Alex, I did discover information that I thought would interest you," Julien said, later that morning. He shared a snippet of the purloined data with Alex. It itemized the monthly transfers from Kadmir and O'Brien's accounts to various individuals, who peddled the crime leaders' influence.

"Fascinating discovery, Julien. I suppose you have this data in a tidy package ready for transmission," Alex said, smiling.

"Able and waiting," Julien said, adding his own smile.

"Yes, but who do we send it to?" Alex mused.

"I vote for President Drake," Julien replied.

"Logical choice, but his hands would be tied if he tried to use Haraken data obtained through back doors."

"I vote for Charlotte Sanderson," Alex said. "She could embarrass a good many people with this information."

"But is embarrassment enough, Ser?" Julien asked.

"Both," Alex and Julien said at the same time, and laughed uproariously at what they intended to do.

"Anonymous, I presume," Julien said, dropping an image over his face.

"The Venetian mask," Alex exclaimed, recognizing the image Cordelia projected during Founding Day. "No, not this time, Julien. I think we need to make a point. Send it from 'Friends of New Terra.'"

"Done," Julien said. He projected a small fedora, but then changed it. Then he changed that one.

Alex watched hats flip over faster and faster on Julien's head, with the SADE's eyes staring up at them as if he was examining each one. "Stop, stop, you're making me dizzy," Alex yelled, between bouts of laughter.

Julien settled on an ancient, straw panama hat, a contented smile on his face. "That information should keep the government, the media, and the populace entertained for quite a while."

"Definitely help them with their vermin infestation," Alex replied, but he wasn't content to exit the system without a final warning to Kadmir and O'Brien. Soon after both men became aware that they were personally devoid of funds, each received a message on his reader. The anonymously sent text hardly gave either man an opportunity to read it before it disappeared in an intricate swirl of color, the reader recording no trace of the message or sender.

The text read: *We are aware of you now. Send your people, drugs, or weapons into Haraken space or anywhere in the Confederation, and we'll hold you personally responsible. Expect our retaliation to be swift and absolute.*

Cordelia took delight in sending Alex's message. Of all the SADEs, she was the most incensed by the events on Espero. That young people could be given dangerous drugs and kidnapped gave rise to a mounting outrage. The emotion was driven by her reorganized kernel hierarchy acquired during her time at Sol and dominated by what was akin to a maternal instinct.

After Alex had dictated his message to Cordelia, he crawled into bed beside Renée, who snuggled against him. As Alex held the love of his life, his thoughts turned to the future. Never one to seek public attention, nevertheless he had been proud to be considered a favored son of New Terra. But that was no longer true. In fact, it was quite the opposite for many powerful and influential New Terrans.

Realizing his presidency might now be a hindrance to the future of Haraken's relationship with New Terra, Alex reviewed his intention to refrain from another term in office. In a year and a half, his presidency would end, and he had to believe it was the right decision. *Time for someone else to lead,* Alex thought.

In truth, Alex welcomed the opportunity to remove the weight of an entire world from his shoulders, but his intuition sensed that the universe wasn't done throwing challenges at him. He chuckled at the thought that the stars might be warning him.

The rumblings of his chest caused Renée to murmur something unintelligible in her sleep, and she stretched an arm over Alex's chest and a leg over his thighs. Alex hugged her close, the warmth of her body and love flooding through him. *Time for a new job too,* Alex thought. *Wonder if anyone needs a good explorer-tug captain?*

Alex's thoughts made him smile. He was no longer a lone captain operating in the deep dark of Oistos. He had friends … good friends, loyal people, who were ready to follow him wherever the next adventure lay. The smile remained on Alex's face as he fell asleep, his arms wrapped around Renée's slender form.

* * *

Before the jump to Hellébore, Julien aided Z with the transfer to his director's avatar. Unsure of the best time to initiate the subsuming of Miranda's persona, Z had left it to Julien to signal the code that would result in his resumption of control.

Julien waited until Miranda retired to her cabin before he sent her Z's code, which returned the SADE's kernel to Z's control. Then he gathered up Z's personal possessions from his cabin and took them to him. None of Miranda's mannerisms were evident in the avatar, as Z moved around the cabin, storing the clothing and accessories Julien brought him.

Installing the necessary cabling between the avatars, Julien waited until Z's director avatar opened its eyes, and his fellow SADE confirmed a successful transfer before he left. What originally was intended to be a perfunctory transfer process now left Julien with a sense of loss.

Z was left alone in his cabin with the Miranda avatar, which lay on the cabin's second bunk. She was dressed in the subtle Haraken wrap she last wore, her eyes wide and staring. Time passed while Z stared at her still form, and, in an uncharacteristic move for him, he stood up and gently closed her eyes.

Sitting down on the edge of his bed, Z reviewed Miranda's memories. Rather than playing the files at his optimum processing speed, he frequently slowed to real time to appreciate some of the nuances of the events. Normally, he would have deemed this action extraordinarily unnecessary, but he couldn't help himself.

At one point, Z wondered if he had become jealous of the Miranda persona and the intimate relationship she enjoyed with humans and the other SADEs. Then, as he examined that response, he realized it wasn't jealousy or envy. Z wanted to be with her.

What have you done? the SADE asked himself. *You've created an alternate persona who attracts you, but you've only the one kernel.*

Z was still wrestling with the emotional impact of his discovery, when he reached the last file in Miranda's memories. Oddly, it was encrypted, which drew his curiosity. His efforts to crack the code were proving futile until he paused to consider Miranda's persona and applied a simple salutation, "Z, dear," which allowed him access to the file.

It was a vid. Miranda stared into a mirror, and her eyes, appearing wistful, recorded her reflection.

"If you're viewing this file, dear Z, then I'm gone again," Miranda said. "Lately, I've wondered where I go. Why don't I meet you? I find these worlds and my existence terribly exciting, and I will miss them."

Z stopped the vid to concentrate. He never meant for the Miranda persona to have such longevity, which had enabled her to build a robust personality. It was an experiment that proved a valuable escort for the Haraken threesome. Now, Z saw his efforts as an error in judgment, an incredible admittance for a SADE, especially for one such as him, who prided himself on the accuracy of his calculations.

Z recalled the words he had often heard from Alex, Julien, and Cordelia — the messy world of humans. *And now I've joined them,* he thought. It occurred to Z to erase the persona rather than store it for another day, but that seemed like cowardice, erasing your mistake so it wouldn't stare you in the face. Unable to come to a decision, Z returned to playing the vid.

"I see the continuity the other SADEs enjoy," Miranda said, "and I've come to believe that I may not be a whole entity, despite feeling that I am. My greatest fear is that I will never return, and, if that's meant to be, know that most of all I will miss meeting you. Be well, dear Z." Miranda blew him a kiss and closed the vid.

Z sat on the edge of the bed for hours, wondering what he had created — mistake or miracle. Deep in his kernel, Z began to devise scenarios by which the miracle might come to pass. After all, he nursed a century-long desire to become mobile, knowing the possibility was extremely remote, yet he walked among humans. His hope was that one day Miranda might too — beside him.

— Alex and friends will return in the novella, *Allora*. —

Glossary

Haraken

Alain de Long – Director of security, twin and crèche-mate to Étienne, partner to Tatia Tachenko

Alex Racine – President of Haraken, partner to Renée de Guirnon, Star Hunter First (Swei Swee name)

Amelia Beaufort – Close friend of Christie Racine

Benjamin Diaz – Minister of Mining, "Rainmaker," Little Ben

Bibi Haraken – Ex-Assembly member, matriarch of the Haraken clan

Brace – Svetlana's companion for a search of Toyo's domes

Cedric Broussard – Z's powerful New Terran avatar

Central Exchange – Haraken financial banking system

Christie Racine – Alex Racine's sister

Claude Dupuis – Engineering tech, program manager for SADE avatars

Cordelia – SADE, Julien's partner

Dane – SADE

Deirdre Canaan – Wing commander

Dubois – Haraken (New Terran) on duty at McCrery Orbital Station

Duggan Racine – Alex Racine's father

Edmas – Teenage boy from Idona adopted by Julien and Cordelia

Ellie Thompson – Wing commander

Eloise Haraken – Close friend of Christie Racine, Fiona Haraken's great-granddaughter

Eric Stroheim – Assembly Speaker

Escobar – Captain, ex-TSF officer, friend of Tatia

Espero – Haraken capital city

Étienne de Long – Director of security, twin and crèche-mate to Alain, partner to Ellie Thompson

Fiona Haraken – The Harakens were named in memory of her

First – Leader of the Swei Swee hives

Flit – Single person grav-drive flyer

Founding Day – Celebration of the founding of Haraken

Francis Lumley – Earther who immigrated to Haraken, *Rêveur* first mate

Franz Cohen – Wing commander
Ginny – Deaf child from Idona, adopted by Julien and Cordelia
Hatsuto Tanaka – Pilot killed at New Terra
Hive Singer – Mutter, who sings to the Swei Swee in their language
Jason – Burn-scarred child from Idona, adopted by Julien and Cordelia
Jason Haraken – Bibi Haraken's son, Assembly member
Jodlyne – Teenage rebel from Idona, adopted by Julien and Cordelia
José Cordova – *Rêveur*'s captain
Julien – SADE, Cordelia's partner
Katie Racine – Alex Racine's mother, Haraken Assembly member
Libre – Celebration day on Haraken for the ex-Independents
Lisbon – Haraken tech searching Toyo's domes for the missing girls
Mallory – Haraken carrying a plasma rifle
Mickey Brandon – Senior engineer, partner to Pia Sabine
Miranda Leyton – Z's femme fatale avatar
Mutter – SADE, Hive Singer to the Swei Swee
Nestor – Trooper killed at the barricade
Nua'll – Aliens who imprisoned the Swei Swee
Olawale Wombo – Senior scientist who fled the UE to Haraken
Oren Gestang – Haraken killed at Toyo's dome
People – Manner in which the Swei Swee refer to their collective
Pia Sabine – Assembly member, partner to Mickey Brandon
Rainmaker – Benjamin Diaz, also called Little Ben
Reiko Shimada – Captain of the sting ship *Tanaka*
Renée de Guirnon – First lady of Haraken, partner to Alex Racine
Rosette – SADE
SADE – Self-aware digital entity, artificial intelligence being
Security Directorate – New Espero security building, twins are co-directors
Sheila Reynard – Commodore
Shera Beaufort – Amelia's mother
Star Hunter First – Swei Swee name for Alex Racine
Svetlana Valenko – Wing commander
Swei Swee – Six-legged friendly alien

Tatia Tachenko – Admiral, ex-Terran Security Forces major, partner to Alain de Long
Teague – Ten-year-old son of Alex and Renée
Terese Lechaux – Medical expert
Tomas Monti – Ambassador to New Terra
Tyree – Deirdre's companion for a search of Toyo's domes
Willem – SADE
Yoram Penzig – UE scientist who fled the UE to Haraken
Z – SADE

Méridien

Confederation – Collection of Méridien worlds
House – Organization of people headed by a Leader
Independents – Confederation outcasts, originally exiled to Libre, rescued by Alex Racine

New Terra

Azul "Mr. Blue" Kadmir – Criminal boss on Udrides
Barber – Peto Toyo's gang team leader
Barnett – Lisa Sparing's alternate voice
Blondie (Jessie) – Aboard the *Bountiful* and killed on Jolares
By-Long Media – Media station Alex and Christie used for their broadcasts
Boker (Scar) – Toyo's man, who later changed his allegiance to Kadmir
Busty – O'Brien gang member killed by Cherry
Charlotte Sanderson – Director of By-Long media station and reporter for Alex's news story
Charles Stratford – Lead biochemist who designed the hallucinogenic drug
Cherry – Roz O'Brien leader on Espero
Chestling – Lenny's friend supposedly killed by the Harakens, according to Toyo
Clayton Downing – Former president of New Terra, convicted and imprisoned
Consuela Ortiz – Wife of Orlando, orphanage owner
Dar – Boss of the Espero club crew

Darryl Jaya – Minister of Technology

Davie – Orphan child, first to test the anti-addiction compounds

Desmonis Distribution – O'Brien company warehouse at Espero

Dillon Jameson – Toyo's head of dome security

Dolan Oppert – TSF general

Downing, Clayton – Former president of New Terra, convicted and imprisoned

Elman Ripard – TSF captain at Jolares

Embracing Arms Orphanage – Orphanage run by Orlando and Consuela Ortiz

Emile Billings – Senior lab chemist

Fangs – O'Brien gang member killed by Cherry

Finian Egan – Assembly representative

Fredericka Tillman Olsen – Investigator for Maria Gonzalez's company

Geron Hanley – TSF prison therapist

Government House – Official residence of New Terran president

Hailey Timmion – New Terran shuttle captain

Henry (Wheezy) – O'Brien gang member

Hezekiah Cohen – Father of Franz Cohen, ex-Joaquin Station director

Janine – Wife of the biochemist Billings

Jessie (Blondie) – Aboard the *Bountiful* and killed on Jolares

Lacey – Receptionist at illegal Espero club

Legs – O'Brien gang member killed by Cherry

Lenny – Toyo's plasma rifleman

Lisa Sparing – Kadmir's mistress

Lunar Restaurant – Dining facility on Toyo's dome where the Haraken girls are found

Lydia Zafir – Assassin on Toyo's team

Maria Gonzalez – Security consultant business president, ex-New Terran president

Marty – Toyo's receptionist at dome's landing bay

McMorris – Former New Terran president who was murdered

Mincie – Billings' daughter

Omi Yakiro – Kadmir's security chief

Orlando Ortiz – Husband of Consuela, orphanage owner
Oslo – Security officer Lydia captures
Peters – TSF major Alex first met during Downing affair
Peto "Craze" Toyo – Criminal boss on Jolares
Portis – TSF colonel
Prima – New Terra capital city
PT Mining Concern – Registry of Toyo's mining company
Roz "Sniffer" O'Brien – Criminal boss on Desmonis
Sarah Laurent – Investigator for Maria Gonzalez's company
Scar (Boker) – Aboard the *Bountiful* and on Ganymede's moon
Serian – Boy who introduces Jodlyne to the dance club on Espero
Sol-NAC – New Terran language
Stan – Lab shift supervisor
Steve Ross – Investigator for Maria Gonzalez's company
Terran Security Forces (TSF) – New Terran system police force
Tessie Bernoulli – Judiciary counsel for the government of New Terra
Trembles – Muscle at the illegal club in Espero
Udrides Resources – Kadmir's mining company
Will Drake – New president on New Terra
Yance Deere – Senior security person with Toyo

United Earth (UE) and Earthers
Bunaldi – *Hand of Justice* mission commander, UE high judge
García – *Reunion* mission commander, UE speaker
Nikki Fowler – Director of Idona Station at Sol
Patrice Morris – Assistant director of Idona Station at Sol

Stars, Planets, Moons, and Stations
Cressida – Moon orbiting Ganymede, heavily mined
Desmonis – Moon orbiting Ganymede, location of Roz O'Brien's domes
Flides – Kephron moon
Ganymede – Huge gas planet in the Oistos system
Haraken – New name of Cetus colony in the Hellébore system, home of
    the Harakens

Hellébore – Star of the planet Cetus, renamed Haraken
Idona Station – An outer rim station at Sol
Joaquin Station – New Terra orbital station
Jolares – Moon orbiting Ganymede, location of Peto Toyo's domes
Kephron – Second planet outward from Ganymede in the Oistos system
Libre – Independents' ex-colony in Arno system, home to the remaining
    Swei Swee hives
McCrery Orbital Station – new Haraken station built to handle freighter
shipping between systems
Méridien – Home world of Confederation
New Terra – Home world of New Terrans, fourth planet outward of
    Oistos
Niomedes – New Terra's fifth planet outward
Oistos – Star of the planet New Terra, Alex Racine's home world
Seda – New Terra ninth and last planet outward, a gas giant with several
    moons
Sharius – Moon and TSF outpost orbiting Seda
Sol – Star of Earth
Udrides – Moon orbiting Ganymede, location of Azul Kadmir's domes

Ships

Bountiful – New Terran freighter that transports Christie and friends to
Oistos
Hand of Justice – United Earth battleship
Reunion – United Earth explorer ship
Rêveur – Haraken passenger liner
Tanaka – Haraken's first sting ship, captained by Reiko Shimada
Travelers – Shuttles and fighters built by the Harakens based on the silver
    ships of the Swei Swee

My Books

The Silver Ships series is available in e-book, softcover print, and audiobook versions. Please visit my website, http://scottjucha.com, for publication locations. You may also register at my website to receive email notification about the publish dates of my novels.

If you've been enjoying this series, please consider posting a review on Amazon, even a short one. Reviews attract other readers and help indie authors, such as me.

Alex and friends will return in the upcoming novella, *Allora*.

The Silver Ships Series
The Silver Ships
Libre
Méridien
Haraken
Sol
Espero
Allora (forthcoming)

The Author

I've been enamored with fiction novels since the age of thirteen and long been a fan of great storytellers. I've lived in several countries overseas and in many of the US states, including Illinois, where I met my wonderful wife thirty-seven years ago. My careers have spanned a variety of industries, including the fields of photography, biology, film/video, software, and information technology (IT).

My first attempt at a novel, titled *The Lure,* was a crime drama centered on the modern-day surfacing of a 110-carat yellow diamond lost during the French Revolution. In 1980, in preparation for the book, I spent two wonderful weeks researching the Brazilian people, their language, and the religious customs of Candomblé. The day I returned from Rio de Janeiro, I had my first date with my wife-to-be, Peggy Giels.

Since 1980, I've outlined dozens of novels, but a busy career limited my efforts to complete any of them. Recently, I've chosen to make writing my primary focus. My first novel, *The Silver Ships*, was released in February 2015. This first installment in a sci-fi trilogy was quickly followed by books two and three, *Libre* and *Méridien*. *Haraken*, *Sol*, and *Espero* the fourth, fifth, and sixth novels in the series and *Allora*, a novella, continue the exploits of Alex Racine and company.

I hope to continue to intrigue my readers with my stories, as this is the most wonderful job I've ever had!

22762295R00255

Printed in Great Britain
by Amazon